THE MUSIC MAKERS

Victorian Timeshift Mysteries

Alexandra Walsh

SAPERE
BOOKS

D1247845

THE MUSIC MAKERS

Published by Sapere Books.

20 Windermere Drive, Leeds, England, LS17 7UZ,
United Kingdom

saperebooks.com

ISBN: 978-1-80055-367-5

To Emma
Blue paint and chilli sauce, innit

We are the music makers,
And we are the dreamers of dreams,
Wandering by lone sea-breakers,
And sitting by desolate streams;
World-losers and world-forsakers,
On whom the pale moon gleams;
Yet we are the movers and shakers
Of the world for ever, it seems.
From 'Ode' by Arthur O'Shaughnessy (1844-1881)

DISCLAIMER

This book is set in 2020, however, as with all novels, while *The Music Makers* exists in a world similar to our own, it is not the real world but an imagined version of events. As such, Sapere Books and myself have made the editorial decision not to include the Covid-19 pandemic in this version of 2020. Instead, I have created a 2020 that might have been.

Alexandra Walsh

PROLOGUE

Cardiff, Wales, 1860

"Is she there?"

Rosie Hardy pulled open the entrance to the octagonal fortune-telling tent, blinking as her eyes adjusted to the purple-tinged gloom, a reflection from the fabric-draped walls.

"Judith," she called, her voice merging into the folds of night trapped within the flimsy walls. "There's something," she shouted to her husband, Cornelius, who had voiced the question. Hurrying to her side, Rosie heard his breath coming in short, urgent bursts as he followed her inside.

By day, the tent was Rosie's domain, a candle-lit haven of female secrets and promises yet to be fulfilled, but in the midnight shadows of the storm, it was a dank, unprepossessing space. Cornelius held up the lantern, allowing a glow of yellow light to ease the murk. The flickering brightness reached out, illuminating the dim corners, exposing the bundle of patchwork cloth. A child, swaddled in the bright cover, gave a sleepy wail as the light found it.

"Esme?" whispered Rosie. "Cornelius, she's left the child."

Darting across the small interior, Rosie reached down to the nest of blankets, gathering it into her arms. Halfway between sleep and wakefulness, the child murmured. Rosie started as something slipped free and fell to the ground, landing with a soft sigh on the grassy floor.

"A doll," whispered Cornelius, showing it to his wife, who was rocking the child, lulling her back to sleep.

The silken dark hair and violet eyes of the doll stared upwards, her face benign, her dress the same as the child's, the two mirror-images of the other.

"A doll," echoed Rosie, "all she leaves the child is a doll." There was a protectiveness in her voice, driven by anger. "It seems appropriate; she always treated the child as a plaything. Esme will be better with us."

Tightening her grip on the slumbering bundle, Rosie hurried from the tent, returning to the bright wooden caravan they called home, leaving her husband to continue the search for the child's missing mother.

"You're safe, Esme," she whispered as she snuggled the little girl into the single bed occupied by her toddler son, Jeremiah. "We will always take care of you."

Esme stirred, sighed, then slipped back into sleep.

Sitting in the chair by the small stove, Rosie watched the children, the doll tucked in beside Esme, thinking over the events of the troublesome evening. The child's mother would not return, of this Rosie was certain, and from tomorrow, they would announce Esme as their own daughter. A child to replace the one she had lost, the tiny scrap of humanity who had breathed for moments before slipping away.

Reaching for her pack of battered Tarot cards, she shuffled them, muttering the French names of the Marseille deck: "*Le Mat, Le Bateleur, La Papesse…*" Well-thumbed and worn, she laid out six cards, her eyes narrowing with each turn: The Empress, The Tower, Death, The Star, the Nine of Cups and the Ten of Coins.

"A mother figure," she whispered. "Loss of status, dealing with issues beyond your control, forced endings, but there is hope." She stroked the card of *L'Etoile*, the Star. "And there is love and family. Yet things are changing and where there is good, there is bad, such as it has always been to balance the universe."

Gathering the cards, Rosie glanced again towards the sleeping child.

"Which are you, my love?" she murmured, stroking a dark curl away from Esme's cheek. "Are you the good or the bad?"

The child did not respond, but outside a roar of thunder caused Rosie Hardy to shudder.

PART ONE: PEMBROKESHIRE, 2020

CHAPTER ONE

"Is this the last?" Eleanor Wilder asked as her father, John, carried in the small box and positioned it on top of the vast pile in the large, airy barn.

"Yes," he replied, "everything else is for the annexe."

"Thanks, Dad," she said, swallowing hard in order to avoid the croak in her voice.

Smiling, her father offered his arm and after a slight hesitation, she took it, leaning on him as they made their way through the boxes to the yard beyond. John slammed and locked the barn behind them, handing Eleanor the key.

"When we've put your pictures on the walls and all the clothes rails and the shelving arrives, it'll be ideal," he promised and Eleanor nodded, her face set in an expression of determination.

"You're right," she agreed as they approached the back of the van where her brother Aidan, older than her by two years, could be heard moving boxes.

A blood red sun was setting in the distance, taking with it the last of the autumnal warmth. Eleanor shivered, pulling her scarf more tightly around her neck.

"You go in," John said, nodding towards the farmhouse. "Aidan and I will finish this. It won't take us long, and you look exhausted."

Opening her mouth to protest, Eleanor knew there was no point. Her father was right; she was shattered and the glowing warmth of the fire shining through the window was too much to resist.

"Hello, love," called Eleanor's mother, Anne, as Eleanor walked into the kitchen. "Boxes all in the barn?"

It was a cheery, smiling enquiry, but Eleanor felt as though each word was a reminder of her failure. The loss of her beloved vintage emporium in a winding lane off the main high street in Richmond upon Thames, Surrey, was the hardest thing to adjust to in the sudden turnaround in her life. As though understanding this, her mother hugged her tightly.

"This is temporary," she murmured into Eleanor's red-gold hair. "By this time next year, things will be different."

Eleanor resisted the urge to argue, to demand to know how her mother dared make such predictions, but there was no point. This was nobody's fault. It was one of those unfortunate events — a stroke of fate which had hit her and changed everything she had ever known. The past months had seen her forced to make difficult decisions, trusting and hoping things would improve.

Collapsing into the rocking chair by the fire in the vast farmhouse kitchen, the flames acted on Eleanor like a spell. As warmth suffused her feet, rising up her legs, she felt the tension of the afternoon easing away.

The family cat, Sandy, a fluffy ginger and white ball of curiosity, leapt onto her lap and stared up at Eleanor with knowing amber eyes. He blinked with slow deliberation, watching with his head tilted as Eleanor replied with an exaggerated blink of her own. This was home, Eleanor reminded herself as Sandy miaowed his approval of her response and curled up on her lap. His purrs vibrated through her as she stroked his silky fur, reminding herself that here she was safe, she was protected and it was the best place to begin again, to rebuild, surrounded by those she loved.

As she closed her eyes, words danced in her imagination: *Safe. Home. Love.* Words she had repeated often, words which on occasion had traction, and she felt them in her heart and soul. Today, however, in the aftermath of watching her life being split between the barn and the annexe attached to her parents' farmhouse, it was difficult.

The back door opened and her brother hurried in on a blast of cool evening air.

"Everything's in," said Aidan. "We can sort it out tomorrow. Dad's finishing off a few things outside," he added, addressing Anne. "He'll be about twenty minutes."

"Thanks," said Eleanor, noticing his inclusion of himself in the unpacking. "I'll be fine, though. You need to open the shop."

Aidan laughed. "It's September, hardly peak season for a surf shop. Chloe has said she'll open up tomorrow," he added, referring to his fiancée.

"It isn't fair to leave her to do all the work..." began Eleanor, but she was interrupted by their mother.

"Are you staying for dinner, Aidan?"

"No, I'm going to head off. I'll see you tomorrow."

Eleanor smiled as Aidan scratched Sandy's head, before he bent down to squeeze her shoulder in a comforting manner. He hugged Anne and shouted a farewell to John before disappearing into the gathering twilight.

Anne handed Eleanor a glass of wine, settling herself in the armchair on the other side of the fire, sipping her own drink. "Things will feel better when everything is unpacked," she said, her voice encouraging.

"I know," Eleanor replied, holding up the wine so it gleamed scarlet in the firelight. "You've been amazing, I'm so grateful."

"Ellie, we don't want you to be grateful," Anne said with a sad smile. "It's a relief we're here to help you retain some semblance of your normal life. Things are strange and frightening at the moment, but they will improve."

"Yes," said Eleanor. "I know." Again, the words felt hollow, but she did not want to be perceived as belittling the huge efforts her family had made on her behalf.

"By next week, the barn will be ready and you can reopen your business," Anne continued. "It might not be in your beautiful shop, but who knows what might be around the next corner? When the time is right, you might find somewhere even more glorious."

Eleanor forced a smile, unable to speak but not wanting her mother to think she was unappreciative.

"Anyway, this will give you more time to continue with your historical research," said Anne as she placed her wine on the small table beside the chair, before returning to the hob to turn down the boiling potatoes. "You might even have time to put together that reference book you've always wanted to write. The history of theatrical costumes during the Victorian era."

Anything historical interested Eleanor; it was what had driven her to open her shop in the first place. It had been her long-held ambition to collate the knowledge she had acquired from her years of dealing with vintage clothing, auctions and running her business.

"I suppose," she admitted, and Anne laughed at her studied nonchalance. "I might even find time to properly catalogue my collection too."

Eleanor's vast collection of theatrical programmes was a family legend. Her interest had begun after a visit to a pantomime in London with her godfather, Steve Evans. Dazzled by the glamour, the lights, the sheer spectacle, eight-year-old Eleanor had treasured the programme from the London Palladium. As she had grown older, her interest in theatre and, in particular, the costumes and the programmes had continued. Throughout her teens, Eleanor would trawl auction websites, looking for affordable programmes, amassing a collection of several hundred which she stored on bookshelves in her bedroom, something which the rest of her family, who had very little interest in the theatre, found both amusing and fascinating in equal measure.

When she was fifteen, Eleanor had discovered a costume within her budget at an antiques market she had persuaded Anne to take her to. The flowing red dress had graced the corner of her bedroom for months, dramatically arranged on a tailor's dummy, with scarves and beads. It was only when she saw a similar costume online and realised it was worth several hundred pounds — far more than the £25 she had paid — that she sold it and the beginning of her business was born.

"You could include these," said Anne, hurrying into the study, which was situated off the kitchen, and returning with a hard-backed envelope. She passed it to Eleanor. "They're the photographs we lent to your cousin Eddie for his party. They were in my mother's things. She showed them to me a few weeks before she died. I'd never seen them before."

Anne's mother, Alice, had died ten months earlier. It had been a surprise because her health had seemed robust. Eleanor pulled out the photographs.

"I'd forgotten about these," she said, examining the collection of faded, sepia-toned images. "They're Victorian, so they must be Nan's parents and grandparents."

"Yes, a few of them are dated and the genealogists who put together the family trees for Eddie's family reunion at Cliffside managed to identify a few others. There's a rough family tree in there too. There are more details in the books we were given at the party."

A few months before Eleanor became ill, she, Aiden, Anne and John had been invited to a gathering at Cliffside. Once a family home, the vast rambling property perched on the edge of the cliff was now a clinic specialising in grief counselling. The owners, Edward Stone and his elderly aunt, Caitlin Bathurst, had hosted a large family gathering. Eleanor and Aidan had grown up knowing Edward Stone, so it had been a surprise when Anne had been contacted and told she was distantly related to the Attwater family who had once owned Cliffside and who Caitlin and Edward were also descended from.

"How are we connected again?" asked Eleanor, unfolding the family tree.

"Through Noah Attwater. He married Hannah Blood…"

"Blood?"

"It's an old Welsh surname," said Anne. "Hannah was the daughter of the Reverend Meredith Blood who had seven children. Hannah, who was the second youngest, married Noah Attwater and we're descended from their eldest daughter, Eleanor. That was how I decided on your name," Anne added. "My mother had mentioned a distant relative called Eleanor when I was pregnant with you and the name stayed with me. When you were born, it suited you."

"Why have you never told me this before?"

"I don't know. It slipped my mind, I suppose, but when I was contacted about the Cliffside reunion, it came back to me, especially when the researchers sent me the family tree."

Eleanor began sifting through the photographs. "Do we have a picture of Eleanor?" she asked.

"The small one," Anne pointed. "It isn't very clear, though."

Eleanor held it up, tilting it towards the light. A slim woman wearing a cloven-crowned hat with a flat brim, similar to a man's trilby hat, smiled shyly into the camera. Her dark hair was arranged in a complicated up-sweep, while her wide eyes glittered with excitement.

"I love her hat," said Eleanor, "and the detail on her dress is extraordinary."

"There's another one you might like too," said Anne, leaning over and rummaging through the photographs. "This one. The woman looks as though she's wearing a theatrical costume."

"This is spectacular," Eleanor exclaimed, studying the image. "What an incredible costume. I'd guess at 1870s to 1880s. It's very risqué. I believe these were known as French photographs — a euphemism for naughty pictures."

The woman was petite with a cheeky grin playing across her heart-shaped face, an expression which was at odds with the way her eyes were turned demurely away. Her dress was an incredible confection of peacock feathers, clinging tightly to her impossibly slender figure, but what would have been shocking for the time were her bare arms, legs and feet. Turning the photograph over, Eleanor was delighted to see faded writing.

"It says, *Esme Blood?*, then, the word *Sister?* but it's been crossed out," she read. "Who's Esme Blood?"

As she said the name, a shiver ran down her spine. It was not unpleasant; it felt more like a connection to an old friend, a name she had known but had forgotten. In fact, she was certain she had read the name somewhere before.

"She isn't on the Attwater family tree, so perhaps she was a relative of Hannah's," said Anne, looking at the printout.

"Esme Blood," murmured Eleanor, turning the name over in her mouth as though it were a fine wine. "Esme Blood, why do

I know her name?" Closing her eyes, she tried to remember where she had heard it before. "It has something to do with Tarot cards," she murmured, "but I can't remember…"

The back door opened, and John arrived with their two sheepdogs, Potter and Webby. Anne hurried over to help clean the mud off their paws before they flopped onto their vast squashy beds in front of the fire.

"I can't say it's a name I've heard," Anne said, returning to the conversation as she opened the oven to remove the chicken casserole. "Perhaps you could join one of those family tree websites and see if you can discover more."

"Perhaps," Eleanor said, placing mats and cutlery on the table, wondering why the name seemed so familiar, eventually dismissing it as something she must have heard at the Cliffside party the previous year.

CHAPTER TWO

"Your parents have really gone for it," exclaimed Nick Chalmers as he and Eleanor walked around the annexe to Anne and John's house that Eleanor was now living in.

"It was quite old-fashioned," replied Eleanor, as she opened the door to the guest bedroom, where Nick would be sleeping.

The two-bedroomed cottage was bright and clean, and there was a lingering smell of paint. Eleanor gazed around, impressed with her mother's ability to completely change the space which had been synonymous with her beloved mother, Alice.

"Mum and I loved each other," Anne had said the previous evening when she and Eleanor had been making up the spare bed for Nick. "I don't need dubious wallpaper and a green bathroom suite to remember her. She's in my heart. My relief is that we have somewhere safe for you to rebuild your life."

"You look pale," said Nick, scrutinising her. "Are you feeling all right?"

"Fine," replied Eleanor with a hint of acerbity.

"Liar," laughed Nick. "Why don't you put the kettle on, while we men finish bringing in the last pieces of furniture."

Nick and Eleanor had been friends for years, crossing paths not long after Eleanor had first moved to London. In order to earn money while she tried to establish her vintage emporium, she had signed on with a temping agency, working during the day and building her business online at night. The temporary work had been dull but reliable until the day she was sent to a large insurance company. Dispatched to the basement to photocopy reports with thousands of pages, she had encountered Nick, who was staring at the piles of paper in amusement. It was not long before the two discovered a shared sense of humour and the realisation their ambitions were greater than working in a windowless room for a faceless conglomerate.

"I want to work in magazines," Nick had declared as he changed the printer cartridge on the photocopier for the third time, while Eleanor sorted the reports into chapters. "Preferably music, but I'd be happy with an interiors title."

Eleanor had told him about the business she had been running since her teens. "I sell things," she had said. "Mostly vintage clothes and smaller antiques, jewellery — when I can afford to buy it at antiques fairs and auctions — but my real love is theatrical costumes and programmes, as well as Tarot cards. There's a surprising amount of Victorian occult memorabilia around; the Victorians loved a séance."

The following day, when the photocopier had broken for the fifth time and the harassed manager had shouted at them both, they had linked arms and walked out of the building without a word. From the safety of the nearby pub, they had called the temping agency to say the job was unacceptable and had remained friends ever since, briefly sharing a flat before both their fortunes had turned around. Nick had been offered a job at the fashionable men's magazine *Axiom*, where he was now editor, while Eleanor's luck had changed at a local auction house.

An auction lot she had picked up consisting of hats had included a selection of bric-a-brac. Inside, Eleanor had discovered a ring with a green stone, surrounded by white heart-shaped brilliants and several watches in battered leather boxes. Suspecting the ring might be an emerald with diamonds — rather than "a silver ring with green stone and glass" as it was described on the inventory — she had it checked by a jeweller friend, who confirmed her suspicions. The stones were valuable gems, and the metal was platinum, not silver. The hallmark suggested Cartier in the 1880s.

The real find, however, were two leather boxes containing watches: a 1950s women's Rolex, set with sapphires and diamonds, and a 1970s men's King Midas 'Tiger's Eye' watch, also a Rolex. Double-checking that the two watches had been included in the original inventory and were definitely her property, Eleanor had approached Christie's auction house in London. The three items were put into specialist sales and three months later had earned her the impressive sum of £60,000: more than enough for her to set up her business properly.

For the next five years, her business had boomed. Her life had expanded, and she had loved living in such an historic area. Only moments away were the buildings known as The Wardrobe, the last remains of the Tudor palace that had once stood majestically on the River Thames, the favourite home of Elizabeth I. A short drive away was the magnificence of Hampton Court, as well as easy access into London. Six months after she had opened her shop, she had met Robbie Hutchinson, an aspiring musician, and she felt things were set for the rest of her life.

It stunned Eleanor to think that in such a short space of time, everything had changed so dramatically. Her problems had begun with a bad cold. Apart from the irritation of having to hire cover for her shop for a few days while she recovered, Eleanor had not given it another thought, until two weeks later when she noticed a tingling in her hands and shooting pains in her legs. This was followed by an overwhelming and inexplicable exhaustion, leading to difficulty breathing. With terrifying speed, the tingling and pains had rapidly absorbed her, making it harder and harder for her to move her limbs until she was struggling to walk. The worst point came when she had tried to stand and her legs had crumpled beneath her.

Within two days of this incident, she had been hospitalised, unable to walk and struggling to breathe, as a creeping paralysis began to shut down her body, including her respiratory system. She was given oxygen to help her breathe, and a week later she was diagnosed with a rare autoimmune condition which had been triggered by her cold.

"It's called Chronic Inflammatory Demyelinating Polyneuropathy," her consultant, Dr Murphy, had explained. "It's incurable, but it is treatable and controllable. You have a period of recovery ahead of you to rebuild your strength and learn to walk again. There will be difficult days but you're young, fit and, apart from the CIDP, healthy, so there's no reason why you won't be able to continue with your life nearly as normal. We'll be here to support you and help, literally, every step of the way."

Three days later, a relapse had seen her rushed into intensive care, struggling to breathe. When she was released, she had a message from Robbie stating that he felt this was the right time for them to end their relationship. The stress of her illness, he claimed, was too much for him and he had his own life and career to consider. When she tried to call him, she found he had blocked her number. This, on top of everything else she was trying to process, sent Eleanor into a downward spiral of depression. She and Robbie had been together for three years, and she was staggered by the callousness of his departure.

Over the next few months, she had worked with physiotherapists to regain her mobility and was given counselling to help her come to terms with the upheaval which had made her life unrecognisable. Eleanor was twenty-nine and her body, the thing she had always taken for granted, had failed her. What was worse was that she had always taken care of herself. She had never smoked, she ate healthily, she never drank alcohol to excess, and after a childhood growing up surfing and swimming in the sea, as well as helping around the farm, she had always stayed fit, swimming at the outdoor pool in Richmond at least twice a week. Her friends had rallied around and Nick visited regularly. He and his partner, Giovanni, stepped in to keep her business running, even though it meant taking leave from their own jobs.

Her parents and brother had hurried to her side too and, despite having spent years living in London, she realised the sense in their suggestion that she return to the family home in Pembrokeshire. Robbie's rejection had been the final blow to her hopes she would be able to pick up the threads of her old life again, but, even now, the memory of handing back the keys to her shop brought a lump to her throat.

"You can use the red barn as a warehouse and run your business online. There's heating and power in there. You can even set up an office and we can all help," John had said, his face pinched with concern.

"My job is coming to an end in a few months because the shop will be shutting when Gwen retires," Anne had added. She worked part-time for a friend who ran a gift shop. "It'll leave me free to help you."

What had made complete sense was moving into the annexe. It was a self-contained two-bedroomed cottage attached to the rambling family farmhouse. It had once been stables but had been converted for Eleanor's grandmother, Alice. When Alice had died, the family had pondered over whether or not to convert the property into a holiday let, but its proximity to the farmhouse made them hesitate.

"We'd be on top of holidaymakers," Anne had said. "They wouldn't have any privacy."

The family's procrastination had led to the perfect solution for Eleanor. All on one level, the annexe would provide a sanctuary for her to recover and rebuild her shattered life, giving her independence but with help a footstep away, should it be necessary. Eleanor had made arrangements to move all of the stock from her shop to Pembrokeshire.

The kettle boiled and as she poured the water into the teapot, Eleanor wondered if she would ever return to her old life. Fatigue was her constant companion and the thought of working the long hours, paying the huge rents and being responsible for her small staff felt terrifying, but so did the prospect of the loss of the life she had built and the friends she had made. In her heart, she knew there were far worse places to recover and that she was lucky to have a family around her who were doing their utmost to make her life continue as normally as possible, but the fact her body had failed her so utterly and her health remained unpredictable, combined with her regular bouts of hospital treatment, were not things she could easily dismiss.

"Are you okay, love?" Anne called, bringing in two bags of food. "I'll grab the rest from the car."

Unpacking the bags, Eleanor began to put away the food, relieved her mother had offered to visit the supermarket. Shuddering and trying to resist the whisper of self-loathing about not managing to do her own shopping, she breathed deeply, thinking through the coping strategies her counsellor had suggested. This was temporary; one day she would feel strong enough to perform these simple tasks again.

It was the small things that had startled her as she adjusted to her new life. Once a lover of busy markets, pushing her way through crowds to secure bargains, she had a shock the first time she and Nick had attended one when she was released from hospital. She had been determined to try and carry on with life as normal, but the jostle and bustle which had once been most of the fun was threatening. Unsteady on her weak legs, she realised the gentlest of nudges could send her to the floor and moments after they arrived, with her arm firmly through Nick's, she had asked him to take her out of the throng. The uneven pavements were a huge obstacle, the crowds of people, even the distance from the car park to wherever they had chosen to visit was longer and harder to achieve.

"Stop it," she muttered to herself as she opened her new cupboards, looking for places to store things. "Self-pity won't get you anywhere."

She had left her beloved childhood home to forge her own way in the world, putting down what she thought were solid roots elsewhere, but it appeared the Universe had other plans for her, and the ties that bound her to Pembrokeshire had wrenched her home.

The sound of a footstep behind her brought her from her reverie and she turned to see Nick, carrying the box containing her Tarot collection.

"Where do you want this?"

"Living room," she said. "It's our project for this afternoon."

Nick wandered off and she heard him speaking to her mother, then he reappeared with the final bags of shopping.

"Here's the tea," Eleanor said, pushing the tray towards him. "I'll sort out the shopping, then when everyone has gone, I need to explain our quest."

CHAPTER THREE

An hour later, when the annexe was resembling a home rather than a furniture storage area, and her family had left, Eleanor refilled the teapot and returned to the living room where Nick was waiting for her.

"So, what's this about a quest?" he said as Eleanor topped up their cups. "Are we going on an adventure?"

"In a way," she said. "Do you remember, before I became ill, I went to a big family reunion at Cliffside?"

Nick was the only person who knew that Eleanor now saw her life in two halves: the time before her illness had wrought havoc, when she had taken her health and mobility for granted, and life after, when her trust in her body's basic abilities had been shattered forever.

"Of course," he replied. "You were interested in tracing your family tree because of the photographs your mum had found in your nan's belongings."

"Well, obviously things have been a bit busy, so I haven't done anything about it, but when Mum showed me the photographs again yesterday, I remembered something."

"What?"

"Last night, I was thinking about this woman." Eleanor pushed the photograph of Esme towards Nick. "Her name is Esme Blood. I thought she sounded familiar, but I couldn't recall where or why, until this morning." Pausing for dramatic effect, Eleanor glanced at Nick, who rolled his eyes.

"Go on then, amaze me," he said, laughing.

Reaching forward, Eleanor opened the box Nick had brought in from the barn which contained her Tarot collection.

Eleanor's fascination with Tarot cards had begun when her grandmother, Alice, had given her the first pack. Based around the stories of the Greek myths, she had rapidly committed the tales and the meanings of the cards to memory, but it had taken her many years to learn the nuances and detail of the packs. What had really drawn her interest were the images, the idea of the journey through life these icons represented and how the cards could offer advice or help her to clarify things if she was unsure about a decision.

"I got these from the last auction we went to before I was ill," she said.

"It was in Kent, wasn't it?"

"Yes, there was the huge antiques market in three large marquees, then the auction in the church hall. I was after the lot that comprised several boxes and a suitcase of vintage clothes. The catalogue said there were costumes, too."

"Was this the one which included the locked trunk?" asked Nick, and Eleanor nodded.

She had fallen in love with the battered Morocco-leather chest and had been determined to own it. Fearing the lot would be beyond her budget, she was delighted when no one else had bothered to bid. When her haul had been delivered the following week, to her delight the boxes had contained more than clothes. There were ornaments, bibelots and postcards from the early 1930s. Prising open the trunk, prepared for it to be empty, she had discovered some old schoolbooks from the 1970s, various stained cookery books and a cardboard box labelled, "Miscellaneous from Grandma".

Feeling a small pang of guilt for trawling through someone else's private collections, she had nevertheless ripped open the box to discover several packs of Tarot cards, a book on the interpretation of dreams, some handmade cardboard runes, playbills and theatrical programmes, and a series of diaries. The covers on the diaries matched the pattern on the back of one of the Tarot packs.

"Last night, when I was getting ready for bed, I remembered why the name Esme Blood was so familiar. It was because I'd read her name in the playbills and on the inside of the diary in the lot we had bought in Kent."

Nick stared at her in astonishment. "How is that possible?"

"Strange things happen," she replied but when Nick looked unsure, she knew she would have to elucidate. "While I was at the Cliffside party, I spoke to Amelia Prentice, who was hosting the party with Eddie Stone."

"Eddie who you snogged at a beach party when you were sixteen?" Nick clarified, and Eleanor laughed.

"Yes, Eddie who I snogged at a beach party when I was sixteen. Anyway, Amelia told me one of her ancestors had called to her, and that was what had drawn her to Cliffside."

"Are you suggesting a ghost spoke to her?" Nick asked.

"No," said Eleanor, trying to remember Amelia's exact words, "not a ghost. She referred to it as a connection."

"And a week later, you bought an auction lot containing diaries and playbills belonging to an Esme Blood, who you think might be your relative?"

"It's an unusual name, so I hope it's the same person."

Eleanor knew Nick was sceptical, but she was sure that these items and the photographs were connected.

Amelia's words came back to her: "One of them might call to you." Is that what Esme was doing? It was odd that the name Esme Blood had found her in two such unexpected ways.

Nick began unpacking her Tarot collection, arranging the boxes of cards on the floor. Many packs were modern, the images based on Celtic folklore and mythical creatures, but there were some packs which were more unusual.

Nick pulled out an early Rider-Waite-Smith deck which was presented in a carved wooden box. The images on this pack were traditionally the most recognised, although they been based on the earlier Marseille pack, of which Eleanor had three different versions.

Delving further into the box, she lifted out three padded envelopes. "Here," she said. "These are the diaries…"

Nick whistled in appreciation as she extracted the four beautifully decorated books. "And these belonged to Esme Blood, the woman who is in the photograph your gran had in her paperwork?"

"Weird, isn't it?" said Eleanor.

She picked up the pack of Tarot cards that had been in the lot with the diaries and spread them before her. As with so many of the packs she bought, they held a faint musty smell, a reminder of their age and all they had seen. The fact the ornate black and gold backs matched the covers of the diaries written by Esme Blood seemed conclusive to Eleanor they had all belonged to her and as she gazed at them, she felt the usual thrill of excitement a new pack of cards always gave her.

Turning the cards, she smiled at the brightness of the colours; while not as vivid as they would have been when they were first created, these were clearer than packs of a similar age that she owned. Dividing the cards into the two packs that made up the whole, she began to lay them out in chronological order to check whether the set was complete while Nick watched her intently.

On one side of the table she placed the Major Arcana; cards that ran from zero (The Fool), to number twenty-one (The World). The ornately decorated icon cards had been the centre of the original game, *Triumphe*, for which the deck had been created in Italy. It was a form of trumps with each card holding a different value. This was a Marseilles deck and as such the names on the Major Arcana were written in French. *Le Mat* — The Fool — began his journey, following the path of life with all its many lessons, ending with *Le Monde* — The World — as he reached completion and understanding.

Next to these, she laid the Minor Arcana, the four suits: cups, discs, swords and wands. The names varied depending on the pack, discs were sometimes replaced by pentacles or coins, wands by clubs, but the swords and cups usually remained the same. These had court cards — king, queen, knight and page.

"They're in good condition," said Nick.

"Especially when you think they're over a hundred years old. It's a complete pack, too; usually there are a few missing."

"Are you going to read them?"

"Maybe," grinned Eleanor. "Let's see if they have anything to tell me."

Staring down at the Marseille pack that she hoped had once belonged to Esme Blood, Eleanor allowed her mind to relax, placing herself in the receptive state she used when she was reading the cards. It took a great deal of focus. Since her illness had begun, she had found it difficult to do a full reading as it drained her energy, leaving her exhausted, but as her eyes drifted across the cards, studying the designs, she noticed something unusual. Bringing her focus to The Fool, the card representing every person's journey through life, she realised there were tiny letters written around the edge.

"Look," she said, picking up the card. "There's writing on it."

Glancing around, she walked over to a bookcase where a few items from her old desk at the shop were sitting, waiting to be found a new home. One was her magnifying glass, the other a jeweller's loupe which she used when checking items at auctions and antique fairs. Holding The Fool under a bright lamp, she read aloud to Nick, "'We are the music makers'."

Intrigued, Eleanor picked up the next card in the sequence: *Le Bateleur* or The Magician. Once again, tiny letters were painstakingly written around the edge, this time reading: 'We are the dreamers of dreams'. A shiver ran down her spine. Leaning over, she examined each card in turn. They all had a line of text secreted around the rim.

"What the…?" she muttered to herself.

"You read them out, I'll write them down," Nick said, pulling Eleanor's laptop towards him.

"Ready?"

Nick nodded and Eleanor began to dictate the words.

"It's a poem," she said when they were halfway through.

"Do you think Esme Blood wrote it?" asked Nick.

"I'm not sure," she replied, her voice curious. There was something familiar about the words. "May I?"

Nick sat back as Eleanor pulled the laptop towards her and flicked open a search engine, typing in the first two lines. A moment later, the poem 'Ode' by Arthur O'Shaughnessy appeared on the screen. She clicked through to a recording of the poem when it had been set to music by Edward Elgar in 1912.

"Let's examine the cards and check it's the same all the way through," said Nick.

"Why? Do you think she might have added her own words?"

"Or a message," said Nick.

Eleanor grinned. "A message across time," she said, her eyes gleaming with excitement.

For the next half an hour, they transcribed the poem from the cards before comparing it with the full version. The entire work had been replicated, but six cards had been left with no text. Eleanor laid these out in a row. Were they a random selection or was there, as Nick had suggested, a message in the cards?

"The Empress, Death, The Tower, The Star, the Nine of Cups and the Ten of Coins," said Eleanor.

Picking up a pen and paper, she wrote down the numbers of the Minor Arcana cards in order to search for supporting cards. It was something she had learned from an experienced Tarot reader many years earlier, a way to join the reading together and give it more depth using numerology. Adding the nine and ten together it came to nineteen, which was the card number for The Sun; adding the nine and one together, she reached ten, representing the Wheel of Fortune and finally, adding the one and zero, to reach one, The Magician.

Glancing at the cards, she made a note of the three lines corresponding to these cards: 'And we are the dreamers of dreams' was etched around The Magician, while on The Wheel of Fortune was written, 'We build up the world's great cities' and, finally, The Sun stated, 'Can trample kingdoms down'. Reading them with as many different inflections as they could manage, they made no sense.

"Perhaps they were random," suggested Nick. "Not everyone uses numerology, and it may not even have existed when Esme Blood, or whoever it was, wrote the poem on the cards."

"True," agreed Eleanor, "but we are still left with the six blank cards."

"What do they mean?" asked Nick.

Staring down at the six cards, Eleanor allowed her mind to clear as she studied the images: the elegance of *L'Imperatrice*, seated on her golden throne with her mace of office; the skeletal figure of *Le Morte* with his scythe ready for him to harvest souls; *La Maison Dieu* with the flames of destruction and the falling people; *L'Etoile*, one of Eleanor's favourite cards, depicting hope even when the sky is dark, followed by two Minor Arcana cards — the nine of cups, or the wish card and, finally, the ten of coins, a significator of family, hearth and home.

Staring at them, she began to decipher the meaning of this sextet of cards, while Nick transcribed her words.

"The Empress is a mother figure," she said, "often representing a strong woman, the Mother Goddess; she offers love and life, the antithesis of the Death card. But she can also be manipulative and controlling, although, from this reading, I don't think that aspect is the issue. She is here as a representation of the protective spirit at the beginning of The Fool's journey, the separation from the Mother Figure and the first step into the unknown..." She broke off, her eyes flickering towards Nick. "Are you writing this down?"

"Yep, and recording it," he replied. "It might be important."

Eleanor felt a rush of gratitude towards him. Nick never questioned her, but always supported and loved her, as she did him. They understood each other's idiosyncrasies.

"Death, as I've told you so many times, doesn't mean someone is about to die, but it's an ending. The final chapter in a section of our lives, usually enforced and giving the seeker reason to grieve." She paused, swallowing hard. When she had been released from hospital, she had laid out her cards and Death had been the first she drew from the pack, followed by a series of cards from the suit of swords, which often presented illness. "Here, Death is with The Tower, which echoes the sentiment of the pulling apart of life, lightning ripping through structure, a loss of status through external events over which the seeker has no control. Although this may make the Tower card seem destructive, it can also symbolise the surge of energy required to move someone out of a rut or a bad situation — the moment of having enough of a bad situation, walking away and knowing that while it might seem an insane move, your instinct tells you it's the correct choice. This is supported by The Star."

"Your favourite card," interjected Nick.

"It is," she said, smiling. "The glimmer of hope in the darkness, the shimmer of light in the night sky. Taking your first step away from the mundane into the magical, though it does have a darker side. If you strive for perfection at the cost of your sense of reason, you can destroy delicate hope with despair. But, seeing as it is placed with the Nine of Cups or The Wish Card, The Star here is offering true hope and with it, the hope of true love. Positioned with the Ten of Pentacles, the card of putting down roots, the love of family, there is a positive outcome to these cards."

"So, to sum up," said Nick, "we have a mother figure, who could have been manipulative, a loss of status and enforced changes that led to a new beginning revealing hope, love and family?"

"Succinctly put," she said, sitting back and staring at the cards.

"What do the three extra cards add? The Sun, The Wheel of Fortune and The Magician?"

"Echoes of the rest of the reading," she replied. "The Sun is a positive card, The Wheel of Fortune is ambiguous, representing both good and bad, depending on where you are with the turn of the wheel, and, finally, The Magician, often thought to be representative of a spiritual guide, is a messenger, a shadow who accompanies you on your journey through life, connecting you with the elements and guiding you when you reach moments of darkness."

Outside, the moon shone through the window. Night had fallen while they were engrossed in their discoveries.

"And the poem?" asked Nick. "Do you think it has any significance?"

"It's possible," she replied, reaching for the diaries, the elaborate metallic patterns on the black leather cover gleaming in the autumn moonbeams. "If these all belonged to Esme Blood, they must be linked."

Exchanging a look of understanding, the two friends settled on the sofa. Eleanor opened the diary and began to read.

PART TWO: LONDON, 1875

CHAPTER ONE

There is little to be said of my birth; I was born, and my life began. Only images remain of the time spent with my mother — fleeting glimpses, fragments, ghosts, the scent of flowers, created in my mind from the stories told to me by other people.

Among those creators of my past were many who suggested my mother's act of abandoning me was one of great sadness. Others would judge it to be a moment of desperation or, perhaps, cruelty. Over the years, I have viewed it as something different. It was a question of survival. The balance of nature has always pointed to the survival of the fittest and, in me, I believe my mother realised she had met her match.

Her departure was her greatest gift. By leaving me in the fortune teller's tent, she bestowed upon me a loving family. A group of people joined by choice rather than blood, allowing me the freedom to be myself, to explore the layers of my existence with no recourse to anyone.

Our world, with its beauty, its contrasting darkness and light, its wonder and its challenges offer the adventure of living. To enable us to exist to the limit of our abilities we have to learn what makes our hearts beat, to be ourselves and to live truthfully within our own skin. My mother gave me this power. The other thing was my doll, Adelaide.

Eighteen-year-old Esmerelda Blood, known to all as Esme, put down her diary and glanced at her life-long companion; some might say she was too old for toys, but she would never be parted from Adelaide. The doll, wearing a frothy dress with a gold bodice and white skirt, made from offcuts of the matching adult-sized dress hanging from the screen in the corner, stared down from the shelf in the tiny dressing room. Her hair remained glossy, but her skin was beginning to fade and crack from age and love.

"Beginners, five minutes!" a young male voice shouted in the corridor, the sound ebbing as he continued through the labyrinthine corridors of the theatre. "Beginners, five minutes!"

Esme glanced at the cheap carriage clock beside Adelaide. It would be twenty minutes before she was needed, but, while she had applied her greasepaint before embarking on what she grandly thought of as writing her memoirs, being laced into her costume took time. Her dresser, Tilly, would be arriving at any moment. She put her diary into the box under the dressing table. This was where she kept her most treasured possessions: her Tarot cards, a letter and the photograph of Aaron. Smiling at the image, she felt a wave of loss and longing, before pushing the thought from her mind. There was a show to perform; this was not the time for mooning over the past.

Esme reached for her black boots, looping golden ribbons around the delicate hooks, ending with a large bow at the mid-point of her calves. Her flowing wrap fell open to reveal the shimmering pink of her loosely fastened corset and underskirts.

"You ready yet, Esme?" came the cockney vowels of her friend, Lynette Mason, as she marched into the dressing room. "Where's Tilly? We ain't got long until we're on."

Lynette was already dressed, resplendent in a costume identical to the golden and white creation waiting for Esme. The dresses were supposed to represent the black, yellow and white stripes of the Russian flag and would be finished with black parasols. The state visit of Tsar Alexander II of Russia was causing a huge amount of interest and in response Esme and Lynette had been given a new number to capitalise on the popularity of all things Russian. Both small and dark-haired, the pair were made up to look as alike as possible to enable them to perform a 'sister' act.

"I'm waiting for Tilly," replied Esme, finishing the bow on her boots with a flourish. "Have you seen her?"

"She was making eyes at Isaac half an hour ago, haven't seen either of them since."

The girls exchanged an amused glance. Isaac was one of the young male actors in the troupe and Tilly had long expressed an interest in his dark good looks.

"I'll help you," said Lynette as Esme stood, shrugging off her robe. "Will you read my cards for me later?"

"Of course," replied Esme, stepping into the costume, and waiting while Lynette tightened the strings at the back. "Romantic problems?" she asked, aware her friend was infatuated with Jeremiah Hardy and was desperate to understand why he continued to show little or no interest in her.

"No, I want to know if someone's going to get rid of Cassie for us."

Esme laughed. "What's she done now?"

Cassandra Smith was Esme's adopted elder sister. Tall, blue-eyed and with tumbling blonde hair, Cassie was a beauty. Popular for her looks and daring costumes, Cassie was wrongly convinced the catcalls she received every evening were in appreciation of her acting and singing, both of which were, at best, mediocre. However, this did not thwart her ambitions to be the female lead in the touring theatrical company where they all lived and worked. At present, the position was held by Rosie Hardy, Esme and Cassie's adopted mother and wife to the proprietor and actor-manager, Cornelius Hardy, who were the biological parents of Jeremiah Hardy.

"She suggested we might like her to join us, 'To add a bit of gravitas'," said Lynette, impersonating Cassie's little-girl lisp, which she thought made her appear charming.

"Gravitas?" snorted Esme. "Where did she learn that word?"

"Probably read it in someone else's review in *The Era*," replied Lynette, nodding towards the theatrical publication that lay on the chair. "Have you heard her latest, though? She keeps hinting she's met a title."

"In her grand plan to catch an earl?"

Cassie was determined to follow in the footsteps of other actresses who had married into the aristocracy.

"You're ready," said Lynette.

Esme walked over to the fogged looking glass in the corner of the room, where she tugged at the front of the dress until it was straight. Lynette joined her and they checked each other in the glass, ensuring they were as identical as they could manage for their act, 'The Skylark Sisters'. There was a knock on the door and a woman's voice called, "Five minutes, Esme. Is Lynette with you?"

"Come in, Winnie, she's here," Esme replied, hurrying to open the door. Lynette's mother, Winifred Mason, smiled; not much taller than Esme and Lynette, with dark hair that was greying at the temples, she was dressed as one of the three witches.

The Hardy Theatricals Troupe was a touring company famous for its updated versions of Shakespearean classics. *The Musical Mystery of Macbeth, The Scottish King* always played to packed houses when they toured the provinces, and since arriving in London it was proving a huge hit with theatre-goers in the capital. After each act, there were further interludes where different members of the troupe performed a series of songs and dances. Tonight would be their debut performance of 'I'm Going to Catch the Eye of the Tsar' — a comic song written by Lynette's father, Marcus, the troupe's musical director.

"It's a lively crowd tonight," said Winifred as the two girls grabbed their parasols and followed her into the chilly corridor. "Watch out for the group of apprentices in the stalls, they're a bit rowdy."

"Perhaps Cassie could calm them," giggled Lynette.

Winifred gave her a mock-stern look. "Now, now, young lady, no need for that, although I suspect Cassie's presence might whip them up into a frenzy."

Lynette smirked but Esme did not react. Despite her best efforts, she and Cassie had never bonded. Esme had tried over the years but their views on everything were opposed, and Cassie was often spiteful towards Esme.

Winifred disappeared into her dressing room to prepare for the next act, while Esme and Lynette made their way to the wings to hear the final bars of 'The Thane of Cawdor will be King' sung by Cornelius and Rosie, who were playing Lord and Lady Macbeth. As Cornelius spun Rosie across the stage, he caught a glimpse of the girls and winked before capering around a table and raising a goblet in unison with Rosie as they reached the final dramatic conclusion of their plan to murder King Duncan. The song had been taken from the original last scene of Act One and explained the Macbeths' plan to ply the king's servants with alcohol until they were blind drunk. Macbeth would then murder the king and they would blame this on the slumbering servants. Cornelius's rich tenor bellowed the final line of the song: "False face must hide what the false heart doth know."

Rosie let out a wild cackle of laughter and they swept off the stage to woops and screams from the packed auditorium.

"Warmed them up nicely for you, my darlings," Cornelius exclaimed in his lilting Irish accent as he and Rosie hurried past, already loosening their costumes as they hurried to change. "Have fun!"

The lights flashed up on the stage and, holding hands, the two girls ran out to an eruption of applause and shouting.

It was midnight. Esme sat on her bed in a voluminous embroidered white nightgown, with a long-fringed scarf around her neck, her dark hair in a heavy plait down her back. Cross-legged opposite her sat Lynette; a similar scarf covered her shoulders, but her nightgown was red flannel. Between them, Esme was dealing a row of Tarot cards. The pack was the French style known as the Golden Marseille design. It had been a gift from Rosie when Esme had become her apprentice in the fortune-telling tent. The connection Esme had with the cards felt natural: her birth mother, Judith, had chosen to leave her in the small octagonal tent and she liked to think some of its cunning had seeped into her during the time she slept there alone before being discovered by Cornelius and Rosie Hardy.

"Temperance, The Chariot, The Queen of Cups, The High Priestess, The Empress, the Eight of Coins and the Three of Cups…"

"Temperance," exclaimed Lynette in indignation, "not likely! Isn't that swearing not to drink gin?"

"It can be," agreed Esme, "but not in the case of the cards. It's more like a state of mind, a moment of peace after a difficult period in your life where you feel safe."

"Is the woman on the card an angel?" asked Lynette, leaning forward to examine the bright card, where a woman in a blue and red dress with golden wings poured liquid from one vessel to another.

"Yes, and she's diluting the wine," said Esme.

Lynette curled her lip in disdain. "What's next?"

"It doesn't really work that way," said Esme, her small hands hovering over the cards, as though warming her palms on the abstract beauty of the images. "I could recite the meaning of each card but that isn't the real way to read them, not if you want them to mean anything."

Lynette narrowed her eyes. "We've left the fairgrounds behind, love," she said. "I'm not some gullible punter."

"Which is why I want to read them properly," replied Esme. Taking a deep breath, she stared down at the five cards, each a familiar friend. The colours, vivid, shimmering, slid together and words began to form. "The love you seek is complex, the innocence and romance you wish to create with your heart is tainted due to the interference of your concerns. You are aware there is a need to push things along, but your heart is pulling in two directions — the need to remain where you are, admiring your love from afar, while also yearning to seek the courage you require to move forward into the unknown. An older woman hovers by your shoulder, offering advice but, beware, although her words are wise, she has her own dreams for your happiness and they may not align with your own wishes. The Eight of Coins is a sign there is hard work ahead if you wish this dream of love to come to fruition. Much strength will be needed, and you must be aware that the shadowy influence of The High Priestess reaches out to warn you of the hidden dangers of this quest. Her influence comes from the combination of the eight and the three."

Lynette looked confused and Esme realised she would have to explain things more simply.

"The Three of Cups is your love for Jeremiah, but he too has his concerns, indicated by The Chariot and the Eight of Coins.

They suggest he is worried about making a commitment to you and his future until he is more financially secure and able to offer you a life of comfort."

"Oh," said Lynette, a small sound of despair.

Esme reached out to take her hand and squeezed it. "Let me finish," she whispered. "Temperance, The Chariot and The Empress combine to suggest that while you currently yearn after a heart that is uncertain, there is still hope. The eight also shows someone who is prepared to work hard for their wages, is humble and is determined to reach his goal; a person who understands their worth. A person who always finds their way."

"So, what does it mean?" asked Lynette as Esme shuffled the cards together.

"Jeremiah likes you but until he's worked out his own plans for the future, which he will, you must be patient."

Lynette flung herself across the room and onto the other bed in the corner. The Tarot reading did not surprise Esme; it perfectly explained the situation surrounding her friend. Esme was disappointed not to see The Star, the hope card, but perhaps if she had done a fuller reading this card would have emerged. Lynette snubbed her candle and Esme blew her a kiss through the darkness, even though her friend could not see the gesture.

Shuffling her cards and straightening them into a neat pack, Esme wrapped them in a silk scarf and placed them in her wooden treasure box. She put a gentle finger on Adelaide's cheek, then settled down. Reaching under her pillow, she pulled out her copy of *Moll Flanders* by Daniel Defoe. The book had been a gift from Cornelius and Rosie for her birthday. It was a tale she had read over and over again, intrigued by the heroine, the irrepressible Moll, and her adventures. However, a few pages later, Esme could feel her eyes closing, and she snuffed out her own candle, plunging the room into darkness. Outside, the sounds of the London night swirled with the mist. Dogs barked, a drunk sang and in the distance raised voices indicated an altercation.

Esme snuggled deeper into her bed, relishing the clean sheets, the warm blankets and the glowing embers of the fire. It was a far cry from some of the places they had stayed in when on tour. No matter how successful they became, often the level of hospitality available in the rural areas they visited was basic and, many times, downright unpleasant. On those nights, Esme and Lynette would curl up together for warmth as they had done since they were children while Cassie griped and moaned. The third bed in the room remained unoccupied tonight and Esme wondered what had happened to her elder sister. *Probably trying to fulfil her ambition to catch herself an earl.*

Esme and Cassie had become sisters because the Hardys, who were kind people, had given the two homeless girls a chance in life. There was no blood connection between them and very little affection. Esme often felt sorry for Cassie, but the sentiment was never returned. Esme had been three when Cassie had arrived in her life, along with Cassie's cousin, Aaron Maclean. Cassie had been living with her aunt and uncle, Seth and Keziah Maclean, when they were unfortunate enough to have a business venture go wrong. At least, that was what Cassie told people; the rest of the troupe were well aware of Seth Maclean's gambling habit, which had landed him and his wife Keziah in debtors' prison. Rosie had insisted the children stay with them until the Macleans were able to improve their fortunes. The two blonde children were welcomed into the Hardy family.

The four youngsters had grown up together: Aaron and Jeremiah were the eldest, Cassie a year younger, then Esme. The Masons had joined the troupe when Esme and Lynette were both eight years old and the girls had been best friends ever since. The group of five had been a gang — squabbling, making up, playing in a world of their own — until the day Aaron's paternal grandfather tracked him down.

"Esme, are you awake?" Cassie's voice broke into Esme's memories.

"I am now," she muttered.

Cassie sat on the bed, the pearly fingers of dawn lighting the sky through the window behind her. Esme could smell stale smoke and gin as Cassie giggled, swaying, unable to keep her balance.

"I know a secret," she taunted.

"Good for you," muttered Esme, pulling the covers over her head and trying to ignore her.

"Don't you want to know?" Cassie hissed, prodding Esme in the shoulder with sharp fingers.

"Then it wouldn't be a secret," Esme replied. She grinned under the covers as the silence suggested Cassie was considering this comment.

"Actually, it's a message, not a secret," came Cassie's voice, all playfulness and teasing gone, replaced with irritation. The bed creaked as Cassie stood up, her feet making a swishing noise as she staggered across the room.

"Tell me then," sighed Esme, emerging from beneath the sheets.

"No."

"Fine."

Cassie was struggling with her dress. Her fingers, uncoordinated from a combination of gin and tiredness, fumbled with the buttons running down her back. Esme watched her for a moment, then her natural kindness surfaced. Without saying a word, she joined Cassie and within a few minutes had freed her sister from her dress and her undergarments, pulling a nightgown over her head, loosening her hair and removing the spikier hairpins before pushing Cassie into bed.

"Thanks," Cassie murmured, then, taking Esme's hand, she squeezed it and whispered, "Aaron's home," before falling asleep.

CHAPTER TWO

Aaron was home.

It had been a week since Cassie had passed on this tantalising piece of news and it had never been far from Esme's mind. While Lynette had always been her best friend, Aaron Maclean had been her heart, her protector, her teacher from childhood. When they reached their teens, a new understanding grew between them. Charming, handsome and with few scruples, Esme had often witnessed how Aaron had manipulated people, usually as he relieved them of their hard-earned cash, before dispensing with their affections once they had served their purpose. In her childish confidence she had never believed he would do the same to her, until the day he vanished into the mist, leaving a pair of red boots behind as the only proof he had ever existed.

Yet, he taught me how to survive, she thought. Her eyes flickered towards Cassie, who was repeating the same line for the third time, encouraged by Cornelius. Other members of the cast rolled their eyes in irritation as each repetition emphasised Cassie's stilted delivery.

Esme drifted back to the past, remembering the day when, after yet another slanging match with Cassie, Aaron had taken her for a walk along the bank of the stream that flowed beside the field where the Fair was camped.

"If you keep giving Cassie fuel to feed from, she'll always come back for more," he had said.

"What do you mean?" Esme had snapped. Aged thirteen, she had yet to learn how to control her temper. For years her fury had run wild, meeting Cassie insult for insult, and, on occasions, blow for blow.

"When Cassie taunts you, it isn't always necessary to reply," Aaron had said. "Yes, you're cleverer than her but with every sarcastic comment you throw at her, all she'll see is you opening yourself up for another chance for her to attack. Remember, Esme, silence isn't weakness, pausing gives you time to think and in those crucial seconds, you take back the power. Sometimes, saying nothing is the best weapon in your arsenal. Trust me, I'll always look out for you, Esme."

Esme was unsure but believed in Aaron, so the next time Cassie needled her, she decided to follow his advice. It was with great surprise that she discovered Aaron was correct. In the storm of Cassie's abuse, Esme had not responded but had smiled sweetly. Her elder sister had been unsure how to react and, in the end, had stalked away. It was the day Esme learned the valuable lesson that controlling herself meant gaining control of a situation.

"Come on, Esme darling, wake up," called Cornelius Hardy, "it's not like you to miss a cue, my sweet. Are you well?"

Esme came out of her reverie, realising everyone was staring at her. "Fine," she replied, her pale cheeks flaming pink in annoyance with herself. She hated making mistakes and tried to always be at her best. *It's Aaron*, she thought. *He makes me forget everything and causes me to daydream on stage and miss a cue.*

"From the beginning of the scene, please," called Cornelius and there was movement as everyone returned to their starting positions, which for Esme was in the wings, waiting with Cassie.

They were rehearsing *The Colleen Bawn*, a melodrama written by Irish-born Dion Boucicault, whom Cornelius admired. First performed in New York at the Laura Keane Theatre on

Broadway, it remained popular with audiences. Esme had a small part with no lines, but her timing was imperative for the smooth running of the performance as she doubled as a stagehand, removing and replacing items from the set as they went along.

"How's your head?" asked Esme as the beginners opened the scene. Cassie had returned home in the early hours again but this time, Esme had been asleep, so she'd been unable to question her sister about Aaron.

"Fine," responded Cassie, her tone bored. "I hope they hurry up; I've got an appointment in an hour."

"Anywhere exciting?"

"Wouldn't you like to know?" Cassie smirked.

"No, not really," Esme replied, her tone soft. "I was being polite."

"If you must know, I have a luncheon appointment with Charles Bartholomew, the Earl of Dunblane. Aaron arranged it. I saw him last night, with his wife."

Cornelius had raised his hand to cue Cassie and she marched on stage, leaving Esme blank-faced and trembling, trying to push away the wave of pain Cassie's words had created.

Aaron was married.

Forcing her attention back to the rehearsal, she allowed the words of the play to flow over her, walking through the part like an automaton. Was Cassie lying? Esme swallowed hard. Why would she lie? To cause pain, which was one of Cassie's favourite pastimes, but this was a huge lie to tell.

This is Cassie, thought Esme, dwelling on the spiteful child Cassie had been, causing arguments, bullying the younger children, then giving a dimpled look of confused innocence when accused of the nastier crimes of their youth. Yet she could not dismiss the fact that Aaron was in London and had not contacted her. Was this the reason? Had their childhood friendship been abandoned? Pushing this thought away, Esme focused on the play. Aaron would never forsake her.

An hour later, Esme was relieved when Cornelius called a halt to the rehearsal. It had taken a huge effort to concentrate, and she was desperate to find Lynette. Her friend would help her through this unexpected storm, but before the troupe could drift away for lunch, Cornelius called them all on stage. Rosie was beside him, a serious expression on her face.

"My darlings," Cornelius exclaimed, drawing their attention, his eyes twinkling, "as you know, for a while now, Rosie and I have been making plans to change the fortune of our touring troupe."

There was a disconcerted murmur, a ripple of voices as looks were exchanged. The Hardy Troupe had been together for many years and were an extended family of performers, artists, musicians, seamstresses and carpenters. Everyone mucked in, taking on several roles in order to make the group work. Married couples raised families, single people found love, everyone looked out for each other. The bond had been created from years of travelling and working together. Rosie would set up her fortune-telling tent, while Cornelius led the team of men in putting together their ramshackle stage where they would perform their unique versions of Shakespeare, accompanied by singing acts, dancing, tumbling and comedy skits. During the winter when the fairs were shut, they performed in shabby theatres around the country.

"We're very happy to say, our touring days are behind us," Cornelius continued. There was a flutter of surprise. "You were told we would be here through the winter but, today, we have signed the lease on this very theatre, The Firebird, and we'll be remaining here for the foreseeable future. This will mean some changes, but all of you who wish to stay with us will find a welcome. Any who prefer to resume life on the road have our blessing to go and may return at any time. We will also be employing new stagehands, costume makers, dressers, the usual crews, so if anyone has any recommendations speak to either myself, Rosie or Simeon Cox, our newly appointed stage manager." He pointed to a tall man with a shock of dark hair, who raised his hand to acknowledge the comment. Cornelius beamed. "All your questions will be answered as we work things out for ourselves but, for now, the programme remains the same, which means we have a show tonight."

With a wave of his hand, he dismissed them, smiling at the buzz of excitement his announcement had created. Cassie rolled her eyes as though this was old news and strutted off the stage, ostentatiously beckoning Tilly to follow her. "I need some help with my new dress," she announced, and Tilly followed with great reluctance.

Cornelius watched Cassie leave, then he and Rosie approached Esme. "You did very well, my darling," he exclaimed. "Perhaps you have a future on the stage, as well as being a singer. What do you think of our news?"

Esme smiled. "Thanks Pa," she said with her usual quiet seriousness, glancing towards Rosie, who smothered a smile. "It's possible Ma might have mentioned you were considering staying here."

"Ah, your mother could never keep anything from you, my little fortune-telling angel," Cornelius laughed. "Do you think you'll be happy to stay in London?"

"Yes, it'll be fascinating to help you and Ma grow the theatrical troupe. There are so many actor-managers in London, to think we'll be part of this new wave of entertainment is marvellous."

"I told you Esme would be excited," said Rosie.

Cornelius gave Esme a one-armed hug, then marched away to speak to Lynette's father, Marcus.

"Esme, are you sure there is nothing amiss?" Rosie asked.

"Honestly, Ma, I'm fine. You know how it is at some times of the month."

Rosie gave a searching look but desisted. Esme knew her mother was unconvinced but Cornelius was calling for his wife, announcing an excursion to a nearby tavern for all who wished to join them in celebration.

"Oysters and stout," he called, but Esme was not in the mood for a party. Cassie's words continued to sting, and she was unsure how long she would be able to hold back her tears.

As she reached her dressing room door, Lynette caught up with her, holding two muslin-wrapped pies and a metal cannister of coffee. "Look what Rosie gave us," she said in delight.

"Why did she do that?" asked Esme.

Lynette shrugged. "Maybe because she loves you and wanted to surprise you," she said, squeezing through the door into Esme's tiny corner dressing room.

A stove glowed in the corner, making the room warm and cosy. Swallowing the lump in her throat, Esme cleared a space on the small table she used for her greasepaint, placing it in the centre of the room and pulling up the two spindly chairs.

"Rosie sent Tilly out for the coffee from The Rainbow earlier," Lynette said, pointing to the steaming canister. Esme breathed in the rich aroma and felt tears well in her eyes. "What's up, Smee?" asked Lynette, slipping back in Esme's childhood nickname as she handed her one of the delicious-smelling pies. "You've been a bit off the last few days."

As a child, Lynette had never been able to pronounce Esme's name; Smee was as close as she could get, and the name had stuck. When Esme had first begun performing, her stage name had been Little Smee, but it was one she had dispensed with a few years earlier, insisting to her parents she did not want to have a career where she perpetually played children, despite her small stature.

"The other night, when I put Cassie to bed, she told me Aaron was in London," said Esme, breaking a piece of the pastry from the crust and popping it into her mouth. "She was drunk, so I didn't believe her, but today she said she'd seen him again. Apparently he's introduced her to some bloke, the Earl of Dunblane…"

"Have you heard from Aaron yourself?" interrupted Lynette.

"No," said Esme. "I keep checking with Ivan to see if he's left a note at the stage door, but today Cassie told me the reason he hasn't been to see me is because he's married."

Lynette's eyes widened in surprise, her hand stopping halfway to her mouth. "Married? But this is Aaron. Being married wouldn't stop him visiting you."

"Perhaps Aaron has tried to contact me, but Ma and Pa have stopped him."

"Why would they do that?"

"They keep forgetting, I'm not a child…"

"You'll always be the baby of the family to them," said Lynette, finishing her pie and pouring out the thick, fragrant coffee.

"Why would they want to keep us apart, though?"

Even as she spoke the words, Esme knew the answer; her parents had always been wary of Aaron's hold over her. When she had been fifteen, they had encouraged her to go on holiday with Lynette and her parents to Brighton. When they returned five days later, Aaron had left the travelling entertainers. Rosie had taken Esme into their caravan and explained.

"Aaron's parents have died," Rosie had said. "They caught influenza in gaol. Aaron's grandfather is going to take care of him."

Aaron's paternal grandfather, Pete Maclean, had arrived a few days after the burial of his son and daughter-in-law and taken Aaron home with him to Falmouth in Cornwall, where Pete had a successful shoe-making business. It was his intention to teach Aaron a respectable trade. Esme had hoped Cassie might have been taken too, but Cassie and Aaron were related through their mothers and Pete took only his grandson.

"Did you know he would be leaving while I was away?" Esme had stormed at Rosie, her heart breaking at the thought she might never see him again.

"He left you a letter," had been Rosie's reply.

The short, scrawled note had become Esme's most prized possession, residing in her box of treasures. *I'll come back for you,* Aaron had written.

For the first few months he had replied to Esme's letters, then on her birthday, he had sent her a pair of handmade boots in the softest red leather she had ever seen. A pattern of handstitched violets ran down the outside and they were laced with scarlet ribbons. After that, there had been silence. Eventually, Esme had stopped hoping a letter would arrive, packing away her red boots with Aaron's letters tucked inside, and she'd tried to put him from both her heart and mind.

A few years later, when they had been travelling to one of the big Golowan festivals in Cornwall, she had seen a local newspaper featuring an advertisement for Maclean and Grandson, with a photograph. Outside a smart shoe shop were Aaron and a man so like him, it had to be his grandfather.

Esme had cut out the picture, keeping it with her until the flimsy paper disintegrated.

"How do you feel about seeing him?" asked Lynette.

For a moment, Esme was silent as she tried to think her way through the haze of emotions Aaron created within her: fear, excitement, fury and another which she refused to acknowledge. What did she feel about Aaron? Part of her wanted to throw herself into his arms and never let him go, but the other part, the pragmatic side, knew it might be sensible to allow her parents to continue to keep him at bay. Aaron was quicksilver, the shimmer of moonlight on water, an illusion, beauty without substance, a dancing shadow offering delight and distraction which could vanish in an instant. And Cassie had told her he had a wife, but Cassie was not above a spiteful lie and Esme did not want to believe Aaron would have fallen in love with another woman. Wiping away a tear, she looked into Lynette's worried face. "Excited, terrified, furious, so many things, but the predominant emotion is anger that he hasn't contacted me. Even if Cassie is correct and he is married, there's no reason to stay away."

Lynette topped up their cups and sipped her coffee. "How about I find Aaron?" she suggested.

"Would you?" Esme could not suppress her eagerness.

"Yes, we can't let Cassie get one over on us," said Lynette, gathering up the crumbs left by their lunch. "Leave it with me, Smee. If Aaron's back in London, married or not, we'll find him."

CHAPTER THREE

"*Twenty tiny toes twinkling their way to the top,*" Esme read the words aloud from the mock-up of the new poster for her act with Cassie, her eyes wide with equal measures of amusement and disgust.

"Cassie suggested it," said Simeon Cox, the stage manager. "It's quite dreadful, but she insists it has a poetic ring."

"Put it next to her name then, not mine," said Esme. "My toes do not 'twinkle'."

"You'd better take it up with your pa," said Simeon, rolling up the poster and disappearing into the wings.

Esme sighed. Cornelius had summoned both her and Cassie the previous week, saying he wanted them to sing together during the interludes of *The Colleen Bawn*. "Your act with Lynette is charming, but it has its limitations…"

"You mean, Lynette has limitations," Cassie had smirked.

"Lynette's talents lean towards acting rather than vaudeville," agreed their father, deliberately ignoring the sting in Cassie's words. "Her parents have asked that she be trained to be part of the cast."

Esme had glanced at Cassie, whose pale blue eyes narrowed in annoyance.

"What about me?" Cassie had snapped. "Am I supposed to sing in the interludes for the rest of my life? I want to be the female lead."

"Your mother is the female lead and Eliza is the second-lead and her understudy," Cornelius had replied. "Cassie, my love, we need you to entertain the boys as your own beautiful self. If we were to put you in the cast, you'd have to be dressed plainly, your hair covered, and no one would be able to appreciate your looks."

Esme had smothered a smile. Cornelius was aware of Cassie's theatrical limitations and by flattering her, he was able to spare her the embarrassment of being unable to perform with enough skill.

Now, Cornelius had summoned them to rehearse the song again. "Come, my darlings, let's try the song again," said Cornelius, leading them to the upright piano that had been wheeled on stage. "We were very close to perfection yesterday but this time, I want you to sing the lead, Esme, with Cassie coming in as harmony. In the musical breaks, we can walk through the dance steps, although I'm unsure whether to leave this in…"

"But Pa, that's the best bit," exclaimed Cassie, who preferred dancing to singing. Esme was proficient at both. "It makes the act classier."

"With our twinkling toes?" asked Esme, her face the picture of innocence. Cassie shot her a look of dislike.

"Yes, my darling, with your twinkling toes," said Cornelius, giving her the smallest of winks. "Sing properly today, please, my darling," he added in an undertone.

Cornelius's fingers danced over the piano keys, picking out the tune, a medium paced, comic song which nevertheless had a complicated soprano lead. The lyrics told the tale of two women discussing what they thought were two different men, until the final verse revealed they had been praising the same two-timing scoundrel. Following the music, Esme did not need her father's nod to bring her in, although she was surprised by his instruction. It was rare she gave full range to her voice, usually toning it down to fit the tunes she sang with Lynette but, today, as instructed, she allowed the music to fill her as she let the tune fly.

The Hardys had been stunned when they had first heard Esme's voice. One morning, not long after her fifth birthday, Cornelius had stood her on a chair next to the piano and begun playing scales. Singing them himself, then pausing for Esme to follow, the sound which flowed from her rosebud lips had astounded the entire company.

"Sing one of your nursery rhymes," Cornelius had encouraged, and Esme had done as she was asked. With each note, her child's speaking voice was transformed into one of bell-like beauty, uncanny butterfly notes floating in the air, pure and clear, as she ran up and down the scales, lilting and magical. As the five-year-old Esme had sung, she had not noticed as her adopted mother had joined them, followed by every member of the troupe who was in the vicinity, including Lynette's father, Marcus, the troupe's composer. Deep inside the music, Esme had lit a flame in her soul, one that would never be extinguished.

On the empty stage, with Cornelius guiding her with the piano, Esme allowed the notes to once again rise pure and clear, enveloping those around her in the ethereal beauty of the music. Whenever she sang, Esme remembered the wave after wave of joy that had run through her when she had discovered this unexpected talent. It tingled like a thousand lights dancing inside her skin: warm, safe, giving her an eerie sense of power as this glorious voice coated her in a protective shell of wonder.

"How am I supposed to make myself heard over her racket?"

Esme stopped.

"Cassie, you're perfectly capable of making yourself heard," said Cornelius, for once unable to keep the irritation from his voice.

"She was behind the beat; it made me miss my cue," Cassie snapped, while Esme gave her a blank stare.

"Why don't you set the pace?" Esme said, after a lengthy pause. "We'll start on verse three. You have the first two lines and I'll follow you."

Glaring in fury at her sheet music, Cassie gave a small, ungracious nod and waited for Cornelius to count her in. Esme followed the tune, acknowledging that her sister's alto voice, while a good match for her own soprano, was weaker and more strained when reaching the top notes.

Reining in her own vocal ability, Esme followed Cassie's lead, allowing her voice to wind around her sister's, harmonising, covering Cassie's off notes until the unpromising beginning became a proper duet. Her confidence growing, Cassie began to act the words and Esme did the same, relieved they had been spared one of her sister's violent temper tantrums.

"Excellent, my darlings!" exclaimed Cornelius. "It's a diamond in the rough, waiting to be polished. We'll make it work, though."

Cassie gave him a sweet smile before glaring at Esme and flouncing off. Esme gathered her music, ready for a break. She decided to walk back to their rented house and relax with the new book of poems she had bought before the evening show, but as she made her way to the wings, she saw Lynette beckoning.

"What's happened?" she asked, as Lynette grabbed her hand and dragged her along the corridor.

"Jeremiah was out this morning, and guess who he saw?"

"Aaron?" Esme breathed, her heart pounding.

"He asked him to give you this." Lynette's voice was trembling with excitement as she passed a small, square letter into Esme's hand.

Looking down, Esme was surprised at the elegance of Aaron's writing, although she noticed the idiosyncratic way he always used a capital 'R' throughout, never a lower case. "Does he want to meet?" she whispered, breathless with fear and anticipation at the contents of the letter.

"Yes," grinned Lynette, "and when Jeremiah asked him if he was married, he laughed and said it was one of Cassie's lies."

Relief swept through Esme as with trembling fingers she opened the note.

Meet me. I've missed you, darling Smee xx

Esme's breath caught in her throat, her eyes came up to meet Lynette's and as excitement coursed through her, so did a whisper of fear.

CHAPTER FOUR

Esme linked arms with Lynette as they strolled down Oxford Street towards John Lewis, the draper's shop. Their quest, if anyone asked, was to find bonnets to match the new dresses Rosie and Cornelius had bought them. "With winter coming, you need something to reflect that you're both young ladies of nearly nineteen," Rosie had said as they selected the rose-coloured wool for Esme and the dark green for Lynette.

Esme was walking towards a bookshop window when Lynette tugged her back.

"Bonnets," she reminded her.

"Yes," agreed Esme, dragging her attention away from the display of Mary Elizabeth Braddon's *Lost for Love* with great reluctance.

Lynette bit her lip and reaching into her pocket, brought out a small gold-coloured watch on a brass chain.

"Isn't that your mother's?" asked Esme in surprise. The watch was one of Winifred's most prized possessions.

"Yes, she doesn't know I've borrowed it," said Lynette, "but I wanted us to keep track of time. Come on, we need to hurry…"

They entered John Lewis and Esme smiled at the assistant as they made their way to the haberdashery department.

"Will you be using this new bonnet to impress Jeremiah?" Esme asked.

"I'm not sure I'm interested in Jeremiah anymore," Lynette said.

"Why not? You only have to look at him when he talks to you to realise you're perfect together. He'll see it soon and then you'll have your happily ever after, like in all the stories you read."

Lynette gave her a withering look. "Happy ever after? It's time you grew up, Smee. There's no such thing, but you can have someone who is kind and works hard. Jeremiah is a gentle person, he's a good actor and he's ambitious. He's handsome, too, and we're friends. These are the qualities I like, but part of me also wants him to think I'm wonderful and worth fighting for. I don't want to go out with him because it's convenient for us both."

"Wait and see," said Esme, "I have faith in Jeremiah." Picking up a length of sky-blue ribbon, she held it up for Lynette to admire. "Oh, this is pretty, it would suit you, Lyn."

Esme and Lynette were a similar height, but their colouring was different. Esme's dark hair, pale skin and blue eyes suggested a Celtic ancestry, while Lynette's lighter chestnut hair and hazel eyes with slightly olive skin hinted at possible Mediterranean roots. On stage, Lynette's hair was darkened with paint or a wig when they were performing as The Skylark Sisters.

"This is more my thing," said Esme, her fingers lacing between a strand of red.

"What about this one?" a male voice interrupted them, picking up a violet ribbon. "It matches your eyes."

Esme gasped. "Aaron," she whispered. Dropping the ribbon into the basket, she backed away. The meeting had been planned with meticulous care by Lynette and Jeremiah, with Esme complicit throughout, but faced with Aaron, she felt her breath catch in her throat. The glamour of his youth had been replaced by the elegance and confidence of a wealthy man. His new-style three-piece suit was expensive, tailored and understated; his Ascot was crimson silk, held in place by a tie pin adorned with a tiny diamond. His boyish blond curls were tamed and, despite the fashion for beards and moustaches, he was clean-shaven, with a nod to hirsute facial adornments in his neat sideburns.

"Hello, Esme," he said. His voice was different, deeper, polished, a far cry from his former mix of West Country burr and fluent Cockney expletives.

"Hello, Aaron," she replied, her voice a breathy whisper which irritated her — she did not want to sound like one of the heroines in the plays they performed.

Another young man emerged from between the aisles, a satisfied expression on his pleasant face. "I knew Lyn and I could find him," Jeremiah said. "Ma and Pa have no idea."

"They're good people," said Aaron, "and they mean well. They took me in when I had nowhere to go and for that, I'll always love and respect them." His eyes never left Esme's face. "Shall we help you young ladies to make your purchases, then perhaps a walk by the Serpentine in Hyde Park, where I believe there is a stand selling the finest hot chestnuts in town?"

Jeremiah laughed. "Chestnuts — do you remember when we used to steal them from the stand at the winter fair in Lewes?" he said.

Aaron grinned.

Esme stared. Her breath was stuck in her throat. Aaron was smiling down at her and her instinct was to run, to admit this was a mistake and her parents had been correct to keep them apart. Danger flared in her heart, and the scrappy, snarly Esme of the fairground days was rising inside her. The angry girl who had lost her best friend, the teenager with an edge to her glare that kept people at bay, the dark-haired fortune teller who held an air of shimmering glamour, the Esme she had learned to control, to keep at bay, the Esme who she knew would always lead her into danger, the girl she could have been if she had not decided to follow in Rosie's footsteps and dwell in kindness and love, rather than fire and challenge.

Her old self was fighting to meet Aaron face-to-face, the glint in her eye as devilish as his own. Even as these thoughts raced through her head and she knew she should resist, Aaron was proffering his arm and she was reaching out, slipping her hand into the crook of his elbow, smiling up at him. She was an adult, after all, a woman with far more life experience than most nearly-nineteen-year-olds, thanks to her upbringing.

Beside them, Jeremiah dared to offer his arm to Lynette, who blushed prettily and accepted.

An hour later, as Lynette and Jeremiah, whispering and flirting, disappeared in search of the chestnut stand, Aaron and Esme sat on a bench by the Serpentine. The December day was mild, and they watched the carriages and the promenaders stroll past.

"Where have you been?" asked Esme, looking up at Aaron.

"You know where I've been," he replied. "Working for my grandfather and running his shoemaking business."

Esme threw him a scornful look. "Your grandfather died two years ago."

Aaron stretched his arm along the bench behind him. Esme felt his fingertips brushing her shoulder and shivers ran down her spine. Two young women, who were walking behind their parents, threw him an appreciative glance. Tipping his hat, Aaron smiled, and Esme felt a surge of jealousy.

"Stop flirting and explain yourself," she demanded.

Aaron withdrew his look from the two women and returned his gaze to Esme. "Do you remember what I said the day we last saw each other?"

His words were scorched into her heart. "You're the only woman I'll ever love," he had whispered to her in the darkness, "but you need to do some growing up before we can be together."

"Yes."

"I meant it."

"Why didn't you reply to my letters, then?"

"Life was busy," he said.

"Busy?" She shot him a disdainful look, furious he could be so flippant about his lack of communication when it had caused her such intense pain and loneliness. "Did that involve finding a wife?"

"Esme, no!" Aaron laughed, enraging her further. "Even if I was married, it wouldn't change my feelings for you."

"How can you make such a statement if you're in love with another woman?"

"Don't be naïve," he snapped. "Marriage isn't about love, it's a transaction. It makes one respectable and, in some cases, wealthy."

Esme narrowed her violet eyes. "Be honest, Aaron. Are you married?"

"No."

Despite his assurance, the amused glint in his eye made her uncertain, but she knew him too well to expect to be given any more information. Instead, shoving her anger to one side, she watched two calvary soldiers trot by on glistening chestnut horses. One glanced in her direction and smiled, speaking to his companion who followed his friend's gaze. Grinning, he whistled a line from 'I'm Going to Catch the Eye of the Tsar'. Esme blew them a kiss and they cheered.

"I've been following your progress in the newspapers," said Aaron and she took great pleasure in the expression of annoyance on his face after the attention of the two young men. "You and Lynette have a successful act, although I'm glad Ma and Pa have finally let you drop the 'Little Smee' act. It was demeaning to someone of your talent. You're far too womanly to be able to keep passing yourself off as a child."

Esme refused to acknowledge his compliment. "Yes, The Skylark Sisters are getting top billings, although I doubt Pa's experiment of putting Cassie and I together in an act will last long." Aaron laughed and Esme, grinning, continued. "I suppose you've heard that Pa has taken the lease on The Firebird."

"He fancies himself as an actor-manager," said Aaron. "It's a far cry from the touring fair."

"Life changes," said Esme. "He and Ma are older; they want an easier life, and the fairs are changing too. There's more competition. Pa's always been a performer; he loves the theatre."

"I came to see *The Musical Mystery of Macbeth, The Scottish King*. It was very good."

"You saw me and Lynette, then."

"Yes, I saw Lynette, but the 'you' on stage wasn't you."

"It's called acting."

"No, it isn't. Why were you singing in such a simple manner? Your voice is spectacular."

"People want sparky and sweet. My voice has to adapt."

"What about you, though?" he said, his eyes curious. "You're different."

"The last time you saw me I was fifteen. Did you think I'd be the same?"

"I thought you'd be fiercer," he admitted. "You were a wildcat when I left, quarrelling with Cassie, making sure everyone knew you were there but now, it's as though you've stepped out of your body and forgotten."

She laughed. "Don't be fooled, my love," she said. "I know exactly who I am, thank you very much. If I choose to show different sides of my personality, it's my business. As for Cassie, why would I waste my energy on her?"

"True, although you might want to watch Cassie. When I moved back in with my grandfather, I learned a few things about her family."

Esme's ears pricked up. "What?" In the distance, they could see Lynette and Jeremiah approaching.

"You know Cassie claimed her mother died of consumption and her father, two weeks later, of a broken heart?"

"Yes," agreed Esme, who knew the story well. "It was why she went to live with you. Your mum, Keziah, and her mum, Margaret, were sisters."

"Exactly, but I have it on good authority from one of my more useful contacts that Cassie's father, Reg Smith, murdered her mother, as well as his parents, and he was hanged."

Esme stared at him in horror. "Does Cassie know?"

"No," replied Aaron. Before they could discuss it further, Lynette and Jeremiah joined them.

"Are you going to tell us why Ma and Pa have banished you?" Jeremiah asked Aaron jovially as they passed round the hot paper cones, crammed with the piping hot, earthy-smelling chestnuts.

"They seem to think I might be a bad influence," Aaron replied with a wicked grin.

"Why's that?" asked Lynette.

"Some of the company I'm keeping," he said. "Cornelius heard I was a businessman and visited me. He was unsure about the rumours swirling around and suggested I consider with care whether my presence in your lives would be advantageous."

"How odd," said Jeremiah. "Pa always had a great deal of respect for you, Aaron. What changed his mind?"

"I have a few side-lines that he found dubious."

"Such as?" asked Esme.

"I arrange things," Aaron said. "People who need services or require short-term loans or might need introductions to help them further their own ambitions. I help them to meet the right people."

Esme glanced at Lynette and Jeremiah, who were wide-eyed. She understood why Cornelius and Rosie would have been cautious. There had been men calling themselves fixers, who would prowl the fairgrounds offering such dubious services. Cornelius referred to them as procurers or pimps, chasing them away from the Hardy troupe. Some of them offered financial services, which never ended well. Esme took in Aaron's expensive clothes and shuddered, wondering what nefarious activity had furnished him so handsomely.

"You're a procurer?" asked Jeremiah, his voice hesitant.

"No." Aaron's tone was firm. "Those men were villains, taking advantage of the weak and the poor. I would never behave in such a manner. I've experienced poverty and the fear of the debt collectors' men, something I saw happen to my parents over and over again before they were shipped off to Newgate, and I swore any money I made would be from those who could afford to lose it. My introductions are made in gentlemen's clubs. Everything is between consenting adults. If one party is uninterested, the conversation ends."

"Quite the Robin Hood…" laughed Jeremiah. Esme saw the gleam of respect in his eyes as he studied Aaron with curiosity.

"Perhaps you could arrange for Cassie to 'catch an earl'," said Esme, and Lynette laughed. "The other day, she told me she was having lunch with Charles Bartholomew, Earl of Dunblane."

Aaron gave her a grin of evil proportions. "How do you think our paths crossed again?"

"No!" gasped Lynette.

"You're lying," exclaimed Jeremiah.

"God's honest truth," said Aaron. "It was the Earl of Dunblane who approached me to see if I could arrange an introduction to the *luverly* —" he said the word in an exaggerated Cockney accent — "Cassandra Smith."

Esme, Lynette and Jeremiah laughed.

"Did he know you were related?" asked Esme.

"Not when he made his first approach," admitted Aaron, "but when I explained we were cousins, he went out of his way to assure me his intentions are honourable." Aaron paused. "Well, honourable enough."

Esme and Lynette exchanged a concerned glance. Cassie might be irritating, but they did not wish her any harm.

"Is that where she's been going?" asked Lynette.

"She's actually done it, landed a member of the gentry?" added Jeremiah, his voice echoing with wonder.

"Unfortunately not," said Aaron. "The Earl of Dunblane is married. He fancied Cassie as a mistress. Cassie is unimpressed about the incumbent countess, but Charles is determined to win her around."

Esme watched Aaron. His voice held no malice, but the coldness in his eyes suggested he was enjoying the joke at Cassie's expense. Despite being cousins, Aaron and Cassie's relationship had been volatile. Esme had often wondered if, should Cassie ever need Aaron's help, a latent family bond would emerge, but this did not seem to be the case. While she felt no need to defend Cassie, her natural kindness hoped Cassie would not be too damaged by the encounter with the Earl of Dunblane.

"You haven't changed," she said to Aaron, who shot her a quizzical look. Then she stood, crumbling up the empty paper cone. "It'll be dark soon; you can walk us back to the theatre."

Lynette and Jeremiah strolled ahead. Aaron tucked Esme's hand under his arm.

"If I were to ask you to come with me, would you?" he said when the others were out of earshot.

Esme stared ahead, her heart pounding in her chest. The sensible answer was 'no', but one flash of Aaron's smile was enough to chase all sense away. "Perhaps," she managed at last.

Aaron squeezed her hand against him. "It's better than I deserve," he said. "Remember, Esme, if you ever need me, I will always protect you."

Esme turned to him, searching his face and, for once, saw sincerity in his eyes. "Thank you, Aaron."

They caught up with Lynette and Jeremiah, and the four reminisced about their childhoods until they turned into Shaftesbury Avenue, the thoroughfare containing many of the fashionable theatres. The Firebird was situated in one of the narrow roads running towards Soho which branched like arteries from the main road.

"I'll leave you here," said Aaron.

To Esme's relief, Lynette and Jeremiah were tactful enough to walk on to examine a poster about an upcoming show.

"Will you be in London long?" Esme asked, the thought of losing him again hitting her like a fever.

"I'm leaving tomorrow," he said. "The Earl of Dunblane has invited me to a shoot on his estate in Leicestershire. This is my business card. Letters sent to this address will reach me."

Esme ran her gloved fingers over the embossed letters: *Aaron Maclean, Esq. Purveyor of Services and Observances.* Underneath was an address a few streets away from where they were standing: Soho Square. Esme felt a physical jolt. He had been nearby all this time. Anger shot through her again. "Is there any point writing? You never reply," she snapped, dropping the card into her reticule.

"For you, my love, I will make an exception," he said. "If you write, I will respond, I promise."

With a bow, he kissed her hand, doffed his hat to Lynette and Jeremiah and disappeared into the crowd.

As Esme, Lynette and Jeremiah made their way to their lodgings a few doors away from The Firebird, Esme could not help but think that while Aaron had assured her he would reply, he had not specified whether it would be immediately or in his own good time. Smiling despite herself, she followed the others inside, unable to shake off her excitement that Aaron Maclean was back in her life.

PART THREE: PEMBROKESHIRE, 2020

CHAPTER ONE

Eleanor stared at the framed poster in her kitchen, tracing her finger over the words.

"Twenty tiny toes twinkling their way to the top," it declared, and written underneath were the names Cassandra and Esmerelda. Looking down at the diary clutched in her hand, a shiver ran down her spine. How was this possible? She had owned the poster for years; it had been one of the first genuine pieces of Victorian memorabilia she had ever bought.

Someone might call to you... Amelia's voice floated back to her.

There was no doubt in her mind that Esme was reaching out to her from the past, but why? The poster was one of three hanging on her wall. The largest was a reprint of a 1951 poster from the London Palladium when Judy Garland had made her debut there, and either side of it were two smaller original posters, one featuring Marie Lloyd in 1886 at The Star Palace of Varieties in Bermondsey, and the other advertising The Firebird Theatre in Glass House Street.

"The Firebird," Eleanor mused as she read the bold advertisement for *The Colleen Bawn* by Dion Boucicault with interludes from not only Esme and Cassie but also 'Isaac The Singing Chimney Sweep' and 'The Delightful Dancing of The Dainty Dolls'. Eleanor gazed at the poster, wondering if in her vast collection of theatrical programmes she had any from The Firebird.

"Why didn't I think of it before?" she said to Sandy, who was sitting on a kitchen chair watching her with amber eyes. "But where would they be?"

If she had been in her shop, she would have been able to walk straight to her collection where everything had been organised and catalogued in order to make it easy for her to help her customers find what they needed with quick efficiency. Unfortunately, the contents of the shop were half-unpacked in the red barn.

Eleanor glanced at her watch, debating whether she could spare half an hour to search, but she knew this was impossible. She had an appointment with her accountant, Andrew, after which she had planned to have lunch with Aidan and Chloe at Wave Riders, the combined surf shop and café they owned.

Reaching Andrew Carver's house, Eleanor breathed in the familiar salty smell around her. It was perched on the edge of the cliff overlooking the wide expanse of Newgale beach and the waves crashed below her, sending up a mist of spray. Even though she had loved running her shop in London, she had always missed the ozone scent of the sea on a windy day.

"Eleanor," Andrew called, walking towards her. "How are you?"

Eleanor noted the concern in his eyes. "I'm fine," she said. "Truly. I was in hospital last week having treatment and today I feel almost back to normal."

Andrew gave her a considered look, one she remembered from her younger years. She had known Andrew for most of her life, as she had grown up with his daughter, Sam, and the look he gave her now mirrored that he had worn when she and Sam would stumble home, late, giggling and trying to hide the fact they had been drinking cider on the beach. After she had started her company, Andrew had overseen her accounts and helped her to negotiate the financial side of things.

"Come on in," he said, "and let's have a look at your accounts. We might need to change a few things now you're online only."

An hour later, Eleanor was feeling more confident about her future. They were packing away when the doorbell rang.

"Perfect timing," said Andrew, gathering their coffee cups. "Arthur and I are going surfing."

"Arthur?" asked Eleanor.

"He's staying in the cottage," said Andrew, nodding through the window to the holiday cottage he and his wife Liz rented out during the summer.

"You don't usually have visitors at this time of year," Eleanor said.

"True, but Arthur was given our name by an old friend. He's an actor but the play he was supposed to be touring with has been cancelled, so he decided to spend a few months in Pembrokeshire."

"Any particular reason?"

"No idea but he surfs, so we've been out a few times. You know how dangerous the tides can be if you don't know them. I feel responsible for his safety."

"Well, I'd hate to come between you and your surfboard," said Eleanor. Shoving her laptop back into her bag, she shrugged on her jacket and after calling goodbye to Liz, she climbed into her car.

Surfing, she thought, as she reversed out. *Will I ever be able to get on my board again?*

It was something she and Aidan had learned as children and throughout their teens they had spent most of their time in the water but now, with legs not only weakened from her illness, but with no reflexes — the mechanism that allowed the necessary spring for running and jumping — she wondered if it would ever be possible again.

There's always a body board, she thought, but using that would not give the true freedom of being able to paddle far out to sea, trying to find the legendary seventh wave which was always supposed to be the strongest, rising high, the surf forming a rainbow of light around you. It had been in those moments that Eleanor had felt she melted into the wave, the roar of the ocean pounding through her, echoing her heartbeat, transforming her into pure light as she flew through the air.

Stop it, she told herself, *stop this. You might not be able to surf at the moment, but at least you can still walk on the sand.*

Flicking on her indicator, she pulled into the wide car park behind the Newgale stones, stopping near to the pathway that led over the sea break. Newgale beach was a vast stretch of sand, low and lethal when the tide was high. The huge pebble bank backing the beach was a storm defence that had been created after a tragic storm in October 1859.

Today, the sea was choppy but there was no danger. Walkways led across the enormous pebble banks to the sands below. Eleanor had never considered she would need these paths; before her illness, she had always scampered over the stones without a thought. She realised how much she had taken for granted: her health, her fitness, her home. Walking with deliberate care, she made her way along the uneven wooden slats, feeling vulnerable on this familiar territory for the first time and wishing she had brought the shooting stick her parents had insisted she put in the car.

"It's not necessarily for you," her father had said, "it's more for other people, so they know not to bump into you."

"It won't look strange," her mother had added. "Lots of walkers on the cliff path use a stick."

Their words had been well-meant, but Eleanor had felt as though they were consigning her to a life she was not prepared to live, one of an invalid, always on the edge, never strong enough to join the crowd. Her stubbornness was such that she would not give in without a fight and, because of this, she had ignored the handmade hazel stick on the back seat of her car. As the wind whipped her hair across her face, causing her to pause to regain her balance, she realised her father had perhaps been right and her refusal was a childish reaction.

With great relief she stepped off the stones on to the sand, heading to a small outcrop of rocks where she and her friends would sit to watch the sea. A man's voice floated to her over the roar of the waves and the hiss of the biting wind, and in the distance she saw Andrew, a small figure in the momentarily flat surf, waving. Raising both arms, she waved back, smiling. Even if she could not join him in the water, it was good to be on the beach and feel the visceral pull of the elements.

Settling herself into a familiar nook, she tucked her hands in her pockets and squinted into the low winter sunshine. In the distance she could make out Andrew's brilliant blue board. Beside him bobbed another man, whom Eleanor presumed was Arthur.

A moment later, a wave rose and both Andrew and Arthur began to paddle, standing as the sea crested, lifting them both in an arc of snowy white foam. They bent into the curve, following the rushing water, flying towards the wide beach. Eleanor felt her heart rise in excitement. She pulled off her gloves and put her fingers in her mouth, letting a raucous whistle screech across the waves to meet the two men. Andrew raised his arms in mock celebration, tumbling gently into the surf with careful precision. His companion, startled by the noise and the unexpected audience, jerked forward, losing his footing and falling headfirst off the board in a tangle of arms and legs. Moments later he emerged, spluttering and laughing.

For the next twenty minutes, Eleanor watched as the two men surfed. Occasionally she would walk a few circuits of the rocks to keep warm but the relief of being alone, breathing in the stinging air and listening to the roar of the elements was soothing her troubled thoughts and energising her mind. *There are worse places to convalesce*, she thought. *My family is here, I have my business to occupy me and there are friends to ensure I don't become isolated. I also have this unexpected search into the past to offer me something new.*

Yet, resentment remained in her heart. It niggled at her that the choice to return home had not been hers to make. The decision had been taken away from her the moment her body had failed. Since then, her life had been one of coping and compromising; it was this loss of autonomy she found so difficult to accept.

"Eleanor!" Andrew's voice floated through the wind and waves. They were walking towards her, two figures, surfboards under their arms, the winter sun behind them, giving their outlines an ethereal glow. "We're heading back," called Andrew. "What time are you having lunch with Aidan and Chloe?"

Eleanor wanted to hug Andrew for not finishing the sentence, for not fussing. Unspoken words hovered between them as she saw the fleeting look of concern on his face, understanding he wanted to ensure she was safe and able to return to her car before he left the beach. Aware her legs were icy cold, despite her thick jeans and long parka, she saw the sense in leaving with them. Once again, she quashed the spark of anger at her neediness, at the fear which swamped her as she imagined not being able to make it back across the stones unaided.

"Anytime from now," she said with a smile.

"This is Arthur." Andrew made the introduction as they drew level.

The man beside Andrew was not at all what Eleanor had expected. Assuming he would be a similar age to Andrew, she was surprised to see Arthur was a few years older than herself. His dark blond hair glistened with salt and silver light, and his deep brown eyes were startling. His skin held the remnants of a tan and as Eleanor looked into his eyes, a certainty washed through her; a feeling she was home.

Never before had she experienced an emotion of such profound intensity, of longing, happiness, despair and joy, wrapped into a shimmering heartbeat as the wind roared in her ears and her world changed. Her mind raced as she stared at this man: she knew him, yet they had never met; he was the missing part of her soul, yet he was a stranger; she was home in his arms, but she had never experienced his touch. Arthur stared down at her and she could see from the jolt of his face, the look of astonishment in his eyes that he too had felt this seismic shift. He was staring at her as though he could not believe what he was seeing. Andrew coughed, bringing them both back to the cold beach.

"Hi," Arthur said, his accent neutral, though he sounded confused.

"Hello," she replied.

"I've been telling Arthur about your vintage emporium, Ellie," said Andrew, and Arthur forced a natural-looking smile.

"It sounds fascinating."

"Thanks," she replied. "It's downsized at the moment, but hopefully it'll survive." Eleanor was thankful her voice sounded normal, even if her insides were squirming with a combination of excitement, fear and joy. All her willpower was required not to launch herself into his arms.

"Your area of expertise is Victorian theatre?" Arthur phrased it as a question and she nodded, fighting to concentrate on his words rather than stare at his mouth. "The play I was supposed to be doing was part of a Victorian revival. It's called *The Colleen Bawn…*"

"By the Irish writer, Dion Boucicault," Eleanor interrupted, momentarily distracted from her abstract feelings to feel the sting of another strange coincidence.

"I was supposed to play Myles Na Coppaleen, the poacher and moonshine brewer."

"The lead," said Eleanor, impressed, "also the part played by the writer when it premiered in New York in March 1860."

"You know your stuff," Arthur said, laughing.

Aware Andrew was hovering and would not leave until he saw her back to her car, Eleanor surreptitiously placed her hands either side of herself in order to push into a standing position. It was not vanity or pride driving this manoeuvre, it was necessity, as the cold was biting into her legs and she was unsure whether they would be able to bring her to a standing position without assistance. Taking a deep breath, she forced her feet into the ground and to her relief, a moment later, she was standing. She saw a look of concern flash across Andrew's face.

"We'll walk you back to your car," he said, and she did not argue.

The wall of stones seemed insurmountable and as she tore her mind away from Arthur, who had fallen into step on her other side, she mentally berated herself for creating a situation where she felt vulnerable. As they walked across the sand, Eleanor's legs began to tremble and, as she stepped over a small stone, her ankle gave way with a sickening jolt. Eleanor let out an involuntary scream as her legs buckled beneath her.

"Ellie!" shouted Andrew in alarm, throwing his board on to the sand as he tried to reach her before she crumpled to the ground.

Trying to stem the tears of humiliation and frustration, she took a deep breath, remaining still as she had been instructed by her physiotherapists. *Stay calm, breathe, assess the situation and the damage. Are you hurt? Can you sit up? Do you need to call for help?* The words flowed through her head, instructions issued by calm professionals, people helping her to rebuild her life, her confidence, her hope.

"Are you all right? What happened?" Arthur's panicked voice reached her through her misery.

"Eleanor's been very ill," she heard Andrew whisper.

"Right," said Arthur. "Can you take the boards?"

A moment later, she was swept off the sand as Arthur scooped her up and headed towards the stone bank. Before she fully realised his intention, he had scaled it with surprising strength and athleticism with Eleanor still in his arms, before slithering down the other side and across the road into Wave Riders, the surf shop and café owned by her brother Aidan.

"We need some help here," he called as he kicked open the door.

"Ellie!" exclaimed Aidan as Chloe rushed out from the kitchen.

Two battered sofas graced the centre of the shop, and Arthur laid Eleanor on the nearest with expert care. A moment later, Andrew crashed through the door behind them, carrying the surfboards, his face wreathed in concern.

"This lady..." Arthur began, but Aidan, white-faced, was already crouching beside Eleanor.

"Is my sister," Aidan said. "Ellie, what happened?"

"The cold," she muttered, "my legs didn't like it."

Aidan reached over and hugged her tightly, pulling a blanket from the back of the sofa and tucking it around her. For a moment, Eleanor leaned into her brother's shoulder, shuddering with the tears she had dammed behind her stubbornness. A moment later, she pushed him away.

"I'm okay," she said. "Really, I'm fine."

Chloe appeared with a brimming mug of coffee and a slice of carrot cake. "Eat," she commanded, "the sugar in the cake will be good for the shock."

Eleanor gave her a shaky smile.

Aidan stood up and turned to Arthur. "Thank you," he said, shaking Arthur's hand.

"No problem," Arthur replied, and Eleanor was aware his eyes had barely left her since their dramatic entrance into the shop.

"This is Arthur," said Andrew, stepping forward, and Eleanor was grateful for the distraction; she did not want everyone staring at her. "He's renting my cottage for a few months."

Eleanor sipped her coffee and flaked a few crumbs of the cake into her mouth. Chloe was right, the comforting sweetness helped ease the shock of falling, but it would not help with her despair or humiliation. Andrew and Arthur were being gently shunted out of the shop by Aidan, who turned the 'Closed' sign around once they had gone.

"Lucky you didn't have any customers," Eleanor said with an attempt at a smile when Aidan sat beside her.

"What happened?" His voice was harsh, and Eleanor knew it was fear.

"I told you, I got cold."

"Mum said you were having a meeting with Andrew. Why were you on the beach?"

Eleanor bridled. "It's only my legs that have stopped working," she snapped. "My brain and my cognitive decision-making processes are fine. I decided to go for a walk and then I watched Andrew and Arthur surfing. It was my own stupid fault. My legs got cold, and I lost my balance on the way back to the car."

"Where is your car?"

"Where do you think? In the car park."

"I'm taking you home," said Aidan.

"No, you're not," Eleanor replied. "Once I'm warm, I'll be able to drive myself."

"Aidie," said Chloe, a calming hand on his arm, "she's fine."

Scowling, Aidan stormed off to the back of the shop, where he could be heard crashing around.

"Sounds as though the bobble hat display is getting what-for," said Chloe, sinking onto the sofa beside Eleanor, a mug of coffee in her hand. "Tell me when you're ready and we'll have lunch, then I'll walk you back to your car, no arguments."

"Thanks, Chlo."

They sat in companionable silence, listening to Aidan working out his frustration on the stock, occasionally grinning at each other, when there was a knock on the door.

"I'll get it!" shouted Aidan and moments later, they heard the low drone of conversation.

"Let's hope it's a customer with a really complex query that will distract him," whispered Chloe, gathering the empty mugs and disappearing into the kitchen.

"Ellie, it's your rescuer," said Aidan as he joined her on the sofas.

Arthur had changed into a heavy fisherman's jumper over dark jeans with chunky boots. He stood awkwardly beside the sofa, looking down at Eleanor with brown eyes full of concern. "Hi," he said. "I wanted to check you were all right."

"Fine now," she replied, aware she was covered in sand and probably had make-up smudged around her eyes from her recalcitrant tears. "Apologies for my dramatic collapse."

"No worries," he said. "Andrew said you'd been ill; I imagine this was part of it..."

"Aidan, can you help me in the kitchen?" called Chloe and with great reluctance Aidan edged away, his blue eyes focused on Arthur until Chloe practically dragged him out of sight.

"Your brother doesn't seem to like me," Arthur said, sitting opposite Eleanor.

"Don't take it personally; he doesn't like anyone who he thinks is making a move on me..." Eleanor could have swallowed her tongue.

Arthur laughed. "Is that what he thinks I was doing?"

"Anyone who speaks to me is treated with the same contempt. He's protective, especially at the moment."

"Do you mind my asking what happened?"

Eleanor sighed. His tone was formal, polite. The intense rush of emotions they had shared on the beach might never have happened. Deciding to get the worst over with, she gave him a very brief outline.

"No wonder everyone is so jumpy around you," he said when she had finished. "I would be too." He stood, smiling down at her. "As long as you're going to be able to get home, I'll leave you to your lunch with your brother."

The bell jangled as he left, and Eleanor felt as though a small part of her had gone with him.

CHAPTER TWO

Eleanor thumped the cushion into a more comfortable shape and Sandy settled himself, curling in a neat ball and gazing at the two women sprawled opposite his chair. Settling into the other armchair, Eleanor accepted the glass of wine offered by her best friend since childhood, Briony Llewellyn. Beside her was the third of their trio, Bathsheba Mundy. Eleanor grinned. The way the three of them were lounging was a tableau left over from their teens when they would sit for hours, laughing, planning their futures and, most importantly, discussing boys.

Where once there would have been a pile of chocolate bars, two wine bottles and the remains of a takeaway were strewn across the coffee table. Beside this was the envelope containing the Victorian photographs, the book Amelia had given Eleanor at the party at Cliffside the previous year and Eleanor's favourite pack of Tarot cards. A row of four cards had been laid out, but these no longer held the interest of the three women. They had returned to the topic of Eleanor's connection to Cliffside.

"It still surprises me that you and Edward Stone are related," said Briony as she sipped her wine. Eleanor noticed Briony's eyes stray towards the cards. Eleanor had been reading them for her.

"Strange, isn't it?" agreed Eleanor. Reaching out, she swept the cards together and returned them to the pack, wrapping them in a purple chiffon scarf and tying the ends together.

"Distantly, though, so you snogging him when we were teenagers isn't incest or anything," said Bathsheba, laughing.

"What a night that was," said Eleanor. "How old were we?"

"About sixteen," said Briony. "He's a few years older."

"I was so angry with you," recalled Bathsheba. "I'd fancied him for ages."

The three women laughed.

"You fancied everyone, depending on the day of the week," said Eleanor.

"Her heart always belonged to Stuart Mackensie, though," gushed Briony, holding her hands to her chest, pretending to swoon.

Bathsheba grinned. "Never snogged him, though," she lamented. "I used to doodle our names together and imagine one day he'd notice me, but he never did."

"I've heard he's single now," grinned Eleanor. "There's time!"

"Stuart has missed his chance," replied Bathsheba, "my heart belongs to Gabe."

She flashed the expensive engagement ring her boyfriend, Gabriel, had given her six months earlier. Bathsheba was home for a long weekend. A scientist who worked in DNA testing at a laboratory in Cheltenham, she had moved to Gloucestershire for both her and Gabriel's careers but with great reluctance, spending as many weekends in Pembrokeshire as she was able.

"They were good times, though," said Briony, her eyes alight with nostalgia. "On the beach, surfing during the day, daring to light a fire at night and have a party. It was a good way to grow up."

"We were quite a gang," agreed Bathsheba. She drained her glass. "Come on then, tell us about this mystery man you met on the beach," she said. "Did you really swoon?"

"No, I did not," retorted Eleanor. "My legs were cold, and it can make them weak. I stepped on a stone and…"

The memory of the beach incident, as she referred to it in her mind, continued to confuse her; the intensity of the feelings between her and Arthur had been followed by his reticence and emotional withdrawal upon reaching Wave Riders.

"What's really upsetting you, Ellie?" asked Briony, her grey eyes gentle.

Eleanor gulped the last of her wine, hoping it would fortify her. These were her oldest friends. They had grown up together, been through everything, from first periods to first boyfriends to first heart breaks. If she were to confide in anyone, it would be to each of them.

"On the beach," began Ellie, "Arthur and I had this intense connection. It's hard to describe but the moment I saw him, it felt as though I'd found my happy ending. Then I fell over and he carried me back to Aidan and Chloe's, but the moment Aidan said I was his sister, it was as though shutters fell over Arthur's eyes and the connection we'd had on the beach hadn't happened."

Briony and Bathsheba shared a glance.

"Do you think I'm mad?"

"No," said Bathsheba.

"Have you heard from him?" asked Briony.

"Not directly but Aidan's offered him a job at the shop, so I've heard about him."

Aidan's glowing reports of his new employee were hard for Eleanor to bear.

"Could he have backed off because of the job?" asked Bathsheba.

It was the logical thought process she had followed herself. Aidan had been looking for someone to help develop his online sales and Arthur had experience, having worked for his stepfather's shop and having built the online side the previous summer, when he had been between acting jobs. The fact Arthur had been brought up in Cornwall, and had surfed since he was a child, also helped.

Eleanor topped up their glasses.

"Tell us," said Briony. "There's something on your mind."

Eleanor considered how much she felt able to share. It was not that she doubted her friends, it was her own ability to keep facing each of these changes in her new world which she found uncomfortable. Arthur was an attractive man, but she was concerned. Even knowing her friends would do their utmost to help and reassure her, how could she admit she doubted her femininity, her ability to be even passably attractive?

"What if it wasn't that?" she began, her voice tentative, twisting the wine glass with nervous fingers. "What if there was another reason Arthur pulled away?"

"Such as?"

"My illness," she said, a lump forming in her throat. "Robbie left me while I was in intensive care. Since then, two men have chatted me up and the moment it's cropped up that I have a chronic condition, they've both run a mile…"

"Robbie is and always has been an idiot," interrupted Bathsheba in a fierce voice. "He was never good enough for you and when you needed him most, he let you down. No good man would ever behave in such a manner. How did Arthur react? You said he asked you about your illness."

"He said it was understandable why everyone was so protective," she admitted.

"Which doesn't sound like a brush-off," said Bathsheba.

"And he did come back to check on you," added Briony.

"Anyway, it's probably for the best," Eleanor said.

"Why?" said Bathsheba.

Eleanor hesitated. "He's leaving in a few months, so it's better not to become involved," she replied, but neither Briony nor Bathsheba looked convinced.

"Tell us about this research you're doing," said Briony, changing the subject. "Your mum said you're trying to trace one of your ancestors."

Relieved, Eleanor opened the envelope and removed the picture of Esme Blood, resplendent in her peacock feathers.

"Amazing dress," said Bathsheba.

Eleanor explained her unexpected discovery of Esme Blood on the poster that had been hanging on her wall for years, along with the diaries and the Tarot cards which had been part of an auction buy.

"Spooky," said Briony when she had finished. "What are you going to do next?"

"There are more diaries, although some of them are a bit of a challenge to read — her writing was tiny. With luck, these will tell me her story. I'm going to try one of those genealogy websites too and have a trawl through my programme collection to see if I have any from The Firebird."

Bathsheba groaned and Eleanor laughed. Years earlier, Bathsheba had offered to help Eleanor catalogue her collection. "No, please," she moaned. "No more spreadsheets, I will never get those hours back."

"I bought you wine," protested Eleanor.

"True."

"Anyway, this is a solo project, it's between me and Esme." Eleanor grinned. "The programmes should corroborate her diary and give them the correct provenance."

"You're beginning to sound like my brother," said Briony in a sarcastic drawl.

Her elder brother, Mark Llewellyn, ran The Dairy, part of the research centre at the nearby Marquess House, while Briony managed the Louisa Woodville Animal Trust, based in a large farmhouse on the edge of the estate. Despite her sarcastic words, Briony and Mark were very close.

"Weren't we at school with some Bloods?" said Bathsheba. "They lived near St Elvis, on the way to Solva."

"Two boys, they were older than us," agreed Briony.

"I'd forgotten about them," said Eleanor. "I wonder if they're related to Esme Blood."

"Was she from around here?"

"Not sure yet." Eleanor yawned. A wave of exhaustion overwhelmed her and the hand holding her glass trembled.

"Enough for today," said Briony, alert to the symptoms. "Anyway, I have to get back to Home Farm. We've got some kittens; they're little scamps and they need a night-time feed. Come on, Sheebs, I'll call us a cab."

Bathsheba was already gathering the debris of their evening and taking it into the kitchen, where she stacked it in the dishwasher.

"I'm fine," Eleanor stated as her two friends bustled around, tidying up, while they waited for their ride. "I get tired, that's all. I won't break."

"We don't want to make you ill again," Briony said, her pale face awash with concern. "After all you've been through, we'd be terrible friends if we made you worse."

"You won't," said Eleanor, understanding their fear. "I'm still me. If it gets too much, don't worry, I'll tell you to back off."

Bathsheba forced a smile and Briony tried to grin too.

"We really do have kittens I need to feed," Briony said, when her phone pinged to indicate the cab's arrival. The two women pulled on their coats, before Eleanor hugged them in turn.

"Leave me to the winter night then, oh faint-hearted friends," she laughed.

With shouts and waves, they clambered into the waiting taxi before disappearing into the frosty night air. Eleanor stood in her doorway, breathing in the familiar sounds and smells of home, the rustle of the wind in the trees and above her, the endless brilliance of the stars in the dark sky. In the distance an owl screeched and as it did, a shooting star lit up the sky with an unearthly brilliance. As she watched, Eleanor wondered if this might be a hopeful sign because at that moment, it seemed her life would never feel normal again.

CHAPTER THREE

With her vintage emporium now fully up and running online, Eleanor was inundated with orders. When she looked around from her newly installed desk, she realised her father had been correct when he had said the barn would be ideal. There was enough room for the rails of vintage clothes and costumes, a huge amount of shelving, which her parents had insisted on paying for, meaning she could unpack a large portion of her stock, with storage for the remainder. Although it was not open to customers, the layout reminded her of her shop and for the first time since her illness began, she felt as though she had some sort of control over her life again.

A buzz from her mobile told Eleanor that Aidan and Chloe had arrived to take her to the local pub quiz. Making her way to the front drive, she was surprised to discover Arthur was behind the wheel.

"Arthur volunteered to drive us," Aidan said when she opened the door. "It's great for me — means I can have a drink!"

When they arrived at the pub, the wind buffeted Eleanor as she climbed out of the car. Taking a deep breath, she waited until she was sure she had her balance. It was the small things which had taken her so much by surprise during her recovery. Something as simple as a rogue gust of wind would be enough to make her stumble, leaving her both furious and nervous about her new-found vulnerability.

Chloe glanced over and slipped her arm through Eleanor's before she could protest. Aidan and Arthur were deep in conversation about a new order for Wave Riders and had not noticed Eleanor's hesitation.

Chloe gave Eleanor a wide grin and Eleanor suspected she wanted to tell her something.

"How are things working out with Arthur?" Eleanor asked as they headed into The Castle pub in Little Haven and were out of earshot of the others.

"Good," Chloe said. "He knows his stuff about boards and because he's travelled and surfed all around the world, he can relate to the customers. He's really boosted our online side, too."

"Great."

"He's asked about you," Chloe added.

"Really?"

"Very interested in your business and you and…"

Before Eleanor could delve further into the information Chloe had dangled, they entered the pub and were greeted by a barrage of noise bringing their conversation to an abrupt halt. Chloe's older sister, Verity, hurried over to greet them and from their favourite table in the corner, Briony waved.

Eleanor, Chloe and Verity made their way through the crowd, dropping into seats on either side of Briony. Aidan and Arthur took the orders for drinks and headed to the bar.

"Ellie, I asked Mark if he'd help with your research into Esme Blood," said Briony, bringing Eleanor from her reverie.

"Bri, that's so kind, but Mark's a professional. I doubt my research into family history is his thing. Anyway, I shouldn't think there'll be anything in his very grown-up archives."

"Mark loves a treasure hunt," laughed Briony. "He was delighted to help."

Eleanor grinned; Briony's brother had been the same when they were children. Set him a puzzle or introduce him to a mystery and he would ferret away until he found the answer.

Aidan and Arthur returned with the drinks, and Aidan introduced Arthur to Briony and Verity.

"Good work, cariad," Briony whispered to Eleanor, glancing towards Arthur as they shuffled up to make room for him and Aidan. "He's hot, no wonder you swooned."

Eleanor laughed, pleased that Arthur had managed to manoeuvre himself into the seat beside her. Leaning back, she looked around at the faces in the pub. She recognised old friends, families she knew by name, two of her cousins — the majority of the crowd was familiar and for the first time, she realised how much she had missed the close-knit community of her childhood and teenage years.

"You all right?" whispered Arthur. She had not realised he was watching her.

"Yes," she replied. "How about you? Not too overwhelmed?"

"It's great," he said. "I thought my hometown, Falmouth, was a small place, with everyone knowing everyone else, but it's the same here. It feels like home."

"Ellie," came a voice and Mark Llewellyn joined them. Briony shifted along, making room for her brother to sit down. As she did, she squashed Eleanor into Arthur, which from the mischievous grin on her friend's face, was deliberate.

"Bri told me about your Victorian quest," Mark said to Eleanor, accepting a pint from Aidan. "I had a look through the Marquess House archive, and you might be quite interested in the things we've discovered."

"Thanks so much, Mark," Eleanor said. "You shouldn't have gone to so much trouble."

"It's no problem at all," he replied. "We're building a Victorian wing in the Mary Fitzroy Heritage Centre, so we've been trawling our archives from this period for a while."

The Heritage Centre was an offshoot of Marquess House, and the plan was for it to become a local resource centre for research, archive storage and access to items that the Pembrokeshire Archives were unable to house. These included delicate documents, valuable items that needed more security and other miscellany.

"Did you find anything?" asked Arthur. "Aidan told me about the diaries and the Tarot cards you found, Ellie," he added, and hearing him use the shortened version of her name made Eleanor shiver with an emotion she could not quite place.

"Some quite unusual things," said Mark, pulling a brown A4 envelope out of his rucksack and emptying out a sheaf of photocopies. "We've got ten minutes before the quiz starts, so I'll go through it quickly, then you can look at it in more detail later. Eddie had given us one of the books from the Cliffside reunion, so I was able to use the family trees in that to help. Bri told me the woman you were interested in was related to the Bloods. Hannah Blood married Noah Attwater, and you're descended from their daughter, Eleanor. The Bloods are an old local family; Hannah's father was the Reverend Meredith Blood, who was married to Blodwen Davies. They had seven children. Hannah was the second youngest and Judith Blood was the eldest."

"Esme's mother," said Eleanor.

"Exactly, and this is where it becomes interesting," said Mark. "There isn't a great deal for Judith before 1858 — I believe Esme Blood was born in 1856?" He looked to Eleanor for confirmation, and she nodded. "But you think her parents were unmarried, and this is why Judith left her with Cornelius and Rosie Hardy?"

"As far as I know from what I've read so far in Esme's diaries."

"The next document I have for Judith is a marriage certificate," said Mark, and Eleanor grinned at the triumph on his face.

"Who did she marry?"

"In 1858, Judith Blood married George Arbuthnot."

"Great name," said Arthur, who had been listening.

"Yes, it's a wonderful name for research because it's unusual," said Mark, "especially as the next document I found relating to Mr and Mrs G Arbuthnot is a ship's manifest."

"To where?" asked Eleanor, surprised.

"They were on board the *Mimosa*," said Mark, but his excited words were met with blank stares. "The *Mimosa*," he repeated, as though this would help.

Briony rolled her eyes at her brother and took a deep swig of her drink, but at the back of Eleanor's mind, a shaft of light shone on a lesson in a classroom when she had shared a desk with Briony. "The ship that took Welsh exiles to Patagonia," she said, and Mark beamed.

"Correct. The *Mimosa* was a clipper that sailed from Liverpool in 1865 to Patagonia. It landed at a port the settlers named Porth Madryn on 28 July 1865. There were 153 passengers intent on building a colony that preserved the Welsh language and culture, although they needn't have bothered — Welsh culture is thriving in Wales."

"And Judith Blood, as Mrs Arbuthnot was on board?" Eleanor clarified and Mark nodded.

"However," he continued, "I think she may have died in Patagonia because on a return manifest, some years later,

George is accompanied by a Mrs Celia Arbuthnot, not Judith. I searched but I couldn't find a death certificate for Judith."

Before they could discuss it any further, a shout from the bar brought their attention to the quiz. As the names for the teams were shouted out — they were Wave Riders Ahoy! — Eleanor wondered if Judith's departure was another reason Esme had been adopted by the Hardys, but it still did not explain why Judith had been with the travelling troupe in the first place or what had happened to Esme's father, the elusive Robert Sutton. Shuffling the papers together, she slid them back into the envelope, feeling as though Mark's research had posed more questions than it had answered.

The cold silver moon shone down as Eleanor and Arthur drove back to the farm. Aidan and Chloe had been given a lift by Verity, and Arthur had insisted on driving Eleanor home.

"It's no problem," he had assured Aidan, while behind him both Chloe and Briony had given her a double thumbs-up.

"Is Mark always that competitive?" asked Arthur as he parked outside Eleanor's annexe.

"Always," Eleanor said. "Aidan can usually keep him under control, though."

Arthur laughed and Eleanor felt a prickle of excitement. Swallowing her nervousness, she said, "Do you fancy coming in for a drink?"

Her heart pounded as Arthur glanced at the clock, then gave a nod.

"Yes, that would be great. Thanks, Ellie. Tea, though, I'm driving."

"Make yourself comfortable," Eleanor said, flicking on a few lamps as they entered, heading into the kitchen to fill the kettle before sidling into her bedroom to check her appearance and surreptitiously apply lipstick.

Looking at herself in the mirror, she wondered what Arthur saw when he looked at her, how he viewed her. He had never known her before her illness; she did not feel the subconscious comparison she saw in the eyes of friends from her childhood. The ones who had known her when she was whole. Returning to the kitchen, she tried to push this thought aside but she could not. She might look the same but, in her heart, she knew there was something missing, a vital element and, despite her best efforts, it would never return.

The concern, conscious or otherwise, displayed by her friends and family was done with love but to Eleanor, it often felt like a judgement. This was not something she could explain to anyone, for fear of upsetting them, especially when they were working so hard to support her and make things as easy as possible. Her thanks for this was something she would never be able to put into words, such was her love for them all, but she continued to wish the illness that had transformed her life had never happened.

Arthur looked up from the message he was typing on his phone, and she wondered what, if anything, she wanted to happen between them. As the kettle boiled and she filled the pot, Eleanor decided to stop fretting and enjoy the moment.

"Tea," she announced.

Arthur took the tray containing her favourite vintage teapot and matching cups into the living room.

Eleanor poured the tea, then settled at the other end of the sofa, tucking her feet underneath her. Arthur was sitting opposite, stroking Sandy, who had appeared through the cat flap in the door that joined the annexe to the farmhouse. When she had moved in, her parents had given her the key, insisting she lock it from her side in order to keep the two properties separate, but as Sandy liked to wander between the two homes, they had agreed to the cat flap.

"How many people in the pub were related?" Arthur asked.

"Probably all of them," Eleanor said, laughing, "but Reece and Jade are our cousins from Dad's side. They were in Double Dragon, who came third. Mark and Briony are brother and sister and they're cousins to Billy and Larry, who arrived halfway through."

"Do you have a large family?"

"Mum's side is quite small, but Dad's is bigger — he has two brothers, and they all have children, so lots of cousins. How about you?"

"Tiny. My mum brought me up with the help of my grandparents and she's an only child, like me. I never knew my dad."

"I'm sorry," said Eleanor.

"My mum never made a secret of it. She had a holiday fling and even threw away the number of the bloke at the airport because she wasn't interested in staying in touch. Unfortunately, a month or so later, she realised she was pregnant with no way to contact him."

"Do you know his name?"

"Simon or John."

"A surname?"

"Possibly Evans or Jones. He told Mum his name was John, but she heard his friends calling him Si, so she wondered if it might be Simon. My mum's name is Wendy, but she told him it was Jamie."

Eleanor laughed. "Your mum sounds epic."

"She was on holiday with a group of friends, and they made a pact to have a riotous time and leave no trace behind, so they agreed on new names and apparently had a great deal of fun. When I was two she married Kevin, and he's always been my dad, but something happened a while ago and it made me realise that without Mum, I would have no blood relations. It was a strange thought, so I asked her and Kev if they would mind me searching for my birth father."

"Won't that be quite tricky if you don't know his real name?"

"I know he was from this part of the world," said Arthur. "It was the reason Kev suggested I stay with Andrew for a while, to see if I can discover anything. It's not that I want a relationship or anything — as I said, Kev is my dad — but it feels as though there's a part of me missing and, if it's possible, I'd like to know who I am."

"It's a big question, and your desire to know is understandable," she said. "From the moment we're born, small seeds of humanity, secrets flow through our blood: our hair colour, eye colour, temperament, all hidden from view, revealing themselves as we grow. Even with two parents to offer us clues to who we are, our development is a constant ever-changing mystery. To be missing half of this blueprint must be even more confusing."

Arthur's silence caused her to look up from topping up their cups, irritated that her hand trembled because of the weight of the teapot.

"You're the first person to really understand," he said. "Most people think it's a lost cause or a flight of madness because I have so little information, but even if I don't discover anything, at least I know I tried."

"My friend Bathsheba is a scientist. She works in DNA testing," said Eleanor. "Have you considered trying it?"

"Yes, it's my next step, but it'll only work if my birth-father is on the DNA register."

"True," she said, then, whether it was the wine she had drunk in the pub or the warmth of his gaze, she found her usual reticence leaving her as she continued, "Rather like you, the question, 'Who am I?' has been on my mind a great deal recently. My life has changed so rapidly, and over the past few months my mind has finally been able to start the process of catching up with the physical changes — both to my body and my geographical location — and it's made me ponder the same thought but for different reasons."

"We're both searching the past for answers," he said, reaching over to squeeze her hand.

As he did so, Sandy leapt from the sofa onto the bookcase, dislodging the pile of Tarot packs Eleanor had been pricing earlier. Arthur leapt up to pick them off the floor, looking down at them with interest. "Briony was telling me you read Tarot cards as well as collect them?"

"They've always fascinated me," she said, "and through various strange twists of fate, I have a pack of Tarot cards that once belonged to Esme Blood, the long-lost ancestor I've been researching. It felt as though the universe was sending me a message."

"Spooky. Do you really believe in it all?" he asked, indicating the cards.

"Fortune telling and predicting the future?" When Arthur nodded, she put down her cup as she gathered her thoughts. "My mind has always struggled with the concept," she admitted. "The sensible, rational being within me states categorically that the future is a concept, so therefore it's unformed and we can never know what will happen, but the more esoteric side of me can't see things in such a rigid manner."

Standing up, she opened the curtains, switching off the lamps and beckoning Arthur to her side, before pointing at the shimmering stars: bright, cold, diamond-hard in the depth of the midwinter sky.

"We're made of stardust," she said. "Every inhabitant of this planet is created from the same chemical elements as the stars, and these are repeated endlessly throughout the universe. The same energy flows through us as surges through the tides of the sea as they respond to the call of the moon. Everything is affected by it, from the deer running from the sound of a snapping twig, to every human being and creature on the planet. To me, this gives us all a connection. We are one, yet we are all separate; we are all the same, yet we are all different."

Arthur was looking up at the stars, his hair shining silver in the luminous beams of the full moon. Eleanor felt her heart race as she glanced at him. There was something familiar about him, even though they had only known each other a few weeks. A feeling of safety; an innate knowledge that she could trust him.

"The First Law of Thermodynamics states that energy can be changed from one form to another, but it can't be created or destroyed," she continued, leading him back to the sofa but leaving the lights low, so they could admire the crystalline beauty of the winter night. "This law also states that energy is always conserved, so if it can't be created or destroyed but can only be converted, where does the energy that keeps us alive go when we die?"

"It's not something I've thought about," admitted Arthur.

"Did you know that at death the body immediately loses twenty-one grams?" asked Eleanor, warming to her subject.

"No."

"The scientist, Duncan MacDonald from Haverhill, Massachusetts, did a number of experiments on this topic. He claimed this twenty-one grams represented the soul. Since then, his work has been largely rubbished by the scientific community, but in 2005, the physician Gerard Nahum followed up on MacDonald's experiments, using electromagnetic weights to try and capture the moment the energy left the body. Although he claimed to have made a discovery, no major organisations were interested in buying his results."

"Why not?" asked Arthur. "This is fascinating."

"Who knows? Perhaps he was seen as a crank, but it's also possible that even now anything even vaguely tainted with hints of the occult is eschewed by the more conservative members of the scientific community. Perhaps they were scared of what this might reveal."

"Are you saying you think there's something in this?"

"What I'm saying is, everything is connected through matter and energy. If energy can only be converted, when someone dies their energy has to go somewhere. If it goes into the air, the ether, the atmosphere, whichever term you prefer, then who's to say we don't occasionally catch a glimmer of that energy, the aftermath of a life, the echo of a soul. Or, if you choose to be secular, the lifeforce. And, if we can get a hint of that, who's to say we can't occasionally glimpse a future event too. Many scientists, particularly Einstein, believed time isn't linear, it can bend and twist, bulge and contract. Perhaps, if you're more sensitive to these ideas and to the rhythms of the universe, you're able to catch the murmurs on the breeze."

"And this is what you think you do when you're reading your Tarot cards?"

"I put my mind in a trance-like state," she admitted. "It allows me to let the energy flow around me more clearly and, yes, I often get strange insights, unexpected knowledge and whispers that usually turn out to be true. I may have read them somewhere, it may not be psychic, but the right information rises to the surface at the right time. Many mediums, especially those who do public seances, research local papers, graveyards and the obituary sections in order to discover what has happened and whether they can tap into something. People who really have a connection might come up with an insignificant detail, but one which is of huge importance to the person who is searching for answers."

"What, like the money's hidden down the back of the sofa?"

Eleanor laughed. "No, more like: you wore my hat to your cousin's wedding."

"What do you mean?"

"I said that to someone once. I sensed a female presence, a grandmother figure, and an image of a black velvet hat came into my mind and the words, 'Tell her she wore it to her cousin's wedding'. It was such a strange thought, but I passed it on and the woman who I was reading for burst into tears because it was true. Her grandmother had passed away a few weeks before a family wedding; the woman had found the hat in her grandmother's wardrobe. She didn't tell anyone where the hat had come from, not at the wedding or after."

Arthur looked impressed.

"And that's before we get to string theory and the idea that every choice we make sends us off on one path while alternate versions of ourselves who have made other decisions live out their version in endless alternate parallel worlds. Time, energy, past, present, future — they are not as clear-cut as people imagine, something that has been proved again and again by scientists. I dwell within the gaps, the possibility and the hope that maybe we are all connected and death is not the end."

Eleanor looked up; Arthur was staring at her with a rapt expression.

"You really know your stuff," he said. "Where did you learn all this?"

"It's a theory I've been developing for years. The iconography of the Tarot cards was what first attracted me to them, then I began to research their history and try to work out how something that began as a simple card game could still exert such fascination over people hundreds of years later."

"Would you read my cards for me?"

Eleanor stared at Arthur in surprise. "Really?"

"If you don't mind? The thought that everything is connected is a fascinating idea. I've never considered it before, and I'd love to know how it feels to tap into that universal energy."

Eleanor was about to fetch her own cards when she changed her mind. Her instincts were drawing her to the Marseille pack, Esme Blood's cards. A rush of energy suffused her as though there was a message waiting, for both Arthur and herself.

"I'll do a small reading to give you a feel," she said, reaching for the cards and beginning to shuffle them, a tingle travelling up each arm as her skin touched the smooth, supple cardboard. "A full ten-card reading takes about an hour, but if you enjoy the short version we can arrange a suitable time to do a Celtic cross with all the trimmings."

Arthur grinned. "Whatever you say," he said. "I'm in your hands."

"Shuffle the pack," she said, placing them in his palm, "then cut them away from you three times using your left hand before putting them back together in any order you choose."

Eleanor took the deck and began dealing from the top: the Ten of Coins, The Star, The Empress. A cold breeze ruffled her hair and she wondered if she should stop, but something compelled her to continue: Death, The Tower and the Nine of Cups.

"No," gasped Eleanor, recoiling from the cards.

"What's the matter?" asked Arthur, white-faced, staring at the Death card. "Is it terrible news?"

"No, nothing like that," said Eleanor, ashamed of herself for reacting in such an amateurish fashion. "This is the Tarot pack that belonged to Esme Blood," she explained, "and she's copied a line of poetry written by Arthur O'Shaughnessy on to every other card except these six."

"Weird."

"It gets stranger," said Eleanor. "In her diaries, she claims these six cards were drawn by her adopted mother Rosie on the night she was abandoned."

Arthur stared at the cards, disconcerted. "Is this what you mean by everything being connected?"

"It's the most extreme example I've experienced."

They stared at the cards, then Arthur broke the silence. "What do they mean? The Death card is quite creepy."

Eleanor reached out and squeezed his hand in reassurance. Arthur started before gently disentangling his hand.

"It doesn't mean someone is about to die," she said, cursing herself for reaching out to him when she was beginning to suspect his feelings on the beach might have been a one-off. Deciding to take refuge in the images on the card, she relaxed her mind and allowed the words to flow.

"As in a traditional pack of playing cards, the Ten of Coins is the final card in the suit before you reach the court cards," she said, her hand hovering over the image as she spoke. It felt strange to be reading a different set of cards, but an energy unlike anything she had ever felt was pushing her on. "The Marseille pack doesn't offer much more than the coins themselves, indicating their origin as a game similar to trumps, however, in the more decorated packs, the Ten of Coins, sometimes called Pentacles, means family, the putting down of roots after a difficult period of change. As this is followed by The Star, the card of hope, which appears when the seeker has been through a time of difficulty, it suggests things are calming down and answers will be revealed soon connected with a family search. This is confirmed by the appearance of The Empress, which represents a mother figure. These three cards together are a positive sign. The Empress, in its most basic form, represents fertility…"

"What?"

"Not necessarily of the pregnancy kind," she said, "particularly as you have no cards here indicating children. It can also be representative of ideas being born, of a desire to push for a new adventure. However, these are tempered by The Tower and Death, both of which indicate a certain amount of enforced change. The Tower is often said to be the card of exile. Again, this can be symbolic, the feeling that the seeker is stuck in a self-created bubble of aloneness as they move through life, unable to share, forced to keep a secret which has not been of their creation. Followed by the Death card, which indicates an ending of some sort, the end of a period in a life which causes sadness. There are turbulent days ahead, which may make you question some of your basic principles. However, the appearance of the Nine of Cups, also known as the Wish card, indicates happiness in a relationship. While this is usually a romantic relationship, it isn't exclusive to matters of the heart; it also indicates family love, reunions and again echoes of the Ten of Coins, the putting down of roots and finding some permanence in a life which has been quite unexpected.

"You've already told me you're searching for your father, but it surprises me there are no kings in the reading, or The Emperor, all of whom represent father figures or older males. Don't be discouraged, though, the Hope card and the two number cards represent family. If I want to add another layer, I can include three more cards."

Eleanor laid out The Sun, The Wheel of Fortune and The Magician.

"Why have you added these?" Arthur asked.

"These are echoes," she said. "Adding the numbers of the ten and the nine, you reach nineteen. Each card in the Major Arcana, the icon cards, has a number and nineteen represents The Sun. Add these together to get ten and this represents The Wheel of Fortune and, finally, the sum of these numbers is one, which is The Magician. These cards back up the original six and again, with The Sun, they suggest success in your quest. While The Wheel of Fortune is at an apex, as you have both positive and difficult cards, it is turning, and I'm confident things are moving in your favour. However, with The Magician, you must be careful not to fall into the trap of self-delusion. Allow events to play out and trust the fact you are on the right path."

Eleanor stopped. Her readings always ended abruptly, as though the universe shut her down when it felt she had delivered the necessary information. She continued to stare at the cards.

"If that was a short reading," Arthur said, his tone one of wonder, "the full one must be incredible."

"Was it helpful?" she asked.

"More than you can know," he replied, but there was a sadness in his eyes. "Would this mean the same for everyone?"

"No," she said, gathering the cards together. "Every Tarot reader has their own way of interpreting the basic meaning of the cards. If I were to lay out the same spread for someone else, their energy would be an influence and other meanings would be more prevalent. There are layers of interpretation, and each card shows a different face depending on the person asking the question."

"You speak about them as though they're conscious."

"No, they're only cards, but they do have an uncanny habit of always being right."

He glanced at his watch. "I'm sorry, I have to go," he said, standing up and reaching for his coat. "I've got an early start tomorrow."

Eleanor felt a wave of uncertainly flow through her. "It's getting late," she agreed.

"Thanks for a great evening and the incredible reading," he said.

As she opened the door, they were millimetres from each other and she breathed in his peppery aftershave, holding her breath, waiting as he paused, tilting her head back, anticipating the brush of his lips against hers.

Arthur hesitated and Eleanor looked up into his gentle brown eyes, then he stepped past her and out into the night, leaving her confused and embarrassed as his car disappeared into the darkness.

PART FOUR: LONDON, 1876

CHAPTER ONE

Esme stood in the centre of the stage, waiting for the first note. A hush fell as Marcus Mason raised his baton and Fabio Campana's aria, *Esmerelda*, rose through the theatre. The piece had been written for the famous opera singer Adelina Patti, based on Victor Hugo's *The Hunchback of Notre Dame*. After several weeks of rehearsal, this evening would be Esme's solo debut, singing under her own name, Esme Blood, rather than Esme Hardy or any of the other aliases given to her throughout her career.

Counting the beats, Esme waited for Marcus to cue her and as he swept the baton down, his arm raised towards her, she gathered her skirts and, swirling them as rehearsed, allowed her voice to fly. All around her, people stopped what they were doing and drifted towards the stage, taking seats in the auditorium, hovering in the wings, pausing to listen to Esme's final dress rehearsal.

It was a year since Esme, Aaron, Lynette and Jeremiah had walked through Hyde Park, eating chestnuts and reacquainting themselves. While Esme and Aaron had continued to correspond, the other development from his visit had been Cassie's acceptance of Charles Bartholomew, Earl of Dunblane, into her life. He was a man of florid complexion, bushy sideburns and a belly of great rotundity. Esme knew her sister would never have given the man a second glance had he not been a wealthy and influential member of the aristocracy.

At first, Cassie had claimed she would never lower herself to become a mistress, but Charles had pursued her with endless flowers, fresh from the new glasshouse at his castle in

Scotland, followed by a pineapple from his estate in Leicestershire. This much coveted fruit was the height of fashion, and as far as Cassie was concerned, sophistication. For a while she suggested it was kept on display at The Firebird to show their level of connections. However, after gentle persuasion from Rosie that it would be wiser to either sell or eat the strange fruit before it began to rot, she had removed it from the plinth in the foyer. Cassie sold it and was delighted with the profit. These gifts were followed by gemstones of increasing value and, when the earl had sent a diamond bracelet delivered with a single pink rose, Cassie succumbed.

Three months later, Cassie had been given the keys to a sumptuous apartment in Piccadilly, where she entertained Charles while continuing her career at The Firebird. Charles offered to invest in the theatre, but Cornelius refused.

"Pa must be losing his mind," Cassie had declared that night as she and Esme waited in the wings to perform their comic singing partnership. "Charles could have renovated this place and made us the centre of fashion."

Esme had not responded. Everyone but Cassie understood the reasons behind Cornelius's refusal; the money had been offered with the condition Cassie would become the female lead and wield more power in the choice of productions. Cornelius felt the price was too high. Instead, he and Rosie had tried to persuade their eldest daughter away from the life of a high-profile mistress, but she had ignored their well-meant words and had the apartment redecorated to her own particular taste.

Her appearances at the theatre were fewer than before, but she could never give up her career entirely — even Cassie was aware of the fickle nature of her current rise in status. Instead, Charles tried to ingratiate himself with the theatrical troupe by sending vast hampers from Fortum and Mason, along with crates of champagne and beer. The tight-knit group treated him like everyone else — while he was treating Cassie with consideration, he was welcome, but the moment he upset her, they would close ranks. Cassie might have an unerring talent for irritating people, but she was one of their own and she would always come before an outsider. It was at this point that Cornelius and Rosie suggested a solo spot for Esme, enabling her to use her full and extraordinary range.

"Thank you, Esme," said Marcus as she finished her dress rehearsal. "Sing like that this evening and the angels themselves will fly down from the heavens to listen."

Esme smiled her thanks before hurrying away, wanting to grab Tilly and make an alteration to her costume. Lynette was waiting for her in the wings. "It could almost have been written for you," she exclaimed.

"Are you rehearsing?" Esme asked.

"Not for another hour. I popped in to see Jeremiah."

Despite Lynette's protestations the previous year that she was no longer interested in Jeremiah, Esme had known her friend had been trying to cover her own disappointment at what she had perceived to be his lack of interest. Jeremiah, however, had realised the error of his ways and after the meeting with Aaron had begun to gently woo Lynette. The couple were edging towards an agreement, but Esme was aware of Lynette's ambitions to join Henry Irving at The Lyceum, and this was what was holding her back from agreeing to marry Jeremiah. As Lynette had confided: "If I'm with Jeremiah, I'm tied to this company, which is wonderful and would ensure my future, but part of me wants to look beyond our footlights and see what it's like on another stage."

"Is it disloyal to think about leaving?" Esme had asked.

"It feels it, but how will we ever have any adventures if we stay under the eyes of our parents forever?" Lynette had responded.

"Exactly, they all took a risk and followed their ambitions. We should, too."

It was a topic to which they often returned but as both were under twenty-one, they did not feel they had much choice but to remain.

"Have you seen Tilly?" asked Esme.

"She's with your ma, fitting a costume."

"Good, I need her to shorten this skirt, it keeps catching on my heel."

"Your mum won't be impressed," said Lynette and Esme grinned.

Her costume was a faux peasant dress with a white blouse, wide belt and a skirt made of a shimmering patchwork of reds, oranges and golds, embroidered with silver and gold thread to catch the light as she moved. It hovered at Esme's ankles and had already been the cause of great discussion among Esme, Rosie and Tilly. Only Rosie felt it was short enough; Esme and Tilly thought it should reveal more of Esme's ankles.

"Why don't you pop in when you've seen Jeremiah? You can help me persuade Ma."

The friends parted ways in the wings — Lynette disappeared behind the flats to find Jeremiah while Esme followed the draughty corridor under the stage. After Esme knocked on the door of her parents' sumptuous dressing room, Rosie called her inside.

"Hello, love," said Rosie, who was standing on a stool in the middle of the room, while Tilly checked the hem she was pinning was level. "What can I do for you?"

"It was Tilly I was after," said Esme. "This skirt keeps catching."

"It's quite short already," Rosie said as Esme twirled around.

Esme and Tilly exchanged a conspiratorial look.

"I understand your concerns, Rosie," said Tilly, "but it would be worse if Esme caught her foot and fell over. If it went up an inch, it would remain a decent length but it would give Esme peace of mind."

Esme looked up at her mother and smiled, her face the picture of innocence.

Rosie looked from one girl to the other in amusement. "Perhaps I'm being old-fashioned," she said, laughing, as Tilly helped her off the stool. "Do what you think is suitable."

Disappearing behind the screen to change, Esme hopped onto the stool for Tilly to pin the hem.

"There's a letter for you," Rosie called. "It's on my dressing table."

Tilly passed it up to her.

"Thanks," Esme replied, remaining insouciant even though she recognised Aaron's flowing script. Tucking it into her bodice, she decided she would open it in private later.

Tilly set to work and when she was satisfied, she circled Esme. "Lift your arms above your head," she commanded, and Esme did as she was asked. The hem travelled up another inch and Tilly gave Esme a complicit grin. "Make sure you use red ribbons in your boots, they'll stand out more," instructed Tilly. "Let me check the bodice."

Rosie reappeared, dressed in a flowing robe. Her eyes narrowed as she examined the hem on Esme's skirt. "Scandalous," she whispered, then laughed.

Tilly straightened up and gathered together her sewing tools. "Drop it in to me when you've changed," she instructed, walking to the door. "I'll hang it back in your dressing room this evening. Cheerio."

"She's in a hurry," commented Rosie.

"Probably meeting Isaac," said Esme.

Rosie beckoned Esme to join her on the chaise by the fire. "Esme, my love, is all well with you?"

"Of course," Esme said, taking her mother's hand and squeezing it in a reassuring manner. "Why do you ask?"

"The cards," replied Rosie and Esme felt a cold swoop of apprehension. Rosie was a talented cartomancer and had taught Esme the skill.

"What did you lay out?"

"The Ace of Cups; The Lovers; The Devil." Esme gasped; this was the card she hated, finding the shadow side of its meaning unsettling. "The Two of Swords; The Knight of Wands and The Wheel of Fortune."

Esme ran through the collection of cards in her mind. There was the positive uprush of love in the Ace, but this was tempered by the trickiness of the Lovers card. A love with complications, emphasised by the shadows of The Devil. *Add to this the Two of Swords*, thought Esme, *the card of choice, even if neither option is appealing and without a decision, Fate could deal a spiteful blow.* It was with relief she remembered The Knight of Wands and the ever-turning Wheel of Fortune. Both indicated change, and The Knight often signalled a move of residence. Whether this move would be good or bad was ambiguous given the selection of cards, and Esme understood why her mother was concerned.

"Not the best selection, Ma," agreed Esme, "but, truly, I'm fine."

"And Aaron?"

Esme shot Rosie an amused look. "Aaron is Aaron and will remain forever unreliable," she replied, "but he will always be my friend…"

From far away, they heard a scream of fury.

"What was that?" said Rosie in alarm.

"It sounded like Cassie."

A moment later, they heard running footsteps and Lynette flung the door open. "Lord, Smee, what have you done?"

"Nothing," said Esme in astonishment. "What's happened?"

"It's Cassie. Charles has chucked her out of her apartment and told her they're finished. She's hysterical and, apparently, it's all your fault."

"My fault? How? I haven't spoken to Cassie for weeks. As for Charles, he always ignores me," exclaimed Esme.

"Cassie's always blamed you for everything," said Lynette, but the usual amusement they shared between them about Cassie was absent.

While Cassie irritated them, neither wished her any harm and the shivering, dishevelled creature who was helped into Rosie's dressing room by Lynette's mother, Winnie, shocked both Esme and Lynette. Cassie was unrecognisable. Her blue eyes were swollen shut with tears, her skin was blotchy and her hair was a greasy tangle straggling down her back.

"Leave Cassie with me," Rosie said. "Esme, change out of your costume. Perhaps when the rehearsal is over, you could go out for a while until things calm down. Lynette, my love, would you and Jeremiah walk through mine and Cornelius's parts, please."

"Of course, Auntie Rosie," Lynette said.

After helping Esme to loosen the strings on the back of her costume, Lynette walked pale-faced to the stage, while Esme hurried to her own dressing room and slipped behind the corner screen. She hid Aaron's letter under a pile of scarves and her wrap, before draping the peasant costume over the screen. As she finished pulling on her red wool dress, there was a knock on the door.

"Esme, my love, are you decent? It's Pa."

"Come in, Pa."

Cornelius appeared, his face white, his eyes serious.

"Pa, what's the matter?" asked Esme. She had never seen him so pale.

"Esme, my love, I must ask you a serious question," he said, taking her hands. "Do you know what really happened to Cassie's parents?"

Aaron's voice rolled through her mind, his tales of murder and hangings. Were these torrid stories he had invented to shock them? To cast even more shadows over Cassie? Would he be so cruel? The answer, *Yes*, floated from her heart.

Biting her lip, Esme replied, "Her mother died of consumption and her father afterwards of a broken heart."

"And you've never heard rumours of anything else?"

"No."

Cornelius patted her hand. "Your sister is very upset at the moment and is saying some spiteful things she probably doesn't mean." Esme chose not to comment, even though she felt her father was misguided in his assumption. "Your mother is taking her home. Perhaps it would be better if you stayed with Lynette and her parents this evening."

"Of course, Pa," she said, kissing her father on the cheek. "Let's not make a bad situation worse."

Cornelius stood but as he opened the door, he paused. "You're sure you've never heard anything else about Cassie's parents? From Aaron, perhaps, when you were young? After all, they are cousins."

"No, Pa," she said, her eyes wide with innocence.

"Very well, very well," he muttered, then for a moment, his normal self emerged. "Your costume is stunning, my darling. You will be a sensation tonight."

A moment later, he was gone. Esme hurried behind the screen to retrieve Aaron's letter, her heart pounding. It was too much of a coincidence this would arrive on the day Charles should so publicly humiliate Cassie. Ripping it open, Esme scanned Aaron's words and gasped.

Esme, there is trouble afoot with Charles and Cass; his wife has had a detective search into her past and they've discovered the truth about her parents. Ma and Pa knew her history, but I am the only other person in our troupe who was aware. Even Cassie doesn't know the truth. If Pa asks you, deny any knowledge. If things become too difficult, come to me.

Below was an address in Kemptown, a smart area in Brighton.

Too difficult? What did he mean? she wondered.

Hiding the letter in her reticule, Esme hurried to find Lynette.

Collecting Lynette's coat, the two girls linked arms and hurried away, cutting across Shaftesbury Avenue and into the main thoroughfare of Piccadilly with its endless flow of carriages and shoppers. Hurrying towards St James's Hall, situated at the quadrant between Piccadilly and Regent Street, they were shown into the luncheon hall for ladies. A few heads turned and Esme noticed other diners whispering, sending them surreptitious glances of interest and shock. Smiling, she focused on the menu before murmuring, "Do you think they're looking because they recognise us from The Firebird?"

"Of course they do," said Lynette. "They're scandalised because we're daring to eat lunch in a public place and us, actresses."

Esme smirked at Lynette's dramatic delivery before flicking a glance around the room. "We add both glamour and a certain thrilling notoriety," she whispered, managing an approximation of her usual cheeky grin.

However, the moment the business of ordering lunch, with a glass of sherry each, was completed, they leaned towards each other, their voices low as they discussed the strange situation at the theatre.

"Did you say anything?" asked Lynette.

"No," retorted Esme. "Did you?"

Lynette shook her head. "Neither did Jeremiah."

"Why would I try to ruin her life with the earl?" Esme snapped. "I was delighted she'd gone."

"Who then?"

"This arrived from Aaron," said Esme, sliding the letter across the table to Lynette.

"Short and to the point," she said, returning it to Esme, who stowed it away.

"He suggested I go to him if things become too difficult. What do you think he means?"

As the waitress approached with their food, they fell silent.

"It makes me uneasy," said Lynette, when the waitress retreated. "Aaron has never been given to theatrics, not like Cassie, and if he's sent you a warning, I wonder if he knows something else."

"Such as?"

"I don't know."

Esme cut up her fish, allowing the flaky white meat to dissolve in her mouth as she considered whether or not to voice the thoughts that had raced around her head as she had watched the rehearsal. Lynette was equally lost in thought.

"Do you think it was Aaron?" said Esme, breaking the silence.

Lynette sipped her glass of sherry before nodding.

Esme ate a few more mouthfuls, then pushed her plate aside and picked up her glass. "Aaron's never said to go to him before or given me any other address, only Soho Square," she said.

"Will you take him up on his offer?" asked Lynette.

Esme shrugged. "It's at times like this, when Cassie's creating one of her storms, I wonder whether it's time to strike out on my own. If Aaron is offering me a place to live, maybe this is the moment. Would you come too?"

Lynette did not answer, instead pushing her food around her plate before she placed her knife and fork together and abandoned her lunch. "Jeremiah's asked me to marry him."

Her dour tone surprised Esme.

"What have you said?"

"I haven't replied," Lynette admitted. "Part of me knows marriage to Jeremiah would be the best offer a girl like me could expect, but…" The sentence trailed away.

"Lyn, should we leave? Go to Aaron? Have a few adventures of our own? Ma and Pa were both on the road when they were years younger than us. Your parents were already performing, following the fairs. All of them, at some point or other, ran away from their folks, from the security of their family, to make a name for themselves."

"But they've given us so much."

"Exactly, 'given'. I want to create something of my own."

Behind them, the clock struck the hour.

"We should get back," said Esme. "Think about it, Lyn."

CHAPTER TWO

"Fifteen minutes, Esme," called Marcus Mason, Lynette's father. "Have you warmed up?"

"Ready when you are," she replied, taking one final look at herself in the foxed-over mirror in her dressing room.

Emerging into the starkly lit corridor, Esme followed Marcus towards the wings. They were in the final week of one of Cornelius's reworked Shakespearean extravaganzas. The bellowing voice of her father filled the auditorium as he sang his duet with The Fool in their musical version of *King Lear*. Cornelius had always felt the play would be much better served with a happy ending and had rewritten the text to finish with a family reunion, rather than a string of terrible deaths. To Esme's surprise, *King Lear and His Merry Daughters* had been playing to packed houses every night.

Cornelius and The Fool danced off stage together, joining Esme in the wings. Marcus gave a nod to Esme. "I'll be down the front, Esme — watch for my cue."

"Esme, my darling." Cornelius caught her arm. "I'm sorry about all this with Cassie. It'll blow over. It always does."

"I know, Pa."

"They're a good crowd," he added.

The band struck up and Esme reached across to hug her father before walking out into the limelight. Nothing else mattered when she was on stage except the music and as Marcus gave her the cue, she opened her mouth and allowed the liquid beauty of her silver voice to fill the theatre. It was only when she finished and there was a moment of spellbound silence, followed by a crashing wave of applause, she became aware of the theatre again. Flowers rained down and after taking several bows, she swept off stage, running back to her dressing room, while the *King Lear and His Merry Daughters'* cast returned to the stage.

Although not a regular member of the cast, the musical numbers for *King Lear* were dramatic and Esme had been enlisted to add her voice to swell the chorus. Dressed as the maid to Lear's youngest daughter, Cordelia, she was in the remainder of the play. Lynette was playing Cordelia and in one scene they re-enacted one of their old Skylark Sisters' songs. On three occasions, the audience had cheered for an encore.

Throwing open her dressing room door, Esme was loosening her costume when she heard a noise behind the screen in the corner.

"Tilly, thank goodness. This costume is tricky, could you unlace me, please?"

There was no response.

"Tilly?" Esme called again.

"You did this, didn't you?" hissed a voice. "You and my horrible cousin. *There is trouble afoot with Charles and Cass. Deny any knowledge.*"

Aaron's crumpled letter was thrown over the screen, falling at Esme's feet. Cassie flew from behind the screen, blocking the doorway, the one path of escape.

"Cassie, what…?" Esme broke off. In one hand Cassie held Esme's *King Lear* costume, in the other, a long, thin, silver knife. It glinted in the flickering gas light. Cassie's blue eyes were wild, her face white and bloodless.

"You little whore," Cassie spat. "You have to ruin everything for me. How long have you and Aaron been peddling these lies? Why do you want to destroy me?"

Esme took a deep breath, trying to control her climbing temper as well as her prickles of fear. "Neither of us want to destroy you, Cassie," she said, her voice as soothing as she could manage.

"Liar," Cassie hissed and with careful deliberation, she sliced into Esme's costume. "My mother died of consumption, my father of a broken heart. They were in love. They loved me."

Cassie's voice began to rise in an hysterical crescendo, repeating the litany with a feverish despair. Esme winced as with each word her sister brought the knife down, slashing again and again and again until Esme's costume was in ribbons.

"They loved me," Cassie screamed, throwing the ruined dress on the floor, "but you and Aaron don't understand love. You dwell in spite, with your secrets, your rumours, your nasty ways. How did you manage it? Did you tell this story to the detective?"

Cassie stalked towards Esme, who looked around for a weapon, anything she could use to protect herself. A hat pin glittered in a tray on the dressing table. Edging towards it, Esme reached behind her to tease it into her fingers, but Cassie loomed in front of her, grabbing her arm, and the hat pin slipped from Esme's grasp.

"Why didn't I see this coming?" hissed Cassie. "It was Aaron who introduced me to Charles. I should have known he'd destroy my happiness in the end."

"Aaron has nothing to do with this," Esme protested, but she knew Cassie was beyond reason — she doubted her sister had even heard her response.

"Aaron, Aaron, Aaron!" Cassie screamed. "It was the same when we were children — always the two of you, sniggering together, making my life a misery. Not anymore!"

All thoughts of Esme's that someone might hear Cassie and come to her aid were drowned out as above them, the deep base of the timpani drums sounded. Her one glimmer of hope was the arrival of Tilly, who should have been waiting in order to help with the quick costume change, but Tilly could be unreliable and often did not arrive. Trying to think of a way to distract Cassie, she was nearly knocked off balance as her sister grabbed her arm and spun her around, pulling her into a tight grip.

"Get off me," Esme snarled as adrenalin surged through her, but Cassie was taller and, in her mania, her grip was like iron.

"Aaron needs to understand what it's like to lose a treasured possession," Cassie whispered in Esme's ear. "No more Smee. Sob. Sob."

True fear engulfed Esme as the cool edge of Cassie's knife was placed against her throat.

"How deeply will I have to cut, do you think?" Cassie crooned. "How long will it take for you to die?"

"Cassie, stop, please," Esme begged. "This has nothing to do with me or Aaron."

"Liar," Cassie sang. "Liar. When I cut your throat, Aaron will realise his mistake and will explain to Charles the truth about my parents, then Charles and I will be reunited."

Aaron, Esme thought, *Aaron. Where are you?* His voice echoed around her head as though he was in the room. *Remember what I taught you, Esme.*

When she and Lynette had turned fourteen, they had attended the Goose Fair in Nottingham, which was the biggest show in their calendar with hundreds of entertainers milling around. Aaron had taken Esme and Lynette aside. "There are some unpleasant people here," he had told them. "Men with no scruples. I'm going to teach you how to protect yourselves."

For the next hour, Aaron had trained the two girls. He pretended to grab them from behind, teaching them how to extricate themselves, how to attack someone's face, to create a hubbub to attract attention. "Don't be shy, gouge at their eyes, scream, shout, kick," he had instructed. His lessons had put the girls on edge, and they had been far more careful that autumn as they traversed the showground. When rumours filtered back to the Hardys' troupe that women were being attacked and a few had gone missing, Esme realised Aaron had been correct to be cautious.

"You could be fighting for your life. Don't be polite. It's you or them," Aaron had said.

You or them.

Esme or Cassie.

"Bye-bye, Little Smee," crooned Cassie, her grip loosening as she changed position, readying the cold blade against Esme's skin. "No more songs for you."

The rattle of the door distracted Cassie and in her sister's moment of hesitation, Esme bought her heel down hard on Cassie's instep, while throwing her head back, smashing it into her sister's chin. Cassie screamed in pain, releasing her grip. A moment later, the door burst open and Isaac and Tilly fell into the room.

"The knife!" Esme shouted as Cassie tried to push past them.

Simeon, the stage manager, and Richard Ives, the director, were running towards the sound of the commotion.

Drums boomed above them as Cassie collapsed into a sobbing heap and Esme, shaking, allowed Tilly to draw her into a hug. Isaac picked up the knife and Simeon helped Cassie to her feet before leading her away; her violence spent, her eyes glazed, docile.

"What was that all about?" gasped Tilly, helping a trembling Esme to a chair.

As the shock of Cassie's attack overwhelmed her, Esme could not speak. Her legs were trembling, her mouth was dry as the realisation that Cassie would have been capable of murder engulfed her. Tilly picked up the *King Lear* costume and shook it out. As it fluttered in ribbons, the shower of embroidery drifting to the floor like a dying rainbow, Tilly fought back a sob. Esme had no idea how long she sat in the chilly room, but suddenly Cornelius was standing in front of her, his face haggard, tears sliding through the exaggerated lines of greasepaint.

"Esme," he croaked.

"I have to go," she said, her voice unexpectedly strong in her own ears.

"Stay. Cassie has gone. Your mother has made —" he struggled for a suitable word — "arrangements."

"No," Esme replied. Her skin prickled. She felt as though the cold metal had left a silver mark across her throat. "Let me be, Pa."

"Esme, you're upset, your mother will be here soon…" Cornelius was floundering, used to passing real emotions to his wife, particularly where their daughters were concerned. Esme loved him for trying to offer comfort.

"Go back on stage, Pa," she said. "We always finish the show. No one must ever know when things are falling apart behind the scenes. It was the first thing you taught us."

"But you could have died." He sounded distraught.

"I didn't, though. Please, Pa." Hugging her tightly, she could sense his relief as he released her.

"We'll have supper at my club after the show," he promised and fled towards the stage, where Esme knew he felt safest.

Tilly continued to hover in the corner, clutching the costume.

"There's gin in the cupboard," Esme said.

"Aren't you going on?"

"No, Lynette can sing a solo tonight, she's more than capable. Pa will tell her. He might even decide to sing with her."

Tilly poured a generous measure into a glass and handed it to Esme, who gulped down half of it, choking as it slid down her throat like slivers of glass. "I've got to help Clarissa with a quick change," Tilly whispered.

"Go," commanded Esme.

Alone in her dressing room, Esme finished the gin before moving methodically around the room, gathering her most treasured possessions: Adelaide, her Tarot cards, her journal and the picture of Aaron. To this she added the few dresses she had at the theatre, shoes, the boots she used on stage and a few of the less bulky costumes. Gathering up her greasepaint, she packed it into its box before scanning the dressing room, ensuring she had missed nothing important. Satisfied, she pulled off her costume and climbed into the woollen dress she had worn to the theatre that afternoon.

Hurrying to the office, she felt around under her father's desk where he hid the key to the strongbox and within moments had claimed her money. It was stored in a canvas drawstring bag with her name written on the top. Unbuttoning the top of her dress, she looped ribbons through the handle of the bag and tied it around her waist, smoothing it down underneath the thick folds of fabric.

"What are you doing?"

Esme spun around. Lynette was in the doorway.

"Get my money, too," Lynette demanded, "quickly. We have fifteen minutes until the show finishes."

"You should be on stage."

"Hepzibah's filling in for me."

"You're coming too?"

"Yes."

Without another word, Esme swept up Lynette's savings and passed them to her friend before turning back to the strongbox and placing a note where her money had been: *Sorry Pa. See you one day soon. Esme.*

Ten minutes later, Esme and Lynette forced open a side door that was usually locked and with a final look at The Firebird, they joined hands and disappeared into the night.

CHAPTER THREE

"Are you sure this is the place?" asked Lynette, looking up at the enormous, white, four-storeyed house in Kemptown, an upmarket area within Brighton.

Esme checked the address, showing it to Lynette for confirmation. "Do you think he's away?"

It was early afternoon, but the windows were shuttered and there was no sign of life. Esme felt a flutter of uncertainty. Aaron's letter had been written a few days earlier. If he was leaving town, why would he have urged her to go to him? Deciding she had nothing to lose, Esme seized the lion-head knocker and banged it hard against the door. A few moments later, it was flung open by a stern middle-aged woman dressed in the traditional black of a housekeeper.

"We're here to see Aaron Maclean," said Esme, handing the woman her card.

"Do you have an appointment?" the woman asked.

"No, but would you inform Mr Maclean that Miss Esme Blood is here to see him," she said, her voice haughty in reaction to the woman's scrutiny, "accompanied by Miss Lynette Mason?"

The woman stared at them for a moment, her eyes registering suspicion. Fingering the card, she gave them a long look, before, with great reluctance, ushering them inside. "You may wait in here while I see if Mr Maclean is in residence," she said, showing them into a parlour. The room was the first to open off the entrance hall, but Esme glimpsed a large staircase and a grandness which took her by surprise.

The door shut behind them with an assertive bang.

"Did you hear her?" said Lynette, her voice rising with indignation. "Not, 'I'll fetch Mr Maclean'." She gave a pitch-perfect impersonation of the housekeeper. "It was 'I shall see if Mr Maclean is in residence', as though he might not see us."

Esme allowed Lynette to bluster and mutter to herself, while she examined the room. The large windows flooded it with light, emphasising the subtle colours of the walls. In niches and on polished occasional tables, ornaments resided, each unassuming but expensive.

"Aaron's done well for himself," said Lynette, gazing around.

Heavy footsteps approached and the parlour door was flung open. Aaron stood on the threshold, unshaven, wearing a tartan robe, his hair wet from being hastily smoothed into place.

"Esme...?" he said, his face white with concern. "Was it Cass?"

Esme nodded and when he opened his arms, she ran into them. The relief of feeling the strength of his body was a balm to Esme's shattered nerves.

"What happened?" he asked.

Lynette gave him a brief outline of events. By the time she had finished, Aaron was trembling with fury.

"What did Ma do with her?" he asked, slipping back into his childhood way of addressing Rosie. He always told her she was more of a mother to him than his own had been.

"Not sure," replied Esme. "Pa said she'd taken Cassie somewhere, but we didn't hang around long enough to find out."

A knock on the door caused Aaron to release Esme, and two maids entered with a tray of tea, cakes and sandwiches. Aaron took one from the plate as they passed, causing the younger of the two maids to giggle. Esme frowned when she saw Aaron wink at her.

"I'm starving," he said, ushering Esme to one of the wide sofas. "We had a soiree last night, hence my dishevelled appearance. There's another this evening, so I was resting. I like to entertain."

Esme did not reply. The younger maid was watching Aaron with a look of such adoration it unnerved her. She glanced at Lynette, who raised her eyebrows in a quizzical manner. Aaron appeared to be oblivious.

"Peggy," said Aaron, and the older girl looked at him with serious brown eyes, "would you ask Mrs Levison to prepare the green and blue rooms for Miss Blood and Miss Mason? They will be my guests for the foreseeable future."

The younger maid's face fell and she scowled, stalking out of the room.

"What's up with her?" whispered Lynette.

"No idea," replied Esme, but she had her suspicions.

Half an hour later, Aaron led them upstairs. "These are yours for as long as you want them," he said, opening the doors to the adjoining bedrooms, "and I'm across the corridor."

His brown eyes twinkled, but Esme gave him a cool look.

"Convenient," she muttered, but she could not deny the rush of excitement as Aaron allowed his hand to brush hers.

"I'm going to make myself decent," he said and disappeared into his room.

The bedrooms were vast and linked through an adjoining door. Esme stood in the centre of hers and stared around in awe, wondering again how Aaron could afford such luxury. Beginning to unpack, she was startled when Peggy returned with two more maids.

"We'll do that for you, Miss," Peggy said, taking Adelaide from Esme's hand and seating the doll on the bed, where she lounged against the mounds of pillows. "Mr Maclean has suggested you and Miss Mason might like a light lunch in the red dining room."

"Lunch? Isn't it a bit late?" Esme said as somewhere in the house a grandfather clock chimed four times.

"Mr Maclean eats at unusual times," said Peggy.

Feeling she was being given no choice, Esme backed out of the bedroom, where she met Lynette.

"Shall we adjourn to the red dining room?" Esme asked in ultra-refined tones.

"Why, yes, Miss Blood, we shall," Lynette responded in kind before they burst into giggles fuelled by nerves and the relief of being somewhere safe. "Blimey, Smee, what have we got ourselves into?"

"Who knows?" Esme replied. "Whatever Aaron's doing, he seems to be good at it. How many people do you know who have to specify which dining room we should attend?"

They wound their way down the wide staircase, then paused, wondering where to find the red dining room. To their left, a door opened, and they could hear the person on the other side continuing their conversation: "…which is all very well, Aaron, but how do you know they won't spill your secrets?"

"Don't worry, Meg, they're sound. We grew up together. I would trust them with my life."

Esme and Lynette exchanged a look of curiosity.

"Meg?" mouthed Esme to Lynette, who shrugged as the door was thrown open and the stern housekeeper, Mrs Levison, appeared.

"Can I help you, ladies?" she asked, her eyes narrowing.

"We've been told to join Aaron in the red dining room," replied Esme.

"In here then, please. Mr Maclean is having a late luncheon."

Esme gave the housekeeper a curious glance, wondering at the relationship between Aaron and this woman.

"Smee, Lyn, come in," Aaron said.

He was dressed in the latest fashion, with, Esme noticed, handmade shoes. Everything about him was expensive but tasteful; no nouveau riche flashiness marred the perfection of his reinvention as a man who came from old money and all the connections it could buy. The day's newspapers were strewn beside his seat at the head of the table, where he was eating a vast bowl of soup.

"Sit, eat, you must be famished, and I can tell you about tonight," he said, dunking thickly buttered chunks of fresh bread into his soup.

Esme's mouth watered at the smell. She and Lynette had eaten a greasy sandwich at the station that morning and a few of the cakes when they'd arrived, but the savoury smell made her realise how ravenous she was after their late-night flight. As Esme took the seat to his right, with Lynette opposite her, the housekeeper, Mrs Levison, reappeared, glaring at them with narrowed eyes. Large bowls of soup were placed in front of them.

"There's no need to be all disapproving," Aaron said to the housekeeper, "we're family."

Mrs Levison gave a curt nod, but Esme saw her shoot Aaron a complicit look. As she walked past him, he gave her hand a surreptitious squeeze.

Esme felt as though she had wandered into a play halfway through and had missed the first act, making the nuances between the characters mysterious and unsettling. Aaron's easy manner did not seem to fit with the suspicious glances of his staff. It was a puzzle, but Esme knew it would not be solved on her first afternoon. Aaron was a man of many layers and the life he had built here would be as complicated to navigate as the man who had created it.

As they ate, the hot food began to work its simple magic and with each mouthful, Esme felt her fears fleeing as the joy of being reunited with Aaron overtook her. Esme gave Aaron a long look and, unable to ignore her desire to know the truth, said, "Is it true, Aaron? Was Cassie's father a murderer?"

"I swear on my life. The man was hanged when Cass was a child," he said. "My mother took Cassie in because she was worried what might happen to her."

"Do you think something like that runs in the family?" asked Lynette, voicing Esme's fears.

"Murder?" Aaron asked.

"Cassie has always been jittery," said Esme, "but I was surprised she could be so violent. If Tilly hadn't distracted her by rattling the door, I'm sure she would have slit my throat."

"Don't," squealed Lynette.

"Yes, don't, Smee," said Aaron, taking her hand. "Are you going to write to Ma and Pa to tell them where you are?"

"Of course. None of this is their fault. They'll worry, and so will Lynette's parents."

"This is your home. You're both safe here," Aaron said, then stood. "I have a few things to complete before this evening's soiree. It would be a pleasure if you would join us. I took it upon myself to order a selection of dresses to be sent to your rooms. Peggy will help you to dress."

"She can't help us both at once."

"All the maids are called Peggy," said Aaron. "It keeps things simple, and the footmen are all John."

Esme and Lynette exchanged another bemused glance.

"Guests will begin arriving about 8pm," he said, "and my soirees are famous for their longevity. It would be prudent to rest this afternoon."

Alone in her room, Esme lay on the vast four-poster bed, Adelaide in her arms, her mind processing what had happened to her. Her flight from her home had been driven by fear and anger, but for as long as she could remember, she had been imagining a life away from the theatre, dreaming of forging her own path. With Cassie's brutal attack, her first steps towards a new adventure had been taken. As she snuggled back against the pillow, the memory of the cold steel against her skin, Cassie's breath and the pressure of her hand on Esme's throat came back like a curse.

Would Cassie have carried out her threat? Esme knew the answer. Had Tilly not rattled the door, the night could have ended in a very different way. The thought was chilling. Was murder a trait that could be passed down through families? Like blonde hair and blue eyes? If so, what secrets were hidden within Esme? Her real parents were unknown, so what had she inherited? Her birth mother's desire to run whenever life threw an obstacle in her path?

Pushing the thought away, Esme's mind flashed to the Tarot cards Rosie had drawn a few days earlier. The Knight of Wands — a change of residence. What else would reveal itself from these events?

As the hour of the party approached, two rather risqué dresses that reminded Esme more of stage costumes than evening gowns were delivered by Mrs Levison. A red velvet and a midnight blue satin. Esme chose the red, intrigued as maids fussed around her, arranging her hair, applying her make-up and lacing her into the low-cut gown. The skirts were narrower than usual, skimming Esme's svelte figure without swamping her petite frame. By the time the two maids had finished and allowed Esme to see herself in the large oval looking glass, she was delighted at the sophisticated figure she presented.

She knocked on Lynette's door and the two girls eyed each other in the same critical way they did before a show, checking each other to ensure perfection. Lynette was swathed in a shimmering emerald-green dress and looked older and more glamorous than Esme had ever seen her. As they stood in front of the mirror, gazing at their reflections, Esme's unease about Aaron's household made her shiver.

"Have we done the right thing?" she asked.

"What do you mean?"

"Leaving The Firebird. Coming here."

"We can always go home, Smee," said Lynette. "Tonight, we'll stick together and no matter what happens, we'll try to have some fun. Aaron would never let us be in any danger."

John, the footman, announced them, causing the girls to laugh. With the theatrical bow they used when performing as The Skylark Sisters, they swept into the room where Aaron was standing beside the fire. Esme read approval in his eyes as the first guests turned to view their entrance. The soiree was in the grand parlour, a large room made even bigger by the cleverly designed doors that could be folded back to allow the two parlours to act as one large space.

"Esme, my love," said Aaron, holding out his hand, "let me introduce you to Sir Wallace Flagstaff, his wife Lady Helena and their nephew, Bill. Sir Wallace is in the publishing industry;

he owns a number of newspapers, including our local Brighton missives."

Aaron introduced Esme as his sister and Lynette as his cousin and Esme wondered again at the game he was drawing them into; each lie wrapping them tighter in his web.

"Jolly good to meet you," said Bill. "Aaron never said he had such a beautiful sister."

Esme turned to look at the young man, and her breath caught in her throat. It had never occurred to her there would ever be anyone in her life whom she would find more attractive than Aaron, but Bill Flagstaff was tall with dark hair and wide eyes of deep green — his smile was disarming but held a twinkle, hinting at a man who viewed life with a curious air and would not be easily forgotten.

"Bill arrived in Brighton last week," said Aaron, his hand warm on her waist, his voice clipped. "He's been living and studying in Liverpool. He's still learning his way around our customs in this part of the world."

The edge of threat was clear to Esme, although she was unsure if Bill heard it. As Helena began discussing the local theatre with Lynette and Bill was distracted by Wallace Flagstaff introducing him to an acquaintance, Esme murmured to Aaron, "If you don't want other men to flirt with me, don't introduce me as your sister."

"You and Lynette are living in my house without a chaperone, and you're both underage. If folk think you're my sister and my cousin, no one will be concerned."

Staring into his familiar brown eyes, Esme felt sick. "Do you see me as your sister?"

"Never," he whispered, "but remember, my love, the show is the most important thing: the lights, the glamour, the illusion.

What happens in the shadows behind the scenes is nobody's business but ours."

A thrill of excitement fluttered through her as Aaron drew his fingers along the inside of her arm, his touch warm, insistent, and her surge of emotion towards Bill was temporarily forgotten.

"Remember the last words I said to you?"

"I'm the only woman you'll ever love," she replied. "We were children, Aaron."

"I meant it, and you've grown up a lot since then, Little Smee."

"Maclean, good to see you…"

A rush of guests separated them, and Esme searched the crowd for Lynette. Standing near the fire, a sherry in her hand, she was holding court with several young men, her eyes sparkling as she laughed, every inch the glamorous actress. Catching Esme's eye, Lynette gave a nod to indicate she should join her, and once Esme was at her side they began their cheeky double act, delighting the guests. Wherever she moved, Esme could feel Aaron's gaze upon her. She lost track of Bill but when, much later, she saw him bidding farewell to Aaron, her heart contracted with misery until he caught her eye and gave her a hint of a smile.

The following day, while Lynette slept, Esme and Aaron walked along the fashionable West Pier.

"You and Miss Gale seemed very friendly last night," she said, having endured a painful hour while the elegant heiress had accosted Aaron and insisted upon his attentions, which Aaron had bestowed with no hesitation, making Esme seethe with jealousy.

"Patience Gale is a ridiculous, self-centred creature who believes every man in the room is in love with her."

"Are you?"

"No, but her father is considering investing in a scheme of mine, so it's prudent to make them believe I'm considering a permanent match with the giggling Miss Gale."

Esme did not respond. Business or not, Aaron had played the part of doting suitor with a proficiency that had caused her and Lynette to wonder. When the Peggys had left them alone, Lynette had joined Esme on her bed as they had done since they were children to discuss the events of the night.

"We need to find out more," Esme had whispered.

"This is Aaron — he's always danced towards the dark," said Lynette.

"Let's hope he hasn't danced over the edge of no return," Esme had replied.

This desire to discover the truth was the reason Esme had agreed to accompany Aaron on a walk. There were too many listeners at keyholes in the house, and Esme needed to know they could speak in confidence.

Aaron tucked her hand into has arm, grinning down at her, and she wondered whether the answers he might offer would be the responses she wanted to hear.

"Don't worry about Patience," he said. "The dream of love between us is enough for her. There will never be anything more."

"*We are the music makers, We are the dreamers of dreams,*" Esme said.

"Arthur's best work," replied Aaron, "but you're right. We were brought up in the world of illusion. When the lights are bright and the costumes are on display, nothing is ever as it seems."

"You say his name as though you know him."

"Arthur O'Shaughnessy is a dear friend," replied Aaron. "We met in London at one of the last parties given by Ford Madox Browne. Browne withdrew from society after the death of his son, Oliver, in 1872, but Arthur and I remained in touch. He is one of the few poets who also works full-time. He's a herpetologist in the zoological department in the British Museum."

"A what?"

"He studies reptiles."

"How fascinating. His *Ode* is wonderful, but then all his poems draw you into new worlds, especially his *Music and Moonlight* series."

"None quite like this one, though," said Aaron. "Inspiration, dreams, hopes passed from generation to generation, conquering lands and welcoming all, no matter whether they are king or peasant. The gift of imagination and the power this creates if we sing our dreams with conviction. His words make me believe I can change the world."

Esme laughed. Aaron's ability to see beyond the horizon was one of the things they shared. A view of what life could be, if your courage did not fail.

"We're music makers, dreamers in the moonlight," she said. "Tell me, my love, how do you afford to pay for your large house and your expensive parties?"

Aaron guided her towards the bandstand, where a small, chilled-looking group of men were playing popular tunes with more enthusiasm than skill. Choosing seats near the back, he listened to the band before turning to her. "I'm a businessman," he said, his tone neutral.

"Indeed, you are," she replied, "but what form does your business take? You once claimed to be a provider of services."

"It's part of my portfolio," he agreed.

"What services do you provide, Aaron? I won't be shocked; we had the same upbringing and have seen more than most people could ever imagine. You were the conduit between Cassie and her earl. Do you continue to work as a match-maker or was your cousin a special case?"

"Cassie was one of many women who have been introduced to men from the nobility," said Aaron, "but it is not a line of work which sits well with me. I prefer to think of myself as a Master of Ceremonies. A provider of a safe space for people to express themselves."

"Aaron, enough," Esme said, sighing. "Tell me plainly, what are you doing?"

"You won't be shocked or disappointed in me?"

"Never."

"My evening soirees are the beginning; this is where we make introductions and where people come to request certain information. Most of the guests have no idea these events are anything other than normal social gatherings, but there is a select group of men and women who have tastes which are not traditional. People with different needs; desires not met by their spouses. I provide certain, special gatherings for these people. They pay a high price for guaranteed privacy and discretion."

"Do you take part?" she asked, intrigued rather than appalled.

The fairgrounds of their youth had provided them both with an unshockable stance as far as the general strangeness of human nature was concerned. Esme had witnessed great cruelty alongside acts of intense kindness. Life was a tide, she had realised, washing you in and out. Sometimes it was your moment to surge forward with the current, while other

146

moments were passages of darkness to endure as you floundered for air with the current tugging at your legs, threatening to drag you under the unforgiving waves. Yet nothing lasted forever, and it was the continuing movement which made life an exhilarating ride.

"I provide the glamorous surroundings, the music, the entertainment and the photography."

"What?" gasped Esme.

"Very few people request the photography," he admitted, "but it's a service we offer, and we are paid handsomely. My house is bought and paid for, and I own the properties on either side too. The basements have been remodelled to provide the venue for my special evenings. From the outside, it's impossible to see or access this space."

Esme did not respond; this was not what she had expected Aaron to divulge. However, she felt it was preferable to the more violent and questionable practices they had encountered in their youth. "Everyone who takes part does so by consent?" she questioned.

"Of course. If anyone becomes distressed or realises these select events are not to their taste, they are escorted home and asked to be discreet."

"And if they're not?"

"There are ways of persuasion." Esme felt a chill at the callous way he delivered these words. "Are you shocked?" Aaron asked after a long silence.

"No," replied Esme, "I expected worse: a brothel, perhaps, women used in degrading manners, but if all those involved are willing participants and paying well for the privilege to indulge their unique tastes, who are we to question them?"

"Will you sing?"

"At your special parties?"

"I was thinking several sophisticated musical evenings with the genteel members of Brighton society in attendance in order to introduce you and Lynette, if she's agreeable, then if there is any interest and you would be willing… You will, of course, be well paid for your considerable skills…" He left the sentence hanging, and Esme laughed.

"You are a terrible rogue, Aaron Maclean."

"You love me, though."

"With all my heart."

PART FIVE: LONDON, 2020

CHAPTER ONE

Eleanor stared into the window of what had once been her shop. Beautiful high-heeled shoes were ranged around, glittering in the twinkling lights of the artistically decorated interior. A wry smile flickered across her face as she stared down at the vintage-style shell-top trainers she was wearing. While she loved them for their quirkiness, they were a far cry from her beloved, trademark high heels. Her feminine identity had been tied to her vintage style and her towering shoes, but with weakness in her feet and ankles from her illness, even the thought of wearing vertiginous heels on uneven pavements made Eleanor feel heart-stopping anxiety.

At first, this had been a huge barrier for her to overcome. Her counsellor had explained what she was experiencing was a form of grief.

"Your life changed unexpectedly and quickly," the counsellor had explained. "Despite making a good recovery, things will always be different from now on, and it will take you time to assimilate this change. Part of your mind is grieving for your old life, the one wrenched from you in the space of a fortnight. There is fear from the loss of control of your body and the fact this one relationship, the one you never thought to question, has been irrevocably altered. Add to this your decision to move back to Pembrokeshire and the changes with your business, is it any wonder you're struggling to come to terms with everything?"

It was another branch of the path Eleanor was travelling as she rebuilt her shattered life, discovering with each step what and who were important to her in her new world. Determined not to dip into bleakness, she turned away from the colourful display of shoes, congratulating herself on saving a small fortune by not buying a pair and having perhaps saved herself from painful bunions later in life.

Glancing at her watch, she began to walk towards the river, deciding to use the more scenic route to get to her rendezvous point with Nick. She was in Richmond for a long weekend of fun, and her first adventure was a pop-up auction at the town hall. Nick had seen it in his local papers and had invited her to stay with him and his husband, Giovanni, for a few days.

Strolling along the familiar river front, she felt a buzz of excitement at the prospect of the sale. Searching for treasure at auctions was one of her favourite parts of running her business. Wandering along the cobbles towards the town hall, Eleanor spotted Nick waving and, aware of the uneven cobbled surface, made her way carefully towards him. Linking arms, they hurried inside and began touring the lots. As it was a specialist sale, there were fewer people than usual but the crowd who were milling around held some familiar faces. Eleanor nodded to a few vintage store owners she recognised from other events but remained with Nick, not wishing to explain the reasons for moving her business to Pembrokeshire. While she was happy for friends and family to know, as well as those people she worked with on a regular basis, she had no desire to be the subject of gossip.

The lots were predominantly clothing and costumes from a variety of eras, with a few items of jewellery, theatrical memorabilia and rare magazines.

"Anything here you think might be suitable?" asked Nick, admiring a silk top hat.

"The velvet coat and the dresses on the rail," she replied. "Everything else is a bit modern for my stock."

"Is that an original Katherine Hamnett *Choose Life* T-shirt?" asked Nick.

"Perhaps. There are loads of fakes around, so be cautious."

Wandering from lot to lot, Eleanor felt happiness bubbling up inside her. There had been times during her recovery that she had thought browsing at auctions with Nick might be lost to her. Squeezing his arm, she said, "This is good, isn't it?"

"Like old times," he agreed, and they both turned away as unexpected tears welled in their eyes. "This would suit you," said Nick, pointing to a gruesome rayon dress in pea-green, forcing their momentary sadness away with laughter.

As Eleanor scoured the room, looking for an equally unpleasant item of clothing to suggest for Nick, a sudden sense of urgency enveloped her. With each step she took around the room, the feeling intensified to such an extent it blurred the edges between pleasure and pain. Eleanor was unsure why this strange sense of anxiety had arisen. Every nerve in her body felt taut, as though she were waiting for an item of huge importance. Yet as her eyes searched the lots, each offered disappointment.

"We'd better go in," she said, forcing herself to quell her rising panic.

Gripping the auction catalogue she had been given as they entered the saleroom with shaking hands, she and Nick took seats at the end of the front row. Unable to shift the rising feeling of fear, she opened the catalogue in the hope of distracting herself. A loose sheet of paper was attached to the first page, detailing a late addition to the sale, and a wave of relief swept through her.

"Theatrical programmes and costumes from London, Manchester, Scarborough, Brighton and Edinburgh," she read, showing Nick. "The reserve is quite low; I might bid for them."

"What's the provenance?"

"A house clearance company; it's gone into liquidation," replied Eleanor, reading the details. "Apparently, the majority of the boxes have been in storage for about fifteen years. This says they were acquired from the closure of an old cinema in West London, but there are no records as to who they belonged to before they ended up there."

"Interesting."

The auctioneer took her place and the atmosphere in the room changed as all eyes turned in her direction. Eleanor loved auctions — the excitement, the tension, the good-natured battling for items — but as the sale of the box of theatrical programmes approached, she felt a desire to own them that was so strong, she felt sick at the thought she might not win. A man she did not recognise put in the first bid, then a woman who she knew by sight from other auctions. Leaving them to tussle for a few moments, the bid was still only at £50, then a phone bidder joined in and the price jumped to £75. The man dropped out and as the auctioneer looked for new interest, Eleanor raised her paddle and heard herself say, "£150."

A flutter of interest ran around the room. The phone bidder added another £10, Eleanor upped her bid by the same and the person taking the remote bid shook her head. The auctioneer offered it up for the requisite amount of time before bringing down his gavel and pointing towards Eleanor. "Number 161."

"What was that all about?" whispered Nick as the auction moved on. "You could have got them for far less."

"I couldn't risk losing them."

"Why?"

"Honestly, Nick, I don't know," she replied. "It was as though someone was pushing me to buy them. Shall we get out of here? There's nothing else I'm interested in."

After dealing with the paperwork and arranging for the delivery of Eleanor's purchase, they pushed their way through the crowd and on to the pavement. Winding their way through the backstreets to Richmond Green, they walked towards the Orange Tree theatre, a small independent venue with a worldwide reputation. It had begun in the upstairs room of The Orange Tree pub, before moving into purpose-built premises opposite. From the moment she had begun living in the area, Eleanor had been a regular visitor. Nick had been offered preview tickets to *The Colleen Bawn* through the magazine and as he knew Eleanor was a fan of the theatre, he had accepted.

"Is there a reception?" she asked.

"Yes, but not until after the show. Come on, let's go into the pub and grab some food, I'm starving."

They hurried into The Sun, another of their old haunts, and Eleanor grinned. Settling at a table, she waited for Nick to bring them their drinks.

"What happened back there?" he asked with no preamble.

"Nick, I'm sorry, I was overwhelmed with the need to buy the programmes," she said. "My instincts are usually good. The last time I felt so strongly about a lot was when I found the Rolex watches."

He gave her a speculative look and she grinned, then he held up his glass and she chinked hers to his before he said, "Let's hope for another incredible find, then. I'll get us some menus."

Eleanor smiled as she watched Nick make his way through the growing crowd. For a moment, it felt as though nothing had changed, that she had walked along the road from her shop to meet Nick on his way home from work for one of their nights out. This was familiar, this was home, then the realisation that it was no longer her life loomed like a shadow. Waiting for the usual pang, it did not come, and Eleanor wondered if she was moving on. Life, she kept telling herself, was a patchwork quilt of discovery, of people and places. Richmond had been her home for a number of happy years, but Pembrokeshire was back in her life again and like an old flame, she was rediscovering both the positives and the negatives, and was becoming more comfortable as she adjusted to her new situation.

When they had ordered their food and more drinks, Nick said, "Tell me about Esme."

For the next half an hour, Eleanor filled him in with all she had discovered in the diaries and the intriguing details Mark Llewellyn had given her about a woman who might have been Esme's birth mother and her emigration to Patagonia on the *Mimosa*.

"I had no idea about Welsh settlers going to South America," Nick said in surprise. "This search is taking you all over the place."

"Esme was an interesting woman," said Eleanor. "She was tough, but there was an innate honesty about her that stopped her crossing the line into criminality."

"Why do you say that?"

"Her boyfriend, Aaron Maclean — well, I think he was her boyfriend — makes her wary. In her diaries, she states he was a money lender and gambler, but I think there might be more sordid revelations to come and, so far, she's distanced herself from the seamier side of his life."

Nick drained his wine glass. "How's it going with Arthur?" he asked.

Eleanor baulked at the unexpected change of subject. Lifting her own glass, she took a gulp of red wine, then shrugged. "It's not," she replied.

"I thought you were both struck dumb when you met on the beach? Giovanni and I were taking bets on when you'd be announcing your engagement."

"We were attracted to each other," she said, "but the moment he discovered Aidan was my brother, he backed off."

"Perhaps he has a girlfriend," suggested Nick.

"It's possible," she agreed.

Nick gave her a conciliatory look and before she could stop herself, she was blurting out what had happened the night after the pub quiz. She trusted Nick implicitly. They had been through too much together for her to worry he would belittle her feelings.

"He didn't even kiss you but ran for it?" Nick confirmed.

"Yep."

"There's more to this, Ellie," said Nick. "Your brother's a good judge of character and he wouldn't have employed Arthur if there was anything dubious about him. Perhaps you need to ask Arthur what's going on."

"Are you mad?" said Eleanor, looking horrified. "There was something I was wondering," she admitted. "I wondered if, assuming he isn't already involved, he might have met someone else around the same time we met and has decided to date them instead."

"Who?"

Eleanor felt traitorous for voicing her suspicions. "Briony."

"No," said Nick. "You two have been best friends since you were born. She might be single at the moment, but she would be the person scaring other people away on your behalf, no matter what her own feelings were. There's something else going on, and the only way you're going to find out is by asking Arthur."

Eleanor changed the subject. "So, tell me about the play."

"It's a revival piece," said Nick, pulling out his phone to check the email with the details. "They're doing a series of Victorian melodramas and this one is *The Colleen Bawn* by Dion Boucicault. It's the first stop before it goes on tour."

"How odd; Esme was in a production of the same play at The Firebird. She was part extra, part stagehand."

"It's a sign," he said as they crossed the road to the small, purpose-built theatre.

For the next few hours, Eleanor sat transfixed, allowing the performance to draw her into its complicated world. Story crossed story, twisting and turning until the final resolve was reached.

Circulating in the foyer afterwards, glasses of champagne in their hands, she and Nick were introduced to the producer and director, Desiree West, a middle-aged woman of great energy. Nick gave her his card, prompting Desiree to tow them around the room in order to meet the cast. When Desiree discovered Eleanor had been the owner of the vintage emporium, she was delighted.

"I visited your shop whenever we were performing here," she exclaimed. "I'm so pleased you're online; some of my favourite clothes were courtesy of your emporium. If we'd realised, we might have come to you for our last-minute changes."

"What happened?" asked Eleanor.

"The tour was beset by disaster, as usual," Desiree said. "Show me a theatrical tour that isn't, and I'll show you a producer who's lying. We had to replace one of the cast."

"Really? How frustrating for you."

"It was unexpected and wasn't an issue I'd dealt with before. It did put things in doubt for a while." Desiree took a bottle of champagne from a passing cast member and topped up their glasses to the brim. "It was a shame because he was a good actor, but when we began taking everyone's details, I discovered his surname was a stage name and it was then we found out he had a criminal record."

"Oh dear."

"I'm all for second chances and it didn't bother me in the least. He'd never been in trouble before or since, so this was a glitch, but it made it difficult as our insurance premiums doubled and I had to replace him. Hopefully I'll be able to work with him again in the future."

More people joined them, and Eleanor saw Nick by the bar, where he was talking animatedly to one of the cast. Desiree turned her voluble enthusiasm to another guest and Eleanor moved away. Tiredness was beginning to envelop her, and she made her way through the crowd to Nick's side.

"Shall we head off?" he asked when the cast member wandered off. "Hey, what's wrong?"

"I'm not sure."

Nick gathered their jackets and they made their way outside, where they climbed into a black cab. "Tell me," Nick insisted.

"Desiree said they had to replace their lead actor as the person they cast had a criminal record," she explained.

"And?"

"When I first met Arthur, he told me he'd been cast in a tour of *The Colleen Bawn,* but it was cancelled."

"Are you guessing that Arthur was the person replaced?" asked Nick.

"Maybe."

"Talk to him," insisted Nick. "You like him, and you need to know what's happening for your own peace of mind."

CHAPTER TWO

Eleanor stared at the boxes in front of her. The lot she had ordered with such determination at the auction in Richmond had arrived and as the delivery driver carried in box after box, she felt they justified every penny of her £170.

"Thanks," she said, signing the docket before wandering among her new purchases.

"Hello, anyone home?" called a male voice.

"Back here," she replied.

"You've been busy." Arthur stood grinning at the multitude of boxes. "Where did these come from?"

"An auction in Richmond. They're theatrical programmes."

"All of them?"

"Not sure yet," she replied. "What can I do for you?"

"Special delivery from Wave Riders," he said. "Come with me."

As Arthur took her hand, Eleanor shivered. Despite her conversations with Nick, she had yet to pluck up the courage to ask Arthur about his past and, if need be, assure him she understood. Everyone made mistakes; it was what those misdemeanours led you to become in the aftermath that mattered. From all she knew of Arthur, he was a good man. Aidan sang his praises, as did Chloe and Andrew; all people whose opinions she held in high esteem.

"Hang on," said Arthur, stopping so suddenly she cannoned into him. "Shut your eyes."

"Why?"

"You'll see," he said, and with great gentleness he took her hand again and began to draw her forward.

"This is ridiculous," she said, but she was enjoying his physical closeness and the strange intimacy of allowing him to guide her. The feelings that had assailed her on the beach began to flutter through her.

"Ready?" he asked, bringing her to a halt, his arms holding her steady. "Open your eyes!"

"My surfboard!" Eleanor gasped, picking up the purple and white board.

"Aidan and Chloe had it restored," said Arthur. "They said it was quite battered when you came home."

A lump had risen in her throat. The board had been an 18th birthday present from her parents and for years it had never been far from her side. When she moved to Richmond the board had gone with her as a reminder of her love of the waves and had stood sentinel behind her cash register. Upon her return, Aidan had taken one look at it and exclaimed in horror at the state of it.

"It looks amazing," she said, running her hands over the smooth curves of the board.

"Perhaps we could go out together sometime," said Arthur and her eyes snapped up to meet his. "Surfing, I mean."

"Of course, although I doubt this would be any use…"

"It's definitely seaworthy."

"It's not the board, it's me," she replied. "My legs aren't strong enough anymore. Perhaps I could try a body board."

Arthur stared at her, an expression of discomfort on his face. "Sorry," he muttered.

"Don't be," she replied, but the easy laughter between them had fractured. "Would you help me to put it behind the desk?"

By the time they had arranged it to Eleanor's satisfaction, the tension had dissipated again and Arthur said, "Have you finished for the day? Do you fancy a drink to make up for me putting my size nines in it?"

Eleanor found it hard to suppress a grin. "I'd love one, but you have no reason to apologise." As she turned to snap her laptop shut, an email popped up with an order. A red flag flickered next to it, meaning the customer had paid for express delivery. "Damn," she muttered. "Do you mind waiting? This is an urgent despatch."

"No problem," he said. "Is there anything I can do to help?"

"Print the labels while I wrap the parcel?"

"Tell me what to do."

A few weeks earlier, Eleanor had bought a stunning hand-painted silk kimono-style dressing gown from an online auction. The sales blurb had suggested it was from the 1920s but when it arrived, Eleanor thought it might be older. The previous evening, she had placed the dressing gown on her website, curious as to whether it would attract any interest. At £500, she felt sure it would languish. It appeared she was wrong; the kimono had been snapped up by someone in America, with an accompanying email requesting it urgently as a gift.

Eleanor spread her packing table with the printed peacock-feather design tissue paper that had become her trademark. When she had begun her business, she had decided to make her packaging beautiful, so each item, large or small, expensive or not, would feel special when it was opened by the purchaser.

Folding the kimono with immense care, she became absorbed in her task. Wrapping the parcel in silk ribbon, Eleanor placed it into a peacock feather box before wrapping it in sturdy brown paper and attaching the Art Nouveau inspired address labels printed by Arthur.

"I can run you to the courier pick-up point?"

"Are you sure it wouldn't be a problem?"

"Not at all…" he began, then there was a thump from the far end of the barn.

Eleanor called, "Hello?" and then turning to Arthur, said, "It's probably Sandy, he loves to hide among the boxes. Sandy…"

Expecting the fluffy ginger cat to come padding out of the shadows, Eleanor was surprised when there was no response.

"Could it be mice?" asked Arthur.

"It's possible," replied Eleanor, "or another animal that's worked its way inside. There are no doors at the back of the barn, but it's amazing what small gaps wild animals can squeeze through. I'd better check we don't have a rogue fox or rabbit roaming around. We'll probably find Sandy hiding in a box and he'll pounce on us when we least expect it. Sandy!" she continued to call, as they walked to the back of the barn. "Anyone here?" She made soft coaxing noises.

Arthur echoed her own calls, but no nervous animal appeared or gave an indication it was cowering in the shadows.

The smaller boxes from the auction in Richmond were lined up on the wide shelving her father had fitted. Nothing was out of place — the larger boxes were positioned on a raised platform to keep them off the floor and protect the contents.

"Maybe the noise was outside," Eleanor said, but as she turned to leave she saw the culprit. "Look." A row of books on one of the shelves had toppled forward, which would have caused the thump. "I bet the vibration from the tractor dislodged them." Eleanor straightened the books and placed a Victorian flat iron in front of them in place of a bookend. "Try moving that," she muttered to the books reprovingly and Arthur laughed.

"Shall we deliver your urgent parcel?"

A thrill of pleasure rippled through her at the idea of spending the rest of the day with him but as she spun around, feeling more like her old self, her ankle gave way and, before she could stop herself, she fell, sprawling into the boxes from the Richmond auction.

"Ellie!" exclaimed Arthur, running forward to help her to her feet. "What happened?"

"My ankle," she said, wincing, feeling tears of shock and embarrassment well in her eyes. "This ridiculous illness."

"Anyone could have tripped," said Arthur. "I stumble over shadows all the time. Life happens, Ellie."

"But I seem to keep collapsing at your feet," she said, trying to make light of her mortification. She tested her ankle, which smarted but held her weight.

"Which is exceptionally good for my ego," he replied, his voice gentle. Reaching forward, he wiped away a tear from her cheek with the soft pad of his thumb.

"And I've split the box," she sighed. "I'm going to have to sort this out. The contents might be fragile."

"Shall I run your parcel to the courier drop-off while you organise the box? Then I could grab a takeaway on the way back and a bottle of wine? It would be as much fun to stay in as it would to go to the pub."

Eleanor wondered whether this was because Arthur was embarrassed to be seen with her in case she fell over again, but his eyes were warm, friendly and concerned.

"Thanks, that would be great," she replied and, after she had given him her courier account details, he disappeared.

Breathing deeply to calm her jangling nerves, Eleanor looked around for a pair of protective gloves. Years of unpacking unknown boxes had cured her of pulling out items with enthusiasm before encountering an item with a less than palatable outer casing. Not wishing to touch anything potentially unpleasant with bare flesh, she kept surgical gloves nearby.

Pulling the ripped box clear of the others, she placed a sturdy stool beside it and, sitting down, flipped open the lid. On top were several cotton dresses, circa 1970, all of which were battered and worn. Wondering if the box would contain nothing but junk, she was about to abandon it altogether when a shiver of anticipation ran down her spine. Placing the dresses to one side to be recycled, she removed several threadbare waistcoats and a fraying tablecloth, adding them to the dismal pile. When she reached into the squashed cardboard box again, her fingers closed on a heavy fabric, and she lifted out a shawl. It shimmered as she held it up to the light, illuminating the delicate pattern of mythical birds flying across the fabric.

"Wow," she murmured, "this is stunning."

Peering into the box, she saw two leatherbound books, well-worn but of good quality, indicating they had been expensive. The first was *On the Origin of Species* by Charles Darwin, and the second was *Moll Flanders* by Daniel Defoe. Below these was another shawl which was wrapped around something hard. Wondering what treasures — or not — were about to be revealed, she reached in, the continuing feeling of urgency unsettling her.

Even before she had unravelled it, Eleanor could see the shawl matched the first she had found, except this one was shot through with purples, golds, reds and oranges, like a fierce setting sun. With careful fingers, she unwrapped the delicate fabric and, as the final layer fell away, she gasped. Staring up at her was a doll with faded black hair, bright violet eyes and a sweet smile. Her sapphire-blue brocade dress was handmade, and Eleanor immediately knew who she was, even though it seemed impossible.

Reaching for the books, instinct told her whose name would be written inside. Sure enough, on the inside cover, there was the familiar, swirling writing from the diaries and the name Esme Blood. Esme, like her, was an admirer of *Moll Flanders*. It was a tiny link, but to Eleanor it felt like another small bond, a will-o-the-wisp leading her to the light. Without any doubt in her mind, she knew the doll was Adelaide, the only present given to Esme by her mother Judith before she was abandoned to the care of the Hardys.

Staring down into the benign face, Eleanor felt a sense of such profound joy that it brought a lump to her throat. Ensuring Adelaide was secure on her lap, she reached in for the final item, a large bible which was unexpectedly light. Gathering the items in her arms, Eleanor made her way to the entrance of the barn, wanting to examine them in the comfort of her annexe. As she opened the barn doors and the smell of the farmyard and noise of the crashing waves engulfed her, a breeze ruffled her hair and she was sure a woman's voice whispered, "We're home," before her phone buzzed and Arthur texted to say he would be back soon.

CHAPTER THREE

Sandy was stretched out on the back of Eleanor's sofa as she hurried in, carrying her discoveries. Arranging Adelaide on a cushion where she could not fall or come to any harm, she placed the books on the coffee table before taking a series of photographs of each item, sending them to her laptop. Before she could examine them further, Arthur's car pulled up outside and there was a tap on the door.

"It's open," she called, taking a few close-up images of the detail on Adelaide's dress as Arthur walked in, laden with several bags. "Look what I found."

"A doll?"

"Adelaide, the doll that once belonged to Esme Blood."

"How is that possible?"

"It's mad, isn't it?" she said, the smell of the food making her realise she was ravenous.

Arthur spread the takeaway out on the table and, after they had served themselves, Eleanor collected Adelaide and the books, leaving the cumbersome bible behind, placing them on the table.

"These were all in the box. If you look inside the books, you'll see they were owned by Esme Blood."

Arthur stared at the serene face of the doll. "Is this what you meant by everything being connected?"

"Yes, I suppose," she replied, "although this feels strange, even by my standards."

Once again, Amelia Prentice's words floated through her mind: *One of them might call to you.* Amelia's journey had led her to Cliffside. What was Esme leading Eleanor towards?

"I've never been a fan of dolls," admitted Eleanor as they ate. "They can be creepy, but Adelaide is compelling."

"Her dress looks handmade," said Arthur as he topped up Eleanor's wine glass, although she noticed he had poured himself a glass of sparkling water.

"The stitches are exquisite. I can't claim to be a seamstress, but I've learned the basics over the years to make repairs, and whoever made this knew what they were doing. It has such fine work and look at the detail on the petticoats." Eleanor cradled the doll, whose dress was made from a smooth, high-quality cotton. The sapphire-blue background was printed with tiny red flowers and trimmed with a lace collar. It would once have been white, but time and age had painted on a yellow tinge, as it had with the lace and cotton of her three layers of petticoats. Each of these were embroidered with white silk, replicating the pattern of trailing flowers on the dress. On her legs were bloomers made from the same fabric and on her feet, small red boots made of the softest leather.

"Where do you think Esme found those boots?"

"Aaron," said Eleanor without thinking.

"Who was her boyfriend?" Arthur clarified.

"Not sure at this stage," admitted Eleanor, "but when he was young, he was apprenticed to his grandfather, who was a shoemaker. Aaron once sent Esme a pair of red leather boots with violets embroidered down the side. I imagine these are replicas."

Turning the doll over, Eleanor ran her fingers over the back of the dress. It was laced with soft ribbons. With great care, she untied the bows, loosening the bodice, wondering how long it had been since the doll was released from the tightness of the lacing.

"What are you doing?" asked Arthur.

"Examining her," replied Eleanor. "Esme was a woman of many secrets. This is her doll; Adelaide is sure to be mistress of a few surprises of her own."

As Eleanor loosened the ribbons, she was interested to see Adelaide's body was made from fabric, a combination of calico and leather. Parting the back of the dress to see if there was anything leaking from her — sawdust or shavings — she was surprised to see another seam running the length of the doll's back, which was also laced together. One end had worked free and, using tweezers, Eleanor began to ease it apart. A moment later, a pocket appeared in Adelaide's back. It was lined, going from back to front in the doll's body.

"Look," Eleanor said in triumph, "there's a secret compartment in her body."

With a pounding heart, Eleanor felt inside and her fingers closed on a folded piece of paper. Pulling it free, she placed it on the table before probing the space for a second time to ensure there were no more treasures to be discovered. Satisfied there was nothing else, she replaced the doll's bodice, tightening the dress and restoring Adelaide to her elegant self. Arthur was staring at her in astonishment. Hurrying to the dresser, she grabbed them both a pair of protective gloves.

"I've never done anything like this before," grinned Arthur as he snapped them on. "It's like being in a film."

Eleanor laughed. "This is the best part of buying things at auctions," she said. "The unexpected discoveries, echoes of lives. Even though we will never know the people who left these ghosts behind, it's incredible the secrets you can discover. Ready to discover Adelaide's?"

Holding her breath, Eleanor unfolded the piece of paper and felt a lump rise in her throat. It was a letter and wrapped inside was a wedding ring. On the inside the letters 'A' and 'E' were engraved, entwined in a circle. Showing it to Arthur, aware of their matching initials, she felt a wave of heat rise up, making her blush.

Eleanor gazed at the unfamiliar looping writing, which was peppered with capital letter Rs, as though the author had never been taught how to write the lowercase version. The words were faded with age, which made it difficult to read but, after a few moments of studying it, Eleanor began to decipher the words with their message of love reaching out across time.

"My Darling Esme, we were always star-crossed, but our love has never been in doubt. You are my wife in all but name. You have owned my heart, my soul since we were children, now we have a child of our own and my love will always protect you both. You may not be able to wear this ring legally, but I want you to have it as a pledge of my lifelong love for you, Aaron."

Tears welled in Eleanor's eyes.

"What does it mean?" asked Arthur. "Why couldn't they get married?"

"I don't know," replied Eleanor. "There are more diaries to finish — perhaps those will tell me more. If not, I'll ask Mark if he can help me."

For a moment, there was a glint in Arthur's eye. "Why Mark?" he said, slapping his napkin on to the table with unnecessary force.

"He's a historian and restorer and many other things to do with research," Eleanor replied, clearing the plates. Adrenalin was pumping through her after these discoveries, and she felt the need to move around.

"Why don't you ask me? I'll help," Arthur offered, but there was a strange timbre to his voice.

"Are you jealous?" she asked, trying to stifle a laugh.

"No…"

"Because there's no need. Mark and I are like brother and sister; we grew up together. His sister, Briony, is my best friend."

Arthur carried the takeaway cartons into the kitchen and Eleanor felt a small flame of hope. Perhaps she had not misread the early signs. Then Nick's words came back to her: *There's something else going on here…*

As she loaded the dishwasher, another thought floated into her mind and she spoke without thinking. "Are you married?"

"What?" Arthur's voice was like a whipcrack. "Where did that come from?"

Eleanor stared at him. He had not replied. "You are," she said. "Is that why you backed off after we met on the beach?"

"No, I'm not," he said, but he looked furious.

"There's something, though," she said. "Things don't add up with you. While I was staying with Nick, he had press tickets for The Orange Tree Theatre and we went to see a revival of *The Colleen Bawn*."

Arthur froze, the colour draining from his face. It was the first time Eleanor had mentioned it, and she was unsure why she felt the desperate need to challenge him, to find out what he had been hiding, especially when the evening had been going so well.

"When we were at the party after the show," she continued, "the director, Desiree West, told me they had been forced to replace their leading man because they discovered he had a criminal record and they couldn't get insurance, which delayed things. Was it you?"

Eleanor watched as a series of emotions played across Arthur's face. Finally, he turned to her, his expression tortured. "It's not what you think, Ellie."

"Is this why you keep pulling away from me? Your secret? Or is it something else? Is it because I'm ill and you find me repulsive?" She was forcing herself not to cry. This was her darkest fear, but she had to know.

"What?" He looked staggered by the accusation. "No, Ellie, please. I think you're the most incredible, brave and resourceful person I've ever met. It's…" He paused. "I'm not who you think I am."

"So, tell me!"

Arthur seemed to crumple before her eyes. He looked terrified. Understanding how easy it was to erect a façade, to pretend all was well, when inside you felt as though you were drowning in darkness, Eleanor reached out instinctively, taking his hand and leading him back to the sofa.

"Whatever it is, I won't be shocked."

Arthur refused to meet her eyes as he spoke, his voice low. "Yes, it was me who Desiree had to replace."

Eleanor felt her breath catch in her throat, but his confession calmed her. There were many reasons people had criminal records and she believed in second chances. Wasn't this the lesson preached by her Tarot cards? *We all make mistakes, but it's how we respond that matters*, she thought. "What happened?"

Taking a deep breath, Arthur looked up, his eyes bleak. "Three years ago, I was part of a tour in Cornwall. We were in a pub after a show when I received a text from my stepdad, Kevin, saying my mum had been taken into hospital. She has asthma and there have been times when it's been very bad. When I was young, one attack was so severe, we thought she might not survive. I was terrified. I couldn't risk not being at the hospital. My mate had gone to the loo and left his keys on the bar, and, in a moment of desperation, I took his car.

Although we'd had a few drinks, I thought I was under the limit."

He paused and Eleanor felt as though she were punishing him by making him confess.

"Did you make it to the hospital?" she asked, but he did not seem to hear her.

"It was raining and I was panicking, desperate to get to Mum, and suddenly there was a cyclist. I swerved to avoid him, colliding with an oncoming car, which was an unmarked police car."

"And the cyclist?"

"I hit him. He was thrown off his bike and broke his right leg and left arm. He was a kid, only sixteen."

"Oh, Arthur, how awful for you both. Were you arrested?"

"Actually, the police were brilliant. They realised I was in a state and agreed to drive me to hospital to see my mum, but they had to breathalyse me. I was three times over the limit."

"And your mum?"

"It was a terrible night. We kept expecting to be told she'd gone but the staff worked miracles and, at 4am, they told us she was recovering and would survive. The next morning, Kevin took me to the police station."

Eleanor reached out to take his hand again. "What happened to the boy?"

"Fully recovered, thankfully, but he should never have been put through such horrors in the first place. I was an idiot — arrogant about being able to hold my drink. I was charged with drink driving, taking and driving a car without permission or insurance and dangerous driving. I was banned for two years and given community service, which I did willingly. In fact, I offered to do more hours than the sentence, as it seemed the least I could do after causing such chaos."

"Is that why you won't even have one drink when you're driving?"

"Yes. I was able to reapply for my licence a few months ago and it feels like a privilege to be able to drive again. Before, I was a bit of a boy racer, charging around the country lanes, taking risks, racing my mates. Not anymore. I drive with care, caution and respect for other road users."

"You're the safest driver I've ever met," she said. "Does Aidan know?"

Arthur nodded. "When he offered me the job, I had to tell him about my criminal record. He was very understanding and treated it confidentially. He said he'd had a near miss when he was younger and understood."

"And Andrew and Liz?"

"They know. Andrew is an old university friend of my stepdad, Kevin. He promised to look out for me, and it's great knowing they're there if I need to talk about things. I suffered from depression and anxiety afterwards, and even now I have bad days, seeing the bike flying over the bonnet of the car."

"It was a mistake. An error of judgement brought about because you were desperate to get to the most important person in your life, your mum. It was a terrible accident."

"Desiree didn't want to sack me," Arthur said. "After I'd explained, she was very understanding, but the budget was so tight that my being there would have sent it spiralling, so she had no choice. It made me feel tainted, unfit to be among other people. Thankfully, Mum and Kevin were on hand, and they suggested I come away for a few months. Andrew is such a brilliant surfer, they thought I could surf my sadness away."

"Is it working?"

"Yes. Meeting you has helped too."

"Truly?"

"Yes. I know things are strange at the moment, but soon I'll be able to explain everything. I promise. Can you trust me?"

Once again, the intense connection which felt soul-deep rose within her. "Yes, I do trust you."

They were centimetres apart and Eleanor turned her face towards him. An emotional battle was raging across Arthur's face. Pain haunted his eyes as he leaned forward and brushed the gentlest kiss on her forehead. "I'd better go," he said, standing up, leaving Eleanor confused and frustrated. "I'll ring you tomorrow."

A moment later he was gone, leaving Eleanor in stunned silence. Gathering Adelaide, the photograph and the next of Esme's diaries, Eleanor curled up on the sofa and began to read, hoping Esme's stories might offer her some insight into her own confused life.

PART SIX: BRIGHTON, 1878

CHAPTER ONE

After her last customer had left, Esme wrapped her Tarot cards in a silk scarf and returned them to the ornate carved box she had bought when she had agreed to do professional readings in Aaron's front parlour.

The door opened and Lynette walked in, her cheeks pink from the cold November wind.

"How was rehearsal?" Esme asked.

Aaron's influences had led to an introduction to the theatre impresario, Mrs Nye Chart, who, after auditioning Lynette, had offered her a starring role in the much-anticipated pantomime at The Theatre Royal. Lynette was enjoying the increase in status this had given her in the seaside town. Her tenure in Brighton would end when the pantomime finished its run in February. She would return to The Firebird and marry Jeremiah. Once she was Mrs Hardy, she would train to become the second lead and understudy to Rosie, while Jeremiah took the same role for his father, Cornelius. Esme was saddened at the thought of her friend's departure but happy for her upcoming nuptials. The time spent apart had proved the depth of feeling between Lynette and Jeremiah.

"Wonderful," Lynette replied. "Mrs Nye Chart is a visionary; I do wish there were more female theatre managers."

"Tea?" asked Esme, pouring her friend a cup.

Lynette accepted it with a smile, cradling the expensive bone china in her small hands. "When we first arrived, I never imagined we would lead such exciting lives," she said. "In my magazines, Brighton seemed too respectable to elicit any fun, but look at us, Smee. Women of mystery. I'm in a pantomime and you're a local sensation with your singing. I bet our parents thought we'd be scurrying home within a week. By the way, Bill was asking after you again."

Bill Flagstaff, the nephew of the local newspaper proprietor, was covering the rehearsal and had escorted Lynette home one evening when a thick sea mist had descended. Aaron had invited him in, and Bill had accepted a glass of sherry. When Esme had appeared a few minutes later, Bill had stared at her in stupefaction. "Miss Maclean," he said, his cheeks turning pink while Esme felt a flutter of attraction flow between them. "How charming to see you again."

"A pleasure as always, Bill," she had replied, placing her hand on his arm as she accepted a glass of sherry from Lynette, delighted to have a chance to needle Aaron, who scowled. Bill left shortly afterwards but had since enquired about Esme on a regular basis.

Esme enjoyed the attention, particularly as it grieved Aaron to witness Bill's adoration. With the continuing myth concerning their sibling relationship, Esme was often forced to endure Aaron accompanying other women to events, to see his flirting and, on occasions, listen to female giggles emanating from his bedroom. While she did not wish to encourage Bill's attentions too far, there was a familiarity about him which she could not quite place and there was no doubt she enjoyed the uncomplicated nature of his company. They shared a sense of humour and his ambition to travel, writing for all the world's most important newspapers, was inspiring.

Outside, there was a commotion as the front door opened, followed by voices in the hallway.

"What's happened now?" said Lynette, placing her teacup on the tray, her eyes sparkling with laughter.

Living at Aaron's was an endless carnival of the unexpected and, as he threw open the door, Esme met his twinkling smile with one of her own.

"Ladies, you're both here; wonderful," he said, beaming. "We have a slight change of costume for the events this evening." He beckoned to an unseen person behind him and a tall, thin woman with brown hair pulled back into a severe bun followed him inside. Behind her was a young man, so similar in appearance he had to be her son.

"Put them there," she commanded, and the boy placed four large dress boxes on one of the vast sofas. Without a word, the boy left, his eyes never rising from the expensive Turkish carpet.

"This is Mrs Simpson," said Aaron but offered no further explanation.

"Perhaps Miss Maclean would like to try her costumes first," said Mrs Simpson, "then I can check the fit."

"Costumes?" asked Esme, her violet eyes meeting Aaron's brown. "I thought it was evening wear tonight?"

"As I said, a change of plan. This was a last-minute request from the host."

Esme flung back the lid of the box and gasped in astonishment at the beauty of the dress within. It appeared to be made entirely from peacock feathers, with a satin lining of emerald-green.

"Where's the rest of it?" asked Lynette.

When Esme held it in front of her, the feathers skimmed her knees and there were no sleeves.

"This is the style requested," said Mrs Simpson. "There's one for Miss Mason, too."

Lynette threw open the box nearest her and pulled out a matching dress.

"Miss Maclean, if we could adjourn to a suitable room for a fitting, I would be grateful. I'm a busy woman."

"We'll go to my bedroom," Esme said. "Aaron, could you ask Peggy to bring up the boxes?"

Stepping into the dress was a revelation. It shivered down Esme's body with a whisper. "Even on stage, I've never worn anything this revealing," she said, staring at her slender arms and shapely calves.

"It's a good fit," pronounced Mrs Simpson. "Does it feel comfortable?"

"Yes. The lightness feels strange, though."

"There's some boning in the bodice to give it shape, but the fabric is too delicate for anything else. You have a good figure; you don't need any enhancements." She helped Esme down from the stool. "There are drawstrings, here and here." She pointed to the seams. "They will make it easier to dress without a maid. The dress is much stronger that it looks, so you can be quite firm."

The second dress was a vibrant red taffeta, narrowly cut to hug Esme's figure. The shoulders were wide and low, enhancing her cleavage, while the skirt skimmed her hips in a long column, flaring out at the bottom for ease of movement. Once again, there were hidden buttons and strings to help her dress with ease.

Esme stared at herself in awe. Mrs Simpson circled like a bird of prey, muttering to herself. Masks to cover her eyes were in the boxes, one to match each dress. It was one of Aaron's rules that they had to wear them when they were performing at the special events in the basement, so their true identities were disguised.

"I'll check Miss Mason's outfits now," Mrs Simpson said and strode towards the adjoining door.

There was a knock on the exterior door.

"Who is it?"

"Me. Strewth!" Aaron was peering around the door. "Esme, you look incredible."

"Are you going to tell me what this is about?" she asked, ignoring the compliment and beckoning him inside.

Aaron made himself comfortable on the bed. "Tonight's event," he said, "is a birthday celebration for one of our richer and more unusual clients, known as The Judge."

They never used people's names, only a pseudonym. Esme gave a small nod to indicate she was listening while continuing to twist and turn in front of the mirror to admire her reflection.

"The Judge's friend and co-host, The Bishop, has made a few tweaks to the original plans. One of which was for you and Lyn to perform one of your old Skylark Sister routines."

"You might have asked us first."

"The request was made less than an hour ago."

"Liar," said Esme, but without rancour, "there is no way that woman could have created these costumes in an hour."

"Oh no, those were always going to be your costumes at some point, but we had to make alterations to the feather dresses so you could dance."

"Fine, which song?"

"'I'm Going to Catch the Eye of the Tsar'."

"It could be worse. And these dresses?" She pointed to her reflection in the mirror.

"For the rest of the music."

"These are extraordinary," she said, before catching a glimpse of Aaron's face with its expression of extreme mischief. "What?"

"Could I photograph you in the feathers?"

"They probably won't fit you," she quipped, "but you're welcome to try."

Aaron laughed. "You should be on the stage, Miss Blood."

Esme gave a theatrical curtsey. "Thank you, kind sir."

He stood behind her and slid his arms around her waist. She leant back into the familiar curves of his body. "Marry me," he said.

"No," she replied.

"Why not?"

"I don't trust you. You claim that wooing all these women is business, but it hurts, Aaron. Every time I see you with one of them on your arm, it's like a knife across my heart."

"There's only you, Esme. You are the woman I love."

"Ask me again next month. And yes, you can photograph me wearing the feathers."

An hour later, Esme made her way down to the vast basement that connected the three houses in a hidden world of red and gold glamour. Clever architecture had created a room that could be used as a concert venue or theatre auditorium, with all the necessary technical equipment required. When Esme entered the sumptuous dressing room, Lynette was already inside, admiring herself in the long mirror.

"Wouldn't it be wonderful to be able to wear dresses like this to go about our everyday business?" said Lynette. "No layers of petticoats or restricting bodices. Freedom of movement and no fear of becoming tangled up in our cumbersome skirts."

"Especially in the summer," agreed Esme, joining Lynette by the mirror, "being able to feel the sun on our skin would be a delight."

With the training of years, the women inspected each other's appearance with professional eyes, ensuring they were as similar as possible.

"Who is this man we're entertaining tonight?" asked Lynette. "Aaron tells you far more than he ever lets on to anyone else."

"This one is being referred to as The Judge, so I assume he's in the legal profession and reasonably high up. He's married and has been for years, with two sons and three daughters, as well as numerous grandchildren…"

"How old is he?"

"In his sixties, I think."

Lynette raised her eyebrows in surprise. "And he's still interested in the kind of capers that go on here?"

"Age is no barrier," said Esme with a wicked smile. "Anyway, he has a 'close friend' who Aaron has been calling The Bishop…"

"No!" exclaimed Lynette.

"I don't think he is really, but he is something ecumenical. He's married with children, too, but the two men have been close friends for years. Aaron said this is the fourth party they've thrown here."

Lynette whistled through her teeth, impressed. Aaron's events were eye-wateringly expensive, so to have used the service more than once showed a level of wealth above the normal earnings of either a high court judge or a member of the Church.

"One of them must be old money," concluded Lynette.

"Five minutes," came the call from outside. "The guests are arriving."

Esme put on her mask and gave herself one last inspection, then picked up the parasol required for their dance. The first time she and Lynette had performed at one of these shows, they had both had to work hard to retain their professionalism. As they sang and danced, the audience, a mixture of well-dressed men and women, had paid them little attention, preferring to hold hands or on occasions, kiss their companions. Despite thinking they were sophisticated young women, both Esme and Lynette had been fascinated by such a vast number of same-sex couples, despite seeing such scenarios throughout their youth. Two women, always referred to as the Sussex Sisters, had lived together quite openly, sharing a bed. Esme knew the penalties for homosexuality were high and felt pity for anyone who was forced to hide their true selves.

As they stepped onto the stage this evening, even Esme, who thought herself to be unshockable, was forced to stifle a gasp. As usual, there were tables spread around the room with a space left in the centre for dancing but this evening, in a prime position on the edge of the circular dancefloor, directly opposite the stage, were two golden thrones. In each of these was a man in his sixties. One was scrawnily built, while the other was obese, his grey-white flesh rippling around him like melting candle wax. What transfixed Esme, however, was their lack of attire. Each person in the audience seemed to be wearing the minimum of their best and most expensive undergarments. She glanced at Lynette, who was staring in such astonishment she had come to a halt. Esme nudged her with an elbow. Their music began and after exchanging a look of intense surprise, they began to dance.

"You could have warned us," Esme hissed to Aaron.

"Were you shocked?" he replied, his brown eyes brimming with laughter.

"Surprised more than shocked," she said. "Is that why you didn't say anything? You wanted to see our reactions?"

"It was funny. Behind your mask, your eyes were on stalks." He laughed.

Esme slapped his arm, but the gesture was one of good-humoured teasing. "Anything else we should know about?"

"All I'll say is that this particular crowd are rather uninhibited," he whispered. "Their tastes are what is known as 'French'."

"Nudity?"

"On occasions," he said, and a look of displeasure crossed his face. "Better hurry, you're on again soon."

As they helped each other dress, Esme warned Lynette about what might be to come.

"Do you think Aaron enjoys making a living this way?" Lynette asked.

"I'm not sure," said Esme, "but since the amusement factor has worn off for us, I'm beginning to find it all quite uncomfortable. Aaron might pay us well, but it's strange. He presents it as though he's helping people, but he charges a huge amount of money and he encourages people to do all manner of things in front of his camera when they're inebriated."

They exchanged a look of unease.

"Smee, why don't you come home with me in February? This has been fun, but I don't like the idea of leaving you here alone."

From the other side of the curtain, their introductory music was playing.

"Perhaps," Esme replied, then they plastered on their professional smiles and stepped through the curtain into the light.

The next morning, Esme was woken up by the newest Peggy, a tall girl with wide blue eyes and an Irish accent, bringing her breakfast tray. Glancing at the clock on the mantelpiece, she saw it was midday.

"Mrs Levison thought you might be hungry," said Peggy, placing the tray on the bed, before moving to the floor length drapes and pulling them aside.

Dull light from the damp day outside filled the room with a murky greyness. "Mrs Levison said to remind you that you have a Tarot appointment with Lady Hay at 4pm."

Esme gave a nod of acknowledgement and dismissal. The event in the basement had continued until the early hours, reaching heights of debauchery which had shocked even her and Lynette, despite their pride that their childhood had meant they were never surprised by anything. The images of the guests and their lack of inhibitions, encouraged by a plentiful supply of absinth provided by The Judge, flashed across Esme's mind and, once again, she wondered about Aaron.

"You're awake."

Aaron stood in the doorway, a shadowy figure draped in an extravagant robe of blue and green silk, smiling at her as though her thoughts had summoned him to her side like a djinn in a fairy tale.

"It's cold in here," he said, throwing coal on the fire before padding across the room and climbing into bed beside her.

"Go away," she murmured, "I'm sleepy."

"It was a late night," he agreed, moving closer to her.

Esme turned her face so they were looking at each other, their heads inches apart. "Is it natural for brothers to behave in this manner?" she enquired.

"In our family, it is," he replied, but Esme caught his hands as they edged towards her.

"Aaron, no, you have to stop this," she said, all sleepiness gone, moving away from him. "I've told you; I'm not fool enough to succumb to your dubious charms."

"When we're married, you'll have to," he replied, his voice muffled from where he had buried his face in the cool cotton of the damask pillowcases.

"I won't marry you until I know you can be trusted…"

"You're wise beyond your years, Esme, my love."

She handed him a cup of tea and, with reluctance, he sat up.

"Do your staff really think we're related?" she asked.

"No," he replied. "They know it's for show in order to protect your reputation."

Esme looked at him askance. "My reputation? With you in bed with me? Or is it because it suits you, leaving you free to romance other women?"

Aaron's eyes narrowed in irritation. "It suits you too, my love," he replied, ice in his voice.

"Meaning?"

"Bill Flagstaff."

"What about Bill?" she replied in a nonchalant tone, although she was delighted the reporter's visits had permeated Aaron's insouciant attitude.

"You've been seeing a lot of him in recent months. Has he been asking questions about me?"

"No, he's never mentioned you," she replied, offering Aaron a slice of her rapidly cooling toast. "He wants to be a playwright; we discuss the theatre."

Aaron shot her a sceptical look.

"Bill and I are friends."

"Friends," he snorted with derision.

"Aaron, you may be incapable of forming friendships with members of the opposite sex, but not everyone has such base needs as you, my love. Let's not forget your many outings with Patience Gale."

They glared at each other.

"Read my cards for me?" He gave Esme his most winning smile.

She stared at him in surprise. "You've never asked me to read them before."

"I'm interested," he replied. "Endless women have been telling me about the talents of my sister, the most sought-after medium in Brighton."

Esme narrowed her eyes in suspicion. "If I don't think you're taking it seriously, then I'll stop."

Kicking back the heavy covers, Esme pulled on her silk dressing gown and walked across to her ornate chest of drawers where Adelaide sat, watching over proceedings with a stern expression. Esme's cards were in the top drawer and a moment later, she was back in bed beside Aaron, who lifted the breakfast tray on to the floor. Unwrapping the cards, Esme shuffled them, then passed them to Aaron. "Shuffle the cards and think about the question you would like them to answer."

His hands, larger than hers, shuffled them with dexterity. Esme knew Aaron's reputation as a card sharp. Games took place with a select few men behind closed doors, often after the more upmarket soirees, but sometimes with rougher looking men, who never entered or exited through the front door.

"Using your left hand, cut the cards three times, moving them away from you, then put them together in whichever order feels right."

Esme watched Aaron closely, ensuring he did not remove any cards from the pack, her slim white fingers closing around his wrist when she saw it twitch. "No sleight of hand," she said. "Either take this seriously or I won't read them."

"Sorry," he replied. "Force of habit."

Esme glared at him and he looked chastened. Taking the cards, now reassembled into a pack, she dealt six facedown onto the coverlet, before placing the remainder of the deck on her bedside table, far away from Aaron. Watching him shuffle and cut her cards had been a strange experience for Esme; it was as though she could feel his fingers on her skin as he touched each card. As she turned the cards, aware of his eyes burning into her, she realised her heart was pounding and her hands trembled.

Ten of Coins; Death; The Tower; Nine of Cups, The Empress and The Star.

Esme gasped, unsure what to make of this spread.

"What is it?" Aaron asked. "Bad news?"

"No," she replied. "It's strange. When Rosie and Cornelius found me…"

"The night your mother abandoned you?"

She swallowed hard, unnerved by the wave of emotion his words created. "Yes, that night. Rosie told me she laid out a spread to see my future. It was these six cards."

Aaron looked startled. "Are you sure?"

"Positive," replied Esme. "We've discussed them many times, drawing out their meaning, and the strange thing is that each time a different card led the spread and the message it gave was altered."

"How can that be? The cards are the cards."

"But time changes the events they are casting their wisdom upon. Nothing is fixed. Not hope, not truth, not love. The questor brings their own unique energy and with each turn of the card the meaning is made anew."

Aaron shifted, his smile faltering as he stared at the six cards. "And what do my cards determine, my love?" he asked.

"Family." Esme began pointing to the Ten of Coins. "And money, the putting down of roots…"

Half an hour later, Aaron left, his step less jaunty and his expression more serious.

"You're remarkable, my love," he said as he reached the door. "No wonder these women are so impressed."

Unsure what she had said to make him so subdued, Esme wrapped her cards and rang the bell for Peggy to bring hot water for her to wash.

A few days after the party, Aaron beckoned Esme into his office, a large well-appointed room on the ground floor of his house. "Look," he said, opening a leather folder to reveal the images he had taken of her in the feathered dress.

Esme stared at herself with a critically professional eye. "Not bad," she said.

"You look beautiful," Aaron said. "What do you think about these?"

Esme's stomach turned as he displayed a selection of images taken from the debauched party thrown by The Judge. People posing in various stages of undress, each smiling into the camera, their bodies floating in harsh shadows from the vast lights Aaron was using as an experiment to photograph people without bright sunlight.

"It's unlikely the photographs will even develop properly," he had assured each model as they had placed themselves in front of his lens during the party. The guests, delighted by these reassurances, had posed in increasingly debauched tableaux, unmoved by the fact these images, if ever revealed, would ruin reputations in a heartbeat. The centrepiece of the evening had been a dance performed by The Judge and The Bishop, involving the two men waltzing with a great deal of enthusiasm but not much panache. The other guests had joined them on the dancefloor and Esme had watched with growing unease as the behaviour of the semi-clad guests grew increasingly lewd.

"Enough," said Esme, not wishing to witness the bizarre spectacle again. The first time around had been sufficient.

Aaron, realising her disapproval, shuffled the photographs away.

"I always knew Aaron danced with the devil," Esme said to Lynette a few days later as they made their way through the bustling streets to buy Christmas presents for their families and friends at The Firebird, "but it seemed harmless fun, like our cheeky quips on stage. After the other night, I realised there's a darkness in his soul and it concerns me."

"What do you mean, Smee?"

"Did you see his face when The Judge began to dole out the absinth as though he were a matron administering medicine to recalcitrant schoolchildren?"

"No," admitted Lynette.

"He looked —" she hesitated over the word — "evil."

"Really?"

"Maybe that's a bit strong, but there was a strange look of satisfaction on his face as though he had them exactly where he wanted them. I know it was their choice but, Lynette, they weren't hurting anyone. They were all adults. We've seen so many curious things and different ways to live — who are any of us to judge others?"

"You're worrying too much, Esme. Aaron knows what he's doing. Anyway, we'll be out of here soon."

But Esme could not stop wondering about the darker side of Aaron's business, particularly after his strange reaction to his Tarot reading. She decided to question Mrs Levison about the ever-changing maids and footmen.

"They're orphans," Mrs Levison said. "He trains them up, then helps them to find positions with a good reference."

"What sort of positions?"

"Usually in service or factories."

"Including the girls?"

"He's most particular about the girls. You don't need to worry, Esme, he won't let them go into brothels. He may bend the law, but he's a decent man."

On a monthly basis, Aaron asked Esme to marry him, but Esme continued to refuse. Her heart, she knew, would always belong to Aaron, but there was so much she felt he was hiding from her and until she could trust him, her answer would remain 'no'. The man Aaron had become was very different from the boy who had protected her in the fairgrounds. While seeming to be a happy-go-lucky charmer without a care in the world, he was, perhaps, the exact opposite. She knew one of his businesses was money lending and was aware he was known to be a man you would not want to cross. Plus, he refused to answer her questions about the nature of his relationship with Patience Gale — a woman whom Esme would have found difficult to like even if she was not always draped on Aaron's arm.

A few days later, finding herself alone in the house, Esme decided to investigate further. Creeping down the stairs, she let herself into Aaron's study and felt compelled to search his desk. Despite her unease at prying, she trusted her instincts and knew this was where she would find answers. The vast partners desk with its emerald-green leather top and its expensive fruitwood inlays was clear of any clutter. Aaron left nothing on the desktop, locking his business paraphernalia away in the desk's deep drawers. Sitting in the captain's chair, Esme perused these; there were three on either side and she knew they would be locked, but Aaron had taught her about the tumblers inside locks and how to revolve them with a hair pin. Pulling one from her elaborate chignon, she bent to the drawers on the left-hand side and, moments later, they clicked open.

With methodical concentration, Esme worked her way through the papers. There was nothing unusual: household accounts, letters of business and endless personal invitations to a variety of charity events, galas and balls. Aaron was well-respected, yet something nagged at Esme. They had grown up together and she always knew when he was keeping a secret. When she caught him out once, accusing him of lying, he had blithely replied: "I didn't lie to you, Smee, I just didn't tell you everything." Esme had been furious.

Abandoning the first set of drawers, she turned to the three on the opposite side. The top drawer only contained stationery but when she opened the second one down, Esme noticed immediately that it was shallower than the others. *A false bottom*, she thought, removing the collection of letters, newspaper cuttings and other detritus. She felt down each side until there was a click and the mechanism sprang forward to reveal a panel hiding a concealed chamber. Lifting this aside, Esme knew she had been correct to trust her instincts. The space below was filled with invitations, laid flat so they would not be damaged. Esme read one with tears blurring her eyes. Her suspicions were correct; these were wedding invitations to celebrate the nuptials between Miss Patience Hortense Gale and Mr Aaron Peter Maclean, three months hence.

Esme placed an invitation on the desk, but as she returned the contents to the drawer, she noticed another piece of paper bearing Aaron's writing. Written on it were the names of the six Tarot cards from the reading she had done for him. Surprised, she stared at it for a moment, then replaced it where it had been before clicking the false bottom back into place. Staring at the heavy cream card with its embossed lettering, Esme found her mind was surprisingly clear. Aaron was the man she loved, despite his shadow side. She was well aware her own nature was made up of darkness and light, yet Aaron was prepared to toy with her, parade her as his sister, woo another woman, even allowing wedding invitations to be printed. Esme doubted if poor Miss Gale would ever become Mrs Maclean, but she was not prepared to be part of Aaron's subterfuge.

She was halfway down the hallway when the doorbell rang. Secreting the invitation in her pocket, she diverted into the red parlour, sliding a book from the shelf.

"Mr Bill Flagstaff is here to see you, Miss," the newest Peggy said with a curtsey. "Are you at home?"

"Yes, Peggy, please show Mr Flagstaff in and ask Mrs Levison to bring tea."

As Bill entered the room at a gallop, his face splitting into a delighted smile, a plan began to form in Esme's mind, and she knew exactly what she had to do next.

CHAPTER TWO

Sitting in the library at St Botolph's Manor in Pembrokeshire, Esme stared out over the rolling fields towards the silver glint of the sea, reflecting on how much her life had changed. Even six months later, her eyes blurred with tears as Aaron stole into her mind and their final conversation replayed.

"I'm leaving," she had said, her voice gentle, her pain concealed.

"Me or the house?" he had responded, glowering at her from where she sat on the edge of his bed.

"Both," she replied.

"And Brighton? Your clients?" he asked, trying to keep his voice steady, nonchalant.

"I've been warning them for several weeks that I might be going," she said, her eyes fixed on his as she had tried to read his heart. "Lynette and I have discussed it. I'll be leaving with her and returning to The Firebird."

"I see," he sneered, bitterness and self-pity tinging his words. "When were you planning on telling me?"

"I was waiting for you. I wouldn't have left without saying goodbye."

"Well, thank you, my lady," he snapped, his voice raw with fury.

"Don't sulk, Aaron. We've both known for months this was coming. The reason you're angry is because I reached this point first. You have been my heart, my soul, but you are draining me, and I need to be free before our love destroys me."

He saw the wedding invitation in her hand. "I've failed you, Esme," he whispered, his voice hoarse with unshed tears. "You trusted me, and I betrayed you. Can I say anything to make you stay?"

Esme shook her head but as he had traced his finger down her cheek, she had rested her face against the palm of his hand, breathing in the smell of him, absorbing the feel of his body, allowing herself a moment of weakness in his arms, before she had closed the doors of her heart and moved away from his embrace.

"You will find me again, Aaron," she had said, raising her hand to silence his protestations. "One day, I will call for you and you will find me, but for the present, we have to be apart."

"Is there someone else?" he had demanded, as she turned to leave.

Esme had laughed. Aaron, with his endless string of giggling night-time girls, his planned marriage to another woman, dared to ask her if there was another man. Staring at him in disgust, she had seen the fury in his eyes as he wondered on whom she had chosen to lavish her love. "No, Aaron, there is no one else," she had replied, her response honest.

At her parting from Aaron, there had been no agreement with Bill Flagstaff. It was later, after she had returned to Rosie and Cornelius at The Firebird, that Bill had begun chasing her heart. Within days of her departure from Aaron's house, Bill had appeared at the stage door, concerned for her wellbeing. Fascinated by the theatrical world, his natural charm and his obvious affection for Esme had soon earned the trust of Cornelius and Rosie Hardy. When he explained his ambition to write a play, Bill was invited to stay and enthusiastically taken into the Hardy troupe.

When, a few days after Lynette and Jeremiah's wedding, Bill had asked Cornelius Hardy for Esme's hand in marriage, tears had sprung into her father's eyes. Rosie, too, had been delighted, as well as relieved, Esme suspected, because marriage to Bill would make her unavailable to Aaron. Esme, continuing to nurse the rawness of her heart left over from her sojourn at Aaron's, had accepted Bill's offer without a qualm, knowing this union would be a sensible decision.

Bill had invited Esme to join him on a trip through Wales and onwards to Liverpool, where his aunt and uncle lived. His uncle planned to buy a string of local newspapers, and, as his heir, Lord Flagstaff was eager for Bill to take on more responsibility.

When Esme held her hand up to the light, her square diamond glittered in the sun. Bill's devotion was a balm to her battered heart and her affection for him was genuine; his kindness, his cheeky sense of humour and his literary talent were things she found attractive. Since their first meeting, a connection had formed between them but, while she felt a strong attachment to him, he would never hold her soul. Marriage had never been a priority for Esme, but she had understood the security and respectability becoming Mrs William Flagstaff would offer. As marriage to Aaron would provide neither, even if it had been possible, Esme had decided life with Bill would be a pleasurable alternative. Esme was enjoying her foray into Bill's world of society with all its foibles and oddities, even if on occasions her heart tortured her with images of Aaron and what might have been.

"There you are!" exclaimed Bill, hurrying into the library. Esme gave a guilty start as she pulled herself away from her memories of Kemptown. "We're ready to go into town. Do you still wish to join us?"

The town of Milford Haven was a bustling street of shops, banks and cafes, the majority of which were linked to the fishing industry that flourished in the vast docks. Many years before, the town had been home to a whaling community from Nantucket, but this had been replaced by a more traditional fishing fleet. The arrival of the railway was causing great interest, with rumours the town would soon be a port for transatlantic travel. To Esme, who had never been this far into Wales, the bustling fishing port and the nearby town of Haverfordwest with its ancient charter and links to the romance of the Mediaeval period, was a revelation. Looking up at Bill, his light brown eyes twinkling, she gave him the full benefit of her dazzling smile. "It would be my pleasure," she said.

"The carriage will collect us in ten minutes," he said. "My aunt will be accompanying us too."

"How wonderful."

Esme hurried up to her bedroom where Gladys, her maid, was waiting, ready to prepare her for an outing. Although Rosie and Cornelius had never allowed Esme or their other children to go hungry, in her youth, money had never been plentiful. She and Lynette had often watched fashionable women, envying them their clothes. Glancing at the open wardrobe, Esme remembered the shopping expeditions she and Lynette had made, buying ribbons to enliven old hats, following the tips in Lynette's magazines to update their old dresses. When her trip had been announced, her parents, finally financially secure thanks to The Firebird, had provided a spectacular array of clothes and Lady Helena Flagstaff had commissioned a vast selection of gowns to add to Esme's new wardrobe. To Esme's dismay, Helena Flagstaff had chosen the styles and colours based on her own preferences for ruffles, bows and flounces, pastel shades and swags of lace — styles which could not be further from Esme's preferred tailored style and jewel colours.

"I've always wanted a daughter," Helena had gushed when revealing the vast and colourful wardrobe. "You'll look as pretty as a picture."

Esme had smiled, relieved Lynette had been nowhere in the vicinity, as they would have been unable to look at each other. Her mind strayed to the sophistication and elegance of the clothes she had worn with Aaron and for a moment, his face hovered before her like a phantom, but she pushed this apparition to one side. If the date on the invitation was to be believed, then Aaron was already married to Patience Gale. The thought slid through Esme's heart like a silver blade.

"All ready, Miss Hardy," said Gladys, and Esme was forced back into the present.

"Thank you, Gladys."

Today she had chosen a dress made by Tilly. The deep rose-pink and matching coat brought a warmth to her alabaster skin while the sapphire-blue hat enhanced the violet of her eyes. *I'm a long way from Little Smee*, she thought, as she gave herself one last glance and her heart ached momentarily for the camaraderie of her old life — the banter and the friendships, the rehearsals, the hard work and the thrill of standing before the lights. But she had made her choice, and the part she was playing now was that of Bill's fiancée.

As they trundled towards Hamilton Terrace, known colloquially as Front Street, where the newspaper offices were situated, Esme gazed down at the docks and out into the haven, the vast estuary used since the time of the Vikings as a place of safe harbour.

"We shall be meeting the newspaper editor, Gregor Phipps," said Bill, taking her hand. "He'll be giving us a tour of the building."

"It's so very exciting, isn't it, my dear?" said Helena. "I find the newspaper offices fascinating."

Esme half-listened as Helena chatted. The words flowed from her like a babbling brook, bright and frothy as she recounted the latest gossip about the royal family, before turning to her favourite topic, the guests who would be attending the grand party they were holding at St Botolph house the following week. "I have some wonderful news, Esme," she exclaimed. "A letter arrived this morning confirming the hire of two pineapples to be used as the centrepiece for our dining table."

Esme shuddered, remembering Cassie's delight at being sent a pineapple by the Earl of Dunblane.

The carriage drew to a halt outside the newspaper offices. Bill helped his aunt first, then held his hand up to Esme. Beaming, he guided her down to the pavement, winking at her as he dropped her hand.

"Have you written to your parents yet?" Helena asked Bill as they entered the offices.

"Yes, although, it'll take a great deal of time to reach them in Patagonia."

"Do you think they'll be able to return for the ceremony?"

"It's unlikely," he said.

"Your father has never had a sense of what is proper. Chasing all over the world with his poor wife. A missionary? What possessed him? Wallace would have taken him on at the newspaper but no, he decided to travel the world spreading the word of God to people who will probably ignore him."

Esme and Bill exchanged a look behind Helena's back of mingled amusement and affection. Her irritation with Bill's parents often caused her to purse her lips, but the kindness of her nature meant she usually followed this disapproval with a comment of concern or praise.

"Wait for it," Bill whispered, squeezing Esme's hand.

"They mean well, though. Bless them."

Esme turned her giggle into a sneeze.

"Are you sure you're interested in seeing how the newspaper works?" asked Bill as they made their way through the busy newsroom to the editor's office, where his uncle was already poring over pages of print and offering suggestions.

"It's fascinating," Esme replied. "Especially for someone who was often in the newspaper."

"Respectable newspapers, though, dear." Helena's voice floated towards Esme from where she had taken a position on the padded chair placed for her use. "You were always in the more responsible publications. Your upbringing was such an adventure and to have played before royalty…" Helena left the sentence hanging, having spoken it at a volume designed to encompass anyone in the vicinity.

"Practically a command performance, wasn't it, dearest?" asked Bill, his eyes wide with amusement.

"Practically," Esme replied with all seriousness.

"Auntie doesn't need to know it was a dissipated Prince Bertie who was there with your sister's dubious beau, the Earl of Dunblane," Bill whispered.

With Helena occupied by the vast tea tray that had been delivered and Bill joining his uncle to discuss business, Esme walked over to the window, admiring the wide-open waters of the estuary. Below her, a carriage stopped and two women alighted, their accents musical as they chatted. Always interested in studying people, ever alert to mannerisms she would once have been able to include in her act, Esme glanced down.

The two women were having an amiable discussion — Esme recognised the gestures and expressions as ones she had often shared with Lynette over the years as they'd decided the order in which they should do their shopping. One pointed to the steps leading towards Charles Street and the shops, while the other, smiling but resolute, indicated towards the docks. Esme leaned closer to the window, willing the women to turn around to face her. As though sensing the weight of her stare, they glanced up at her.

Esme's breath caught in her throat and she blinked several times, trying to clear her eyes, but each time the vision remained unchanged. The two women had hair as dark as her own, with eyes of bright blue. They looked uncannily similar to Esme. An emotion of raw, feral need swept through her as her instincts told her to run to these women, to embrace them, to feel their arms around her, to go… She hesitated, but the word was clear in her mind: *to go home.*

"Esme, we won't be much longer but…" Bill had appeared at her side. "What's the matter?"

"Those women," she whispered, "who are they?"

Bill stared at her in confusion. "Who, dearest?" he asked, peering out of the murky glass.

The women had gone. Esme stared down at the empty pavement, a pang of loss engulfing her like a physical pain. She forced a smile and turned to Bill. "No one," she replied. "It must have been my imagination."

As Bill led her to the chair beside Lady Flagstaff, Esme itched to return to St Botolph's Manor, to lay out her Tarot cards and try to discover who those women were and why she felt as though she knew them.

CHAPTER THREE

"Esme, are you awake?"

Her feet sinking into the thick wool carpet, Esme tiptoed to the door, opening it enough for Bill to slip inside. Shivering with pleasure as he pulled her into his arms and kissed her, she leaned into him, breathing in the scent of his spicy cologne.

"What a relief," he sighed. "My aunt has gone insane."

Esme laughed. "Our engagement party is very important to Aunt Helena," she chided. "Ever since we had drinks at the theatre with my family, she's been determined to have a celebration of her own."

"Are you sad your family won't be here?"

"No," replied Esme. "They'll be at the wedding; this party is your aunt's moment in the limelight."

"I thought it was ours," said Bill, settling himself on Esme's bed.

"Foolish man," she replied. "The party is always about the hostess, never the guests, and certainly never the people in whose honour it is being hosted. Has she consulted you about the guest list?" Bill shook his head. "Suggested you might like to invite your friends?' Again, his answer was in the negative. "Exactly."

Bill grinned. "You're a wise woman. Although Aunt Helena is more astute than you might believe. This morning, she summoned me to the drawing room and informed me that tomorrow the 'younger set' will be arriving and gave me a list of people she's invited."

"Are they people you know? Or people she feels are suitable?" asked Esme.

Bill laughed. "A mixture of both. At least it means we won't be as bored as I'd anticipated. You'll be able to get to know everyone before the ball on Saturday."

"Which shortens our rehearsal time," she said.

As the plans for Helena's ball had gathered speed, Bill had asked Esme to teach him to dance. Esme had been startled. "You can't dance?"

"No," he had replied. "My parents didn't give it much thought and when I went to live with Aunt Helena and Uncle Wallace, they assumed I knew, but…"

"Very well," Esme had said, fondness for her betrothed filling her heart as she looked into his woebegone face. Taking his hand, she led him to the centre of the room. "Dance lessons it shall be."

Bill had proved a fast learner with an easy, natural rhythm and a graceful style.

"Off the bed, you," she demanded. "Your waltz is not yet perfect. You keep skipping instead of gliding."

"When I proposed, I had no idea you were so relentless," Bill groaned as he hauled himself into a standing position.

"Professional," she replied, "not relentless. Never go on stage under-rehearsed."

With no music to accompany them, Esme counted them in and began to sing, her voice filling her bedroom as she twirled and dipped. Bill guided them through a Viennese Waltz, each rotation increasing his confidence.

"It's a shame we're not at The Firebird," she said as they finished. "Pa would have had you on stage as quick as you like."

"Perhaps we could work on a double-act, like the one your parents used to perform," suggested Bill.

Tales of Esme's childhood left Bill enthralled. As they began again, gliding around the large bedroom, he spun her into his arms. "Was your childhood always happy?" he asked. "You make it sound idyllic."

Esme thought back to the occasions when they had fled in the night to avoid villains and thieves, of the cold seeping through the walls of their horse-drawn caravans, of curling up with Lynette for warmth in barns when beds were unavailable, of the days of hunger and cold that went hand in hand with the tawdry world of the fairs. All reasons why Cornelius and Rosie had worked so hard to make themselves respectable to enable them to fulfil their dreams of a better life for their assorted offspring. And then there was the night Esme's mother had vanished.

"There were moments it wasn't," she said, "but it was a long time ago."

The clock on the mantelpiece chimed.

"I'd better go," said Bill, kissing her. "Afternoon tea will be served shortly."

He bowed deeply from the waist before hurrying back to his own room, leaving Esme laughing. Sitting at the dressing table, she pushed a few stray curls back into her elaborate hairstyle, considering how she would dress it for the ball. The house was filling up with guests, close friends of the Flagstaffs who were excited to meet Bill's bride-to-be. Esme was glad to have had years of theatrical training and experience behind her, because each time she appeared downstairs, Helena had a new well-wisher delighted to make her acquaintance. The endless small talk and chatter about weddings was becoming a torture and was beginning to take its toll on her nerves. It took all her acting skills to pretend she was interested.

Esme plastered on a smile as she made her way downstairs to tea.

"Esme," called Helena as she came down the wide curving staircase, "quickly, my dear, before Bill arrives, there is something we must discuss."

Wondering if they were once again going to have their amiable argument about bridesmaids — she just wanted Lynette, while Helena wanted an array of friends' daughters whom Esme had never met — Esme followed Helena into the library.

"Oh, my dear, I have such news," Helena exclaimed, grasping Esme's hands in excitement.

"Wonderful," enthused Esme.

"Bill's parents will be arriving on the morning of the ball. It's a surprise. He believes them to be in South America, but they have travelled home. My brother, Bill's father, suggested we keep it a secret. I am beside myself with excitement. Wallace will distract Bill on the morning of the ball so I can secrete his parents into the house. They are very excited and can't wait to surprise him. It will be an ideal opportunity for you to make their acquaintance. They will adore you as much as Wallace and I."

Esme stared at Helena in astonishment. From the descriptions of Bill's parents, she had formed an image of cold, dour, humourless missionaries who had abandoned their son to be brought up by relatives, but Helena's description suggested this was not the case.

"Very well, Aunt Helena," said Esme. "We will do all we can to surprise Bill."

"My dear, you look ravishing." Lord Wallace Flagstaff offered Esme a sherry as she entered the Lady Emma Room the following evening.

The manor was bursting with guests and this evening marked a formal dinner to welcome those who had made the journey to Milford Haven for the engagement party. In honour of this, Esme was dressed in a gown supplied by the Flagstaffs and she was not happy. Despite Helena's good intentions, Esme was beginning to feel as though she were providing a hobby for Bill's aunt. After exiting her bath earlier, Esme had returned to her bedroom to discover Helena deep in conversation with Gladys.

"We're deciding the best style for your hair," Helena had enthused.

"I know what I'd like," said Esme, opening the copy of *Myra's Journal*, a magazine Lynette had sent her. "This style with the curls is very fashionable…"

"Far too exotic, my dear," Helena had interrupted. "We've decided on something more suitable that will flatter your gown. Please don't disappoint me."

"But…"

Helena had hugged her, then floated from the room, leaving Esme torn. It was her hair, her choice, but as Gladys set to work, she realised the girl was following the instructions issued by her employer. Summoning up her sweetest smile, Esme turned to Gladys. "Perhaps," she had suggested, "with your extraordinary skills, we could combine the two styles."

Flattered, Gladys had looked over Esme's shoulder at the magazine. "Your suggestion is far prettier," she agreed. "Leave it with me, Miss."

Moving away from Wallace, Esme caught a glimpse of herself in a large oval mirror above the fireplace and felt like weeping. The insipid pale blue gown with its bows, ruffles and flowers reminded her of a dress she had worn onstage during her days as Little Smee. It had been covered in similar over-fussy decorations. A dress had been made for her doll, Adelaide, who had taken a starring role with Esme, but, she thought, *I was supposed to be a doll, too, and I was ten years old.* It had been the beginning of the tradition to create matching costumes for Adelaide. The style was far too young, and Esme was thankful neither Lynette nor Cassie could see her — Cassie would sneer, and she could almost hear Lynette cackling.

Bill appeared by her side.

"Don't say a word," she murmured as his eyes twinkled at her gown.

"Your hair looks nice," he replied, suppressing a smile.

"Stop it," she said, feeling better as they giggled together.

Guests circulated, Bill introduced her and Esme's face began to ache from smiling. After endless wedding chat, they had decided to escape to the glasshouse for a few minutes when an arrogant upper-class voice cut through the hubbub, causing Bill to stop in his tracks and Esme to skid into him and curse under her breath. Horrified, she looked up in case anyone had heard, but the only person near enough was the man who had hailed Bill and his eyes were brimming with amusement.

"Billy Boy!"

"Crispin Baron," exclaimed Bill. "What the devil brings you to this part of the world?"

The two men shook hands with enthusiasm.

"Pleasure, dear boy. You know me, never one to miss a party. When Lady H wrote to say you were taking a trip up the aisle, I decided to see for myself who'd captured your heart."

Esme squeezed Bill's hand, very aware of Crispin's eyes roving over her and the amusement she was creating. It was as though she could read his thoughts, and they were dismissing her as a timid creature, innocent, sheltered and unworldly. *If only you knew*, she thought.

"This is my fiancée, Esme Hardy," she heard Bill saying and forced herself back to the present. "Darling, this is the Right Honourable Crispin Baron, degenerate, gambler and heartbreaker."

Esme lowered her eyes, deciding to continue with the image of simpering innocence presented by her dreadful gown. "Hello," she murmured.

"Pretty," said Crispin. Esme wondered if he thought her too dim-witted to hear him, even though he was standing feet away from her.

"Bill," Helena's voice floated over the crowd, "would you join us, please?"

"Crispin, old man, look after Esme for a moment."

Bill disappeared before Esme was able to protest. She stared up at Crispin Baron.

"Drink?" he asked, beckoning over a footman and holding up their empty glasses.

"Don't mind if I do," she replied in her best stage Cockney, enjoying the shocked expression on Crispin's face. "Or I could be an innocent colleen from the mists of Ireland?" she suggested, switching accents.

Crispin raised an eyebrow in amusement and Esme studied him. He was tall, slim and moved with a feline grace. He was aware of his beauty and the arrogance this produced took the edge from his physical perfection.

"You didn't choose the awful outfit, then?" he remarked. "That was Helena's doing."

"She means well," replied Esme.

"Indeed she does," he said, passing Esme a second sherry and scrutinising her. "You look familiar. Are you part of the Hardy family at The Firebird?"

"Yes. How do you know The Firebird?"

"I have a house not far away in Gerard Street. The theatre has provided me with many an entertaining evening. You're the singer and you performed with your sister, Lynette?"

"Lynette's not my sister, but we did have an act called The Skylark Sisters, so the mistake is understandable. Cassie Smith is my sister."

"I bet she's a handful," he said, laughing.

Bristling slightly, Esme decided to change the subject. "How do you know Bill?"

"We were at school together," said Crispin. "Bill was a few years below me, but he's a decent chap. Sweet William, we called him…"

"What scandalous rumours are you pouring into Esme's ears?" Bill had returned. "Esme, my dear, your presence is required by Aunt Helena. Good to see you, Baron. Billiards later, perhaps?"

"If your good lady has no objection."

Esme smiled, relieved to be leaving Crispin Baron's side. His confidence reminded her of Aaron, but there was an edge to him which left her uncomfortable.

Throughout the evening, she was aware of Crispin's gaze following her and it was unnerving. When Helena suggested an early night, she agreed with no protestation, leaving Bill to a enjoy a night of drinking and billiards with his friends.

As she bade Bill good evening, Crispin shot her a look of such smouldering intensity, she felt her skin scorch pink. As a satisfied smile spread across Crispin's face, she fled, wondering why her heart was beating with such frenzy at his crass attentions.

CHAPTER FOUR

Entering her room after breakfast, Esme saw her trunks were in the process of being packed. They would be departing after the ball, taking a train from Haverfordwest to Carmarthen, where Wallace was interested in buying another newspaper and a print shop. From there they would travel to Cardiff before wending their way to Liverpool and the vast estate that Esme would call home once she was married to Bill.

Esme knew she loved Bill, even if it was in a different way to the intense passion she felt for Aaron but, despite the impending nuptials, the reality of her life as Bill's wife was one she was not yet ready to face. The moment she said, "I do," even the possibility of marriage to Aaron and a life with him would be lost to her. Whenever she tried to consider the years stretching before her as Mrs William Flagstaff, a strange sense of claustrophobia overwhelmed her.

"Pull yourself together," she muttered to herself. "Aaron is married to Patience Gale; he's been lost to you for a long time."

Throwing herself into an armchair by the fire, Esme wondered how to spend the rest of the morning. Bill was being distracted by Wallace to enable Helena to smuggle his parents into the house, and Helena had requested that Esme, too, stay hidden, so that it would be more of a surprise.

On her bedside table was a large black bible. Flipping it open, Esme took out her Tarot cards which were hidden inside it in a neatly cut-out square. While Helena found Esme's Tarot cards thrilling, Wallace was less impressed. A regular church goer, he claimed the fashion for spiritualism was bewildering and, while he had not voiced his displeasure at Esme's skills, his frown deepened whenever his wife praised her abilities. It was Helena who had provided the bible and Esme had grown even more fond of her for it, enjoying her cheeky subterfuge.

Shuffling the deck, Esme cut the pack with deft fingers before laying out three cards: the Three of Swords, The Devil and the Five of Cups. She stared at the images. The Three of Swords suggested an uprush of spite or gossip being directed at the seeker, unexpected discoveries often leading to painful choices. Then there was The Devil, which Esme loathed with its brooding menace. Looking at the chained captives on either side of the glowering demon, she imagined the heat of its foul satanic breath on the back of her neck. It was a card indicating the need to face an inner darkness, a shadow on the soul, a moment of living hell. She had never been able to see past this to its supposed vital and positive side of triumph from despair — to her, this card represented fear.

Finally, there was the Five of Cups. Not wanting to contemplate the meaning of this card, particularly in connection with the other two, Esme shuffled them back together, replacing them in their hiding place in the bible before throwing herself on the bed. Closing her eyes, trying to block out the images, her imagination instead presented the three cards, dancing before her. The Five of Cups suggested a rupture in a relationship through the discovery of a betrayal or secret, a wrenching apart of desire.

Esme tried to rationalise her fear — these were cards, they meant nothing. They had power only because she infused them with wisdom and knowledge from her own mind during her readings. The cards themselves were inert, nothing more than images on paper, a game. Yet a feeling of fear began to wind itself into Esme's heart until, with a shake, she scolded herself, imagining the disappointment in Rosie's eyes, should she discover this moment of superstition.

Rummaging through one of the bags, she pulled out the poetry anthology she had taken from Aaron's house. Opening it to Arthur O'Shaughnessy's 'Ode', she began to recite aloud but as she reached the end, her mind strayed again to Aaron. One evening at a recital they had performed the poem together. The following morning, he had made her a gift of the book.

"It's our poem," he had said. "Whenever you say it, think of me."

Idly she counted the stanzas — nine in total, each one eight lines long. 72 lines in total. A shiver ran down her spine — there were 78 cards in a Tarot pack. A difference of six, and six cards spun into her imagination: The Tower, Death, The Empress, The Star, the Nine of Cups and the Ten of Coins. Rosie's cards for her; her cards for Aaron.

Hurrying to her writing desk, she removed her Tarot deck from inside the bible and sorted them into chronological order. Then, with great care, she began to transcribe the lines of the poetry onto her cards, leaving blank the six images from the readings. Each line bound her closer to Aaron, entwining their lives, their souls. Aaron might be married to another woman and Esme might be about to marry Bill, but it did not stop her love for Aaron or his for her. Their hearts had shared one beat since their childhoods and every time she looked at her Tarot cards, she would be reminded of their soul-deep connection.

When she had finished, she felt the need to escape from the strange cloying feeling in her bedroom. Gathering her bonnet, she darted out of a side door, breathing in the fresh, salt-tinged air, before taking the path leading to the walled garden. Rounding the corner, she came across a bower of roses and honeysuckle with a seat giving views over the garden towards the glimmering sea. Settling back to enjoy the sensory beauty of the garden, she allowed herself to relax. "Perfect," she sighed, breathing in the sweet scents of the flowers that reminded her of the bouquets sent to The Firebird from admirers.

The world she had known all her life at the theatre felt very far away and she realised how much she missed being on stage. The months with Bill and his family had been pleasurable but there was nothing like the adrenalin of a performance, the roar of the audience, the camaraderie of the troupe. A wave of unbearable homesickness overwhelmed her. It would be many months before she saw the Hardys again and, when they were reunited, she would be a bride, her name changed to Esmerelda Flagstaff.

As she contemplated this, a conversation with Bill returned to her. When he had met her family, Rosie had explained the dynamic of the Hardy family to him. "Jeremiah is our son," she had said, "but we were never blessed again. We had a daughter, but she died. Esme was the daughter of a woman who travelled with us for a while, and then a few months later, Aaron and Cassie arrived with Aaron's parents. They were old friends of Cornelius, and we adopted the children when they were in difficulties."

Bill had been interested. "So your name isn't really Esme Maclean?" he questioned. "Aaron is not a true brother?"

"No," Esme replied, "he insisted we used his name in order to protect our reputations while we lived with him."

"Names are funny things, aren't they?" he had mused. "Mine is an endless source of family trouble." He had not explained what he had meant and when Esme had pressed him, he would smile, dazzlingly, and change the subject. A slipperiness Esme admired as much as it annoyed her, this edge to his personality adding an interesting layer to his otherwise amenable disposition. "He'll have to tell me on the wedding day," she muttered.

"Talking to yourself, Miss Blood?" came the arrogant tones of Crispin Baron.

"Reciting a poem," she replied, moving along the bench to make room for him. "How did you know my name?"

"You performed as Esme Blood after your sister had left The Firebird."

"You're extremely astute, Mr Baron."

Crispin grinned, then said, "Have you met Bill's extended family?"

"Not yet, but they'll be here this evening."

"Lucky you."

She found his Aaron-esque quality and his knowing smirk irritating.

"Will you be returning to London after the ball?" asked Esme, refusing to rise to his deliberate provocation.

"Perhaps," he replied, "although I may pay the family home a visit. I haven't been back for a while, and I want to check on my younger sister, Delphine."

"And your parents?"

"The Mater and Pater," he said with an icy spite. "No, I don't want to see them. I try to visit when they're away."

"Do they travel much?"

"Yes, between the houses my mother brought to the marriage. She was the heiress; my father came from a good name but no money. It was a marriage of convenience, as are most marriages. My elder brother and his wife are the same — they can barely tolerate each other. How they managed to have a string of children is beyond me."

"And you?"

"No doubt marriage will come my way soon," he replied. "It's why I'm a little envious of you and Sweet William. You actually like each other, it's extraordinary."

Esme stared at him. "Don't most married couples?"

"For all your sophistication, Miss Blood, you are rather naïve about the marriages of the upper classes. No one in my family has ever married for love. They were all business transactions, rather like the marriage of your friend Aaron Maclean," he finished, taking Esme by surprise.

"You know Aaron?"

Crispin batted the question away and his expression became serious. "Remember, Esme, we all play a role — you know that better than anyone. Should you need help, don't be afraid to ask." He was gone before she could comment, leaving her with a growing feeling of unease.

"My dear, what a very sophisticated dress."

Esme could hear the hint of disapproval in Helena's tone but, for once, she hardened her heart. Helena had been dictating her wardrobe for the past month and this evening, when she would finally be meeting Bill's parents, her pride would not allow her to appear in one of the frilled monstrosities chosen by the Flagstaffs. Instead, she was wearing a gown of oyster satin, made by Tilly. It was simple, understated and elegant, worn with long kid gloves. Around her neck was a moonstone necklace given to her by Rosie and Cornelius for her eighteenth birthday. It was her favourite piece of jewellery and she kept it for special occasions.

"Thank you, Aunt Helena," Esme replied with a dimpling smile, misinterpreting the comment with charming intent.

"Bill's Welsh family will be joining us for drinks before the ball begins."

Esme was aware of the plans; Helena had been reciting them like a litany for the past week. A family gathering, with the added excitement of the introduction of Bill's parents, who were currently hidden upstairs. Nerves fluttered through her again. Her interlude with Crispin had left her bemused and, in order to avoid further conversation with either him or Aunt Helena, Esme had retired to her room, claiming she wished to rest to be fresh for the festivities that evening. For a while she had lost herself in the pages of her favourite book, *Moll Flanders*, but even Moll's adventures failed to hold her interest for long. Eventually, she had fallen into an uneasy slumber, waking when Gladys arrived to begin the preparations for the evening ahead.

"Esme, you look wonderful." Bill's hand slid around her waist as he beamed down at her.

"Thank you," she demurred.

Wallace hurried into the room, his usually stern expression replaced by one of twinkling delight. "The Reverend Meredith and his family have arrived," he said to Helena.

"What a delight," Helena said. "It's been so long since we've had a proper family gathering."

The butler, Cuthbert, his Welsh vowels lyrical, announced, "The Reverend Meredith Blood, Mrs Mariah Blood, Miss Aelwen Blood and Mr Gawain Blood."

Esme felt a jolt of surprise, then scolded herself. Blood was a Welsh name; it was not unusual to discover people with the same surname as her own.

A tall man in a long black coat depicting his ecumenical position entered the room. Despite the harshness of his garb, his high-cheekboned face held an ascetic beauty, enhanced by his reddish hair and unusual golden-brown eyes. Beside him his fair-haired wife was lavishly dressed in the latest fashion, which surprised Esme as the contrast between them was stark. A younger man followed, who was strikingly similar to his father, and a young woman, who stood behind her mother.

As Esme stared at the young woman, a shiver ran through her. She was one of the women she had seen a few days earlier in Milford Haven. Though her hair was lighter than Esme remembered and her eyes held hints of green in their blue depths, the similarities between her and Esme were remarkable.

"Meredith Blood is the most boring man in the world," Bill muttered as Helena and Wallace greeted the new arrivals. "His sanctimonious son, Gawain, is worse. Try to avoid him at all costs. Mariah isn't quite so awful and Aelwen can be fun but, if you want to have any enjoyment this evening, keep away from them as much as possible."

Bill took Esme's hand and led her forward. "This is my betrothed, Miss Esmerelda Hardy," he said, smiling to the assembled group. There was a stunned silence.

"Esme is a singer. She has performed for the Prince of Wales," bubbled Helena, who was the only person not to have noticed the strange atmosphere as the Blood family flashed their eyes between Esme and Aelwen. "Wallace, perhaps you could arrange things as we planned?" she continued, ushering Esme and Bill towards the large window nearest the doors, coaxing everyone further into the room. "We have more guests arriving."

On a signal from Wallace, the butler opened the double doors. A tall man with blue eyes blazing from a tanned, handsome face stepped into the room. Beside him was a petite woman with reddish-brown hair and eyes identical in colour to those of Reverend Blood. Both were simply dressed but the quality of the fabric suggested their wealth.

Bill stared as though he had seen a ghost, then he ran towards them. "Mother, Father!" he exclaimed, throwing himself into their arms.

With undisguised love and adoration, they embraced, tears streaming down their faces. All three beamed with delight and love at being together again and Esme watched them in wonder. She had never been deprived of love — Rosie and Cornelius had adored her — but the depth of the bond between Bill and his parents was not an emotion Esme had never before witnessed.

Disentangling himself from the loving embrace, Bill reached for Esme's hand. "Esme, these are my parents, Celia and George Artbuthnot. And this is Esme Hardy, my wife-to-be."

"Hardy? I thought you said your fiancée's name was Esmerelda Maclean," said Bill's mother.

"A mistake — she was staying with her adopted brother, who is a Maclean. They don't share the same surname."

"My dear, how wonderful to meet you. My son has chosen a beauty…" began George.

Blushing at such an introduction, Esme smiled, bobbing a curtsey. With great solemnity, George bowed from the neck, before pulling Esme into an unexpected embrace.

"Forgive my brother," trilled Helena. "He's been away from society for too long. He is untameable."

Esme smiled, enjoying the warmth of the greeting. "The pleasure is all mine," she said.

Celia walked forward to greet Esme with a kiss on her cheek. "Welcome to our family, my dear," she said, but her greeting was stilted.

Unable to help herself, Esme stiffened in Celia's swift embrace. As she caught the quizzical expression on the older woman's face, the atmosphere between them shifted and Esme felt the withdrawal of Celia's affection. The card of The Devil swam into her mind, but she forced herself to dismiss it. Celia Arbuthnot had been travelling for many days — she would be tired.

"Wallace, call Cuthbert with the champagne," Helena said, her cheeks pink with delight and excitement.

Esme gripped Bill's hand, her nails digging into his palm, halting him in his tracks. "I thought your surname was Flagstaff, like Wallace…" she began.

"His real name is William Arbuthnot," interrupted Gawain. "He changed it for financial gain."

Fury sparked in Bill's eyes. "I did no such thing," he exclaimed. "While we are dealing with business associates, I use the professional name of Flagstaff as it is a family business, but Esme will be Mrs William Arbuthnot."

The two men glared at each other, but further hostility was avoided as the champagne was served. After toasts to Esme and Bill, the family moved from their private gathering to the ballroom, where the guests were beginning to assemble for the elaborate five-course dinner that would precede the dancing.

Esme was separated from Bill and seated between Crispin Baron and a business associate of Wallace. She watched the Arbuthnots throughout the meal. Celia doted on her son and Esme wondered why, if they loved their only child with such devotion, they were prepared to leave him with his aunt and uncle while they travelled abroad. "Tell me," she whispered to Crispin, "do you know much about Bill's parents?"

"A little," he replied. "They're missionaries. I believe they went to South America on board the *Mimosa* in 1865. Bill was quite young, and Helena offered to be his guardian — she felt it was safer for him here. Helena and Wallace weren't able to have children, so Bill is Wallace's heir. He was Arbuthnot at school, but most people refer to him as Flagstaff these days."

"Where do the Blood family fit in?"

"His mother."

"Celia is a Blood?"

"Yes, but this is the odd thing, I'd always been led to understand that Bill's mother was named Judith…"

Esme choked on her wine, but the conversation halted as the plates were cleared and by the time Esme had been furnished with her pineapple-shaped iced dessert, Crispin's attention had been engaged by the dowager on his other side, while Esme was left to fend off the friend of Wallace's who was a regular at The Firebird when he was in London. Throughout his bluff advances and admiration of Cassie, Esme tried to push away Crispin's words. A shiver of suspicion ran down her spine but with determination, she forced it aside, assuring herself it was her imagination and the names were a coincidence.

At last, the ball began. Helena was beside herself with excitement as the band struck up and after an announcement from Wallace, Bill led Esme on to the dancefloor.

"Imagine we're in the glasshouse rehearsing," she whispered as he took her in his arms, his face pale with nerves at the idea of dancing before such a vast crowd. "Look at me and forget anyone is watching."

Within moments, Bill relaxed and other couples joined them until the dancefloor was full. An hour later, Esme had danced with a variety of guests, her feet throbbing from having been crushed beneath those of clumsy partners. Casting around the throng, searching for Bill's light-brown hair, she walked over to Crispin.

"Have you seen Bill?" she asked him.

"Library, I think," he replied, "with his Pa. They were heading in that general direction, or it may have been the terrace."

Esme decided to check the library first but when she opened the door, it was not Bill but Celia who was seated there, staring into the fire. Hearing the door creak, she looked up, her face a mask of misery. Her golden eyes, faded with time, looked deeply into Esme's. Silence hung between them, and terror began to beat in Esme's heart. Finally, in a voice trembling with fear and confusion, Celia spoke. "Oh, dear God, it is you."

Esme could not speak. She stared at the woman with growing understanding.

"In Bill's letter — the final one we received before we set sail — he told me your surname was Maclean," Celia continued, her voice rising in an hysterical wail. "How would I have guessed it was you? Esmerelda is your middle name. The chances of you and Bill ever meeting were ludicrously small."

Esme was suffused with cold as the meaning of Celia's words reached her startled mind. "My middle name?" she gasped. "What do you mean? How do you know this?"

"Your name is Rose Esmerelda Blood Sutton," said Celia and every word she spoke caused Esme physical pain.

"Rose?"

"I named you after Rosie Hardy. She was like a mother to me when I needed help the most but in order to avoid confusion, it was she who began calling you Esme, using your middle name."

Esme stared at the woman, her heart pounding. How was this possible? This was her mother.

"But it doesn't make sense," Esme gasped. "Why did they call me Blood instead of Sutton?"

"To hide you from the men who murdered your father."

Esme turned away. Who was Rose Sutton? It was not her. She was Esme Blood. "Why have you changed your name to Celia?" she demanded, trying to realise sense from chaos.

"It's my middle name," she said. "Oh, my dear, all I wanted was for you to be safe."

"Safe?" Esme's voice was hard. "You left me in a tent in the middle of the night. Anything could have happened to me."

"You don't understand," Celia implored. "Rosie's fortune-telling tent represented safety to me. I knew you would be found, no matter what happened." When Esme did not respond, Celia, breathing hard, spoke into the growing void between them. "When I fled, there were men after me. Frightening and dangerous men who would use any means to achieve their desires. Your father, Robert, owed money. We ran away to get married and were returning to fetch you when we were attacked and your father was stabbed."

Esme stared at this woman, this stranger, who was spewing forth a story that had shaped the entire course of her life.

"I was scared the men would come after me, after you," Celia said, rocking in her chair. "Leaving you with Rosie and Cornelius seemed the safest option, as did changing my name. Rosie must have thought the same thing and used your middle names to hide your parentage."

Realisation was washing over Esme. "If you're Judith Blood, my mother…" she said, her voice fearful as the ends tied themselves into a hideous cat's cradle of deceit, "then Bill is my half-brother…"

Celia's head jerked as though pulled upwards by an unforgiving puppeteer. "No, you must let me explain..." she began, her voice desperate, "the lies we have told run so deep."

Esme did not know what Celia was talking about, but she did not want to listen. Aaron had masked their relationship as that of brother and sister, an idea which Esme had always found repugnant but now, unwittingly, she had become engaged to her half-brother. Her stomach heaved and she ran towards the fire, where she was violently sick into the coal scuttle. Empty and shaking, Esme reached for the brandy decanter and poured herself a healthy measure, gulping it down and wincing as its fire hit her throat. Her brain no longer seemed to be functioning. In place of her thoughts there was a swirling cloud of anger. Then words began to spill from her mouth — resentments and fears she had pushed into the shadows at the corner of her mind were unleashed at last.

"All my life," she said, "I applauded you for walking away, for thinking you couldn't cope with a child, for choosing survival. Not once did I imagine you settled, married, happy and with another child, working as a missionary. Hiding from the men who had murdered my father, while you left me alone to take my chances." Celia flinched as though Esme had struck her. "You have a loving husband and a son, upon whom you dote. You told them you were a widow..."

"I was," Celia interrupted, her voice more like the cry of a wounded bird. "Your father was murdered..."

"And what did you tell them about me? Did you even mention me?"

"I said, you were..." Celia gulped. "I said you were dead."

"Dead?" Esme's anger had risen, her voice reaching a crescendo of pain. "You told your new husband I was dead!

You have denied me for your entire life. You kept your son and you buried your daughter!"

Esme's love for Bill was draining away, corrupted by these revelations, replaced by anger, jealousy and disgust. A bitterness she had no idea she could feel gripped her heart. Shaking with such violence her teeth chattered, Esme stood up straight and with deliberate slowness, turned to face her mother.

Celia had not moved. She stared at Esme, her face rigid with shock. This time, Esme held the power — she knew that if she so desired, she could destroy this sweet, loving family. Trample them into the dirt, her revenge exacted swiftly and brutally, punishment meted out on the mother who had abandoned her.

Yet, she knew she could not do that. She did not care about Celia or Judith or whatever she chose to call herself, but she had loved Bill. He and George were innocents in Celia's schemes, and she did not feel it was her place to reveal the cold heart lurking within the woman they both adored.

"You don't understand," Celia sobbed, breaking the growing silence. "The men who murdered your father were evil. I met George and married him for safety. We fell in love later, and when we were offered the chance to live abroad, I seized the opportunity, hiding Bill with the Flagstaffs."

"And these men? Do they continue to pursue you?" Esme asked, unsure whether to believe in these shadowy creatures of destruction.

"No," Celia said. "They stopped chasing me a long time ago…"

"So why didn't you come back for me?" Esme yelled. "Why didn't you love me? Why didn't you at least send me a message?"

Celia buried her head in her hands and did not respond.

It was time for Esme to leave, to walk away from her mother as Celia had walked away from her all those years ago. To inflict upon her as much pain as she had on Esme. "You can tell Bill why I'm leaving," Esme said.

"No," Celia implored. "He adores you…"

"He's my brother," Esme snapped.

"No, Esme, you must stay," Celia said. "You don't understand…"

"What is there to understand?"

A shadow fell across Esme; Bill was beside her, his face streaked with tears as he reached out his hands to them both. His expression was one of pleading desperation and disbelief. Beside him stood his father. "Tell me it's not true," Bill gasped. "Please, tell me it's not true."

Esme shook her head, horrified by his sudden appearance. "Where were you?" she asked. "You were supposed to be on the terrace."

"I wanted to show my father this room. We were behind the bookcases in the corner, we heard everything," he whispered. "It's not true. It can't be true."

"You've seen your cousin, Aelwen. How many more are there in your mother's — our mother's — family who look like me? Did you never notice?" Esme's voice was shrill with despair. "They're my cousins too!"

Bill and George turned to Celia who, with a slow nod, sealed their fate. George swore under his breath, before reaching forward to place a comforting hand on Celia's shoulder. Bill swayed, his face grey with despair. Esme moved towards him but stopped, realising he was no longer hers to comfort. Instead, she stepped aside and allowed Celia to pass, watching as, without a glance in Esme's direction, she enveloped Bill in a hug. George stepped forward and encircled them both in his arms before holding out a hand to Esme, to draw her in.

"We can explain…" he began, but Esme had heard enough.

She fled, sobbing for the little girl left alone, for the years of justifying her mother's actions, for the loss of a family and for the broken heart left behind after the split from a man she loved. A man she would never be able to see again. This cruelty seemed the greatest of all; to love and lose a beloved was a common occurrence, but to find and lose a brother as well was beyond her comprehension. The card of The Devil hovered in her mind: a darkness, a shadow on the soul.

"Esme, are you quite well?" Helena's voice reached her through a buzzing in her ears as she ran towards the front doors.

"I feel faint," Esme managed as Helena caught her arm, "perhaps some air."

Her knees were trembling so much she was unsure whether they would support her. Lifting her skirts, she ran through the open doors on to the vast terrace, away from Bill and from the horror unfolding around her. She did not care that it was dark, that she was in the middle of the countryside. Nothing could entreat her to stay, not now she knew the truth.

"Esme, wait!"

Bill was chasing her. Esme paused at the stairs leading from the terrace into the grounds, giving Bill one last sorrowful look, then, fighting back tears, she disappeared into the night.

PART SEVEN: PEMBROKESHIRE, 2020

CHAPTER ONE

The words of Esme Blood's diary stayed with Eleanor for a long time. *How would I feel*, thought Eleanor, *if Mum and Dad had chosen between me and Aidan? I would be devastated.* And there was worse. Bill was Esme's half-brother. A cold sweat broke out on Eleanor's forehead as she thought of the implications. It was with relief she remembered how Esme, for all her self-proclaimed unshockability, had spurned Aaron's sexual advances and, she hoped, apart from the occasional kiss, Esme had kept Bill at bay, too.

Sitting in her office in the barn, her mind strayed to the many boxes not yet unpacked from the auction. Adelaide sat on a cushion with Esme's books in a pile beside her. Reaching over, Eleanor pulled the bible out from the bottom of the pile. Esme's diaries had distracted her from checking to see if this, too, had once belonged to her. The lightness was unusual for such a large book and when she opened it, Eleanor saw why — the centre had been hollowed out and lined with paper.

"Helena's bible," exclaimed Eleanor, but what surprised her more was the writing in the base of the hollowed-out square. The letters were tiny, and Eleanor reached into her desk drawer to dig out her magnifying class. "Unbelievable," she muttered. "The six Tarot cards she drew for Aaron: The Tower, Death, the Nine of Cups, The Empress, the Ten of Coins and The Star." These were the six Tarot cards from Esme's Marseille deck which had been left blank. The other cards featured the lines of Arthur O'Shaughnessy's 'Ode', the poem beloved by both Esme and Aaron. Eleanor felt there was something here she should understand, but the meaning of these coincidences remained beyond her grasp, as though she was being asked to complete a jigsaw puzzle with only half the pieces and no knowledge of the image.

"This is madness," she sighed, feeling she was creating more mysteries than she was solving.

Walking to the back of the barn, she glanced at the boxes from the Richmond auction that were still waiting to be explored. A trip to hospital for treatment and her ongoing desire to read the diaries had halted Eleanor in her exploration of them. As the spring rain pattered on the barn roof, lulling her with its gentle music, she pulled on a pair of protective gloves and began to organise her unexpected haul. The methodical sorting would be a perfect antidote to her whirring mind and confused thoughts.

Several boxes and a stack of early 1970s theatrical programmes from a long since defunct regional theatre later, Eleanor was wondering whether, as far as her business was concerned, they had been a waste of money. The pinging of her phone was a welcome distraction; it was a message from Mark Llewellyn: *Are you in the barn or your annexe?*

Barn. Where are you?

In my car, I didn't want to get soaked running between the two. See you in a mo.

"I've found more information about your missing ancestor," called Mark as Eleanor heard the barn doors open and close.

"Back here," she replied, and Mark appeared around the rails of clothes, pulling a folder from his rucksack. He paused when he saw the boxes.

"This looks fun," he said, an eager expression on his face.

"Would you like to help me go through them?"

"Of course," he said, pulling off his jacket and hanging it on a nearby clothes rail. "I can show you my discoveries afterwards."

Delighted to have some company for what was turning out to be quite a dull task, Eleanor threw Mark a pair of protective gloves, explaining the provenance of the boxes. When she had finished her tale and had brought Mark up to date on the diaries, he was astounded.

"That is quite a story, Ellie," he said. "Perhaps I should see if we can get the diaries transcribed at Marquess House — we have a huge staff there. These are incredible historical documents."

"Let's see how it ends first," said Eleanor as she felt an uncomfortable prickle at the back of her neck, unsure whether she wanted to share Esme's story.

"Fair enough," said Mark, opening his rucksack and pulling out an A4 notebook ready to catalogue his finds.

Eleanor was far more ad-hoc, opening each box and giving a fast assessment before moving on to the next, working out an order for further investigation. Every box would be thoroughly inspected, but her first foray was always to find the obvious before searching for the secrets. After having more luck with her current box, discovering piles of theatrical programmes and newspapers from the 1920s, Eleanor reached for a square, flat box.

It was lighter than the others and she braced herself for disappointment, but as she lifted it towards her, the same feeling of longing and recognition, the sense of urgency she had felt at the auction rose in her like a snake. Having read the Tarot cards for so many years, Eleanor was aware of the strange coincidences the universe sometimes threw at people, herself included, and she wondered if this was one of those moments. The small hiccups in time where events so unexpected evolved, prompting the phrase: *if this was in a film, you wouldn't believe it*. Her fingers were tingling, and it was as though she could sense there was a secret awaiting her discovery.

Flipping open the lid, she gasped. Mark looked up. "Dresses," she said. Her hands were shaking. "Costumes, but it can't be…"

Lifting up the first dress, she stared at Mark, who looked equally as stunned. As the feathers caught the light, the iridescent greens and blues shimmered while the lining, a faded emerald-green silk, shivered at her touch. It would once have been as brilliant as the peacock feathers, flashing and moving under the limelight.

"The peacock feather dress," said Mark. "Surely it can't be the same one as the photograph?"

Eleanor draped the dress over the back of a chair and pulled out a second, followed by two battered eye-masks. They stared at them in wonder.

"Anything else?" asked Mark.

"Nothing," she said. "Oh, wait, look, a calling card with a photograph."

"Who is it?" asked Mark.

The man's hair was long and he had neat sideburns, but it was his intense brown eyes that caught Eleanor's gaze. They pierced her across time; the knowing, mocking expression exuded a dangerous charm, hinting at a steely resolve; a man whom it would be unwise to cross. Turning it over, she saw his name was printed in swirling italics.

"Aaron Maclean," said Eleanor, before turning to Mark and answering his question. "Yes, there's no doubt in my mind these dresses belonged to Esme and Lynette. These were the costumes they wore on the night of Aaron's party at his house in Kemptown. Why else would Aaron's card be in the box?"

"Extraordinary," said Mark. "Did you say Esme was a fan of Arthur O'Shaughnessy's 'Ode', the one about the music makers?"

"Yes, why?"

Mark returned to the neat pile of items from the box he had been examining and passed her a leatherbound book. "An anthology of poems, including the 'Ode'."

The rush of longing returned as Eleanor took the book. Opening the cover, she was surprised to see both Esme and Aaron's names inscribed. In the books she had found with Adelaide, Esme's name alone had been written in the covers.

"This is extraordinary," she said, turning the pages with gentle fingers, eager to see whether there were any clues in the book.

It fell open to the familiar poem and Eleanor shivered as she read the words. Turning the page, she was surprised to see tiny letters written around the edge. Squinting at the flowing words, she read aloud: "*Aaron, Theodore, Poppaea, Crispin, Bill, Delphine, Harriet, Elizabeth*. We know about Aaron and Bill. Crispin was a friend of Bill's, but I've no idea about the rest."

"Nor me," said Mark, "although as they're obviously connected to Esme, they might be useful in discovering more about her. Shall I show you what I've found?"

Returning to Eleanor's desk, she cleared a space while Mark pulled up a second chair and opened his laptop. "Aaron Maclean," he said, spreading out printed versions of the pages he had brought up screen. "He was Esme's lover?"

"Possibly, I haven't finished the diaries yet, and I'm still hoping they'll get married…"

"Aaron did get married," said Mark, arranging copies of certificates in front of Eleanor. "In fact, he made a habit of it."

Eleanor stared at the documents in surprise. "How much do I owe you for all this?" she asked. "It costs quite a lot to order all these original documents."

"Nothing. We have several accounts at Marquess House. Perdita and Piper said I could order as much I liked, although they did ask that if we find anything you're willing to share, whether we could borrow it for The Mary Fitzroy Heritage Centre? They're planning a Victorian wing because so much changed socially during this period, particularly for women."

"Would they really be interested?" Eleanor had not met the twins who had inherited their grandmother's manor house, but she was aware of them as both Mark and Briony worked for the estate.

"Yes, they're determined to discover as much about local history as possible, and as the Bloods were from Little Haven, they're intrigued."

"It's really kind of them," she said.

Turning her attention back to the row of certificates, she felt a stab of disappointment when, rather than Esmerelda Blood, she saw the name Patience Hortense Gale next to Aaron's on the wedding certificate. It seemed the wedding did go ahead.

"The problem with this marriage," said Mark, "is that it was later declared invalid."

"Why?"

"Because Aaron Maclean had two other wives living at the same time and had never at any point got divorced or annulled the unions."

"What?" Eleanor was incredulous, then she remembered Cassie's spiteful words to Esme, saying she had met Aaron's wife.

"He was a bigamist," said Mark, "many times over. Look at the dates — some of them are only a few months apart and the marriages took place all over the country."

Eleanor stared in fascination. "Why, though?"

"Most of them were heiresses, not to vast fortunes but when put together, he would have had access to large sums of money."

"Esme's diaries suggest he was not quite the charming businessman he liked to present to the world, and this must have been one of his scams. Wasn't bigamy an arrestable offence?"

"Not always," replied Mark. "The marriage laws in the Victorian times were remarkably complex, likewise the attitudes to bigamy — many couples lived together even though they might not have been married. Often one partner had been abandoned by a spouse or the marriage had broken down. If the new relationship was thought to be honourable, it would be accepted by family, friends and the local community."

"I suppose divorce was prohibitively expensive?"

"Quite right, so this was often the solution to relationships that had gone awry. In the 1860s, many novels and plays featured a bigamy theme. It was a source of fascination for the Victorians. There were lots of books and plays: *Lady Audley's Secret, Mary Ellen, The Colleen Bawn...*"

Eleanor suppressed her wince: *The Colleen Bawn* again. "Aaron's behaviour would have been deemed as scandalous, surely?"

"Yes, but from the way you've described him, would he have cared? There are no records suggesting he ever came to trial, not that I've been able to find, anyway." Mark riffled through the print-outs and pulled out a list. "I've been doing some digging into Aaron, and his first wife died from consumption, or pulmonary tuberculosis as we know it. He had a second wife, who also died, but in childbirth, along with the baby."

"Oh, Mark, that's so sad."

"It is. I suggest Patience might have been suspicious of his behaviour around this time, and it was shortly after this that their marriage was annulled, which means when he married Lady Jessica Courtenay, a year later, it was legal and valid."

Eleanor thought for a moment, working out the timeline. "If Aaron was widowed twice and then his marriage was annulled, why didn't he marry Esme? After she discovered the truth about Bill, she would have been free to return to Aaron."

"Perhaps for all their childhood and teenage infatuation, when they were adults she discovered she didn't want to marry Aaron?" suggested Mark.

"But that doesn't follow when you think of the letter and the wedding ring I found inside Adelaide."

"Remember, Ellie, that was Aaron's letter to Esme; perhaps she no longer reciprocated the feelings."

"Do you think Aaron married Lady Jessica out of spite?" mused Eleanor.

"Possibly, but remember, Aaron was making a career out of marriage, and she was by far the richest of his wives. Lady Jessica Courtenay was an heiress of considerable fortune but, and this is the sad part, she became very ill not long after she gave birth to her only child, a daughter, Poppaea Esmerelda."

"What was wrong with her?"

"She was admitted to an asylum with 'melancholia' — in other words, depression."

"An asylum, how awful," shuddered Eleanor.

"It wasn't the kind of barbaric place we associate with Victorian asylums. It was a private hospital, very small, and she wasn't there for long. Afterwards, she lived in the family home and in the 1881 census there is a host of medical staff also living at the address, but no Poppaea. I haven't found a death certificate for her, so she must have been elsewhere."

"Any sign of Esme on the census?"

"Not yet, but it doesn't mean she isn't there. She might have been married, in which case she'll have another name. She's proving trickier to locate on the marriage register. I did find something unexpected about Esme," he added. "I don't want to upset you, though."

"What?"

"It was a court case."

"What was it for?"

"Child abduction."

Eleanor stared at him in horror. "There must be a mistake."

"It was a common crime back then — children were becoming more sentimentalised than at any other time and, as such, the business of childhood became a thriving industry: expensive clothes, shoes, jewellery. Children were often kidnapped for their clothes, which could easily be sold. Other cases detail ransoms being demanded, but the crime was taken seriously and dealt with promptly."

"What happened to Esme?"

"I'm searching for the outcome, but you might have more luck with her diaries."

Eleanor was struggling to take in these new discoveries. Aaron's philandering, at least, offered an explanation for why he had written the letter to Esme, saying he could never marry her, but as having multiple wives clearly was not an obstacle for him, had the reason they had been unable to wed actually been because Esme was in gaol?

"There must be an explanation," said Eleanor.

"Do you think Aaron could have persuaded her to commit a criminal offence on his behalf?" asked Mark.

"From what I've read about her so far, I don't think so," said Eleanor, "but I hate to think she might have become so desperate later in life that she'd allow herself to be manipulated in such a manner."

"I'll keep searching," said Mark, "but you might need to brace yourself in case it isn't the happy ending you hoped for, Ellie. Remember, these were real people, and not everyone gets the fairy tale."

CHAPTER TWO

"Ready?" called Chloe through the changing room door.

"You might have to help me, Chlo," Eleanor replied, undoing the lock.

It was the first time she had attempted to put on a wetsuit since her illness had begun, and the weakness in her hands was apparent. Pulling on the constrictive rubber had always been a challenge, but now it was almost impossible.

Chloe squeezed through the door, locking it behind her. "Come on, then!" she said, her tone matter-of-fact, experienced as she was in helping people, usually novices, into wetsuits.

Ten minutes later, Eleanor and Chloe headed out from Wave Riders to the beach, where Aidan had gone ahead with the boards.

"Do you really think this is a good idea?" asked Eleanor.

"Yes. Aidan and I will be right beside you. Nothing can happen. At some point, you have to get back in the water. You love surfing."

When Eleanor had mentioned she would like to try body boarding as an alternative to her old board, which stood like a sculpture in the barn where she could brood over it when she was at work, Aidan and Chloe had responded with enthusiasm. In her heart, Eleanor had hoped she would go in the sea for the first time since her illness with Arthur, but as she had not heard from him since the night of his revelation, the offer from her brother and his fiancée was a perfect second choice.

"The surf's good today but the wind is gentle, so the waves shouldn't be too overpowering," said Chloe as they made their way over the vast stone barricade surrounding the long golden sands of Newgale beach. "By the way, I hope you don't mind, but we let a few people know you were well enough to go back in the water and the response was rather enthusiastic."

"What? Who?" Eleanor knew this gesture was meant with kindness, but her nerves were taut at the thought of entering the churning waves on weakened legs, unsure how well she would be able to survive in the ebb and flow of the tide. Would she immediately topple over and feel the sick sweep of humiliation as her body failed her yet again? The idea of being surrounded by people while this happened was daunting.

"People who love you and want to make sure you're safe, as well as celebrating your return to the water," Chloe said, putting her hand on Eleanor's arm and bringing her to a halt. "Ellie, we know this has been hard for you and we want to help you recover. You've been so brave; this is our gift to you."

"Chloe … I…" Eleanor could not speak; emotion, nerves and fear robbed her of her voice.

"You'd better brace yourself," Chloe continued, "there's quite a crowd waiting."

As they rounded the stones and had a clear view of the beach, Eleanor's mouth dropped in astonishment. Coloured windbreaks flapped in the breeze where a camp had been set up and people milled around, laughing and talking. To her surprise, there was a pile of body boards, but no full surf boards.

Bathsheba saw her first and let out an ear-piercing wolf whistle, causing a cheer to go up as Eleanor and Chloe approached. Beside Bathsheba was her fiancé, Gabriel, and her younger sister, Eve, while Briony beamed from behind her. Stuart Mackensie hovered near the back of the group with Chloe's sister, Verity, and beside her were Edward Stone and

Amelia Prentice, who was holding the leads of their greyhounds, Nero and Lara. The biggest surprise, however, was Arthur, who was standing behind Aidan and Andrew.

"Oh, my goodness," Eleanor gasped, overwhelmed as they surrounded her. "You're all amazing."

"We thought you'd appreciate the company," said Aidan, grinning.

"It's overwhelming," Eleanor said, feeling tears well in her eyes.

"Let's get going, then!" said Stuart Mackensie, grinning broadly and taking her hand.

Eleanor glanced at Bathsheba and Briony, who were giggling, and out of the corner of her eye she noticed Arthur scowl.

Aidan shouted instructions, handing out the body boards, and Eleanor found herself in the middle of a crowd, wading into the shallows. Only Amelia stayed on the beach, settling down with the dogs to watch.

"Are you ready?" asked Chloe, who was beside her. "If it gets too much…"

"I'll say," said Eleanor and as the waves lapped her knees, she shivered in excitement.

When she had been lying in her hospital bed, an oxygen mask helping her breathe, drips in her arm and no movement in her legs or arms, she had dreamed about surfing — the moment of weightlessness when the water lifted her board, surrounded by sky, spray and water, borne through the air on the cry of the gulls, until she plunged back into the laughing waves. This time, it would be different; the body board was a gentler experience. It did not matter, though; she was back in her beloved waves, the swell surrounding her, buoying her up, giving her back her sense of self.

With a squeal of pleasure Eleanor launched herself into the water, gasping as the cold enveloped her. Floating in the foam, she spluttered and laughed as a small wave crashed and broke over her.

Arthur appeared at her side. "Are you okay?" he asked.

"Yes, thank you for coming today."

Before Arthur could reply, Aidan's voice interrupted, "There are some good ones coming in...' Followed by others:

"Look for the seventh wave..."

"There's no such thing..."

"It's the best wave..."

"Here's one..."

"Ready..."

Eleanor allowed the shouts of her friends to merge with the roar of the elements. Waiting with the board positioned in front of her, looking over her shoulder for the wave, as it began to surge forward, she kicked off. Feeling it lift her, she rose through the spray as the water rushed past. Closing her eyes, she allowed the wave to carry her forward, as those around her cheered. A shriek of pure joy escaped her lips and, in that instant, Eleanor knew she would survive the frustrating and frightening prospect of a lifetime of illness, because she was not alone. All around her were friends who loved her, who had chosen to share this moment and, as she was dumped into the mercurial ocean, she rolled over on to her back, stared up at the scudding white clouds in the wide blue sky and laughed.

An hour later, Eleanor was exhausted. Staggering up the beach, she flung herself down beside Amelia. The dogs were asleep, snoring gently in the afternoon sun.

Amelia passed Eleanor a hooded towel. Eleanor wiggled out of her wetsuit and, under the long towel, managed to drag off her wet bikini and pull on jogging bottoms and a fleece. Taking the hot chocolate Amelia offered her, the two women watched the antics of the surfers for a while.

"How are you getting on with your family tree?" Amelia asked.

"Honestly," said Eleanor, turning to her, "it's becoming quite strange. It's as though Esme is reaching out to me through time."

"I know that feeling," Amelia laughed, "it makes you question your sanity."

"Exactly." Eleanor sipped from the enamel mug.

"Remind me how Esme is connected to Cliffside?" said Amelia.

"Through Hannah Blood, the wife of Noah Attwater," replied Eleanor. "Judith Blood, who was Esme's mother, was Hannah's elder sister."

While they waited for the others to return from the waves, Eleanor told Amelia what she had discovered, including her unexpected meeting with Esme's doll, Adelaide. "I wonder if I should stop searching now."

"Do you want to?"

Eleanor stared out to sea, where the sun was beginning to dip and the temperature was dropping. "No, but I'm scared of what I'm going to discover."

"Esme has come to you for a reason," said Amelia, "as I believe Osyth came to me. I was at my lowest ebb, and she took me home. Perhaps Esme is doing the same for you; trust her, you need to see it through."

Home, thought Eleanor. Was this what it was all about — finding her way home?

An image of Arthur flashed across her mind, which was interrupted by the real Arthur and Aidan looming over her.

They shook their heads, spraying Eleanor with seawater from their hair.

"Stop it!" she yelled, but there was laughter all around them.

"You girls used to do it to us," grinned Aidan, "when we were all forced to have short haircuts for school. Revenge is mine!"

With much laughter, they struck the encampment and headed back towards Wave Riders.

"We'll do the final sweep!" Eleanor shouted as she and Bathsheba walked around the area where they had been sitting, checking for litter, forgotten clothing and any other detritus.

Half-buried in the sand was a wallet. Eleanor flipped it open — the name on the bank card was Arthur Pengally. Scooping it up as Bathsheba joined her, Eleanor waved the wallet before putting it in her pocket. "Arthur's," she said.

"There's nothing else," Bathsheba said. "We'll hold his wallet to ransom for a couple of bottles of lager."

Laughing, they made their way back across the sand, scrambled up the wooden pathways and into the car park, heading for Wave Riders. Eleanor stumbled at the top and Arthur's wallet fell out of her pocket, spreading its contents on the sandy floor.

"You grab those, I'll get these," said Bathsheba, running after the bank cards which had skittered further afield.

Eleanor bent down to gather business cards and pieces of paper. The top card was for the National Probation Service, Cornwall, with a telephone number scrawled on the back in pen and the name Kenny Monrose written underneath. Eleanor assumed this was to do with Arthur's conviction. Fluttering in the breeze was a folded piece of paper which she grabbed before it could be whisked away, but when she glanced down at it the words seemed to leap out and her heart felt as though it had stopped.

This can't be true, she thought, willing herself to have misread it. Eleanor fished her phone out of her pocket and took a series of snaps of the page before refolding it and replacing it in the wallet.

"Come on, the others will wonder where we are," said Bathsheba, handing Eleanor the bank cards.

Bathsheba chatted as they crossed the road, heading for the surf shop, but Eleanor did not hear a word her friend said as the list danced before her eyes. It contained six names written in Arthur's handwriting — two had been crossed off, one had a question mark beside it and there were three others. Trying to block out the sick feeling that was growing inside her, she wished she had never seen the piece of paper but now she had, it could not be unseen. Finally, she understood Arthur's reticence about becoming romantically involved, because the heading on the list read *Potential Fathers*, and at the bottom was her own father's name.

CHAPTER THREE

Checking her emails to distract herself, Eleanor was reading one from a toy restorer she had contacted with the possibility of having Adelaide restuffed when there was a ping. Nick was video calling her.

"Hiya," he said, when she answered. "What's happened?"

The previous day when she had discovered she could surf should have been a moment of great joy, one of the small victories associated with recovery, part of her endless mantra of realistic expectations and easy steps. However, the shock of finding the list in Arthur's wallet had clouded everything. All evening, as an impromptu party took place at Wave Riders, she had avoided Arthur. With so many people there, it had been easy. For once, he had not been able to offer to drive her home and it was with relief she had scrambled into a cab with Briony.

"I've discovered why Arthur's holding back," she said.

"Is he married?"

"No. He might be my brother." Despite every effort not to break down, she dissolved into tears.

"What?"

Explaining what had happened and texting Nick the picture of the list, her sobs subsided as she spoke, each word drawing the shock from her heart, and by the time she had finished, she was calmer. "It reminds me of Esme's diaries," she said. "She discovered Bill was her half-brother. Maybe this is why she's been haunting me."

"The chances of it happening to you both are quite odd," Nick agreed.

"The thing I don't understand though is, if we are related, why did we have such a strong reaction to each other on the beach when we first met? Do you think there's something wrong with me?"

"Actually, no," Nick replied, "there's a scientific explanation."

"Really?"

"It's called Genetic Sexual Attraction; it's the phenomenon of intense attraction between biological family members when they're reunited after a long period of separation."

"And you know this, how?"

"I wrote a feature about a brother and sister who had been separated at birth and when they were reunited as adults, they fell in love. There's this thing called the Westermarck Effect which turns off the sexual attraction part of a person's brain to relatives when they're raised together as a family, so they label their affections differently. When separation occurs early within families, especially when siblings are separated and adopted by different families, this effect doesn't happen. As basic human attraction tends to be towards those who have similar physical attributes, individuals can be attracted to birth family members. They see them as family in name and biology only, but without the shared experiences and social conditioning that would normally develop — in other words, no 'ick' factor — they can sometimes have intense feelings and fall in love."

Eleanor stared at him in astonishment. "I feel better knowing there's a scientific explanation," she replied. "At least I'm not a sick and twisted individual, fancying my potential half-brother."

"Or you might not be related and your reaction on the beach was because you genuinely liked each other."

"True," she said, with a hint of hope in her voice.

"On a more serious note, have you mentioned this to your dad?"

"No. How would I even begin that conversation?" she said. "Do you think I should tell Arthur I've seen the list? Would it be lying by omission if I didn't mention it?"

Nick shook his head. "Would you rather he thought you'd been going through his wallet?"

"It was accidental," she replied.

"Ellie, he asked you to trust him. When he's ready, he'll tell you one way or the other."

"You're right," she sighed. "At least it explains his reticence."

Feeling better after her conversation with Nick, Eleanor showered and dressed, wandering next door into the farmhouse where her mother, Anne, was sitting at the kitchen table surrounded by photographs.

"Hello, love," said Anne, "I was coming to find you in a minute."

"Why's that?"

"I've got news. Uncle Steve is coming home in a few weeks."

"Great," said Eleanor, who always enjoyed seeing her godfather. "Is this a permanent homecoming or between jobs?"

"Between jobs. They'll be back for a few months, then he's off to Egypt."

Eleanor sat beside her mother and picked up a picture of the four of them on holiday when Eleanor and Aidan were aged seven and nine. "What's prompted this?" she asked, her gaze encompassing the piles of snaps.

"It's something I've been meaning to do for ages," Anne said. "Your father bought me photo albums for Christmas three years ago, and I'd forgotten about them until they fell off the top of the wardrobe yesterday. I decided it was a sign to stop procrastinating and at least make a start on organising all the photos. Now I've finally started, I'm enjoying myself. Look, these are from your christening."

Eleanor examined the image of her parents with her godfather, Steve, who was holding her, his face bursting with pride. Aidan, a toddler in her father's arms, looked bored. She shuddered, thinking about Arthur. Should there have been another child in attendance? Pushing this disturbing thought aside, she forced a smile and reached towards the piles of photographs. "What else have you found?"

Her mother pushed a torn and faded photograph wallet towards her. "Look at your dad in those."

Eleanor flicked through the images of her father on holiday with his friends. One group shot was particularly striking. A group of young men in their late teens and early twenties were all dressed for a night out in a variety of pastel shades, their spikey hair glinting with highlights. "Why have I never seen this before?" she asked, before adding in a horrified tone, "Did Dad have blond highlights?"

The back door opened and John came in, depositing a basket of fresh eggs on the table. "What have you got there, Ellie?" he asked, taking the picture and laughing. "I remember that holiday. We had a blast!"

"It was shortly before you met me, I think," said Anne.

Eleanor listened idly as her parents reminisced about friends from their teenage days. Turning the picture over, Eleanor read out the list of names on the back of the group picture. *Waxy, Mike, Two-Lanes, Max, Si and Bugs.* "Why do you and Uncle Steve call each other Max and Si?" asked Eleanor, handing the photograph to her mother, who pasted it into an album.

Her father laughed. "It's from when we were teenagers. The lads called me Mad Max after the film, on account of my driving, and we called him Psycho Steve, because he was wild."

A chill ran through Eleanor — were these the men Arthur's mother had met on holiday all those years ago? The two groups of friends meeting, having fun and parting, not realising the legacy they were leaving behind?

CHAPTER FOUR

"Hello!" Eleanor called a few days later as she pushed her way through the plastic sheeting covering the entrance to the south wing of The Mary Fitzroy Heritage Centre.

"Hi, Ellie," called Mark. "We're through here."

When Mark had emailed asking about the possibility of displaying the dresses with a brief outline of Esme's career, Eleanor had agreed. Despite extensive searching online, Esme Blood was not as well remembered as other music hall stars, and this was a failing Eleanor wished to remedy. Depending on what the expert thought, Mark had said, it might be possible to restore the dresses and masks to their original glory.

Mark was standing with a tall, red-haired woman. They turned and smiled as she approached.

"Ellie, this is Piper Davidson," said Mark.

"Hi, Ellie, thank you so much for letting us see the dresses," said Piper. "Mark's been telling me about your ancestor. What a story."

"It's been an emotional ride," admitted Eleanor, "and we're not at the end yet. There are a few more diaries for me to read, which I hope will fill in the gaps from the records online."

"You can't trust everything that's in the public domain," agreed Piper. "Original sources are always more trustworthy for finding the truth. May I see the dresses, please?"

Eleanor put the dresses on the two tailor's dummies in the middle of the room.

"Wow, these are extraordinary," exclaimed Piper, as Eleanor put the battered masks beside them. "We have a dress restorer in the workshops at the moment — would you mind if I called her over for an opinion on these?" Piper wandered off, her phone clamped to her ear.

"Actually, while Piper's busy, I've done a bit more digging about Esme," Mark said.

"Have you found out what happened at her court case?" Eleanor asked.

"No, not yet, but I did discover something quite odd in the 1881 census," he said, beckoning her over to a laptop on one of the tables. "As I couldn't find Esme, I decided to search for her adopted parents, Rosie and Cornelius Hardy."

Eleanor peered at the screen. Rosie and Cornelius Hardy were listed as living in Haymarket and under the 'Other Household Members' section, there was a list of children: Poppaea Esmerelda Maclean, Lady Rosalind Blanchard, Theodore Cornelius Baron and Nicholas Hardy. All were young children and beside each was listed either 'Grandson' or 'Granddaughter'.

"Nicholas Hardy must be Lynette and Jeremiah's child," said Eleanor. "We know Poppaea Esmerelda Maclean is Aaron's daughter from his marriage to Lady Jessica Courtenay. Do you think she's with the Hardys because her mother was in hospital at this time?"

"I think you're right," replied Mark. "The most interesting discovery is Lady Rosalind Blanchard."

"Was she Esme's daughter?"

"No, she was Cassie's. Cassie married a viscount, and I discovered something very strange about that."

Opening the attachment Mark had pulled up on screen, Eleanor read the short newspaper cutting with interest.

Death of Viscount Blanchard

The body of Henry Etherington, Viscount Blanchard, was discovered by his groundsman this morning. The Viscount was found floating in his ornamental lake. Upon removing the body, it appeared to have knife wounds, suggesting foul play. It is thought he may have disturbed poachers. He leaves a wife, Cassandra Etherington, Viscountess Blanchard, formerly Cassie Smith, actress at The Firebird, Piccadilly, and a daughter, Lady Rosalind.

A second cutting read: *Cassandra Etherington, the widow of Viscount Blanchard was today charged with his death.* The feature then listed Cassie's career, the time she spent recovering from 'nerves' at a sanatorium and the story of her father's murderous career and subsequent hanging. Mark pulled up a final cutting: *Cassandra Etherington was released by the Metropolitan Police, with their apologies, on the orders of her husband, Viscount Blanchard.* "From what I can gather, the viscount disappeared and a body was found in the lake at their estate with stab wounds. At first, the police assumed it was the viscount…"

"Couldn't they tell?" interrupted Eleanor.

"No, it didn't have a head."

"How revolting."

"Cassie's history was released to a newspaper, and she was practically found guilty by association with the violence committed by her father. Then, suddenly, the missing viscount reappeared, he and Cassie were reunited and, well, I don't know if they lived happily ever after, but they went on to have three more children."

"And the corpse?"

"As far as I can discover, it was never identified. I've been through the coroner's records for back then and they're quite patchy. If all this was going on at the time of the census, then it would explain why Lady Rosalind is with her grandparents."

"Extraordinary," said Eleanor. "Any luck with a marriage certificate for Esme?"

"Nothing yet, and I've tried all the names we've discovered so far," he said. "Blood, Hardy, Maclean, even Flagstaff and Arbuthnot."

Realisation dawned as the revelations of Esme's diary rushed back to her. "Try Rose Esmerelda Sutton."

"Where did that come from?"

"The diaries. Her mother named her for Rose Hardy but to avoid confusion, Rose called the little girl by her middle name, Esmerelda, or Esme for short. Blood was her second middle name, but her correct surname was Sutton. Her father was the Right Honourable Robert Sutton."

"Brilliant idea," said Mark, pulling up the search page on a genealogy website.

Eleanor leaned over his shoulder, watching as a list of results appeared. "Look," she said in excitement, "Rose Esmerelda Sutton married…"

Mark clicked on the link. There was no marriage certificate, but there was a list of names indicating people in the same page of the register. Eleanor stared at one she recognised.

"But how is that possible…?" said Eleanor as they looked at each other in astonishment.

PART EIGHT: SHROPSHIRE, 1878

CHAPTER ONE

Spring was giving way to summer and the fields lining the roadside were a waving sea of golden wheat. Flowers wound their way through the hedgerows and, as she looked out of the coach window, Esme thought about all the fields they had stayed in during her childhood. The hectic days of rehearsing and performing, helping Rosie in her fortune-telling tent before running wild with the other children, creating mischief but never meaning any harm. It seemed very distant from the life she had fallen into since her departure from The Firebird. Her thoughts then led from that departure to another.

As she had fled across the lawns at St Botolph's, ignoring Bill as he called her name, Crispin Baron had emerged from the night, his face full of concern. Capturing Esme in his arms, he had soothed her and, with an efficiency she had not expected, arranged to transport her to safety in a coach borrowed from the stables.

"Esme, I was on the terrace, I heard…" he had whispered by way of an apology as they fled through the night.

Since then, she had been unable to fault Crispin; he had given her a wall to hide behind as she recovered from the shock of her discovery. It was not long, however, before his less than altruistic reasons were revealed. "Marry me," he suggested one morning as they walked along the seafront in the picturesque seaside town of Tenby.

"We've known each other a week," she had replied.

"Think of it as a business transaction. Unless I am married by my twenty-fifth birthday, I forfeit my sizeable inheritance."

"How old are you?"

"I shall be twenty-five in two months' time."

"You're cutting it fine."

"Remember what I said, Esme. No one in my family has ever married for love; they've all been business endeavours. We're one step ahead of the rest — at least we like each other." When she had not replied, he had continued, "If we're married, it'll stop Bill coming after you."

Coming back to the present, Esme flicked through her newspaper before placing it on the seat. "My sister is married," she said, looking out of the carriage window at the passing countryside.

"A real sister or an adopted one?" Crispin asked.

"An adopted one, Cassie. She's married to Henry Etherington…"

"Viscount Blanchard? She's done well for herself. How old is your sister?"

"A few years older than me."

"Henry's in his early fifties."

"It might be a love match," Esme suggested.

"Unlikely, my dear, highly unlikely," replied Crispin. "He's five foot tall, bandy-legged and suffers from gout. However, he is one of the richest men in England."

Esme laughed, silently congratulating Cassie on achieving her ambition to marry into the aristocracy. Perhaps the demons of her beautiful but unstable sister were under control. She determined to write to Rosie, for the sanitised version of events, then to Lynette for the truth. Wondering how Rosie would feel when she heard Esme's unexpected news, her heart squeezed with sadness.

"Not far now, my dear," said Crispin, and she was surprised to hear a hint of fear in his voice. "I'll sign the paperwork and pay homage to Mater and Pater, then we can be away on our toes with a fortune in our pocket and back to London to live among civilised folk."

"Are you sure? Will it really be this easy?"

"The solicitor gave me very clear instructions. Under the terms of Grandfather's will, I must marry before my twenty-fifth birthday, then my money will be released. No bride, no bounty."

The carriage drove through wide, wrought-iron gates and Crispin leaned back against the seats as though trying to hide. Esme could understand why. The sentinels beckoning them forward to Baron Hall were gnarled blackthorn trees. Twisted and macabre, the cruelty of the long spikes on their branches was hidden below a canopy of snowy blossom and shimmering leaves.

"I hate this place," he said.

"Why?"

"Memories, bad ones," Crispin muttered. "You'll understand when you meet the Baron clan. There was never a happy day in this house when we were growing up."

Esme reached for her gloves, turning the large sapphire ring around on her finger so the stone nestled into her palm in order for the kid gloves to sit smoothly over her wedding and engagement rings. The weight of the gold felt strange, as did her new name, Mrs Baron. Both reminders of a decision made in haste to protect herself from the horror of all she had discovered on the night of the ball.

The carriage crunched to a halt. Esme glanced at Crispin, whose usually laughing countenance had been replaced with brooding malice. Reaching across, she placed her hand on his arm. "We'll face them together," she said. "I'm your wife, after all."

Baron Hall was large and jumbled, but it was far more impressive than Esme had imagined from Crispin's description of it being "a rotting pile". Staring up at her new home, she sighed — this was not where she had expected to be as the summer swept its beauty over the countryside. She had anticipated being at the Flagstaff family home, preparing for her wedding to Bill. While her love for Bill had never been as intense as her passion for Aaron, her fondness for him had been genuine and, despite their shocking discovery, she missed him. She hoped Baron Hall would offer her protection while time cured her heart.

The vast double front doors were thrown open and a slim girl with hair as dark as Crispin's threw herself into his arms, squealing with delight. "Crissie, you're home," she trilled. "I'm so relieved!'

Crispin introduced Esme and Delphine to each other. He had filled Esme in on the journey. "There are three of us," Crispin had explained. "Absolom, the heir; me, the spare and Delphine, my younger sister." His voice had hardened when he spoke of his brother but softened on discussing Delphine. "Mater and Pater have never taken much interest in Delf, so she's a little fragile."

"And Absolom?"

"Married to Dilys, with four daughters: Eve, Mary, Ruth and Harriet. They live in Baron Hall most of the time."

When Esme held out her hand to Delphine, the girl averted her eyes, refusing to meet Esme's gaze. With a trembling hand, she reached for the amethyst cross she wore around her neck, gripping it until her knuckles whitened. It was then Esme noticed the scar tracing its way across Delphine's cheek, a jagged line marring her delicate pink and white beauty.

"Esme is my wife," said Crispin, in a voice in which there was a hint of pride and a touch of malice as he continued, "She's Pater's worse nightmare, a showgirl."

"Your wife?" Delphine exclaimed.

"Yes, we were married in Cardiff last week. Mater and Pater in residence?"

Delphine shook her head, tears welling in her eyes as she fled around the side of the house.

"Well, it went better than I expected," Crispin said with no hint of irony. "I think she likes you."

Esme was stunned. "How can you tell?" she asked. "She was terrified."

"She didn't curse you in her made-up language," he replied, shrugging.

Esme looked for a hint of humour, but when she realised he was serious, she tried to swallow her growing unease.

Crispin took her hand and led her into the house, where they were met by a tall thin man wearing butler's livery, hurrying towards them, flustered at not having been there to open the door.

"Master Crispin," he exclaimed.

"Fraser," Crispin replied and there was genuine affection between the two men. "Apologies for the unexpected arrival, but I have some exciting news. This is my wife, Esme."

Fraser blinked away his surprise. "You are very welcome, Mrs Baron. Let me call Mrs Fraser and she can discuss arrangements with you."

"Actually, Fraser, would you organise some tea in the Long Room? We're parched. Perhaps Mrs F could visit us there? I thought Esme could have the Rose Suite."

"Very well, sir, we shall arrange it."

Ten minutes later, Esme and Crispin were seated in an elegant, galleried room, while an army of staff provided enough food for ten people. Esme smiled and nodded as Crispin introduced her to each member of staff.

"Thank goodness for them," he said as they were left alone. "They've been more of a family to me and Delf than Mater and Pater have ever been. When I'm away, it's a relief to know that Fraser and Mrs F are here to care for her. Otherwise, I'd take her with me."

"Sir," came a voice, and Esme turned to see a slim woman with blonde hair caught up in a severe style, accentuating her high cheekbones and delicate features. The beautifully tailored black dress, indicating her status as housekeeper, gave her an unmistakeable air of authority.

"Mrs F!" exclaimed Crispin in delight.

"We thought you must be on your way," Mrs Fraser said, beaming back. "A number of trunks arrived bearing the name Esme Hardy, and we realised you might have fulfilled the instructions in your grandfather's will. Not a moment too soon, my dear, if I might be so bold."

"A few more weeks and the money would have been lost," Crispin agreed, taking a bite from a heavily buttered fruit scone.

Esme followed Mrs Fraser up the main staircase towards the east wing of the vast mansion. A maze of corridors opened from the first-floor landing like the veins in a leaf, winding away to hidden corners, twisting and turning through centuries of repairs and additions.

"These are your rooms," said Mrs Fraser at last. "Master Crispin is opposite."

Further down the corridor, Esme saw a young man watching her with hooded, angry eyes but as she glanced towards him, he disappeared with an echoing slam of his door. Mrs Fraser glanced towards the noise but made no comment.

Throwing open the door of the Rose Suite, Esme wondered if she had stepped on to a theatrical set. The walls were papered with enormous pink roses, rose-pink velvet curtains hung at the huge window, and in the centre of the room was a vast four-poster bed covered in a bedspread that matched the wallpaper. Thick pink carpet covered the floor and the collection of chairs near the fireplace were upholstered in the same fabric as the curtains. The effect was overwhelming.

"If you and Master Crispin plan to stay long, perhaps we could change the room to suit your own preferences," said Mrs Fraser, and for the first time Esme felt as though this woman might be an ally. There was a sparkle of amusement in her voice and Esme offered her a tentative smile.

"Yes, I think it might be fortuitous to remove some of the pink," Esme replied.

Mrs Fraser gave her a wink. "Don't worry, Miss Blood," she said. "You'll get used to it."

"You know who I am?" Esme gasped.

"Mr F and I are big fans of the theatre. We used to watch the touring performers at the fairs, but whenever we're at the London house, we like to visit the shows. You've always been one of our favourites. The act you did with your sister, Cassandra Smith, was a waste of your talent. Your voice is spectacular. The Barons are very keen on musical evenings. It would be wonderful if you could perform."

"Thank you, Mrs Fraser," Esme said. "For you, I shall."

As Mrs Fraser closed the door, Esme felt a wave of relief wash over her. At least she had one person in this strange house on whom she could rely. Staring at the pile of trunks, she realised the Flagstaffs must have sent them on once they had read about her and Crispin's marriage in *The Times*. She hurried to the luggage, aware a maid would arrive at any moment to begin unpacking. A smaller box sat to one side and Esme flipped it open, removing first the Bible containing her Tarot cards and then her doll, Adelaide. Running her fingers down the back of the doll's dress, Esme allowed herself a secret smile — the money, hidden in the pocket she had created in Adelaide's body, was safe.

Aaron had insisted on paying her and Lynette for their performances, and that combined with the savings she had brought with her from The Firebird had become a sizeable sum of money. These white bank notes, now folded and hidden in Adelaide, were her safety net. Should anything happen, she would have the wherewithal to keep herself safe. As she stared around the overwhelming pink bedroom, she knew this was more important than ever since her marriage into the Baron family.

Esme checked herself in the large oval looking glass. The sapphire blue dress was the least ruffled creation given to her by the Flagstaffs and with her own alterations — the removal of the bows and fabric flowers — the basic shape was acceptable. Her new maid, Hester O'Leary, reminded her of Tilly at The Firebird and together they had sorted through Esme's wardrobe, discussing how to turn the additions from Lady Helena into more elegant and wearable gowns.

"Leave it to me, Mrs Baron," Hester had said. "These are good quality; we'll have them up-to-date in no time."

When Crispin collected her, he smiled. "Very pretty, dear wife," he said, "and blue. My brother will be pleased. He feels all women should dress in the colour of the Virgin Mary."

"What?"

"You'll see," was all Crispin would say in response.

Esme felt her temper rising. She was tired and her preference would have been to have an early night, but a full dinner lay ahead.

Crispin took her hand. "Ready?" he asked.

He led her through the room known as The Grey Parlour — a square, depressing space with grey walls, brown furniture and family portraits — onto the terrace where his brother and sister awaited. Delphine gave Esme a shy smile and walked over to stand beside her, pushing a small pink rosebud into her hand.

"This is for you. We can be friends," she whispered, and Esme's heart ached at the loneliness in her voice.

"Yes, we can," Esme assured her.

"Crispin, bring your wife forward," boomed a voice and Delphine flinched, taking a small step behind Esme as though for protection.

Crispin led Esme forward to the centre of the terrace.

"I am Absolom Baron."

Esme's immediate thought was to say, "So what?" imagining Lynette beside her giggling, but glimpsing the pleading expression on Crispin's face, she gave a demure smile and lowered her eyes. Short in stature and whippet thin, Absolom Baron had pale mousy hair, protruding grey eyes and pasty skin the colour and texture of cold porridge. The one hint of contrast on his pale face were his bulbous red lips. To Esme's surprise, Absolom Baron wore a clerical collar. She had always thought it was the second son who was forced into the clergy or military service, not the heir apparent.

Hovering to the right of Absolom was his wife, Dilys. Dull brown hair scraped back from her face in a severe and unflattering style could not disguise her fine bone structure, wide green eyes and full mouth. Her dark blue dress was drab and unflattering, while a yellowing shadow on her cheekbone suggested the ghost of a bruise. Her dreary appearance was accompanied by an air of such intense sadness, Esme wanted to hug her. Dilys gave a small curtsey in greeting, her pale lips breaking into a nervous smile, and her eyes briefly held Esme's, as though questioning why she had chosen to marry into the Baron family. The fleeting look vanished, replaced by a blank expression.

"How are you settling in, my dear sister-in-law?" Absolom asked.

"Very well," Esme responded.

"Good, good," Absolom replied. "In Mater and Pater's absence, I am head of the family and, as such…" Before he could continue, there was a movement in the doorway. Fraser had appeared and was looking agitated. Moving forward on silent feet, he whispered in Absolom's ear. Esme watched as the little colour in Absolom's face drained away, leaving him cadaverous.

"That is most irregular but welcome, nevertheless," Absolom stammered before beckoning Dilys, Crispin, Delphine and Esme forward. "Mater and Pater are home, three days earlier than we expected."

Esme stared at the Baron siblings. Terror emanated from them like a curse.

"Fraser, tell the kitchen to delay dinner until Pater is ready to dine, and send for my daughters," said Absolom.

The Baron children fell into line — Absolom and Dilys at the front, Crispin behind, clutching Esme's hand with such force that she winced, while Delphine, behind her, whimpered. Absolom led the way into the Grey Parlour, where they were joined by four young girls.

"These are our daughters," whispered Dilys, pointing to the tallest, then down the row, "Eve, Mary, Ruth and Harriet."

Esme looked at the girls in surprise as they took their places in front of their parents — their ages appeared to be very close.

"Mary and Ruth were born at the beginning and end of the same year," whispered Delphine, who seemed to have read her mind. Esme felt both compassion and revulsion for Dilys.

The door to the Grey Parlour opened with a prolonged creak. Priscilla Baron entered first, her long russet gown sweeping the floor. Dilys curtseyed and behind her Esme heard the rustle of Delphine's dress as she did the same. Crispin nudged her and after shooting him a look of fury, Esme bobbed a curtsey too. Priscilla Baron was a tall woman, handsome rather than pretty, with faded blue eyes and gleaming silver hair swept into a complicated style. She glanced at each member of her family, who dropped their eyes as her gaze fell upon them before finally reaching Esme. "You are married then, Crispin," Priscilla stated.

"Yes, Mater," Crispin croaked. "This is Esme."

"An unusual name," said Priscilla. "We have never had an Esme in the family before. I hope you understand the honour which has been bestowed upon you, being allowed to join our hallowed enclave."

"I'm beginning to realise your family is…" Esme hesitated, then finished, "unusual."

"You must meet my husband, Osgood; the head of our family," Priscilla continued, her voice resonant.

From the shadow of the doorway, a man emerged, his footsteps slow and deliberate. Each member of the Baron family vibrated with dread, and Esme felt her breath catch in her throat as she wondered what terrible hold this man had over his children.

Osgood was tall and enormously fat with a florid complexion. He extended his hand towards Esme, as though in a blessing. His heavily embroidered coat, aping his ecclesiastical robes, struggled to contain his wobbling stomach. "Bless you, my child, welcome to our noble family," he lisped. Esme shuddered with revulsion as he kissed her hand, but he gave her nothing more than a cursory glance, instead sweeping his narrowing, disapproving eyes to Crispin, who could barely speak from fear.

As Osgood interrogated his younger son, Esme watched, transfixed; in an instant, she was transported to another time, another life, when she had sung with Lynette, wearing a mask and a dress made from peacock feathers, and two men had graced golden thrones in the privacy of Aaron's basement ballroom in Kemptown. As the name, The Bishop, floated into her mind, Esme forced herself to suppress a smile of triumph.

The following day Esme and Crispin stood, shoulder to shoulder, while Osgood Baron surveyed them from behind his vast captain's desk. His office was positioned at the top of one of the unexpected flights of stairs in Baron Hall, alone, isolated, an eyrie in the centre of the house, where if he left the door ajar he could observe the double-height staircase, monitoring the movements of his family. It was a gloomy space, with heavy lace curtains at the narrow windows. A feeble gas lamp gave a soupy yellow glow, throwing shadows onto the collection of taxidermy animals in varying positions of teeth-bared terror.

"Your grandfather was under the impression you were a 'confirmed bachelor'," Osgood said to Crispin, whose face was white, his lips drawn into a tight line as he avoided looking into his father's eyes. "It was why he added this new condition to your inheritance. Crispin, it is time for you to prove you are as virile as your brother before your money will be released. Your brother has fathered four children. However, we need a male heir to continue the name — daughters are unacceptable." With a wave of his pudgy hand, he dismissed the existence of his four granddaughters and Esme understood why Crispin was so protective of Delphine. "You will remain at Baron Hall until such time as..." Osgood paused, and Esme knew he could not remember her name.

"Esme," she said with a wide smile, her violet eyes meeting the pale watery blue of her father-in-law's, "daughter of Judith Blood, who was the eldest child of the Reverend Meredith Blood Senior, and the Right Honourable Robert Sutton, deceased."

"Robert Sutton?" Osgood questioned. "The son of Sir Dudley Sutton of Sutton Court?"

"Yes, he was murdered."

"He was. How very interesting. Do you see your Sutton relatives?"

"No."

Osgood stared at her, as though appraising a brood mare. "You are a suitable vessel for the Baron heir. You will both remain within Baron Hall until such time as you are gravid, Esmerelda."

Crispin grabbed Esme's hand and dragged her away.

Esme and Crispin did not speak until they were in her suite of rooms.

"The evil old flapdoodle," swore Crispin, his fists clenched. "He didn't put any of these restrictions on Absolom."

"Absolom was married before your grandfather died," Esme said. "I bet he made some restriction. Did he leave instructions for Delphine?"

"He didn't leave her any money."

"He's definitely an evil old flapdoodle, then," she said in Delphine's defence, her sorrow for the youngest Baron increasing.

"Esme, I'm sorry," said Crispin. "My offer to you was genuine — a home, security and, when we felt it was suitable, separate lives. I am very aware your heart belongs to another, as does mine, but through various quirks of fate — also known as my evil grandfather — we are, as yet, unable to be with our beloveds."

Walking to the window where Delphine was meandering through the formal garden, trailing her fingers along the low rosemary hedges and seemingly chattering to invisible friends, Esme considered his words. They had known each other three months and this was his first suggestion that he was in love with someone else. It was not a surprise; she had long harboured suspicions about her husband.

"And now, Pater's holding us here until you're with child." Hatred towards his family laced every syllable, making Esme wince.

"All may not be as bleak as you believe," she said, feeling this was the pertinent time to voice her suspicions. "We have already consummated the marriage." Crispin stopped pacing and turned to look at her. "I believe we may have fulfilled the terms of your grandfather's will."

"You do?" asked Crispin.

Esme nodded, her hand straying unconsciously to her skirts, smoothing them with gentle hands.

"When will you be certain?"

271

"Ma always said you could never be certain until you felt it quicken. At present, that hasn't happened, but I've missed my monthlies."

"Speak to Dilys — she's had four children, she'll know the signs," Crispin said, his eyes regaining their lustre. "Until we're certain, it'll be necessary for me to spend my nights with you. Father's words suggest he will position his shadows to watch, ensuring we are sharing a room with determined regularity."

"His shadows?"

"They are staff loyal to Father," he said, and Esme noted a tremor of fear in his voice, "who monitor the rest of the family."

A chill ran down Esme's spine. "He spies on you? On us?"

"Yes." Throwing a log on the fire, Crispin made himself comfortable on the large wing-backed armchair, placing his elegantly shod feet on the footstool. Esme sat in the smaller chair opposite. "Who has your heart, Esme?" His tone was gentle, brooding, his eyes fixed on the fire. "It isn't Bill. Despite the unfortunate circumstances of your parting, it was clear that while you and he were great friends and enjoyed the thrill of attraction, he did not command your heart."

Esme was surprised at Crispin's astuteness. "You know who holds my heart, Crispin."

"Aaron Maclean?"

Esme nodded. "You know him, don't you?" she said, wondering where two such different men might have shared an encounter. "When we were at St Botolph's, you mentioned him."

"I know of him, rather than being personally acquainted," said Crispin.

"And you? What did you do for your family to tie your money up so tightly?" she asked. "Caught you in a molly house, did they?"

Crispin winced. "Not quite," he said. "I've never had to pay for my pleasures."

An image floated across Esme's mind of the young man who had watched her with such distress when she had first arrived. "The boy along the corridor?"

"You saw him?"

"When Mrs Fraser showed me to my room, he was watching me and he looked sad."

"His name is Donald," Crispin sighed. "We met at school. He was the son of my housemaster, Mr Clements. Our feelings are illegal and our devotion must be hidden. He serves as my valet, enabling us to be together with the minimum of suspicion."

Crispin turned away, but not before Esme had glimpsed the pain on his face. *What a pair we are*, she thought.

"Very well," Esme said. "We shall share a room until such time as I am certain that I'm with child. Although, as my courses haven't arrived since after we were married, it seems likely I'm expecting. I shall speak to Dilys and perhaps Mrs Fraser. She seems a sensible sort."

"She and Mr Fraser have six children; her advice will be invaluable."

"What will happen to our child when it is born?" she asked.

"What do you mean?"

"It was our plan to return to London as soon as your finances were settled. We had hoped that would be in a matter of weeks, but this doesn't seem possible."

"We'll take the baby with us and hire staff to look after him."

"I suspect, if it's a boy, your father will want to oversee the Baron heir."

Crispin considered her words, then shook his head. "Let's see if there's a baby first," he said. "These are decisions to be made once the child is in our arms, then we will be in a better position to bargain."

"You are not using my child to score points over your father," Esme snapped.

"*Our* child, darling, our child. It will be a Baron, remember."

Esme's hand strayed once more to her lap, wondering again at the wisdom of her decision to marry Crispin Baron.

CHAPTER TWO

The grand piano in the music room was a place of refuge for Esme. Running her fingers along the keys, she felt a wave of homesickness entirely different from the nausea caused by her pregnancy. Two doctors had confirmed her condition and both Osgood and Absolom Baron had insisted the family pray together every morning to ensure she would deliver a boy: the longed-for Baron heir. Using her delicacy as an excuse, Esme refused to kneel on the unforgiving stone floor of the chapel while the father and son ecumenically took it in turns to intone the more violent passages of the Bible to their cowering families.

Stretching her fingers, Esme played a chord, a ripple of pleasure flowing through her, transporting her to the past. Lynette's father, Marcus, had taught them both to play the piano from when they were big enough to sit on the stool. At Baron Hall, she was discouraged from speaking about her past on stage — an instruction she ignored with a steely-eyed defiance, instead choosing to practise and play the simpler tunes in her repertoire.

"Aunt Esme." A quiet voice came from the doorway.

Looking up, Esme smiled, beckoning Harriet, the youngest of Absolom Baron's daughters, to her side. Hugging the little girl to her, Esme winced at the child's thinness beneath her utilitarian brown dress.

"Will you teach me another tune, please?" Harriet asked.

"Where are your parents?"

"Father has gone to town with Grandpapa, and Grandmama is in the garden with Bolter."

Bolter was the gardener and it amused Esme that Priscilla was often in his company; the two shared a passion for the vast gardens surrounding Baron Hall. Esme wondered if they shared anything else.

"Where is your mother?"

"Mother is in her bedroom, resting."

Esme remained unsure whether Harriet's mother, Dilys, was an ally or an enemy. Although Dilys quaked with fear whenever her pitiless husband was in the room and she displayed bruises and cuts with alarming regularity, she appeared loyal to Absolom. At present, Dilys's wrist was bandaged and a bruise was blooming over her swollen and closed right eye. She had announced at dinner the previous evening that she had fallen in her room and bumped into the door handle, but Esme had seen such injuries before and she was certain Absolom was behind his wife's mishaps.

"We're safe for an hour, then," whispered Esme, shuffling over on the piano stool so Harriet could perch beside her.

Esme had discovered Harriet in the library one afternoon, hiding among the shelves, her face screwed up in concentration as she tried to read *On the Origin of Species* by Charles Darwin. It was difficult to say which of them had been more shocked, Esme because she had never seen any of the sisters individually, or Harriet, who had cowered in fear, trying to hide this most controversial of books.

"Harriet, you're safe with me," Esme had whispered, kneeling down beside her, heartbroken at the thought Harriet assumed she was a bully like the rest of the adults who dominated the girl's narrow world. "Whatever you're doing, I won't tell anyone."

Harriet had swallowed, her eyes flicking from side to side as though looking for a way to escape. "Father says that to read any book other than the Bible means we will go straight to hell, but I can't believe it," she whispered. "If books are so terrible, why does Grandpapa have this library? He's a bishop in the Church and he reads other things."

Taking her trembling hand, Esme sat on the floor beside her. "Reading and educating yourself won't send you to hell," she had reassured Harriet. "It will give you knowledge, confidence and new views on life, which is perhaps why your father and grandfather are frightened of you reading. It could make you question things."

"You ask questions all the time, Aunt Esme," Harriet had said. "Father says you're a fallen woman who used to cavort on stage and you will definitely go to hell. What does cavort mean?"

"I was a singer and dancer," said Esme, anger towards Absolom seething in her chest. "I acted, too, and your father doesn't approve, but if I'm going to hell and you're going to hell, it can't be too bad because we'll be together."

Harriet had laughed.

"Shall I tell you a secret?" said Esme, who felt Harriet needed an adult to trust in the eerie passages and whispering darkness of Baron Hall. Harriet nodded, too excited to speak. "My bible isn't real. If you open it, there are Tarot cards hidden inside."

Harriet's hands clamped over her mouth in shock, her eyes glittering with questions she was too afraid to ask. After this, Esme and Harriet had often met in the library and when Harriet had asked if Esme could teach her to sing, she had agreed. If nothing else, Esme had thought, watching Harriet skip away in excitement, it would annoy Osgood and Absolom.

Harriet wriggled excitedly beside Esme. "Could you teach me one of the songs you sang when you were Little Smee?" she asked.

In exchange for information on the Baron family, Esme had told Harriet about her eclectic upbringing. Harriet's secret in return had been to explain that her hair was not the drab brown displayed but was naturally blonde. Her mother painted all the girls' hair, as well as her own, with a homemade solution of bitter oak and ash to give it the dull brown colour.

"Mother and Ruth have the same colour hair as me. Eve's is brown, and Mary's is a pretty golden red. But Father says God punishes prettiness. It was the reason he cut Aunt Delphine's face when she was a girl. He said it was better that he punish her on earth rather than being tortured for all eternity by God."

Esme had felt sick at this revelation and in order to avenge herself on her cruel in-laws, she had decided to teach Harriet every song in her repertoire and to take the girl with her when she left Baron Hall, possibly to encourage her to join the performers at The Firebird.

"One of my favourite songs was written by my friend Lynette's father. It was about my doll Adelaide and was called 'My Friend'."

Harriet's pale face lit up with excitement and Esme realised she would be a beauty without the drab, lank hair. As her fingers danced across the keys, she wondered if there was a level of protection in Dilys's strange action of colouring her daughters' hair. The scar on Delphine's face served as a livid warning of what the Baron men were prepared to do.

The notes filled the music room with a rainbow of sound. Esme sang each line alone, then repeated it with Harriet, who then sang it by herself. This was the way Marcus had taught her and Lynette their pieces before they were old enough to read. Harriet was a fast learner, and less than half an hour later she and Esme were singing the cheerful ditty. A discreet cough behind them caused Esme to turn around.

"The master and his son are returning. Their carriage has been seen at the east gate. They will be home in a few moments, and Lady Baron has finished supervising Bolter. She is returning from the garden," said the calm voice of Mrs Fraser.

"Run upstairs with your sisters, Harriet," Esme said, but there was no need as the little girl was already halfway across the room. "Thank you, Mrs Fraser."

"It's good the child has someone to turn to," Mrs Fraser said. "You've made such a difference, Mrs Crispin." In order to differentiate between the wives, the staff referred to Esme and Dilys as Mrs Crispin and Mrs Absolom respectively, while Priscilla Baron was Lady Baron or Her Ladyship.

The scraping of the front door indicated the return of Osgood and Absolom. Esme hesitated — she had no desire to encounter either man. Deciding to wait for them to move through the grand hall, she remained at the piano, where she knew she could not be seen from the doorway. Neither realised she was in the music room and continued to speak.

"At least he's managed to impregnate the showgirl," said Absolom. "It should stop all the nasty rumours."

"She's a pretty little thing," replied Osgood. "Perhaps when the child is born, I may consider initiating her into our flock. We could do with some new blood."

Absolom gave a cold laugh. "Didn't think she was your type, Pater. I thought you had an eye on Crispin's bit of fluff, the boy, Donald."

"Not for me, dear boy, for you. The boy Donald will no doubt bend to my will in the end…"

Revulsion and fury roared through Esme at the arrogance of the two men.

Absolom departed up the stairs, his smug laughter ringing out, and in a moment of pure anger, Esme turned to the piano and began to play. Osgood paused, listening. Aware he was standing on the other side of the half-open door, she began to sing. Her voice was liquid silver, slicing through the dusty air with the glitter of a blade.

"There's Russia in the air,
Bears, snow, the dream of romance
A fairy-tale prince walking the streets
I'm going to catch the eye of the Tsar.
Palaces of gold, gemstones galore
Sleigh bells ringing as the Cossacks dance
A fairy-tale prince walking the streets
I'm going to catch the eye of the Tsar…"

In her mind she saw herself and Lynette, first on stage at The Firebird, then in their glorious peacock feather dresses in the red and gold basement of Aaron's house in Kemptown. The tune had been bright and funny as they had danced in unison, twirling parasols, but now, in Esme's slower, more dramatic version, each word issued a challenge.

The door was pushed open and Osgood entered, quivering with emotion.

Under normal circumstances, Esme went out of her way to avoid her father-in-law, finding excuses to leave any room he entered. Dinner was the place she encountered him with tedious regularity, but as Absolom tended to dominate the conversation, she was usually able to eat in silence. On the few occasions Esme had encountered Osgood, he had tried to question her on her faith, a subject she refused to discuss.

"That is a haunting tune, my child," Osgood wheezed, taking slow steps towards her as she continued to play. "Was it something you once heard at the theatre where you flaunted yourself?"

Esme did not respond, but she made an alteration in the lyrics, replacing the original placename, Moscow.

"Dancing at the summer ball,
In the red and gold where Kemptown calls
A fairy-tale prince walking the streets
I'm going to catch the eye of the Tsar…
We'll twirl through the white nights,
Entwined in love and lost in dreams,
My fairy-tale prince walking the streets
I'm going to catch the eye of the Tsar…"

"Kemptown?"

The word was strangled and Esme looked up, her violet eyes challenging Osgood's. His face had changed colour during the execution of her recital, flushing before settling on a stark white. He stepped forward, a hint of betrayal in his pale blue eyes. Esme continued to play.

"A childhood favourite, I presume," he repeated as though in a trance, his voice low with menace.

"Oh no," Esme replied, continuing to play but this time in the jaunty major key in which the song had first been written, "it was part of an act I used to perform with my friend, Lynette. We were known as The Skylark Sisters."

Osgood blanched at her words. Esme reached the end, finishing with a theatrical flourish before allowing the silence to grow between them. "Is it a common tune?" he asked.

"It was written especially for us by Marcus Mason, Lynette's father. As far as I'm aware, we're the only duo who sing it." Esme felt a cruel satisfaction watching her father-in-law's face sag. It was a moment of revenge for Delphine, for Harriet, for Dilys and her daughters, and the fear that had haunted their lives. "You really should be careful, Father-in-law, dear," continued Esme in an icy voice. "Women in peacock masks have a habit of appearing in the most unexpected of places."

Osgood gave her an unpleasant smile. "'Then he will say to those on his left, depart from me you cursed, into the eternal fire', the book of Matthew, chapter twenty-five, verse forty-one," he quoted, taking a step nearer with each word until he loomed over her.

For a moment, Esme thought he was going to slap her across the face, but then the door to the music room was thrown open and Priscilla entered, her face thunderous.

"My dear Esmerelda," she said in a voice of ice and fury, "would you accompany me, please? There are matters of great urgency which must be discussed."

"But…" began Osgood, who continued to snarl at Esme.

"This cannot wait," snapped Priscilla.

Esme rose to her feet, startled as Priscilla gripped her arm and dragged her up the stairs.

Moments later, Priscilla all but flung Esme into her pink bedroom. Behind her were Mrs Fraser, Hester, Dilys, Delphine and Crispin.

"You foolish girl!" admonished Priscilla. "You couldn't resist taunting him, could you?"

Esme stared at Priscilla in astonishment. Mrs Fraser and Hester had sped past Esme and she could hear them crashing around in her bedroom, packing. "I don't understand…" she began.

"Of course you don't," said Priscilla, "and I should have explained sooner, but I thought you were safer not knowing, for now, anyway. Your pregnancy is enough to protect you at present."

"Protect me from what?" Esme turned to Crispin. His face was white, his eyes darting around the room. "Will someone explain what is happening?"

Priscilla took a deep breath, steadying herself before turning from Esme and issuing instructions. "Dilys, prepare a bag for Harriet, then ask my maid, Sawless, to help you prepare for a journey to Cambridge to see your father. Ensure the girls travel with you."

"Yes Cilla," said Dilys, and Esme watched in astonishment as Priscilla gave her a heartfelt hug before Dilys gathered her skirts and flitted from the room.

"Mrs Fraser," called Priscilla, and the housekeeper appeared in the doorway to Esme's bedroom. "Leave that to Hester, please. Would you run to Delphine's room and collect her bag?"

Mrs Fraser nodded and left.

"Now, my sweet, we must disguise you," said Priscilla, looking at Delphine.

"Esme, could you help?" asked Crispin. "Would you be able to hide Delf's scar with your greasepaint?"

Esme stared at them in wonder. Priscilla was holding her daughter's hand and Crispin had a protective hand on his mother's arm. "Not until you tell me what is happening," she snapped.

Exchanging a look, the three Barons moved to the chairs grouped around the fire, beckoning Esme to follow. Priscilla smoothed out her skirts and began to speak. "My dear Esme, we were remiss in failing to warn you. Your revelation downstairs could cost us all dear and we must protect the innocent, yourself included."

"What do you mean?" asked Esme, beginning to feel ripples of fear. She who so prided herself on being able to read people, to wield her power of observation, honed over years of studying the Tarot cards, of offering people solutions and helping them towards their dreams, appeared to have misread this situation in the most catastrophic manner.

"My husband, Osgood, is a bully of the worst sort. He will discover what you love, and he will use this to destroy you. His method is never to threaten you directly but to hurt those around you. It is the reason, why in public and particularly in the presence of my husband, I withdrew all affection from my children. However, I surrounded them with people I trusted would protect and care for them."

Crispin's words came back to Esme: *The staff have been more like family…* Their kindness and care were deliberate, organised by the mother who was forced to watch them from afar.

"Do not think for one moment I did not care," said Priscilla, "particularly about my daughter —" she reached for Delphine's hand — "but things are not as they appear."

Esme stared at her surprise.

"I have never forgiven myself for what Absolom did to his sister…"

Crispin made a noise that was almost a growl.

"He and Osgood cut Delphine's face as a punishment for being too beautiful," Priscilla said, her voice close to tears. "I was away, visiting my father, who was dying. When I returned, it was to find Delphine confined to bed, swathed in bandages, and Crispin incarcerated in the attic, where he had been locked when he tried to challenge his father and brother. Without the

Frasers, who had been clandestinely caring for them, both my younger children would have died."

"Why have you stayed?" said Esme, aghast.

"To leave would have been a death sentence for my children and grandchildren. Osgood would have had free reign. My father was a good man but he misjudged Osgood, believing that as a man of God, he would be a gentle husband. His error became apparent after Absolom was born. Osgood threatened to kill the child."

"What?" Esme exclaimed as prickles of revulsion travelled across her skin.

"He believed I was showing him too much love," Priscilla said. "It was then I realised his true nature. As Crispin has probably told you, the family money is mine. Osgood was furious when my father died and he discovered that, while he had been left a sizeable allowance, the bulk of the money came to me. My father left nothing to Absolom, knowing he would inherit from his father, but the reason for Crispin's codicil was to offer him protection. With a wife necessary before he could inherit, it was unlikely Osgood would be able to force him into an unhappy marriage as he had done with Absolom and Dilys — what family would choose a husband who was only marrying their daughter in order to release his inheritance? Delphine will be more than protected by my will and shall be a very wealthy woman. You see, Esme, my husband has never been faithful to me but then, I have never been faithful to him either. Crispin and Delphine are my children, but not his. I have long loved a man who has loved me in return, but to reveal this would endanger them further."

Esme looked at Crispin and Delphine, with their glossy dark hair and dark brown eyes. "Bolter, the gardener," she whispered. Priscilla gave her a complicit smile. "You knew this?" Esme asked as she turned to Crispin, who nodded.

"I told Mama that it would be safer to tell you, but she felt it was better to wait. Your pregnancy was protection enough from Father and Absolom, but we were planning to allow you into our secret very soon."

Esme felt the world rocking beneath her feet. The firm foundations on which she had built her knowledge of the Baron family were tipping her off centre. She was floundering, trying to make sense of all she was being told and, as the danger of her predicament surrounded her like a storm, she reached for a firm anchor. "We should leave," she said. "My parents will let us stay with them…"

"Esme, you don't understand. If you flee to the Hardys, Osgood will destroy them, as he did your real father, Robert Sutton."

"What?" Esme stared at Priscilla.

"Osgood was infatuated with your father. When Robert fell in love with your mother, Osgood wanted his revenge."

"Osgood was in love with my father?" asked Esme, unable to take it all in.

"Oh no. Osgood is incapable of love. Infatuation ruled his heart, the desire to control. When, in Osgood's view, your father spurned him, he decided to have his revenge. Your father was never in debt to Osgood; it was a rumour my husband spread to give him power to hurt your father. Osgood proposed to punish Robert through you and your mother. You had been born out of wedlock and Osgood threatened to kidnap and kill you. In fear, your parents married, then planned to flee to America with you, but Osgood's men caught up with them before they could collect you."

Blood was roaring in Esme's ears as Priscilla's words crept into her soul. "You're lying," Esme whispered.

"No, I'm not," Priscilla replied. "While I didn't know your mother, I knew your paternal aunt, Victoria Sutton, and she discovered the truth a few years ago. When I saw your marriage to Crispin announced in *The Times*, I knew it was time to return home to protect you both. Osgood has a long memory. He is aware of who you are and that chills my heart."

"What should we do?" asked Esme, terror creeping through her as she realised the extent of the shadow hanging over them.

"When you sang to him, you laid down a challenge that Osgood will not be able to ignore, but we have a small window of opportunity. This afternoon, Osgood and I are due at the Arnolds' house for the christening of their third grandson. It is twenty miles away and we will be staying overnight. I shall insist Absolom accompanies us, something he will leap at, as there will be a number of senior clergy in attendance. It also gives them time to plan their next move against you, Esme."

"But where shall we go?" asked Esme.

"Donald and I can go to his mother in Scotland," said Crispin. "His father died some years ago and his mother returned to her family in the Highlands, but we can't take the others with us."

"Very well," said Priscilla.

Esme was on her feet, pacing, her quicksilver mind ignoring her panic as she made plans, her survival instinct coming to the fore as she plotted a viable escape. "I have my greasepaint in the other room; I'll be able to disguise Delphine by hiding her scar. Harriet should come with us, too. We can wash the dye from her hair. We'll need warm clothes of reasonable quality.

We shall be three sisters who work together in service and are visiting our ailing grandmother."

"Where will you go, though?" Priscilla asked.

Esme paused. Her instinct was to hide in a theatrical troupe, but she pushed this aside, aware that with a child growing inside, the time had come to stop running. The information Priscilla had given her about her parents changed her view on events. "My mother's family," she said. "The Bloods are a huge clan and they live in a remote village in Pembrokeshire. I've only met a few of them, but I'm sure they will help."

"Very well," said Priscilla.

"There is one more thing," said Esme, "we must contact Aaron Maclean."

"What?" Crispin's response was one of fury and Esme wondered, fleetingly, if her attachment to Aaron bothered Crispin. "Why?" he demanded.

"Your father is a man with many evil connections," Esme said. "Aaron is also a man who is not to be crossed. If we need protection for the darker side of the world, Aaron will be our best chance."

"Do you know how to contact him?"

"Yes, but we must act with caution. Send this to his address." Esme hurried over to her writing desk and scribbled down the names of the six Tarot cards from Aaron's reading, the same cards drawn from the pack by Rosie on the day her parents left her in the fortune-telling tent: *The Tower*, *Death*, *the Ten of Coins*, *the Nine of Cups*, *The Empress* and *The Star*, followed by the word, *Home*. "He will know these are from me and if he can, he will find us."

Priscilla took the piece of paper and tucked it into the bodice of her dress. "Osgood, Absolom and I shall be leaving after luncheon," she said. "Everything must continue as normal until then. Once we have left, wait for an hour, then set out."

Esme remained in her room where Mrs Fraser brought her lunch, along with a dress of dark green calico.

"It belongs to one of the maids," Mrs Fraser explained. "I shall ensure it is replaced."

Esme forced herself to eat, knowing it might be a long time until she had such a wholesome meal, before helping Hester to finish packing. However, as she wrapped Adelaide in one of the shawls given to her by Rosie, Esme sent Hester to the other room before removing the neatly folded pound notes from their hiding place. Tucking a few into her reticule, she hid the remainder in a small canvas pouch and, when Hester helped her to change into the dress provided by Mrs Fraser, Esme discreetly tied it around her waist for safekeeping.

When Delphine had finished her own lunch, she hurried to Esme, who transformed her sister-in-law, disguising the scar under a layer of greasepaint, blending the edges until Delphine's skin was smooth.

"I look different," was all Delphine managed when Esme held up a mirror, but the sadness in her eyes was devastating.

As instructed, they waited until the coach containing Priscilla, Osgood and Absolom left, then a tap on the door from Mrs Fraser summoned Esme.

"There is a carriage waiting in the stable yard," Mrs Fraser said. "Crispin has collected Harriet. He will take you as far as Welshpool, then you must find your own way to Pembrokeshire. Will that be possible?"

"Of course," replied Esme. Delphine looked terrified.

Throughout their journey, Esme shepherded the two younger girls, protecting them as best she could, sticking to the busier roads, taking trains where possible, coaches when they were not. By the time they arrived in Little Haven, Esme was exhausted. They walked into the village and, to her relief, the first person Esme saw was Aelwen Blood, standing outside a shop and laughing with two other women who, from their colouring, were related to her in some manner.

"Aelwen!" Esme called, exhaustion overwhelming her as they reached their journey's end.

Her cousin turned in astonishment. "Esme," she said. "What are you doing here? Your mother is here, but George Arbuthnot has returned with his sister and her husband to Liverpool."

"And Bill?"

"With his father."

Esme sighed with relief. "Why has my mother remained?"

"Grandmother is ill. Your mother has stayed to be with her."

Aelwen led them to her mother, Mariah Blood's, house. "Mother, we have visitors. Esme has returned."

Mariah hurried forward. "Esme," she said, hiding her surprise.

"My mother is here?" Esme asked.

Footsteps behind them caused her to look up. Her mother, dressed in a simple grey gown, stood in the doorway. "Why are you here?" Celia asked, her voice quavering with nerves.

"To listen," said Esme. "I know what Osgood Baron did to my father. In a moment of panic and despair, I married his son, Crispin. We have run away from Baron Hall. This is Delphine and Harriet Baron. Will you help us to hide?"

"Of course…" began Aelwen before her mother interrupted.

"You're safe here," Mariah said, but Esme was looking at her mother, whose eyes were swimming with tears. Taking a step forward, Celia opened her arms and with the minutest of hesitations, Esme stepped forward.

"Welcome home, Esme," Celia said. "Welcome home at last." Her arms were tight around Esme, and they hugged until they cried.

Esme awoke the next day to find her mother sitting in a rocking chair beside her bed, knitting a shawl from soft blue wool.

"Esme," Celia said, "how are you feeling?"

"Where are Harriet and Delphine?" Esme asked, her mind blurred from tiredness and nausea.

"Delphine is with Aelwen, and Harriet has been taken to the beach by Elen and Dewi to catch crabs."

"Who are Elen and Dewi?"

"Your cousins, the children of my brother Owain and his wife Ceri."

"How many brothers and sisters do you have?"

"I'm the eldest, then there's my brother Meredith, who you've met, then Owain, Edmund, Patrick, Hannah and Blodwen, named for mother."

"Seven of you," said Esme.

"It was a noisy upbringing. It's good to hear my real name again, although they are careful to call me Celia in front of my husband."

"What shall I call you?"

"Oh, Esme, you may call me whatever you think is appropriate. I have no right to ask you to call me Mother."

"Priscilla Baron told me what happened, why you and my father were running."

Celia's face became a mask of regret. "Not a day has gone by when I didn't think of you," she sighed. "Coming back would have put you in more danger."

"And Bill? Was that the reason you left him with Helena and Wallace, changing his name to Flagstaff?"

"There's something else, Esme. If you had stayed, we could have told you both, made it right. Bill is not your brother."

"Enough lies, Mother. If we're ever to forgive each other, we must be honest."

Putting aside the shawl, Esme's mother leaned forward and took her hands. "The night your father was murdered, I took refuge in a church. It was the safest place I could think to hide. I curled up in one corner and slept. In the morning, I was woken by George Arbuthnot. He had come there looking for help with his three-week-old son. The boy's mother had died, but she and George had not been married. It would be untrue of me to say we fell in love at first sight, but I think we recognised a certain need in each other. I offered to look after his son in exchange for a roof over my head. Three months later, he proposed and we agreed to bring Bill up as our own. Until the night of your engagement ball, Bill had no idea I was not his real mother."

Esme watched as her mother shrank into herself with the telling of this tale. "Bill and I aren't related?" Esme said in wonder.

"Not through blood, no, but he is your step-brother."

"I needn't have married Crispin," Esme whispered, her words exhaled like a breath. "I agreed to marry him to protect both Bill and I from any scandal. Oh, Mother, this is a mess."

"Surely the marriage can be annulled?"

"I'm pregnant," Esme hissed. "This is Crispin's child. Your lies, told so long ago, have trapped me in this bizarre marriage.

My child carries the name of the family who murdered my father."

"Oh, my dear, what have I done?"

Esme stared at her mother, the woman who had abandoned her, not through selfishness, as Esme had always imagined, but through love. A scared young woman, desperate to protect the people she cared about, a woman forced to make a desperate choice, as she, Esme had felt compelled to do. As these thoughts engulfed her, a glimmer of understanding rose in Esme.

"Can you ever forgive me?" her mother asked, her voice quavering with unshed tears.

Squeezing her mother's hands, Esme hesitated, then with a tentative smile, she whispered, "I think I can, Mother."

CHAPTER THREE

"Aunt Esme, look what I've caught." Harriet's voice filled the cottage as she raced in, holding a mackerel.

"You clever girl," Esme said, smiling. "Shall we cook it for your supper?"

"Yes, please," Harriet trilled. "I'm going to show Delphine."

Esme laughed as Harriet hurried from the room.

"She's a different child," mused Aelwen, who stood behind Esme, folding the washing she had taken from the mangle.

"Thank goodness," replied Esme, catching the end of the sheet and folding it with her cousin.

"Have you heard from your mother?"

"A letter arrived yesterday," replied Esme. "They will have set sail by now."

"And how is Bill?"

"Recovering, as am I," Esme said. "He thinks he will have a better chance if he begins again in Patagonia."

Being part of the Blood family had been a revelation for Esme. The connection of blood, both in her veins and her surname, gave her a sense of belonging she had never before experienced. Her maternal grandparents, the matriarch and patriarch of the family, had welcomed her without question, enfolding her into the warmth of the family with all its complexities of love, friendship, rivalries and laughter. It had taken her a while to adjust to the rural way of life, but the year she had spent in the peace of the village of Little Haven had been the balm she needed to recover from her many adventures.

Not long after Esme's arrival, Blodwen Blood, her grandmother, had recovered from the ague troubling her and, knowing her mother was safe, Celia had decided to return to George and Bill in Liverpool.

"I will write every week," she told Esme and had been true to her promise, keeping her up to date with the family news, including their decision to return to South America. Esme was relieved the relationship between them would have a chance to grow gradually. There were many years of misunderstanding and hurt to put right and the scars would take time to heal.

To Esme's surprise, regular letters arrived from Crispin in Scotland. He and Donald were renting a hunting lodge and were reinventing themselves as Scottish lairds. From Priscilla, there was the occasional note, informing her of their movements and delivering the news that Dilys and her other three daughters had made a permanent move to her father's house in Cambridge. After Esme's initial fear that Osgood and Absolom would find her, nothing was heard from them, and Esme began to relax. From Aaron, there was silence, and it was his desertion which hurt more than anything else.

A wail from the corner drew her attention.

"Theodore Cornelius Baron," Esme said, a smile lighting her face, "you are always hungry."

She scooped up her son, rocking him in her arms and making him giggle. From the moment he had been born, the love she had felt for him had astounded her. It was this uprush of maternal feeling which had given her new respect for both her mother and mother-in-law. Due to the malignant influence of Osgood Baron, both women had been forced, in different ways, to distance themselves from their children. She understood how Priscilla had found the strength to retreat from her children in order to protect them, how her mother had taken her chances, trusting Rosie Hardy to protect Esme, when she was scared for both their lives. Esme knew there was nothing she would not do to protect Theodore.

Before she could take her son upstairs to feed him, Meredith Blood and his son, Gawain, with Delphine holding Gawain's hand, entered the cottage. Everything about Delphine was different. She glowed with confidence and happiness. From the moment they had arrived, Esme's cousin, the dour Gawain, had been smitten with Delphine. Helping her to recover from the horrors inflicted upon her by her father and brother had softened Gawain and a month earlier he had proposed marriage, which Delphine had accepted with delight.

"Esme, my dear, have you seen the newspaper?" asked Meredith.

"No," Esme replied, unnerved by the seriousness of their expressions. "Has something happened?"

"It's your sister, Cassie," said Gawain. "She's been arrested. It happened a few days ago and things look very serious. The charge is murdering her husband."

A shiver of cold steel seemed to pass across Esme's throat as she remembered the night of Cassie's fury. "No," she gasped. Her hand was steady as she reached out for the newspaper. As she read the description of the headless corpse being discovered in the lake on the Blanchard estate, wearing a night shirt belonging to the viscount, Esme found herself squeezing Theodore more tightly than usual. "This is impossible," she said when she had finished reading. "Cassie would never have been able to do this."

"What do you mean?" asked Gawain. "You've told us yourself how she threatened you with a knife."

"True," Esme conceded, "but she was incensed, and she's much taller than me. If she had succeeded, there's no way she would have been able to hide my body."

"You know about bodies, do you?" asked Meredith, his tone sharp.

"Not really," Esme replied, "but I do know that dead bodies are difficult to move."

"How do you know this?" asked Gawain.

"We were on tour in Cornwall when Lynette, Aaron and I discovered a body." She looked back through time, remembering how they had sneaked out early to swim in the sea and on the edges of the camp had seen one of their temporary stagehands, seemingly unconscious from drink. Giggling, they had approached, their laughter turning to horror as they realised he was dead. "There were no signs of foul play. Pa thought he'd probably had a fit. The men wanted to carry the body back to the Hardy encampment in order to deal with him with dignity, but it proved difficult because he was so heavy and unwieldy. Eventually, they used part of the stage to carry him. Cassie would never have been able to move a body alone and if she'd decapitated him, she would have been covered in blood. One of her staff would have seen."

Silence greeted her words.

"It says in the newspaper Cassie's real father murdered her mother," said Gawain.

"Yes," agreed Esme, "that is what I've been led to understand."

Theodore grizzled in her arms, but Esme could not tear her eyes away from the newspaper. It made no sense. Rosie had written to her recently, delighted to deliver the news that, despite people thinking Cassie had married Henry for his title, they had grown fond of each other, and she had given birth to a daughter, Rosalind.

"Sergeant Evans brought the newspaper," said Meredith. "He's outside and he wishes to speak to you."

"Why?" asked Esme.

Aelwen took Theodore from Esme's arms and with Meredith by her side, Esme hurried outside into the summer sunshine.

"Mrs Baron?" asked a tall man with full moustaches and heavy sideburns.

Even though she knew she had done nothing wrong, the appearance of a policeman was never welcome. "What's happened, Sergeant?" Esme asked with a feeling of foreboding.

"A report has been made that you have abducted two children," said Sergeant Evans, causing Meredith to give a derisive snort.

"Abduct two children? What nonsense is this?" he snarled. "Go inside, Esme, I will sort out this stupidity."

Without needing to be told twice, Esme hurried back inside and took her son from Aelwen. Delphine was waiting.

"A report has been made that I have abducted two children," said Esme, and Delphine narrowed her eyes.

"Theo and Harriet, no doubt."

"Sergeant Evans hasn't said as much, but yes."

"You can't abduct Theo, he's your son," said Aelwen, "but Harriet?"

"You haven't abducted her either," said Delphine, then with hesitation, she continued, "Harriet's your step-daughter."

Esme looked at Delphine in surprise. "No, Delf, she's my niece through marriage…"

Delphine shook her head. "Harriet is Crispin's daughter," she said.

Esme and Aelwen stared at Delphine in amazement.

"When they were younger, Dilys and Crissie were friends," Delphine explained. "Everyone thought they would marry one day, and a tentative arrangement was made between Mater and Dilys's father, Harold. Dilys had an older brother, Roland, but when he died from a fever, Dilys became her father's heir. He's a very wealthy man and, while Crissie was away at university for a few terms, Absolom and Pater decided it would be advantageous to arrange a match between Absolom and Dilys. No one was in favour, but then, unexpectedly, Harold agreed and the marriage went ahead. Crispin and Dilys were both devastated."

"Considering what your mother told us about the things your father has done in the past, I bet he threatened Harold," said Esme.

"Without doubt," agreed Delphine. "After Dilys and Absolom had Eve, Ruth and Mary, Absolom went away with Father for several months and, during the summer they were absent, Crispin and Dilys renewed their friendship. Harriet was the result."

"Does your mother know?" asked Esme, wondering again at the endless depths of lies and secrets hidden within the Baron family.

"Why do you think she sent Harriet with you? You're Crispin's wife, Harriet's his daughter, so you're legally one of her guardians. She was safer with you than Dilys."

Esme reeled. Since her arrival in Little Haven, she had viewed any thoughts of the Baron family as a contagion to be avoided, forcing herself to think of other things should they ever haunt the edges of her psyche, but as Delphine spoke, Esme could see her words were the truth.

"Let me see what this man has to say," said Delphine, hurrying past Esme. "I know the levels of vindictiveness Pater will reach, and I will not let him hurt any of us again."

Esme watched, open-mouthed, as the once fragile and nervous Delphine marched out to discuss matters with the two men. Theodore began to cry, and Esme took him upstairs to feed him. As she sat on her bed, the window ajar to enable her to hear what Sergeant Evans was saying, Esme's spirits sank.

"Bishop Baron claims your niece has kidnapped his granddaughter and grandson," the sergeant was saying. "There's pressure being put on me from very senior members of the police force, as far away as London, to arrest Esme."

"London? As if we care what they think," scoffed Meredith.

"These men are serious," said Sergeant Evans. "I know these charges are ludicrous, but they are determined to take Esme and the boy. If they can get the girl too, they'll think it's a bonus."

"Sergeant Evans, this is my father taking revenge. There is no case to answer," interrupted Delphine, explaining Harriet's parentage to the astonished men.

"You may well be correct," said Sergeant Evans, when she had finished, "but if I don't arrest her, they'll send men from Carmarthen, who'll be less understanding."

"How much time can you give us?" asked Meredith, urgency in his voice.

"I can't delay for long — perhaps two days if I say I keep missing you, but after that, I'll be risking my job."

"Thank you, Tequin," said Meredith.

Esme did not hear the remainder of the conversation but ten minutes later, there was the clip-clop of hooves as Sergeant Evans departed.

Upon returning downstairs, Esme discovered Meredith talking to Delphine, Gawain and Aelwen.

"We think it might be better for Delphine to take Harriet to Crispin," said Meredith with no preamble.

"To the Highlands?"

"Yes, Gawain will escort them."

"Very well, if you think that is the safest thing for Harriet." Esme would miss the little girl, but her protection was paramount. "And Theo?"

"Could you go to your adopted family in London?" asked Meredith. "While I would once have suggested our remoteness was an advantage, this situation makes me uneasy. You will be better lost in a crowd."

"I agree," said Esme, fury at Osgood Baron rising within her. This man had been the shadow on her life since her birth. As his image rose in her mind, so did the card of the Devil. She angrily pushed the thought aside.

"Very well," Meredith said, "I shall make the arrangements."

Esme watched as her uncle strode from the cottage.

"We will stop my father," Delphine said. "He has done enough damage. I shall send a telegram to Mater to warn her that he is using his power to try and hurt us."

Delphine and Gawain followed Meredith from the cottage and, while Esme admired Delphine's resolve to fight back, she wondered what power they would have to wield against this man. As a senior member of the Anglican church, with influential friends, at present Esme could not fathom a way to avoid the threats.

"Why is he doing this?" asked Aelwen as Esme placed a sleepy Theodore in the cot by the fireplace and turned again to the newspaper.

"He wants Theo," replied Esme, "the male heir."

"The man is mad," Aelwen snorted.

"Quite possibly," agreed Esme, "but he is also powerful. He will do everything he can to secure my son."

"Do you think he's the one who has had your sister arrested?" asked Aelwen, nodding towards the newspaper.

"Without a doubt," replied Esme, but another realisation was creeping over her. As she once again faced the intrusion of the Barons in her life, the cruel bullies who felt they could do as they chose — delivering threats, planning murders and terrifying anyone they wished to destroy with impunity — she realised that her strength had returned. She was ready to fight her corner to defeat her enemies and protect those she loved, no matter the cost to herself.

CHAPTER FOUR

Esme sat in the first-class compartment of the train, Theodore asleep on the seat between her and Aelwen, their chaperone, sitting opposite them, reading a newspaper. When Esme had suggested she and Theodore travel alone, Meredith had given her a look which broached no argument but, at the same time, made Esme giggle. Having come to know Meredith, she had discovered a kind and loving heart under his austere demeanour.

"You will travel with Aelwen and with Mr Noah Attwater," he had told her.

"Who?"

"Noah is married to my younger sister, Hannah, and he lives not far from here at a house called Cliffside. He's a respectable businessman and makes the journey between Pembrokeshire and London on a regular basis. He will take you to The Firebird."

"And Aelwen?"

"She will stay with the Attwaters until such time as we feel it is proper for her to return."

Noah Attwater proved to be an interesting and charming travel companion and, despite Esme's bitter feelings at being forced to have a chaperone, his presence proved useful.

They were not long into the journey when a large man loomed at the entrance to their compartment. With a racing heart, Esme clasped Theodore to her, fearing it was Osgood Baron. Noah blocked the entrance, ushering the man away by explaining that more family members were boarding at the next stop. The large man backed down, but not before his eager eyes roamed between Esme and Aelwen with disappointment.

"Men like him give the rest of us a terrible reputation," said Noah, seeing the panic in Esme's eyes and trying to comfort her by making light of the situation, but as he reclaimed his seat, Esme noticed his white knuckles and clenched fists.

Noah Attwater delivered Esme and Theodore to The Firebird without further incident. After hugging Aelwen goodbye, Esme was welcomed into the arms of the people she considered her real family, the men, women and children who had been part of her life since her childhood. She and Lynette stared at each other in wonder, each holding their baby for the other to admire.

"The Skylark Sisters and Sons," laughed Lynette as she bounced Theodore on her knee while Esme cuddled Nicholas Hardy.

"Don't say that anywhere near either of our fathers," laughed Jeremiah. "Your dad will be writing the music, Lyn, and mine will be working out the dance steps!"

"It's good to be home," said Esme as the theatrical world tumbled around her in all its colour and wonder. "Have you heard from Aaron?" she added, trying to keep her tone light.

"Not for a while," said Jeremiah. "He dropped in to see Ma a few months ago. There's something you need to know, Smee."

"He's married," Esme replied. "I saw the announcement in *The Times*."

"His wife was expecting a baby when we saw him," said Lynette, her tone as gentle as she could manage. "She was near her term. I'm sorry, Smee."

"I can't really complain, can I?" Esme said as Theodore gave a wail of hunger. She wondered if that was the reason Aaron had not responded to her summons. "Patience Gale got her wish, then."

"Patience Gale? The woman with the annoying laugh?" asked Lynette. "Aaron's marriage to her was annulled. Aaron's married to Lady Jessica Courtenay."

Esme stared at Lynette in astonishment. For the first time, she wondered if perhaps her bond with Aaron was finally broken. Had he truly fallen in love with another?

A week later, a letter arrived. Esme was in Rosie's dressing room with Theodore, minding Nicholas while Lynette rehearsed. She was singing them a simple tune, encouraging them to clap their hands when Cornelius entered, followed by Rosie. Both of their faces were ashen.

"What's happened?" Esme asked.

Cornelius held out the heavy blue paper and Esme felt fear clutch her heart as she recognised the cramped handwriting:

Dear Esme, you have a simple choice, deliver the Baron heir to our London address or your sister will hang. We have it in our power to clear her name. Yours, Osgood Baron.

"No," Esme exclaimed.

"What are we to do?" wailed Cornelius.

Rosie squeezed her husband's hand and pushed him onto the chaise, where Nicholas reached towards him, distracting him, before turning to Esme. "You will not be handing Theo to anyone, not even for Cassie's sake," said Rosie.

"But Ma, she'll hang," said Esme. "These are the men who murdered my father."

"You will reply to this man and tell him if he wishes to see you, it will be on your terms and it will be here. Only then will you discuss his threat."

"It's a daring card to play."

"True, but I suspect he'll accept. This is a man who admires a protagonist who is ready to challenge and play his game of cat and mouse. If you notice, he hasn't included a date or time. He's expecting you to negotiate."

"Very well," replied Esme, and together they composed a short reply inviting Osgood to The Firebird the following day.

'I'm Going to Catch the Eye of the Tsar' was playing when Osgood Baron walked on to the stage where Esme was waiting. Theodore and Nicholas were both absent from the theatre, being cared for by Lynette. Esme knew there was a multitude of people in the wings ready to rush her aid, should it be required.

Rosie escorted Osgood centre stage, then stood a few steps behind Esme.

"Where is the Baron heir?" boomed Osgood, refusing to look at Esme.

"His name is Theodore and he is not here," replied Esme, her voice clear while her heart pounded.

"Child, I am not here to negotiate," said Osgood with a sneer. "You have two days to deliver the boy to the Baron London home in Piccadilly or your sister will end her life at the end of the hangman's noose. Her death will not be the end; we will destroy everyone you care about, one by one, until you are alone. However, if you hand me my grandson, your family will be safe."

Esme felt the words forming in her mind, threatening to fly out of her mouth like furies, to tell Osgood that Theodore was not his grandson, that he was not Crispin's father, but she did not want him to unleash his wrath on Priscilla or Bolter.

"My eldest son and I will await your response," Osgood continued, "although, if I were you, I shouldn't think about it for too long. Not while poor Cassandra's life is in your hands. Tick tock, little Songbird." Osgood turned around and stalked away.

"Songbird was your mother's stage name," said Rosie, holding Esme's arm and preventing her from following Osgood. "We must be careful."

"I'm going to kill him," said Jeremiah, marching from the wings, his face puce with fury. "No one comes into our theatre and threatens us."

"Calm down," snapped Rosie. "We'll think of something."

Esme looked at her adopted mother but for the first time, the indomitable Rosie looked shaken. "I'm going to fetch the boys," said Esme.

"I'll come with you," said Jeremiah.

The pavements were heaving with people as they pushed their way through the side door. It was a hot afternoon and the shops were crowded. Esme preferred it this way. It was easier to lose yourself in a crowd. Lynette's parents had a house not far away in Greek Street. Walking as quickly as the crowds would allow, desperate to feel Theodore in her arms, she did not see when two men intercepted them, blocking her from Jeremiah's view. It happened in an instant. One moment Esme was forcing her way between sightseers and shoppers, the next she was being lifted from her feet. A sting on her neck made her cry out. The world blurred and one name rose to her lips, the name of the person who she felt sure could help her, if he had not forsaken her forever.

"Aaron…" she whispered before everything went black.

CHAPTER FIVE

The tiny piece of stone scratched the finest of lines on the wall, but it was enough. A mark for each day, a record of her life, to prove she was here, breathing, fighting to survive.

"Twenty-one days," murmured Esme, running her fingers over the marks.

These faint scratches were her spell of protection, her promise she would escape this hell. Esme huddled in the corner of her cell, staring around the miserable space. For three weeks she had been incarcerated here with a straw mattress filled with lice, fleas and things she did not want to think about; her skin raw with bites and sores, her hair lank around her face and the rough wool of the grey dress offering no protection against the chill damp of the air. Even her boots had been taken from her, replaced with shoes with holes to allow the damp to seep inside, freezing her to the bone.

When she had awoken, furious with Osgood Baron for kidnapping her in such an underhand manner, but angrier with herself for not realising he would take drastic action, she had rattled the door and screamed for help, but no one had responded. For a day and a night, she had been left alone, until as the grey fingers of dawn pushed their way through the slit of a window at the top of one wall, a hatch in the door had opened and a tray of watery gruel had been shoved inside. Esme had fallen on it, gulping it down, both desperate for sustenance and revolted by the gloopy, greasy mess.

It was then she began marking the wall, determined to retain her sanity in this battle of wills with Osgood Baron. The small hope which kept her fighting was the knowledge that

Theodore had not been at the theatre and with luck, Lynette, Jeremiah, Rosie and Cornelius would have whisked him away to safety. Any alternatives were too dreadful to contemplate.

"He is safe," she whispered to herself each day. "Theo is safe."

As for the rest of her family, she had no idea. Where was Cassie? Was she somewhere nearby in a similar cell? Had Osgood carried out his threat and had her executed? She knew neither Rosie nor Cornelius would agree to Osgood's insane orders to swap Theodore for Cassie. And yet...? As time passed, Esme wondered. Would they forget about her and save Cassie? In moments of hope, she knew this was impossible, but in the dark hours of night, of which there were so many, fear stole around her, like the noxious stench from the Thames on a summer day.

She would push these thoughts aside, focusing instead on other things: naming the cards in the Tarot pack; reciting every play she could remember from the repertoire from both her travelling days and those at The Firebird; counting to 500 forwards and backwards and forwards again until she sank into an uneasy slumber. In the hours when sleep eluded even these devices, her mind would roam unchallenged to dark places, down corridors of shadows, into the corners where the demons crouched, each a smaller, blacker oubliette until she came to the most sinister of all, the place marking Aaron's betrayal.

When she had fled from the Barons, leaving the cryptic messages for him, she had expected he would follow but he had never appeared. Perhaps the message had never reached him, perhaps he did not understand it, or perhaps he no longer cared...

Whenever this thought sliced through her, it felt like ice on her skin, scalding and freezing in one terrible touch. The loss of Aaron was debilitating in ways she could never have imagined, engulfing her in intense despair, absorbing her soul, her heart, her very essence of being, leaving no room for anything to exist except the pain.

Love, decided Esme, *is a quicksilver emotion. Beautiful and creative; cruel and destructive. A madness, untameable and capricious but able to be caring, healing and more powerfully good than any other force in the universe.* "No wonder we will kill for it," she murmured. "No wonder we will risk all. When the madness of love strikes, we no longer care. We reach out for the soothing, golden feeling that permeates the soul and leaves us with the clarity of that pure moment of belonging, of knowing nothing can harm us again, nothing, that is, except losing love. To regain it, to feel its golden light, we will gladly fight to the death."

Aaron had married Lady Jessica Courtenay and they had a child. *But I married Crispin*, she thought, *and had Theo, and it hasn't changed my love for Aaron, so perhaps his love for me remains untarnished.*

Esme realised that to give in to her fears was what Osgood desired. Instead, she would fight back. The thing that had most upset Osgood was her voice and so, one day, she decided to sing, a task she repeated each day. This morning, leaning back against the slimy wall, Esme closed her eyes, thinking of the people she loved and as the ghosts of their laughter reached her, she gave full flow to her extraordinary voice.

"There's Russia in the air,
Bears, snow, the dream of romance
A fairy-tale prince walking the streets
I'm going to catch the eye of the Tsar…
Palaces of gold, gemstones galore

Sleigh bells ringing as the Cossacks dance
A fairy-tale prince walking the streets
I'm going to catch the eye of the Tsar…
Dancing at the summer ball,
In the red and gold where Moscow calls
A fairy-tale prince walking the streets
I'm going to catch the eye of the Tsar…
We'll twirl through the white nights,
Entwined in love and lost in dreams,
My fairy-tale prince walking the streets
I'm going to catch the eye of the Tsar…'

As the final note died, her cell door slammed open. Esme screamed, curling into a defensive ball.

"Miss Maclean?"

A young woman was standing before her. She was tall with a wide, blue-eyed gaze and a sweet face.

"Peggy," gasped Esme, and the girl's face creased into a broad smile.

"You know, Miss, it always amused me that we maids were all called Peggy at Mr Maclean's house, but it is actually my name."

It was few moments before Esme could gather her wits to form a sentence. "What are you doing here?" she whispered.

"Mrs Levison placed me here a few days ago," replied Peggy in her lilting Irish accent as she pushed the door shut. "It's a temporary position."

"You're in touch with Mrs Levison?"

"Yes…"

"What about Mr Maclean?"

"Not directly, but Mrs Levison passes on my messages. She's his step-grandmother. They're very close."

Aaron had never mentioned his personal connection to Mrs Levison, but Esme had often noticed Mrs Levison huddled with Aaron, chatting in a conspiratorial manner, and now she understood. She reached her hand out to Peggy. "I must get a message to Aaron or to my parents, to find my son," she said. "Can you help?"

"Of course," Peggy replied. "Why do you think I'm here? We've been helping your family search every gaol in the country trying to find you. After the trumped-up trial convicting you of child abduction and you being sentenced to life imprisonment, Mr Maclean has been fair mad with worry."

"What trial?"

"It was a sham, Miss, brought about by Osgood Baron. Did you realise he visited Aaron's club as The Bishop with his friend The Judge? Vile creatures. Well, The Bishop died a few weeks ago of apoplexy but his friend The Judge, who really is a judge, so it seems, insisted you be punished and brought someone else to the dock, posing as you, and sentenced you to life imprisonment."

Esme stared at Peggy. "Osgood Baron is dead?" she whispered.

Peggy nodded.

"And The Judge?"

"Alive, but you don't need to worry about him anymore. Mr Maclean has dealt with him. Do you remember the photographs? The ones he took at the evenings in the basement?"

"Yes," said Esme. The images were scorched on her mind. The Judge and The Bishop prancing naked, the lewd dance, the acts which had shocked Lynette to speechlessness. All these, captured by Aaron and his staff on the photography plates.

"Mr Maclean had a quiet word with The Judge, showed him the photographs and suggested he might want to rethink your trial and the accusations made against you, as everyone knew they were false."

"Aaron did that for me?"

"Oh yes, Miss, he's been demented with worry. He wrote and wrote to you after you sent him the list of your Tarot cards, but you never replied."

"He wrote...? But I didn't receive any letters," she whispered, then realisation dawned. Despite thinking she was hidden, it was apparent that Osgood Baron had known her location, but rather than follow her to Pembrokeshire, he had bided his time. It would not take much to bribe a Post Office worker to steal Aaron's letter; his distinctive writing with the capital 'R's scattered through his words would have been easy to spot. This had all been part of Osgood Baron's plan to hurt her by making her think Aaron had betrayed and forgotten her. Priscilla Baron's words returned: *He will discover what you love, and he will use this to destroy you.* Yet, Osgood Baron was dead and his plan had failed. Aaron had not forsaken her; instead, he had used every device available to him to save her.

"Anyway," continued Peggy, "The Judge was angry at first, then Mr Maclean explained he had the support of a powerful newspaper magnate who was willing to publish the images as well as the story of the parties in the basement..."

"Uncle Wallace?" gasped Esme.

"Yes, Miss, he and Lady Helena have been helping the search, too. The Judge agreed to exonerate you of all charges but the only trouble was, no one knew where Osgood Baron had sent you."

"Where am I?"

"You're in Cornwall, Miss. Bodmin Gaol. I'm so glad I'm the one to have found you. I always loved listening to you sing when you were living with Mr Maclean. The Russian song was always my favourite, so when I heard it, I knew it must be you and you were safe at last." Peggy beamed and pulled Esme into an enormous hug.

"My son? Theo?" Esme said, tears welling in her eyes as she realised her incarceration was over. "Where's my son?"

"With your parents, quite safe," said Peggy.

"And my sister, Cassie, Viscountess Blanchard?"

"Back with her husband."

"He's alive?"

"Oh yes, Miss, there was quite a bother when he came back to England. He'd been abroad, to France, I think they said. When he returned and discovered what was happening, he summoned Osgood Baron to him and demanded an explanation. It was while that horrible man was trying to talk his way out of the mess he'd made that he collapsed and died. Your sister was being held by Osgood's son at their house in Much Wenlock. The viscount went straight there, and the son has been arrested too. I'm not sure what's happened to him, but Mr Maclean said it would be dealt with. I've never seen Mr Maclean so angry; it was terrible to behold, Miss, that it was." Peggy glanced over her shoulder; footsteps indicated another warder was on their way. "I'm going to have to lock the door, but don't you fret, Miss. You'll be home in no time."

Mrs Levison was the person who arrived to escort Esme to freedom. Her stern face crumpled with despair when she saw the meanness of the cell and Esme's dishevelled state.

"Don't you worry about a thing," she said, fighting back her tears before taking Esme's arm and leading her along the dark, labyrinthine corridors, into a waiting carriage. "We've sent for Aaron and he's bringing Theo."

They drove to a large white house, where Esme was washed, deloused and dressed in a clean, crisp nightdress.

"Sleep," Mrs Levison said, tucking her into a wide, soft bed. "All will be well in the morning."

"Are you really Aaron's grandmother?" Esme asked.

"I was his grandfather's housekeeper," Mrs Levison said. "Peter Maclean was a good man. He protected me from my drunken husband. We never married but we lived together and were accepted by our community. Aaron was a boy who needed a great deal of love and we provided it. When Peter died, Aaron and I decided to sell the business and we've been looking after each other ever since."

Her words soothed Esme to sleep and when she awoke the next morning, Peggy was once more at her side. She encouraged Esme into a crimson dress, arranging her hair in a simple but elegant style.

Esme made her way downstairs and Peggy settled her in the Morning Room, where a fire blazed. To Esme's amazement, her bible with the hollowed-out centre and the volume of poetry from Aaron's house were on the occasional table beside her chair. Opening the bible, she saw a battered piece of paper on top of her Tarot cards and recognised it as the note she had sent to Aaron listing the six Tarot cards: *Death*, *The Tower*, *The Empress*, *Nine of Cups*, *Ten of Coins*, *The Star*. Lifting it out, with her familiar cards, she saw written in the hollowed-out section, in Aaron's distinctive script, these names repeated like a prayer.

"New beginnings, changes, the mother figure, love, family and hope," she murmured.

Replacing them, she picked up the poetry book and smiled — written inside the cover were both their names. Esme flicked to her favourite poem and allowed the words to flow around her, thinking of all they represented, when the door clicked open and she heard a cry.

Her heart leapt and she was on her feet, tears in her eyes as she saw him, saw them. Aaron stood in the doorway, holding Theodore. A sob escaped from Esme as she ran towards them, taking the weight of her son in her arms, breathing in his baby scent, squeezing him so tightly he squawked in protest. As Aaron's arms enclosed them both, his tears dropping in her hair as he sobbed with relief, she leaned into him, Theodore between them.

"You're the only woman I will ever love," he whispered, his voice cracking.

"You're the only man I will ever love," she replied.

"I love you, Esme Blood," he said, kissing her. "I have come for you as you told me I would, and I will never leave you."

Tears of joy, relief and delight were coursing down Esme's cheeks as she returned his kisses over the head of her protesting son. "I love you, too, Aaron Maclean, and I will never leave you again, either."

PART NINE: PEMBROKESHIRE, 2020

CHAPTER ONE

Eleanor hugged the diary to her, tears streaming down her face. "Oh Esme," she whispered, "you and Aaron found each other at last."

Love, she thought, *will I ever find it again?* Eleanor's mind flitted towards Arthur. Arthur, from whom she had not heard for two weeks. Arthur, who, according to Aidan, had returned home to Cornwall without saying goodbye.

"For good?" she had asked.

"I don't think so," Aidan had replied, "but as we're quiet, it seemed a good idea for him to have some time off. Anyway, he won't be here forever, will he? He'll be off on tour in some play, I expect."

Aidan spoke the words without knowing the pain he caused, as these were thoughts she, too, had acknowledged, although if the list was correct and one of the men on it was Arthur's father, then he might be in their lives for longer than they had imagined.

For the past few days, Eleanor had been in hospital for treatment, and it had left her feeling tired. The reaction varied — after some visits she would bounce back within hours, but at other times it took a few days. Apart from checking for any urgent orders, she had decided to spend a few days resting, which had been the ideal time to finish reading Esme's story.

Placing the final diary on the table, Eleanor gathered together all the belongings of Esme's she had accumulated, including the photographs which had begun her quest. Looking at the image of Esme wearing the spectacular peacock feather dress made her smile — she was still amazed that she had discovered the real thing. Eleanor hoped Esme would approve of her decision to allow the dresses to be displayed at the exhibition in The Mary Fitzroy Heritage Centre.

"They're dazzling," Piper had said. "They may not be perfect, but who wants that? These were worn; they were used for performances. Who knows what tales they could tell?"

"What tales indeed?" said Eleanor to Sandy, who had sauntered in through the open front door. He narrowed his eyes at her and fled to the bedroom. "What had happened in the end?" she mused.

Opening the letter she had discovered inside Adelaide, Eleanor read Aaron's words again, this time with more understanding:

My Darling Esme,

We were always star-crossed, but our love has never been in doubt. You are my wife in all but name. You have owned my heart, my soul since we were children, now we have a child of our own and my love will always protect you both. You may not be able to wear this ring legally, but I want you to have it as a pledge of my lifelong love for you,

Aaron

Both were married to other people, so who was the child of their own? She remembered the list of names in the poetry anthology, and she read them aloud: "*Aaron, Theodore, Poppaea, Crispin, Bill, Delphine, Harriet, Elizabeth.*" She had mentally ticked off each person until she reached the final name. "Elizabeth? Was she Esme and Aaron's child?"

Reaching for her laptop, she was about to open a genealogy website when Anne knocked on and opened her front door. "Ellie, I have a surprise for you."

Eleanor looked up; having grown up with people wandering into each other's houses, announcing themselves with a cheery, "Hiya," it did not seem odd or intrusive that her mother would not ring her doorbell. It was one of the things she had missed when living in Richmond: the unexpected visitor. "What's that, Mum?" she replied, smiling.

"Look who's here!"

"Uncle Steve!" Eleanor struggled to her feet but before she could make it across the room, the man had reached her in two strides and pulled her into a tight hug. He released her, staring into her face, his eyes brimming with concern.

"Your mum said you've been in hospital," he said.

"It's a regular occurrence, Uncle Steve. We're all going to have to adapt."

Steve Evans was of medium height, stockily built, with close cropped silver-grey hair. His blue eyes stood out in his suntanned face, a deep brown from working in the Middle East in the oil industry. When the refineries in Milford Haven had begun to close, Steve had been one of the first to take his chances abroad and the gamble had paid off, providing him with a comfortable income. He had met his wife, Inez, while he was abroad and they were the proud parents to three daughters: Jacquetta, Maisie and Joanna.

Having grown up a few doors away from John, Steve considered Newgale to be his home. Close friends since boyhood, Steve had been best man at Eleanor's parents' wedding and he had always taken his role as her godfather seriously, never forgetting a birthday or Christmas, writing her long letters and sending photographs from the many countries he had worked in.

"What's going on here?" Steve asked. "Your mum said you were resting."

"I am," she replied. "This is pleasure, not work — it's the historical research I've been doing, including the family tree."

Eleanor sat down and Steve pulled up the chair beside her. The photographs were spread across the table, and Steve's eyes moved to the image of Esme in her peacock feather dress.

"Who's she?"

"Esme Blood, an ancestor. She's connected to us through the Attwaters from Cliffside."

"Cliffside over near Nolton Haven? Eddie Stone's place?"

"The same."

Eleanor outlined Esme's tale, finishing with the discovery of the dress in the photograph.

"Strange," Steve said, staring at the picture. "She looks familiar. Did you ever have this on show?"

"Not as far as I know. They were Gran's. We'd never seen them before." Sorting through her pages of research, Eleanor found an image from a small piece she had discovered online, captioned *Esme Blood, Music Hall singer*. "This is a bit clearer," she said, pushing it towards him.

As he stared at it, Steve looked puzzled. "She definitely looks like someone I've met, but I can't place it. Must be my age," he sighed. "Right, love, we're coming to Sunday dinner, so I'll see you in a few days, although Inez might pop in with the kids. Until then, you take care."

Eleanor walked him out into the front garden. It adjoined the farmyard where her father was climbing down from his tractor. Potter and Webby, the two border collies came dancing towards Steve and Eleanor, barking in excitement.

"Good to see you, Si," John said, embracing Steve.

"You too, Maxy-Boy!"

"Anne's invited us for Sunday lunch."

"I'd better get a few crates of wine in, then!"

Amid much laughter, Steve climbed into his car and with a cheerful toot of his horn, drove away. As Eleanor headed back to her annexe, her phone buzzed with a message from Briony: *I've got loads of stuff about Esme from Mark to show you this evening. Sheba and Gabe are home for a few days, so she's coming too.*

A shiver of anticipation ran through Eleanor as she wondered whether Mark had discovered the end of the story.

"We've brought wine and crisps," announced Briony when she and Bathsheba arrived a few hours later.

"And a box folder," said Eleanor, looking at the bag on Briony's shoulder.

"Yes, from Mark."

In return for Eleanor agreeing to display the dresses in the museum, Mark had enlisted some of his team to help with her research, with others in the process of transcribing the diaries.

Eleanor opened the wine, pouring out glasses while her friends arranged themselves at the dining room table. Adelaide was seated on one of the armchairs, watching. Eleanor felt she was a connection to Esme, and while she was there, nothing bad could happen.

"Tell us all," said Bathsheba, shovelling a handful of crisps into her mouth.

Eleanor explained what she had discovered in the diaries. When she had finished, Briony stared at the pages around her.

"I think these might fill in some of the gaps," she said. "Mark's numbered them." She passed the first page to Eleanor. "He's discovered that Esme had another child…"

"A daughter?" asked Eleanor.

"Yes, but Mark isn't sure who to claim as her father, because her name was Elizabeth Rose Maclean Baron." Briony looked to Eleanor, hoping she could elucidate.

"Elizabeth's father was Aaron Maclean," said Eleanor, showing her friends the letter, "but Esme was still married to Crispin Baron, so perhaps to spare Elizabeth from being illegitimate, they used Crispin's surname and added Aaron's surname, Maclean, as a middle name. Esme's mother did the same with her."

"Is this why Esme and Aaron couldn't marry?" asked Bathsheba.

"It must be," said Eleanor. "Aaron was also still married to Lady Jessica Courtenay, who suffered from severe mental health problems."

"People were restricted in so many difficult ways back then," said Bathsheba. "The law was against everyone except the rich."

"What do you mean?" asked Eleanor.

"It's sad Esme and Aaron couldn't divorce their partners and marry each other."

Briony riffled through the pages in front of her and passed several printouts to Eleanor. "These are the census records for the Baron family," she said.

The top page gave a summary of the Baron family after Osgood's death.

"This is wonderful," Eleanor exclaimed. "Priscilla Baron was able to marry her long-term lover, Percival Bolter."

"Lover?" said Briony.

"Not only lover," grinned Eleanor, "but father of her two younger children, Crispin and Delphine. He lived at Baron Hall and was the Head Gardener."

"Very Lady Chatterley," said Bathsheba. "Did she keep it quiet so she wouldn't be thrown out and lose her home?"

"Hardly — the money and house were hers," said Eleanor. "According to the census records, prior to it being named

Baron Hall after her marriage to Osgood, it was called Hargreaves Hall for several centuries, which was Priscilla Baron's maiden name."

"What happened to the rest of the family?"

Eleanor scanned the pages, grinning as she read the fates of Delphine, Dilys and the girls.

"Delphine married Gawain Blood and they had four children; Dilys also remarried — I wonder what happened to Absolom? — and she had two sons." Flicking through the images, she stopped at one of an elaborate memorial in a church. "Look," she said, passing it over, "*To Dilys Wentworth, beloved wife of Roderick Wentworth, Esq. Mother to Eve, Ruth, Mary, Harriet, Roderick and Samuel.* Let's hope her second marriage was genuinely loving."

"If she married again, what happened to her first husband?" asked Bathsheba, topping up their glasses.

Eleanor read further down and grimaced. "He was arrested after the death of his father and he hanged himself rather than face the ignominy of going to trial."

"How awful," said Briony. "What about Esme's husband, Crispin?"

"Mark's written: *Finding Crispin was more of a challenge, but we tracked him down in Wester Ross in the northwest Highlands of Scotland. He lived in an old sixteenth-century hunting lodge with a variety of staff including Donald Clements. Harriet Baron was staying with them in the 1891 census, but she was listed as 'Daughter', which I think might be an error. He lived here until 1902, when he died from throat cancer.*" Eleanor smiled — the diaries had explained this strange anomaly, and Mark's facts mixed with Esme's tale explained the oddities of the lives of the Barons.

"Do you think Esme stayed in touch with Crispin?" asked Bathsheba.

"Probably, as he was Theo's father," said Eleanor, "the longed-for son and heir. Do we know what happened to him? There's nothing here about him or Harriet."

Briony checked Mark's list. "Harriet Baron is on page five and Theodore Baron is next, here." She passed over some more paperwork.

"Harriet Baron married Sir Peregrine Talbot in 1897 and in the 1901 census they have a son, Gerald. By 1911, they have three children, but there isn't much else, and Theo —" Eleanor put out her hand and Briony passed her the printout — "is always listed with his mother and Aaron at their house in Soho Square, with Elizabeth and Poppaea. By 1911, he's living at the renamed Hargreaves Hall, which he must have inherited when Crispin died. He's married to Lady Persephone Blanchard, who is Cassie's youngest daughter. I bet they were terrified of telling their parents they'd fallen in love."

"But weren't they cousins?" asked Briony.

"Not by blood. Cassie and Aaron were cousins, but there was no blood connection to Esme or Theo," said Eleanor.

"Is that everyone?"

"Dilys's three daughters all married and had children," said Briony, but after a cursory glance, Eleanor put these to one side.

"The question is, what happened to Esme and Aaron?" Eleanor said, disappointed to see there were no more printouts.

"Which is a question I am not at liberty to answer, because Mark said it's a surprise for the preview of the Victorian wing of the museum," said Briony.

"I could look it up myself," said Eleanor.

"Please don't," said Briony, her eyes sparkling. "Mark has found a few things, but he needs to check them before he tells you."

Eleanor looked at Bathsheba, who grinned conspiratorially. "Fine, I'll wait," she said, forcing a smile, but as they cleared away the paperwork and moved to the sofa, Eleanor felt a wave of disappointment. She was desperate to discover what had happened to Esme and Aaron after her release from gaol.

CHAPTER TWO

Eleanor tied the string around the final box and stood back to admire her handiwork. A rush of orders had kept her busy over the past few days, as had a series of online auctions, where she had been delighted to secure some beautiful vintage clothing. Looking around the barn, she grinned. With the door open and the summer breeze blowing in the scent of home, Eleanor felt contentment suffuse her.

It had been eighteen months since she had become ill, and her life had changed in ways she could never have imagined but, at last, she was at peace with all that had happened. While she did not subscribe to the belief that illness can be a gift — there was too much darkness involved for her to ever be grateful for the changes it had wrought — she was aware that life was good. For the first time since her legs had given way on that terrible night, she felt she had options, and that her life would continue in a way of her own choosing.

Her father appeared in the doorway. "How are you doing with the parcels?" he asked.

"Finished," she replied. "Are you sure you don't mind sending them, Dad?"

"Your Mum and I are going into town anyway, so it's no problem, and you'll be here for the auction."

"Thanks, you're the best," she said, hugging her father.

"Best Dad Ever," he said, kissing the top of her head. "I have the mug telling me so — Aidan bought it for me, remember."

Eleanor giggled; the mug was a hideous monstrosity, but it was a family joke that had been running for years.

An hour later, the auction was over, and Eleanor had bought several dresses and a number of hats from the 1920s. With a quiet afternoon ahead, she wondered if there was another diary of Esme's somewhere in the barn that would finish the story, or even the battered remains of the note Esme had sent to Aaron listing the Tarot cards. She suspected this had long been lost to the mists of time. There were five boxes which she had not yet had time to unpack. Gathering up Adelaide, who she felt might act as a supernatural magnet and draw her previous owner's belongings to her, she wandered to the rear of the barn.

Snapping on some protective gloves, Eleanor began to sort through the boxes. The first presented surprises of its own: four entangled necklaces, followed by a pile of chiffon scarves and below them, three parcels of silk. She put them all aside, deciding to offer them to Piper in case they might be useful for one of the displays at the museum.

The next three boxes contained a jumbled collection of old pantomime costumes and programmes from the 1960s and 1980s. Reaching for the final box, Eleanor braced herself for disappointment. Ripping off the parcel tape, she reached inside and pulled out a pile of theatrical programmes. As she touched them, a shiver ran down her spine.

"The Firebird," she gasped, tracing her fingers over the emblem, familiar from the poster in her kitchen. "I knew it. I knew they were here somewhere."

Leaning over the box, she began to sort through the stacks of programmes, her fingers tingling with each layer she removed. Finally, when she had them all laid around her in a giant circle, she saw a wooden box bearing The Firebird emblem at the bottom of the box.

"What have we here, Adelaide?" she said, her voice brimming with excitement.

The box was heavy, and she needed both hands to lift it out. Placing it on the chair she had put beside her, she pulled herself into a standing position and opened it. Inside were old-fashioned gramophone records in paper sleeves. With trembling hands, she took out the first one and, as she read the label, felt a burst of happiness: *I'm Going to Catch the Eye of the Tsar, Performed by The Skylark Sisters (Esme Blood and Lynette Hardy). Musical arrangement: Marcus Mason.*

Eleanor stared in incredulity. It had never occurred to her that there could be a recording of Esme singing. She thought such things were later than the Victorian era, yet here they were, captured forever. Moving to her packing table at the front of the barn, Eleanor laid the records out, five of which bore Esme's name. Two were as The Skylark Sisters with Lynette, two were by Esmerelda Blood, then, to her surprise one label read: *Esme Blood and her daughter, Elizabeth, the Miniature Songbird.*

"Elizabeth," she gasped. Reaching for her phone, she dialled Nick's number. "Talk to me about early gramophone records," she said when he answered.

"Hello to you too," he replied. "What gramophone records?"

As she explained what she had discovered, Nick's enthusiasm rose to match hers.

"I'll speak to Giovanni; he must know someone. Package them up and I'll send a courier to collect them. Esme will sing again."

Giovanni was a music professor at Roehampton University, and his specialism was early recorded music.

Hanging up, Eleanor returned to the programmes left strewn across the floor, determined to delve into the world of The

Firebird. Moving back to her packing table, which was far larger than her desk, she replaced the records in their wooden box and sorted the programmes into chronological order.

Skimming through the first pages, she found advertisements for everything from soap to photographic services. A thrill rushed through her when she found a cast list for *Romeo and Juliet, A Rollicking Romance written by William Shakespeare and Cornelius Hardy*, which made her laugh. It seemed Cornelius had been determined to give all the Shakespearian tragedies a happy ending. She read Lynette's name alongside those of Jeremiah, Rosie and Cornelius Hardy, and Isaac Cooke, who, Eleanor thought, must have been the Isaac for whom Tilly had nurtured a soft spot. These people felt real to her, as though she had lived the adventure with them.

She was beginning to give up hope of finding Esme's name when she picked up a programme dated September 1888. This time, the cast list was for a revival of *The Ticket-of-Leave Man* by Tom Taylor, a melodrama first performed in 1863. At the top of the cast list were Mrs Lynette Hardy and Mr Jeremiah Hardy. At the bottom of the page there was an advertisement with a sketch of two women. The words read: *By special request, Mrs Esme Baron and the Viscountess Cassandra Blanchard will revive their successful double act for the delight of their fans and for their parents, Rose and Cornelius Hardy. Sponsored by Aaron Maclean Esquire.*

"Esme, you went back," she laughed. "You performed with Cassie. You forgave her."

Eleanor could not describe why this reunion filled her with such intense elation. Despite everything, Esme, Cassie, Lynette, Jeremiah and Aaron had been reunited in a special performance for Rosie and Cornelius.

She was distracted from her discovery by the sound of footsteps. She looked up, expecting to see her father, but her heart began to thud when she saw Arthur framed in the doorway.

"Hello," he said, his tone hesitant. "You have every reason to tell me to leave. I shouldn't have vanished in the way I did, but things were confusing."

Eleanor stared at him for a moment before her brain caught up. "Come in," she said, her voice soft. "You don't owe me an explanation."

Relief washed over his face as he joined her by the packing table. "Perhaps," he said, "but the way things have been between us has been difficult. I asked you to trust me, and I hope you can continue to a little longer. Soon, everything will be made clear."

Eleanor's heart was pounding. Had he found his father? Were they related? Her mind travelled to Esme and Bill, their disastrous engagement and Esme's subsequent marriage. While she was not about to do anything as desperate, it continued to concern her that her reaction to Arthur was as intense now as it had been on the beach. A feeling of knowing, trusting, the completion of herself. Was that love, or her genes recognising their own? A family connection, rather than romantic love? It was a moment before she realised Arthur was speaking.

"My intention had always been to spend a few weeks at home, but Mum was poorly again and I had to leave in a hurry. I'm so sorry…"

"Arthur, stop apologising," Eleanor said. "How's your mum?"

"Fine, thanks," he replied, then, noticing the pile of programmes, he added, "Sorry, am I disturbing you?"

There was a nervousness in his voice, a humility which made Eleanor want to hug him. Instead, she leaned forward and opened the box of gramophone records.

"Look what was in the last box — recordings of Esme singing," she said, unable to keep the excitement and delight from her voice. "Throughout my research it never occurred to me that I might be able to hear Esme. I thought the time period was too early, but I looked it up online and, apparently, the first commercial recordings were made as early as 1889. These were wax cylinders and the first gramophone, or phonograph records, as they were known then, were available commercially from the end of the nineteenth century. Nick's going to ask Giovanni if they can be digitised. I know he's cleaned up audio on other old records. We might actually be able to hear Esme sing." Her excitement bubbled at the thought of being able to listen to Esme and Lynette singing 'I'm Going to Catch the Eye of the Tsar'. "And these are programmes from The Firebird Theatre." She pushed them towards Arthur, and his face took on a curious, closed expression.

"Lynette and Jeremiah," he said, running his finger down the cast list. "You might be interested to hear that since I told my mum about your research, she's been inspired to research our family tree, too."

"Really?" said Eleanor. The familiar prickle of unease had returned, and she noticed Arthur's voice had become strained. Icy fingers traced down her spine as she said, "What did she find?"

"My grandmother's photos," he replied, "which have been in a box under the bed for as long as Mum can remember. She thought they'd be snaps from the 1950s and 60s, but many were a great deal older." He reached into his jacket pocket and pulled out a padded envelope, which he upended on the table, pushing the photographs towards Eleanor. Goosebumps ran up her arms as a different young woman in the peacock feather dress giggled at her from across time.

"Lynette," she gasped.

Arthur nodded. "And I think this is Jeremiah," he said, sorting through the images and passing one to Eleanor. It showed the same young woman, this time more formally dressed, standing beside a nervous-looking young man, who, even in the old black and white photograph, could be seen to have ruddy cheeks.

"Arthur, these are incredible," she gasped, staring at the images which felt familiar.

"There's this, too," he said, passing her a more battered image.

It was cracked and faded with age, but the people were visible. The formal portrait showed a woman with dark hair seated on an ornate chair, holding a small girl, who in turn held a doll. The child and doll were wearing matching clothes, outfits which Eleanor recognised because the doll was sitting not far from them in the dress from the photograph. Behind the woman, leaning on a half pillar, was a tall, good-looking man. On either side of the adults were three more children — a boy with dark hair flowing to his collar and wide eyes, who bore a startling resemblance to the woman; a slender girl, her demeanour shy, with light brown hair and a sweet face; and a smaller girl, who was the image of the man.

"Esme," Eleanor gasped. "It's Esme and Aaron."

"I thought it was but until you'd seen it, I didn't want to get my hopes up," he said. "The question is, who are the children?"

"The boy is Theodore Baron. The little girl on Esme's lap is probably Elizabeth — Esme and Aaron's daughter. The other girl, who looks like Aaron, is probably his daughter Poppaea, and I would guess the older child is Harriet Baron."

"Who?"

"Arthur, I have so much to tell you," Eleanor said, clicking on the kettle. "We could be a while."

By the time she had finished, Arthur was astounded. He was a good listener, she thought, reacting in the right places, keeping his interruptions to a minimum and embracing the story with whole-hearted enthusiasm.

"These are only a few of the pictures," he said. "There are more, and there's one of Esme in an evening gown wearing an incredible diamond necklace — perhaps it's one from their days in Kemptown."

"Perhaps," she replied, finishing her tea. "The question is, Arthur, why did your grandmother have a photograph of Esme Blood?"

Arthur did not reply. Instead, he pulled up an image on his phone and showed it to Eleanor. Looking back at her was Arthur with a woman. The woman reached his shoulder, and her eyes were a blue that was almost violet. Her dark hair was cut in a bob, streaked through with silver, and she and Arthur were laughing. "My mum, Wendy Pengally," he said.

Eleanor dropped the phone on the desk as though it were contaminated. "Oh God," she moaned. "Arthur, I know the truth. When I found your wallet on the beach, I dropped it by mistake and your stuff went all over the place. Sheba and I gathered it all together, but I saw... I saw your list. I'm so sorry."

"Why are you telling me this?" he asked, his face ashen.

"Look at the picture of your mum," she said. "Your mum is the image of Esme. You're clearly descended from her, we're both related to her, we're…" but she could not finish the sentence.

Arthur looked horrified. "Ellie," he said, his voice as tightly controlled as her own, "it's not what you think. I'm sorry you saw that list, but the reason I showed you this is because you're right, we do have shared ancestry. You're descended from the Blood family, and I'm descended from Elizabeth Maclean Baron and Nicholas Hardy. Esme and Aaron's daughter married Lynette and Jeremiah's son — I'm a direct descendant from Esme and Aaron."

In that instant, Eleanor saw his resemblance to Aaron — the golden hair, the sleepy brown eyes and the charm — but whereas Aaron, even in the battered photograph, exuded an air of devilment, Arthur was calmer, his daredevil behaviour taken from him on a stormy night long ago when he had lost control of a car.

"So we're related?" she whispered.

"We share ancestors," he said. "But this will come good."

"Come good?" she replied. "How?"

Arthur looked desperate. "Please," he said, "trust me?"

And, despite everything, as she looked into his brown eyes, she felt she could trust him with her life.

CHAPTER THREE

Noise, laughter and the occasional bark or miaow spilled from the farmhouse. Eleanor walked through the unlocked door from the annexe carrying a cauliflower cheese, while Chloe followed with a bowl of roast potatoes.

"Thanks, love," Anne called, as she and Inez strained the vegetables, "I don't know how we'd have cooked it all if we hadn't had your kitchen for overspill."

In the living room, John and Steve were opening bottles of wine and Aidan was playing Cluedo with Steve's three daughters.

"I'll put it in the dining room," Eleanor called, carrying it through and placing it on the hotplate. "Do you think Mum's done enough food?" she said to Chloe, who adopted a mock serious expression and looked at the groaning table.

"We could always make everyone a sandwich if there isn't enough," she replied.

Anne's Sunday roasts were legendary, and she always cooked enough for an army.

Aidan joined Eleanor and Chloe. "Ellie, I've been meaning to ask you, have you heard from Arthur lately?"

"Yes, he popped in a few days ago," she replied. "Is there something wrong?"

"I hope not," said Aidan, helping to load the food onto the table and point everyone to their seats. "He sent me an odd text, and I was a bit concerned." Aidan lowered his voice. "He said you knew about his —" he hesitated over the word — "accident and how he suffered from depression and anxiety afterwards."

"Yes," she replied.

"He's a decent bloke. If he was having trouble again, I'd want to help him."

"If he calls, I'll let you know," she said with a twinge of nervousness, wondering why Arthur had not gone back to work since his return to Newgale.

Two hours later, Eleanor thought she might never be able to eat again. As she walked into the kitchen with the pudding bowls, her phone buzzed. "Arthur," she said, moving into the living room where she would not be overheard.

"Ellie." His voice was tense. "Where are you? I'm at yours…"

"Come into Mum's. We've been having Sunday dinner; there's loads left if you're hungry."

"I think I've found my dad," he said in a rush. "See you in a sec."

Eleanor pushed her phone back into her pocket, her hands shaking. Surely, if it was her father, if they were related, he would not have sounded so delighted, but her heart was pounding as she hurried to the front door to let him in.

To her astonishment, Arthur grinned, before pulling her into his arms and kissing her, full on the mouth. After her initial shock, Eleanor responded, her stomach fluttering in excitement.

"I've been wanting to do that for so long," he said. "You've no idea, but I couldn't until I was positive. The results of my DNA test are back and, thanks to the database and the charity who have been helping me, I've found my father's name."

"Who is it?" asked Eleanor, her own excitement growing.

"A man called Steven Evans, and he's from Newgale. Can you believe it? I came to stay here because of Andrew, but I stumbled into the right village. I wondered if you or your parents knew him."

"Steven Evans?" Eleanor asked, her joy evaporating.

"Mum heard his mates calling him Si, so she thought his name might have been Simon, but it's Steven…"

"Si, short for psycho…" murmured Eleanor.

Suddenly, an ebullient voice said, "Somebody taking my name in vain?"

Eleanor turned to see her godfather in the doorway. Arthur leapt away from Eleanor.

"You didn't tell me you had a new boyfriend, Ellie," Steve said. "Let's hope he's not such a waste of space as the last one. I'm Eleanor's godfather, Steve Evans, and, believe me, I'm even more protective than her father."

Arthur stared at him in incredulity. "You're Steve Evans?" he asked.

Eleanor's eyes flickered from one to the other, watching as all colour drained from Arthur's face.

"Yes. Why? What's the matter?"

"Uncle Steve, you might want to sit down," said Eleanor. "This might be difficult. Arthur, you'd better tell him."

Clearing his throat, Arthur said, "Are you the Steve Evans who had a holiday fling with a girl calling herself Jamie?"

Steve stared at them as though they were mad, then recognition of the name filtered through his brain and he turned to Eleanor. "Jamie? Yes, that's it," he said. "Your picture, Ellie, the woman with the dark hair wearing the feather dress — she reminded me of Jamie."

Eleanor nudged Arthur, who pulled his phone from his pocket and showed Steve the photograph of his mother. Eleanor was suddenly aware of the silence; everyone was listening to their conversation.

Steve turned to Arthur. "Your mum?" Steve asked as he looked from Arthur to the picture, his voice serious as realisation dawned on his face. "What about your dad?"

"I've never known my dad," said Arthur. "Mum discovered she was pregnant a few weeks after she got home — my birth father was her holiday romance."

Eleanor moved to stand beside him, slipping her hand into his, offering moral support.

"Until now?" Steve phrased it as a question.

Arthur nodded and reached inside his jacket. He gave Steve an official-looking letter bearing the results of the DNA test. "You're on the database," Arthur said, his tone bordering on apologetic.

Steve unfolded the letter before handing it to Inez, who had appeared beside him. She leaned over, absorbing the information. "I put us on there," she said. "I wanted to trace our family trees; it seemed an interesting thing to do."

Steve turned to her, his face ashen. "I didn't know, Inez," he said. "We never even told each other our real names."

"Steve, it was years before we met," Inez said, soothing the panic in his voice. "It's a shock, but you've always wanted a son." She reached for Arthur's hand. "Your wish has come true. Welcome to our family, Arthur. You had better come and meet your three sisters: Jacquetta, Maisie and Joanna."

Arthur and Steve seemed dazed, staring at each other, then they moved as one, hugging each other tightly.

"My son," said Steve, wiping his face with the back of his hand. "You're my son." He stared at Arthur as though he could not quite believe what was happening, then he turned to Eleanor and said, "It's lucky you're my goddaughter and I love you, otherwise I don't think anyone would have been good enough for my son."

Terrible joke though it was, Steve's comment broke the tension. Eleanor could feel the relief flowing around the room.

"I'm sorry to have been so secretive," Arthur said, turning towards Aidan. "It's just that for a while, I thought we might be brothers. The only clue I had when I began looking was this photograph." He showed them a picture almost identical to the one Eleanor and her parents had discovered so recently. "My mum doesn't know I have this. Her friend, Jane, gave it to me when I asked her about the holiday. Jane couldn't even remember which one was the unknown Si. For the past six months, I've been tracking them all down and trying to discover who might be my father. I'm sorry to have dropped such a bombshell on you," Arthur added, turning to Steve and Inez. "It never occurred to me that you would be here when I shared the news with Ellie."

"Serendipity," replied Steve. "As Ellie is always telling me, everything in the universe is connected."

Several hours later, Eleanor and Arthur let themselves through the adjoining door into the annexe, locking it behind them. Dusk was painting the living room with shadows, but neither moved to turn on the light.

"From the moment I saw you on the beach," said Arthur, taking Eleanor in his arms, "I knew I wanted to spend the rest of my life with you. Discovering you might be my half-sister was devastating."

"I couldn't understand why you pulled away," she replied. "I thought it was because of my illness."

"What? Why would that matter? To me, it shows how incredibly brave you are, that you've continued to cope with it every day, never letting it stop you achieving your dreams."

Eleanor felt tears well in her eyes. "There's something else," she said, leading him to the sofa and finally clicking on a lamp, suffusing the room in a golden glow.

"What?"

Reaching for Esme's Marseille Tarot pack, Eleanor began to sort through them, pulling out the six unmarked cards: *The Empress*, *Death*, *The Tower*, *The Star*, *Nine of Cups* and *Ten of Coins*, followed by *The Magician*, *The Sun* and *The Wheel of Fortune*. "I understand the message now," she said, a shiver running down her spine, the beam of the light casting a golden haze around Adelaide, who sat on the bookcase, a tangible link to Esme Blood.

"The interpretation you gave me seemed quite clear..." Arthur began, but she shook her head.

"What I understand is why Esme called out from the past. I thought it was because of my connection to her, through Hannah and Noah Attwater and their daughter, my namesake, Eleanor Attwater, but the real reason is you."

"Me?" He looked perplexed.

"You're her direct descendant; you have her and Aaron's blood in your veins. Esme brought us together, I'm sure of it, leading you here and drawing me to her belongings. Despite everything that happened to her, she never stopped loving Aaron. She knew, eventually, they would be together, and she wanted to ensure you found love, that we found love, together."

Arthur looked sceptical. "How can you be sure?"

"Sometimes you have to trust your instincts," she said, "and read the signs." As she spoke, there was a whispering noise and, as they looked up, Adelaide shifted position on the bookcase. Arthur swore and even Eleanor felt a shimmer of unease, until Sandy appeared from behind the curtain with a miaow, causing them both to exhale, then exchange a nervous giggle. "Esme believed love would win," continued Eleanor. "Love triumphed for her and Aaron."

"And for us?" asked Arthur.

"We have to trust our instincts," she said as Arthur leaned forward to kiss her and the circle was complete, at last.

EPILOGUE

Eleanor smoothed down her dress as Nick helped her from the cab, peacock feather patterned chiffon whispering over the emerald-green silk as she moved. The red ankle boots, made from the softest leather and embroidered with violets, with a small heel, made her feel more like her old self. Her pale red hair was swept up on top of her head, and around her neck was the shimmering diamond necklace she had discovered with the rest of Esme's belongings.

Tonight was a party at The Mary Fitzroy Heritage Centre, a preview of the Victorian gallery for all those who had loaned or donated items. Esme and Lynette's dresses were one of the main displays in a room created especially for them.

"We have a few surprises for you," Mark had said a few days earlier. "I hope you'll like it, Ellie."

He would not be drawn further than this, but she was aware he and Arthur had been in cahoots, and she suspected Arthur and his mother, Wendy, might have added some of their photographs to the mix.

As Giovanni opened the door, Eleanor could see her parents, Aidan and Chloe talking to Steve and Inez.

"We're meeting Arthur, his mum and his stepdad, Kevin, here," Eleanor told Nick, searching the crowd for the familiar blond hair, but there was no sign.

"Won't that be awkward for Steve and Inez?" asked Nick, taking a glass of champagne from a passing waiter.

"It was Inez who suggested it," Eleanor replied.

"Quite the family party."

"In so many ways," laughed Eleanor as Arthur appeared and moved towards them.

"There you are," he beamed. "Come and meet my mother." He took her hand. "You look beautiful."

"Thank you," she said, conscious of their entwined hands and the occasional glance from people she knew, including Briony and Bathsheba, who were on the other side of the room. They gave her an unsubtle double thumbs-up, which made Eleanor laugh.

"Mum, this is Ellie," said Arthur.

Wendy and her husband, Kevin, were admiring the vast mermaid figurehead that dominated the central space of the first room of the museum. As Wendy turned, Eleanor started. Slight in stature, with a sharp bob of glossy dark hair shot through with moon-bright silver steaks, Wendy Pengally's bright blue eyes and dimpled cheeks were unnervingly familiar.

"Hello, Ellie, it's wonderful to meet you at last," she said, her voice low and melodic. "Arthur has told me so much about you."

Eleanor took Wendy's outstretched hand and found herself drawn into a hug. Kevin was next, then Steve and Inez arrived, and she stepped back to allow Arthur to make the introductions.

Mark appeared at her side, brimming with excitement. "Come with me a minute, Ellie," he said. "There are a few things I want to show you before we begin the tour."

He led her through the theatrical red curtains that separated the new Victorian wing from the main museum and Eleanor gasped. It was as though they had stepped back in time. A beautiful exhibit replicating a Victorian drawing room stood before them, warm and inviting.

"This is based on some of the things Perdita and Piper discovered about the local area. It leads through to another exhibit down there." He pointed to a shadowy corridor. "But I wanted to show you this and tell you the final part of the story."

"What do you mean?" she asked, following him along a curving passageway. "We know what happened." As they rounded the corner, she felt her stomach tighten in excitement — before her was a stage and on either side were the peacock feather dresses, displayed on tailor's dummies. Behind them were enormous blown-up photographs of Esme and Lynette wearing the dresses. Between these was another image, one she had never seen before, of the two young women in longer dresses, holding parasols, and posing as though dancing. "The Russian flag dresses," said Eleanor. "Where did you find this?"

"We've been trawling archives, picture agencies, private collectors, not to mention the things Arthur's mum discovered in their attic."

"How did you know where to start?"

"I managed to discover why so much of Esme's stuff was in the same place. I traced the company who sold the lot at the pop-up auction in Richmond. They owned the building where the boxes were found and it was set to be demolished, hence the reason for them being cleared out and sold. Originally, it had been a cinema before becoming a large antique market. In the basement there were several rooms no one ever bothered to explore, and all these boxes were in there."

"Where had they come from?" asked Eleanor.

"A clearance company had bought them from a restaurant in Soho in the 1990s. The building was being renovated, and a section of the basement had once been part of an old theatre..."

"The Firebird?"

"Yes, but what's so fascinating is that after The Firebird closed down in 1934, it was converted into a private dwelling and was owned by Mr Aaron Maclean until his death in 1940, when it passed to his wife, Mrs Esmerelda Maclean, who died in 1942."

"They did get married!" exclaimed Eleanor, suffused by warmth and happiness. "Esme finally became Mrs Aaron Maclean."

"At some point they did, yes," beamed Mark. "Esme's stuff must have been put into the basement and forgotten, especially as part of the house was bombed in 1943 during World War II."

"Amazing, thank you, Mark. This is incredible."

"I also found her will and, from the bequests left, it seemed they adopted Harriet Baron, too."

Mark took her hand and led her to another exhibit containing a photograph of Esme. She looked to be in her late forties, wearing a long gown, the diamonds which hung around Eleanor's neck sparkling back at her through time. Beside Esme was Aaron, handsome, dignified, but with the same twinkle in his eye. The grip of his hand on Esme's waist showed his love and adoration of the woman in his arms.

"Mark, thank you," Eleanor said. "This is wonderful."

"We'd better get back," he said, glancing at his watch. "The tour's about to begin."

Eleanor found Arthur. "Did the meeting between the families go well?" she asked him.

"Yes," he replied, hugging her tightly, "better than I'd ever have dreamed. There's something else I wanted to tell you, Ellie."

"Not more family secrets?"

"No, it's a decision I've made. I'm going to stay in Newgale."

"But what about your career?"

"It'll still be there when I want to go back," he said. "Aidan's offered me a job over the summer and Mark has said they need someone here to do the tours, especially in the Victorian section and…" He hesitated. "I want to be near you. Now I've found you, I want us to be together. If that's what you want?"

A rush of happiness filled her and she stared into his brown eyes, feeling a sense of completion. "There's nothing I want more," she said, reaching up to kiss him.

For the next half an hour, the gathered guests followed Jenny Procter, the chief librarian and archivist from Marquess House, around the museum, admiring the exhibits, listening to their stories, until they reached a sign reading *The Firebird*.

"I hid it before," said Mark as Eleanor turned to him in surprise.

As they admired the dresses and heard the shortened version of Esme Blood's adventures, Eleanor watched the crowd swirling around her. All the people she loved best in the world were listening in rapt attention to the tale she had discovered, the story of her and Arthur's joint ancestor, a woman who had become real to her. Then, without warning, Esme's silver voice rose through time, filling every corner of the room, holding the crowd spellbound.

Eleanor felt Arthur reach for her hand as the tune changed and two perky voices began to sing: 'I'm Going to Catch the Eye of the Tsar'. In her mind's eye, Eleanor could see them all: Esme, Aaron, Lynette, Jeremiah, Cassie, Rosie and Cornelius, dancing across the stage at The Firebird. As Arthur encircled her with his arms and she leant back into his familiar hold, the song came to an end and it was followed by the laughter of the two girls and a voice with a hint of a London accent, saying: "We got it right that time, Lyn."

"You did," sighed Eleanor. "Esme, you got it right for us too."

As the crowd applauded, she stared at the photographs and at the people around her, the people she loved. She thought about all that had happened over the past few years, all she had discovered and the perspective it had given her. When she'd begun her quest for Esme, it had been a search for herself as much as for this unknown woman who had called to her across the void of time.

As a new song flooded the room, this time combining the beauty of the voices of Esme and Elizabeth, the Miniature Songbird, Arthur tightened his arms around her and Eleanor listened as Esme sang: "*I knew your love would last a lifetime, You stole my heart but you brought it home again.*" Eleanor knew it was the same for her — love had been the last thing she had expected to find, but it had found her, and as a sense of peace settled over her, she realised that, with Arthur, she was home.

A NOTE TO THE READER

Dear Reader,

Thank you for taking the time to read *The Music Makers*. I hope you enjoyed joining Eleanor as she discovered Esme's story.

This is fiction, but I have included historical detail. It was a delight to research the Victorian theatre as it was a topic in which I was already familiar, having first discovered its charms many years ago during my Theatre Studies A-level. The Victorian era was a period of huge change in every aspect of society and the theatre was no different.

While The Firebird was not a real theatre, the plays and turns performed there are taken from the correct period. Cornelius Hardy is an amalgamation of a number of actor-managers from the period and his love of rewriting Shakespeare was inspired by the work of Nahum Tate, who in 1681, rewrote Shakespeare's *King Lear* to have a happy ending. Tate's version of Lear was performed for hundreds of years, until Shakespeare's original ending was reintroduced in 1823 by actor Edmund Kean, and in 1838, William Charles Macready, actor, purged the text entirely of Tate, leaving only the Bard's words. Cornelius took things a few steps further and added music, too.

Likewise, 'Twenty tiny toes twinkling their way to the top' was provided by my dad, Tom Walsh, who is a huge fan of theatre and particularly variety. He first saw this epitaph on a poster in the early 1950s; however, the original had the two sisters 'tapping' their way to the top. As Esme and Cassie were a bit too early for tap dancing, my small tribute to my dad was altered to 'twinkling'.

Crispin's insult to his grandfather as 'an evil old flapdoodle' comes from *Chambers Slang Dictionary* by Jonathan Green: a flapdoodle was a very rude Victorian reference meaning a sexually incompetent man, who is either too young to have had sex or too old to attempt it.

Eleanor's illness, Chronic Inflammatory Demyelinating polyneuropathy, is an illness I know well, as it is one which invaded my life many years ago. For this story to work, I needed an illness serious enough to drive Eleanor back to Pembrokeshire and the support of her family, but which would enable her to continue to live a relatively normal life. It is always said you should write what you know, so I have. While Eleanor and I share the same chronic condition, she is not me and her reactions are not mine.

The information about bigamy and child abduction were from fascinating essays on JSTOR and the examples used refer to real cases.

The poem, 'Ode' by Arthur O'Shaughnessy is part of his *Music and Moonlight* series and the full work can be found in Louise Chandler Moulton's *Arthur O'Shaughnessy: His Life and His Work with Selections from His Poems* (Leopold Classic Library).

The magazines which so fascinate Lynette were from the wonderful Margaret Beetham and Kay Boardman, *Victorian Women's Magazines: An Anthology* (Manchester University Press, 2001).

The Tarot readings are my own. The Tarot cards have fascinated me since my teens, and I have studied and read them for many years. As with all interpretations, there is no wrong or right, and these are my readings for these characters and this story. Other readers may find different meanings, all of which I hold in great respect.

Thank you to my brother, Jonathan, for his advice on music, audio and the transferring of ancient records into the digital world.

Thank you to my fellow Sapere Books authors Michael Fowler and Simon Michael for their advice on Arthur's crimes. It helped hugely to have a former senior police officer and a barrister to offer ideas, thanks chaps!

Thank you to everyone who has helped me with *The Music Makers*, particularly Amy, Caoimhe, Richard, Natalie, Matilda and Helen at Sapere Books and Sara Keane, my lovely agent. It has been a huge and thoroughly enjoyable task. Once again, any mistakes throughout the text are mine. Please forgive me.

If you have enjoyed the novel and would like to leave a review on **Amazon** or **Goodreads**, I would be so grateful as reviews are very important to authors. I love hearing from readers, so if you would like to contact me, you can through **Twitter**. You can also follow my blog on my website.

Thanks again for reading *The Music Makers*.

Alexandra Walsh

www.alexandrawalsh.com

Sapere Books is an exciting new publisher of brilliant fiction and popular history.

To find out more about our latest releases and our monthly bargain books visit our website:
saperebooks.com

Made in the USA
Columbia, SC
27 April 2023

15837950R00193